SOLO

SOLO

BY STANFORD WHITMORE

Harcourt, Brace and Company

NEW YORK

To J.

for a time

Chicago. Night. December.

The Loop is quiet now. Its glass-and-granite gorges echo the wind. And down frozen tunneled streets prowl yellow-eyed cars.

Above the brass-studded red leather door a banner fills with wind. A man emerges from the door and walks away. Two more men come out of the door and stand indecisively scraping their shoes on the cement. In their hands are rectangular black cases. When another man comes out all three start walking. A Checkercab turns the corner, blinks its lights at them. They shout at it, pile in, and the cab leaves in its wake a rag of smoke which twists and furls and fades into the hard blue air.

Back at the door stands another man with a cigarette in his face. He stamps first one foot and then the other. His fingers take the cigarette—flick—and the coal-point tumbles lazily, scatters sparks against a fire hydrant. He pushes the door. His words puff. In a time he is joined by another carrying a black case. They walk.

The Loop is quiet again.

Above the red door the banner swells. It says these are the men. It says they play the music.

ONE

I

On a foggy and sulphurous night he came into the city alone. He wore a leather jacket and carried only a cardboard suitcase. At first he lived in a one-flight-up hotel that smelled of calcimine and wet cigars. After three days he took an apartment on the far South Side near the lake. Impersonal and bleak, the rooms were above a barbershop whose owner passed the day combing himself and arguing with a mangy green parrot. The red brick street was never really busy. Nothing exciting had happened since summer, when a woman had been decapitated by an Illinois Central train.

He kept to himself. Early every morning he ate at a restaurant across the street from his rooms, and it was not long before his presence made the waitress uncommonly nervous.

When he came in she saw a muscular, fluid-moving towhead whose hands hung like grappling hooks from the sleeves of his leather jacket. He looked not more than twenty, and tough. His face was pale and hard and rarely clean-shaven; the waitress guessed that the stubble was an attempt to hide the small white scars around his mouth. His strangest physical quality, however, was in his eyes. They were set too far apart. A clear, penetrating blue, they were so wide-spaced that more than once the waitress wondered how much he could see without turning his head.

But what unnerved her most was his attitude.

For three weeks he had had both a cough and a severe head-cold; his clothes were not nearly warm enough for a Chicago winter; his meals were always the cheapest, and once she had seen him making tomato juice out of ketchup and water. It would have been natural if he had complained at least once, about something, during these three weeks—but he never complained, was never irritable, and in fact seemed simple-mindedly happy about everything. When he came in his thick nasal voice would say what a fine day it was, even when she could see for herself sleet or snow or weather as cold as frozen iron. And burnt toast tasted all right, and so did bitter coffee and oatmeal so rubbery she held her breath when she served it.

Nothing bothered him, and it annoyed her. She told the cook, and together they started watching and thinking too much. After a day or so they began to resent him. He was just too satisfied to be normal. He was probably a little off in the head.

But when he said his name was Virgil Jones they paid little notice to it. Names were names, and customers were customers, and this one could not be really important.

Early one December Thursday Jones woke in the hot darkness of his rooms. He turned on a gooseneck lamp near the bed, and for a moment his eyes scanned the room with the flat stare of a snake. Then he blinked, became human, put his feet on the stiff rug. He slept in a sweatsuit. He dressed by pulling trousers and shirt over the sweatsuit. In the bathroom he lifted warm water to his face. After brushing his teeth he touched, and took down, two white handkerchiefs from a length of twine strung across the room. He stuffed the hand-kerchiefs into a hip pocket, and at the windows pulled back an edge of one shade.

Along the curbs thin snow swirled like ashes. No snow was

in the air, but the wind from the lake was strong. Above the stores tin signs swung creaking. On the street scraps of paper moved nervously with the dark gusts. He released the shade and sat on the bed to put on clumsy crepe-soled shoes. Ambidextrously, and with the unwasted motions of routine, he made the bed and raised it into the wall and closed the dark varnished doors. Before leaving he drew on his jacket and a pair of thick-fingered brown cotton gloves.

When he reached the sidewalk the air struck him so that his eyes watered instantly. Light from the restaurant cast a yellow patch on the red bricks of the street. The air was freezing. The neon sign above the door crackled brightly as he passed under it.

At the near end of the counter two garage mechanics looked up from their hotcakes. The cook peered out. The radio in back spun from the news to a sweep of violins, and with the appassionata came the waitress: rouged, rust-haired, bringing water and a face that said she wasn't interested in anything Jones might have to say this morning.

"A waffle and black coffee." He looked along the counter.

"You want tomato juice?" she asked stiffly.

"Ketchup."

"To put on your waffle."

He grinned. "You don't want me to get away with anything, do you?"

"We sell tomato juice, you know."

"But I don't like it." His secretly amused eyes looked into her bewilderment, yet he did not seem to be laughing at her. It was as if he enjoyed thinking of all the remote, sober rules and doctrines of society he had offended by wanting to make tomato juice without paying for it. So he drank the water and waited by staring at the neat rows of cereal boxes in a metal rack next to a pie-cage. The waffle came crisp brown and hot. He made it spongy with syrup. He did not bother to watch as the waitress filled thermos bottles with coffee and returned them to the mechanics. After she had taken their checks they put toothpicks in their mouths, saluted, and went out.

The waitress was having coffee and the *Sun-Times* at the end of the counter. Jones quickly finished eating. He blew his nose loudly and wiped his eyes. It was 6:44 by the wall clock. He put the exact change by his plate. At the cash register he took a toothpick and held it up until the waitress saw. Then he went out into the still dark street.

Where he went and what he did was a mystery. The neighborhood knew he got on a bus that ran toward the steel mills, but since he wore no badge and carried no lunchbucket or sack, nobody had a mind to say what sort of work he did. He was gone all day.

In the evening headlights picked him out briefly as he got off the bus, crossed the street and merged with late shoppers, blank-faced commuters and groups of red-mouthed, jabbering schoolgirls. A small brown dog stopped, ears up, then trotted at his heels for several yards before tossing its muzzle to *chinkchinkchinkchink* in another direction. Jones stepped into the shallow entrance and thumbed the doorlatch, climbed the stairs.

The apartment was dark and hot. He turned on the lamp, removed his hat and leather jacket. The room was clean but faded. Near the windows sprawled a velvety purple sofa flanked by unmatching floor lamps. There were also two overweight armchairs with stringy skirts, and a coffee-table with cracked glass. On it lay several copies of *The National Geographic* and an oversize magazine devoted to color photographs of beautiful homes. A pair of flame-shaped tan lightbulbs stuck out of the flowered wallpaper. There was a green rug.

He took off his cold stiff clothes and threw them on the

14

sofa. Naked he went to the bathroom and turned on the shower and let the needlespray strike him directly at the crown of his thin hair. When he got out of the shower the room was hung with damp gray mist. He wiped the mirror, looked, and said something into the towel.

After he had dried he pulled down the bed and slept for an hour.

When he awoke it was colder in the room. He dressed in khaki pants and a cheap houndstooth sportcoat which showed below the worn leather jacket. He went out bareheaded. His cold was so thick his mouth had to hang open for air.

In a week it would be Christmas. Most of the stores were open but not very busy as he passed, walking straight-toed and eyes now shifting to see everything, his ungloved hands hidden in the warmth of his pockets. He did not stop at any of the stores, and, after a few blocks, he began to walk faster. Under blaring colors of a theater marquee, past slick flashing traffic and more stores and people, sounds of horns and gears, and finally halted.

The music store was open. Its double windows shone with rows of phonographs and radios; on each wall, frowning at the entrance, were enlarged color portraits of classical musicians. Through the glass the store was wide and deep. Only three people were visible.

Against one wall was an upright piano. Jones went in.

The counter was thirty feet from the piano and faced a series of listening-booths. The proprietor was talking to a young woman with short dark hair. Suddenly he looked up, put his right hand to his glasses, and broke off the conversation by pointing. The girl turned. Her face was tanned and beautiful. Briefly her eyes lifted toward the other man beside her, the tall man of about twenty-nine who was wearing a frame of expensive built-up clothes and whose thin face was now like that of a scowling Cherokee.

Jones pulled back one end of the bench and sat down. Without looking toward the counter again he kneaded first his left hand, then the right. They were big powerful hands with bony, square-tipped fingers. They came up, spread, poised over the keyboard—flashed, struck a savage dissonance, and again and again slammed the keys.

The swift stabbing chords began to form, took shape, mounted on one another, rose louder—stopped. And again the wild discordance.

Then nothing, no heel, no movement to mark the beat—but still it was in the silence . . . ponderous and certain . . . four slow, steady pulses, and then he began playing *I Cover the Waterfront* softly and gently, drawing out the high notes without use of pedals, hunched over the keys with his wide eyes straight ahead, never watching his hands.

He played cold and emotionless and fixed on the sounds—block chords and startling transpositions to a minor key, but never, not once losing the beat, never abandoning the clean, essential lines of the melody. For a quarter-hour his hands created almost every conceivable variation on the theme, and there were no mistakes, no uncertainties. It was pure, strong jazz piano.

When he finished there was silence in the store. Jones rested his hands in his lap and looked at the keys.

An angular woman had come out of one of the booths and waited, ignored, for service. She looked briefly in the direction of the piano and compressed her lips. By clearing her throat into her fist she finally got the attention of the proprietor.

His name was Seymour Schwab and he was in his early thirties. He had a sad, blunt, Semitic face and a spiky haircut. A brown tweed suit and thick-framed glasses made him look like a displaced graduate student. He was polite but moved nonchalantly as he got the woman's request from the rack.

Before returning to the booth the woman screwed her face into affronted dignity at all four.

The dark girl lounged against the counter and stared toward the piano as if trying to will Jones' attention. The tall man with her put a cigarette at the center of his mouth but did not search for a match.

Schwab came back to stand nearby. "That's him."

"He looks like a tramp," the girl said guardedly. Worried, her eyes shifted to the man beside her. He did not seem to notice.

Schwab began, "I'll tell—"

Without preliminaries Jones attacked the keys. Again the same slow tempo, powerful and clear, but this time no standard ballad. It was classical and not classical. It was complex but somehow free of obscure intricacies. It was, above everything, confident. He played as though he didn't care what anyone thought of it. On and on and on, breaking away from progressions he had developed only partially, interpolating great splashes of chords, winging away with blinding arpeggios, and never once losing the rhythm.

Almost instantly after the final chord his hands shot up and spread, pounced: and he was off on a wild, upbeat rendering of *Tea for Two*—all alone and hammering, driving the whole piano before the violence of his hands. There was no let-up for a long time, yet all the while his face held no sign of excitement, his feet were not pounding the rhythm. He played like a fantastic machine.

And after a time it was suddenly finished.

Jones stood, moved out, then carefully replaced the bench. He gave a shy little nod toward Schwab and for several seconds stared at the girl. Then he went out.

The street was bright and crowded and cold. He came close to a head-on collision with a package-blind woman whose mouth gaped and who waited for the apology that did not

17

come. A man went up on tiptoe, looked over heads in both directions, shrugged and lowered himself.

After two blocks Jones slowed to a normal walk. He made fists and put them in his jacketpockets, and walked with his head down.

The heat had come on again in his rooms. He did not switch on a light. At first by touch alone, he moved past the furniture and wall-corners and laid out his clothes for the next morning. Then he undressed.

Outside were noises of the street. The drawn shades glowed and faded with the diffused lights of passing cars. There was the wind. A bus hissed.

For awhile he sat on the edge of the bed. Then, as he stood, he suddenly reeled and clutched for support but found nothing and sank helplessly to one knee. He tried to stand but toppled sideways into a sitting position. It was some time before he turned and braced and got to his feet and once more sat on the bed in the dim light.

"——do you think?" Schwab's sand-colored eyebrows arrowed at the centerpiece of his glasses. His face was directed toward the girl, Helen Kostakos, but the right to answer clearly belonged to the man. Both she and Schwab looked at him.

Six feet two inches of wiretight nerves and with a starved, strong face, Ross Jaeger at twenty-nine was one of the five best jazz pianists in the country. "Who is he?"

"No one seems to know," Schwab said, "but of course facts seldom bother people when they want to discuss someone, especially if he doesn't 'fit in.'" He turned down his mouth. "All I know is what I hear on the street, and that is, his name is Jones, he's been in the neighborhood about a month, and, naturally, I suppose, he's a kind of odd-ball. Because no one really knows him."

"You were starting to tell us about him when he came in," the girl said.

"You said you've talked with him," Jaeger said.

"Only once, Mister Jaeger. A——"

"Ross. I've been in here enough for that."

"All right, Ross. A week ago this Jones came in and told me he'd like to play the piano. Mind you, he told me. No cringing request. Well, I liked him for it and said it was all right provided he knew more than *Chopsticks*." He smiled with embarrassment at the memory. "As you've just heard, he knows considerably more . . . or am I judging something I know not of? This jazz being your department."

"He's good," Jaeger said quietly.

The girl Helen said nothing. Her smooth brown face was unnaturally calm. She was wearing a blotchy yellow-green-tan tweed coat that looked as though she kept it under a mattress. On her left hand was an outsize ring of black stone.

"Yes—" Schwab pushed himself from the counter and began to stalk before the long high rows of records, moving his hands "—he has a great gift. Something could be done with him."

"You sound like a patron," Helen said. "Or a promoter."

"No, not a promoter. Patron? I don't know . . . but certainly not a promoter of that—no offense, Ross—that . . . elaborate aphrodisiac sort of thing—" He stopped as the angular woman came out of the booth and unfolded two ten-dollar bills. The woman's eyes strayed to the girl and Jaeger, then to the vacant piano, back to Helen and Jaeger. Schwab handed over the paper carrying-case and the woman went out with another glance at the piano that had exploded in her ears.

"I confess I've never heard your records," Schwab took up again, "but I like to argue, Ross." He impaled the sales-slip on a tall spike. His eyes were at the top of his glasses as he remained in a bent position.

Jaeger shrugged, obviously indifferent to this kind of argument.

"I don't think," Helen put in with deliberation, "you can argue away that *I Cover the Waterfront,* the first thing Jones did tonight. Call it anything you like, but it was beautiful and honest. Awfully honest."

Schwab straightened and pointed at the flat brown package in front of her.

"And that?"

Her teeth flashed in a smile. "We can't buy Mozart and Debussy and talk like this, is that it?"

"Unless you're willing to be unreasonable." He stretched his lower lip between thumb and forefinger. "I'm beginning to think I don't know you well enough, both of you. How long have you been coming in here? About five . . . since July, anyway. Not very long, is it? And you, Ross—how is it that you've turned your back on your years at Juilliard for the life of a jazzist? And yet still come shopping for the classics?"

But Jaeger had turned away and began to stroll around the store inspecting things from a distance.

"Forgive me," Schwab said to her. "I really am sorry for trying to be so damned . . . oh, I don't know what. I try too hard too much, that's my trouble, Helen. I didn't mean to antagonize Ross."

"He takes things seriously."

"I can see that."

"But don't let it bother you. Just forget it."

"I only hope he does." He started, stopped pacing, pressed both palms on the counter, leaned forward. "But I will admit this Jones' technique was . . . uh . . . quite advanced. Some of the ideas, too, were intelligent and well-developed. Now I don't know about the 'honesty' you mentioned—but then I'm not on speaking terms with these blues. Or whatever they are. It strikes me that they cry when they lose a lover and cry when they find a lover. It all sounds the same. But maybe I'm just a sterile dilettante. That can happen, Helen."

Her deep eyes had drifted as he spoke. Now they came back to Schwab and the counter and her package on it. And, apprehensively, to Jaeger as he was suddenly beside her.

"Do you know where he lives?" Jaeger asked.

"No, but—" Schwab began.

"Can't you find out?"

"—I think he'll be in again," was the relaxed answer. "We didn't chase him out or hang over the piano to watch his fingers, and I imagine he appreciated that. He'll be back. And who knows? I may become a jazz-addict and serve gin and sandwiches, hold rent-parties, let Jones set up light housekeeping in one of the booths. Why, I . . . well, it was something to say, anyhow."

She had not been listening, and Jaeger made no reply. Now she lifted her package from the counter and walked with Jaeger toward the door. Schwab hurried to be beside her, his eyes furtively at her face as though wanting some signal before he spoke again. They reached the door and he had said nothing.

"Would you let us know," she said, turning, "anything new you find out about this Jones? I'll be in again."

"Soon," Jaeger said past a cigarette.

"Fine," Schwab said. "But just one thing, a last something-or-other. Is it possible to compare this with the truly great music?" He had no sooner asked than he flung down his hand. "I didn't want to ask that, not at all. Of course you can't. Pure academic nonsense . . . Goya and George Petty, right? Probably. But wine, candles—small talk among the pygmies." He shivered as Jaeger opened the door. "Come back and we'll see about this erratic. Let me think about him. And see that you don't break those records."

He moved his hand jaggedly, closed the door and went back behind the counter. In the next half-hour five people came in and played three times the number of records they bought. To all of them he was courteous but never ingratiating. When the last customer left fifteen minutes before closing-time, Schwab saw him out and locked the door. He was alone again.

Morning was a year away. He did not want to go home. He did not want to go there because morning was a year away.

He stood alone in his darkened store.

In June Schwab and his wife of two years had gone on vacation to a cool, sun-glittering lake in Wisconsin. It had been their first vacation since marriage, and they were planning to start a family when they came back to Chicago. The weather was perfect. On the second morning she went for a swim while he sunned himself on the warm white sand. She swam far out and waved to him. He sat up and waved back. Her arm was pale and tiny. She was small and dark-eyed and gentle. He turned to brush sand off the blanket, and when he went to wave again he could not see her. He did not see her for four days, and then she looked like nothing he had ever known.

Now he worked late, and read, and tried to make jokes. There was nothing else to do.

As he passed the cash register he stopped at a miniature plaster bust. Above its pupil-less eyes rose a massive, smooth forehead. He leaned over in the silence and touched the sullen mouth with the tip of his index finger.

"Look at you," he whispered. "You've nothing to say about this Jones, have you? Naturally not. I suppose I shouldn't expect it. You've already said enough for a hundred men—a hundred thousand men. Certainly. Well, you and I will wait and see. You don't mind? Good."

Gently he rested his fingers on top of the cold head. "Maybe Jones won't be a waste. So much is wasted, isn't that so? Lost forever, by everyone, everywhere—lost. A man is everything he has lost; he is the sum of it. Isn't that a truth? Everything he has had and lost. Isn't that so? Isn't it?"

And he whirled and walked to the door and left in the darkness the blind white eyes.

At ten o'clock the next night, the buses and streetcars, the offices and factories waiting on Monday did not matter. Inside

23

the shadowy cellar nightclub, the zouzou, it was warm and crowded and smoky, and on the stand the sextet was jamming.

Helen sat alone in the back of the big U-shaped booth where the musicians usually drank between sets. She drank dry wine, and her face said she was not going to be able to drink as much as she needed.

She sat up in the booth as heavy applause spattered from massed shiny faces of the audience. On the stand she saw Ross slumped at the piano, Allred shaking out and wiping his trumpet as he chatted with tenor saxophonist Dave Britton, Nick Augustine flexing his lips and making lizard-eyes at the women up front. At the edge of light lounged Leonine Jackson, his mouth an ivory crescent, his enormous hands silhouetted against the white bass. Juan Reuben bent close to his drums and tapped softly, tightened, tapped and adjusted again. They all relaxed, readying for one more, unhurried and apparently indifferent to the requests piped from the crowded cardtables.

Finally Allred glanced at the inside of his wrist. Then toward the piano and Jaeger. Ross moved his mouth. Allred nodded. The others looked at him. He spoke right, spoke left, came front.

His heel: one, two—and they were in it, Jaeger's *Iceberg T*, all of them together, soft and clean and cool, gliding along at half-throttle in the shadows. After the first chorus Britton came on solo, blowing in his private, subtle tone, holding the gold tenor straight up in front of him and riding through thirty-two bars before Allred came on for his chorus, his brass nibbling at the thick air. Then it was Jaeger himself—quick, escaping passages marked by unusual intervals and a nervous quality of phrasing that seemed uncertain, yet when he finished he had brought it all with him and it was complete.

They played for a good long time before winding it up

24

because of Nick Augustine. Nick was young and handsome and blew a trombone that endangered every plateglass window in The Loop. He had been with the sextet only two months—joining up just before the West Coast tour—and Jaeger still had hopes of taming him. Now he set his feet wide and blasted his choruses right into the faces. He was a rough, swinging, blowing fool. "Go, man, *go!*" the audience shouted, and Nick went—all trombone, hips and stomp, blowing off to a world of his own.

When the entire smoke-hung room was pounding she saw Ross look up at Allred. Charlie took two short steps and brought the bell of his horn near Nick's shoulder and began blowing the word. It got through. Nick tapered off and let the others get with him for the final chorus. Then it was finished. The crowd was still set up high, excited, calling for more. The sextet left the stand.

Jaeger nodded his way through bowties and *Real fines* and got to the booth. He had on a chocolate four-in-hand tie and a beige drape suit. Lee Jackson was with him. The goateed Negro made a pistol of his hand, dropped the thumb.

"What you say, girl?" Jackson said, his eyelids going down and up like windowshades.

"Not much, man," she answered automatically. "Hello," she said in an intimate, almost shy voice as her eyes found Jaeger's and as she felt the hard, clean, tan rush of him sit next to her, felt a light unyielding pressure against the length of her leg. Jackson sat at the edge of the booth and started a cigarette. A round of drinks came just as the intermission pianist started his job.

"Augustine." Jaeger slowly shook his head in exasperation.

"Mahn, but he blows up a storm . . ." Jackson's head lolled and his fingers twitched on the tabletop. "Oooweee."

"So does a factory whistle."

"Sure, but look at all the cats start movin' when it does."

25

"Nick is big-band," Helen put in. "Kenton, or—"

"Right," Jaeger said. "But right now Nick is goofing. He could be learning, thinking. He's got only five of us to blow against."

"Hell, Ross," Jackson said with lazy amusement, "you two side up against me. This chick's gone on you instead of me. Now how'm I going to cut that kind of deal?"

Jaeger waved his hand in dismissal. "I'm serious, Line. There isn't anything wrong with blowing the way it's written, or if it's just a head arrangement, with the *mood* of the thing. Any man who blows a lung out every chorus might sound like the greatest to all these—these people, but he's not thinking, he's not giving himself a chance to feel the music, and on top of that, he's convincing all the squares that jazz is always loud and fast and rough." Jaeger grasped his drink, rattled the ice. "The trouble with Augustine is that he was born thirty years too late. He's got the idea jazz is still getting wigged and shutting your eyes and blowing up a storm. He won't discipline himself. I don't like to put any man down, but he . . . well, what difference does it make . . ."

She knew his tired irritability was not because of Augustine's destruction of the careful, serious work Jaeger put into all his compositions. What was really bothering him was Jones.

"You know something?" she heard Jackson ask Ross.

"What?"

"Tell the girl why Nicky gassed you in the first place."

Jaeger laughed, turned to her. "Because he blew. For all the reasons I'm criticizing him now." Then, in a lower voice: "Did you pick up those arrangements from Werre?"

"Both," she said, still grinning at space. "I left them on your phonograph before coming down tonight."

For some time none of them spoke. Although she was looking at the rim of her glass Helen was aware of Jaeger's again-

26

harried eyes and of the sad, intense plodding of the intermission pianist. With a glance she found Jackson's eyes, sent a message.

"I got to cut out." Jackson finished his drink, slid out of the booth and read his wristwatch. "Looking for my number and a nice little lady. We got time."

"Sure," Jaeger said. "Only I've had your number for a long time now, dad. And what nice little lady is going to mess with you?"

Jackson snapped into a fighting stance, threw a short left hook. "Oh—oh. Dig that? Glad you was there and it was here, ain't you? Well now. You got any idea what this hand going do next?"

They watched the hand.

"Damn if I know. . . ." His face stretched in a grin. "Gone," he said, and was.

She did not order another drink. She watched Jaeger worry the joints of his fingers. His face was averted. Thin lips parted, his bony face on guard, the high cheekbones faintly pitted with smallpox-scars, a thick lock of black hair over his forehead.

"I read," she began, not wanting to plunge yet, "that *Downbeat* review of *I Surrender*. And someone told me Old Butterlips had a few good things to say about it the other night." Old Butterlips was Roger Henneberry, whose nightly record program was the most powerful influence in Chicagoland jazz. It was said he could make or break almost any upcoming musician, or keep an established jazzman in the spotlight. He was, understandably, hated by most of the musicians.

"It wasn't too bad." Jaeger made a wan smile as he referred to the recording. "I lagged on that second eight behind Dave, but it wasn't too bad. We can do all right if everyone works at it." He took a glossy photograph thrust at him, scribbled, and handed it back to a heavy-lipped girl wearing glasses that looked bulletproof.

Helen was silent. *'We can do all right.'* She knew it was not false modesty, and she wanted to tell him not to be too hard on himself—but she had said that before. It seemed as if she had said everything before, and still he was the same. After four years Ross was unchanged. It had been a long, often-lonely effort for him to come this far, and he was not satisfied yet. He asked too much of himself. Jazz was his religion, and he wanted his heaven now. He never stopped trying to reach it. And in her mind, as always, was the truth she had found, had had to find: she would go with him, would do anything that might help him find himself, for he was alone on his search—no matter the time or the money or the fame or the ways she made love to him, he was always alone with the piano. No one could play it for him.

She looked at him. "He'll come back."

"Who?" The question was so unconvincing that he lowered his eyes and began pulling nervously at his right ear.

"Jones," she said quietly. She watched him frown, sip his scotch, grunt into the glass. He set it down. Shook his head and shrugged. His morbid jealousy of rivals had made him an encyclopedia of jazz pianists; more than a few times he had driven miles to a sagging roadhouse or a desolate tavern simply to hear some pianist he had heard of. When any man put jazz on a piano, he had Jaeger in the audience sooner or later.

"I can't read his style," he said. "He doesn't sound like any-body I've ever heard. What do you think?"

She thought hard but had to agree with him. She couldn't see any clear trace of an influence on Jones' style of playing.

"Impossible," Jaeger said when she had finished. "He had to get his ideas from somebody. A man can't be com*plete*ly original. That's right, isn't it?"

28

She said it was right. Her mind groped for something with which to divert the steady rush of Ross' insistence. He was punishing himself.

"You think he cuts Crawford?" Jaeger demanded.

"Maybe." She bit her upper lip. "I guess so. Yes."

He pursed his lips and slouched against the shiny leather of the booth. Lighting a cigarette, he let smoke seep out as he spoke.

"Who else?"

"Honey, I don't know—I'm only a listener. I can't rate him."

"Not Lennie . . ."

Her eyes burned and she wanted to cry *No, not Tristano not Tatum not Oscar not you, Ross, he couldn't cut you. He might be better than the others, but not you.* But Jaeger was no fool. Flattery never distracted him. And it was almost as if he wanted to believe the worst for himself.

"Ross—" she talked into his eyes, saw them give way "—I can't compare simply because you want me to. I could say yes or no and yes and no all night, and you'd still want to decide for yourself. The only thing to do is to go back and try to track him down and hear him again. That's all you can do. You won't find out by asking me." Her hands trembled. She felt watery inside.

Jaeger said nothing. He looked apologetic, but said nothing.

Almost at once she wanted to add something to soften the anger of her words, but instead she felt forced to say one more thing, the final one now that she had come this far.

"I wish you wouldn't make such a war out of everything. Believe me, it's wrong. Nobody can be perfect, especially in this. Don't worry about what others say. All you can do is the best you know how—and you know it's pretty damned good —and if someone like Henneberry happens to rate some other

29

pianoman higher . . . well, that's only one opinion. You can't satisfy everybody."

A flicker of something that could have been resentment lit his brooding eyes for an instant, but he remained silent.

In the background the piano had been hacking feebly at the mass of crowd noises. Now it stopped. There was sporadic, indifferent applause. She could see Britton already hooking the neck-cord to his tenor, Augustine moving toward the stand with his elastic walk. Reuben was talking to Jackson over the ride cymbal. Gradually the crowd quieted.

Jaeger stood. He held the fingertips of his left hand lightly against the fine short hair at the back of her head.

"You going to stay for this set?"

"No." She moved her head and kissed the inside of his thumb. "You don't mind? I've got to get some sleep."

"Sure. Get some sleep." He touched her hair again.

"Call me tomorrow?"

She saw his hand clench air, his eyes darken and grow heavy as they burned at her mouth. Then he softened.

"Around two. Sleep warm."

She smiled. Faces turned as he moved between the tables; heads converged, whispering. He was Ross Jaeger, the biggest man there. People listened when he played. He was a lot of piano.

Then he was on the bench, blinking at the lights, his delicate hands feathering the keys. Allred strolled to the center of the stand and talked with his back to the audience.

For a moment she regretted having asked Ross to go with her to Schwab's. If he hadn't been there he would not have heard Jones. But even as she speculated she knew it made no difference. Sooner or later Ross would have heard—yes, because she would tell him. She would have to tell him because she was now part of him. It was what she had asked for when they met over two years ago. It had been her choice, and making it had wrenched her from one life into another. For having seen this man Ross, she could not unsee him. And having seen with the same vision her family opposing everything outside its orthodoxy, she could not unsee that if she submitted to them, her one life would be no life at all.

As the overheads dimmed she left the booth and circled behind the crowd. The faces of four men turned and showed teeth as she swung past the cut-glass brilliance of the bar. From far off—too far, it seemed—came the opening bars of music. She did not recognize the melody, and did not care, for in her mind was mounted the two wide eyes in the face of Jones.

3

Jaeger left his North Side apartment at two o'clock the following afternoon. The day was bright and windy and cold. From
the Outer Drive he could see on his right the slablike, spire-
topped façade of The Loop. On his left frothed the lake, and
where it was not white it was the color of olive paste. The
wind whipped at the water and the stark brittle trees and
at the canvas top of his Cadillac as he drove south through
thin traffic. The sun glared without warmth. The day was
miserable. He had always hated the sun because it made his
eyes ache; the cold he hated by definition. When they worked
together it was a catastrophe. It was as if someone had thrown
the wrong switches. The ornament lit up and that was all it
did. At the same time the blowers went on and it was twenty
degrees colder.

With the heater on full, he adjusted the sun-visor and
entered the windblown shadows of Jackson Park. He tried
to center all his attention on driving.

When he locked the car Jaeger was immediately a stranger
to the listless, routine movements of the neighborhood Saturday afternoon. He was a blue Cadillac convertible, an ash-
soft overcoat cut in the lavish style of professional entertainers. The car and the coat did a lot for him. They gave him the
appearance of a healthy bank-account and a permanent locker

at some athletic club, but did their best work in diverting attention from his face.

In daylight it was a sick face. At one time it had been young and not unhandsome—and that was the worst part of it, because the young strength could still be seen, only now losing ground to a peculiar starved quality around his eyes. It was a deadly serious face. The skin was blotched by the cold, and the sunlight was too sharp. He made no attempt to control his thick dark hair in the wind.

When he went into the store he still had no clear idea of what he was going to do. The simplest thing would be direct questions, but he didn't want that. He wasn't sure of what he wanted. His throat was nervous, and he swore at himself. Suddenly he thought of Helen and the telephone. He shrugged, decided to call later. After probing at the sheet-music rack and noting the piano, he went to the counter. Most of the booths were occupied, and at the counter a woman was reading a catalogue with her forefinger.

Jaeger picked up a Columbia booklet and glanced several times at Seymour Schwab.

The proprietor was cleaning his eyeglasses with a handkerchief, holding each lens to the light and squinting. Two pinched red marks were on the bridge of his nose. He looked up, hastily fitted the thick glasses and smiled with recognition.

Jaeger mumbled hello. "Has he been in again?"

"No," Schwab said, "not since night before last—Thursday. But I *have* found out something . . ."

"Where he lives?"

"Where he works, or at least is supposed to work. The mills—the steel mills. As a laborer, of all things. Now isn't that an anomaly for a man with his talent? Of course I don't pretend to be a judge of—"

Jaeger stopped listening. Schwab annoyed him. It seemed that the proprietor had already seen through to the core of his fears and was praising Jones in order to aggravate them. Yes, Jaeger thought, Schwab was enjoying himself—the problem was not his. If Jones was a great pianist, it made no difference to Schwab. He would lose nothing. Dislike for all Schwabs swelled in Jaeger; he knew many of them. The outsiders. The ones with all the answers and none of the risks. It was always easier to discuss something when you weren't involved. Why worry about mistakes? Try again. Answers were cheap. Mouth it around again. The outsiders never had to find an answer. They could always give up and discuss some other problem they weren't involved in. Even Helen. Even her.

"This is a lot of talk." As Jaeger said it he saw a look of childish hurt on Schwab's face, and it gave him a feeling of repayment and satisfaction. "Who knows this Jones?"

Schwab shook his stubbled head.

"He has to talk to somebody," Jaeger prodded.

"I understand he does. Apparently he talks to everybody, but when he's through they still don't know anything about him—by that I mean the usual facts such as where he lives, where he came from, what he does for a living . . . This steel mill thing is more of a rumor than an established fact."

"Then what *do* they know about him?"

Schwab shrugged. "He's friendly, never in a bad mood, seems to enjoy life, thinks pretty much of himself. Has a lot to say, and believes in it—a little wildly, too. Very strong personality . . . sort of a preacher."

"What does he preach, music?"

"No. Himself."

"Himself?"

"So I'm told."

"I suppose he told you all this."

"No—the old man who washes my windows in the mornings." Schwab was beginning to look apprehensive as he

34

studied the gaunt pianist. "But he doesn't know where Jones lives."

"All *right*. You said that." He did not care that Schwab looked at him strangely. He did not care because suddenly his mind forgot how to care. It did not know how to act. It was dead. He shook out a cigarette and put it between his lips, and with the flare of the match his mind came alive again, only this time overwhelmingly full. The flame dwindled and went out. His mind refused to organize itself. Desperately he tried to fasten onto any single thing which would sustain his attention, but always, as he clutched, the one spun out of reach and whirled, drifted with all the others. At last he got hold of something—the neat thin trademark of the cigarette—and it was enough to bring him back. He decided he had to have a drink.

"Come back again, won't you, Ross?"

Jaeger turned toward the voice and discovered he didn't remember walking away from the counter. He realized he had acted like a man in a trance.

"I will, thanks. Sorry," he mumbled, not knowing himself why he said it. Then he walked out into the cold blue shadows of a dying winter afternoon, and at a tavern three doors away drank four hot searing quieting whiskies without taking his hand from the shotglass.

When he left the tavern the cold air cleared his head, and he suddenly remembered that he had eaten nothing all day. He walked toward the restaurant up the block.

A radio was playing in the kitchen. The waitress was dumpy and had wilted reddish hair. He would have hardly noticed her if it hadn't been for her odd habit of staring about six inches above the eye-level of people as she took their orders. When she did it to Jaeger it made him wonder if his hair had blown off. The idea was crazy; he laughed to himself, relaxed. He waited, conscious of being watched because of his expensive clothes.

As Jaeger ate, however, the fragmentary and half-defined fears came on him again.

He could not have said exactly what or why they were—he was too involved. All he knew was an inseparable mixture of insecurity and discontent, and he felt it more than he understood it. It was a feeling of something wrong. He felt that things could be set right again if he could only get hold of, if he could only hear more of Jones and the dimensions of his piano.

The truth was that Jaeger was afraid. He was afraid Jones could be so good that Ross Jaeger would be forgotten.

"More?" The waitress held the squat glass container above his coffeecup.

He nodded, tried to swallow and speak, but his mouth was full of frenchbread, and she was gone. On an impulse he had thought to ask if Jones ever ate here, but when she left he gave up the idea. How would she know anyway? he thought. She never looks at faces. So over good bitter coffee and a rich, strong, lung-deep cigarette he read the entertainment pages of a discarded evening newspaper. When he finished it was almost totally dark outside.

The wind had quieted. Gently the black air stirred with promise of snow. He felt better at night. Everything was subdued, slowed in softer colors and sounds. Peaceful. He thought of the zouzou and its crowds and noise and the bright battering lights—but when it was over, when there was only the night again, it was peaceful. Night gave a man a chance to do nothing but exist.

A half-mile east, at the same time Jaeger pulled away from the curb, a bus turned onto the wide street and began speeding rubberily toward his car.

Delayed by a double-parked truck, Jaeger swung around

36

it and continued in the direction of South Shore Drive. The Drive ran parallel to the lake and, a mile north, became the Outer Drive along the lakefront. As usual he drove too fast. After two blocks, at a wide avenue bisected by the street-level tracks of the Illinois Central Railroad, Jaeger suddenly guessed that he could save almost a mile by making a left turn here rather than going all the way to the Drive. He did not see the bus.

Facing him, it was at the curb across the street. It had stopped to discharge passengers. With a great gasp it started to move just as Jaeger wheeled in its path.

It was as though a searchlight had been snapped on outside his right side window. His whole body drained of strength but his foot jammed on the accelerator and he felt the car surge and then in his headlights gleamed a leather jacket and he wrenched blindly wildly at the wheel and it was over. His hands were slippery and cold. One at a time he wiped them on his overcoat. His mouth was open. He heard himself breathe.

"I could have killed him." His voice was distorted, thick. "I could have killed that guy."

Gradually his mind calmed. Soon he was able to hear his tires on the asphalt. He stayed behind a slow-moving green car with an Indiana license. Above and ahead, as far as he could see, streetlamps glowed like a twisting double strand of beads. After some miles his emotions were normal.

"I could have been killed," he whispered.

The big roman-numeraled clocks on State Street read six-thirty as he entered The Loop. Saturday night, and he passed the queues already beginning to form in the hard white lights of theaters. There was no line in front of the Telenews. He left his car in a subway garage and walked two blocks and pushed a dollar bill into the glass booth.

Luckily he came in not two minutes before the football pictures started. They were all of professional games, and in one—the Bears-49ers thriller—McElhenny of the 49ers reeled off a beautiful 92-yard kickoff return. The kick was low and hard and as he came up to take it he was already sprinting. He took it at waist-height and came straight up the middle like a bull out of a chute and at midfield ran over the only man to touch him. After the football pictures there were scenes of a fire on the New Jersey docks, of the President of the United States flattering God, of a second set of triplets, of a beagle that liked to smoke a meerschaum pipe and watch the boxing matches on television. There were hazy, jiggling films of some war in a jungle, and there were spotlighted scenes and ecstatic words about puffed sleeves at a fashion show in London. He saw it all through, even the feature on water-skiing at a mossy Florida swamp, and after watching the last man trampled again, he looked at the bluish-haloed clock on the wall of the theater, and left.

The films had taken his mind off Jones, but as Jaeger drove to the zouzou the idea of the pianist returned to depress him. Who was he? Why was he burying his talent in the steel mills—if he really did work there? What sort of man would do that? *He preaches himself,* the Jew had said. *Himself.* The word tumbled in his head like a sharp rock.

Brooding, he thought of Helen. She knew good piano, and she too had heard Jones. Even now, Jaeger thought, even to-night—as she was smoothing her stockings or painting her hot damp mouth or just relaxing in her apartment and wearing nothing under her silk robe—even now she was comparing: Jones vs. Jaeger. She could not help comparing. Every-one compared all the time, in everything.

The nightclub had just opened. A few eager couples sat as close to the stand as they could get. The low-ceilinged room was good and dark and there was no smoke yet. The bartender said hello and kept working at a glassful of cloth. Angelo, the owner, was not in yet.

Jaeger stood at the bar and drank scotch-and-water and looked at the satiny rear ends of the waitresses as they passed. All of them had a smile and a hello for him. Dispassionately he concluded that they would be easy, and he did not flatter himself. A jazzman seldom had to go hungry. But he did not want that kind of food. He did not want the frustrates and the worshippers and the neurotic fertility-goddesses; he had had, and had not enjoyed, the vocalists who had given themselves to him in a kind of comradeship of jazz. The trouble was that none of them had seemed able to be complete as a woman. They had always given him the feeling that they loved it not because of him, the real him, but because of what they thought he was. And if they did it on that basis they would not be around long if he ever fell short of living up to what they thought of him. No, he did not want to live with that threat hanging over him. He wanted a woman to be a woman. He did not want their wiles and pressures. He wanted Helen. He finished his drink.

It was nearly an hour until the first set, and he didn't enjoy the thought of being in the open where autograph-hunters could fire on him. He started toward the back room.

"Hey Ross!"

Jaeger turned beneath a modern painting and saw four white young faces gaping at him from a front table.

"Real cool tonight!" said one face.

O Christ, he said to himself. But he waved and dipped his head as if it meant something, and went into the back room. Where does he get off calling me Ross? Well, he thought, that was part of what you had to pay. For a two-fifty mini-mum, sometimes nothing at all, they owned you. But then again, it was better than being old and respectable. Or a failure. Then they never shouted at you. Then you walked in silence.

He hung his overcoat on a thick wooden hanger and loosened his tie. Then he counted the sticky cards of a deck on the cardtable, shuffled them twice, and started solitaire. In the middle of the second game the washroom attendant came in. Jaeger asked him to bring back a couple, yes two, drinks. When the quiet old Negro returned Jaeger told him to have one, and no arguments. Neither of them spoke after that. They drank. Jaeger kept trying to put up the deck, but he couldn't fill out the diamonds. The attendant excused himself and went out. Jaeger muttered a reply to the chair where the old man had sat. He looked at his wristwatch and decided he had time for one more try, this time deliberate, careful.

"Green seven on that purple sixteen, mahn."

A long, licorice-colored finger appeared in front of his eyes. He squinted up through the smoke at Jackson.

"I'm trying to beat this thing." He slid three, turned over a worthless red nine.

"Sheeit, I can cut that game any old time."

"Sure you can." He uncovered the Ace of Clubs. "Jackson rules."

"Naturally. They got to have special rules for the king of that game, and I am *it*." Jackson wandered around the room, the steel taps on his heels sounding slow and precise. "How you feel, Ross?"

"So-so." Jaeger put a fresh cigarette in his mouth and lit it from a stub.

"Wish I did, but mahn, I feel the least. Got a sore ear. Aches."

"Been listening to yourself."

"You just play that game there without none of your jive . . . I *do* wish I was back in Frisco, though . . ."

"That help your ear?" This time the hearts were stubborn.

40

"Sure, don't you know that? It's the fog. Packs your ear so's you don't have to wear no cotton at all."

Jaeger looked up. "Hell, you're not wearing any *now*."

"Yeah, but I'm thinkin' about it."

Jaeger made a face and put down the pack and rested his chin in the V of his big hands. Silently he watched Jackson awhile. The bassist was his best friend. In some ways it seemed like Jackson was all a man could ask for in a friend. He was a listener and a talker and a conscienceless genius of a liar whose inventions were designed to make the dullest night a strange and marvelous thing. He was an untiring prowler ready to go anywhere, any time, and for any reason, and he seemed to know everybody. He got a lot out of life without even trying.

"What's crossin' your mind?" Jackson wanted to know.

"You."

"*Well* then—take your sweetish time. Just sit there and see me parade."

Jaeger went back to his game. Noticing Jackson flop into a chair, he wondered what fantasy would come next—probably cancer of the eyeball, or a new bass without strings.

"You know—" Jackson hadn't waited long "—I think I'll shave me this goatee off. They ain't so stylish no more. Grow me one of them beards . . ."

"Good deal," Jaeger mumbled. The game was fading on the table before him.

"That's right. Next year all us cats is wearing big beards and derbies. I seen it in *Esquire,* sure enough. Last month's."

"Great. You can carry about five sticks of gauge in the beard."

"Oh, hell . . ."

The door opened and both Jackson and Jaeger said hello to the shy smile of Dave Britton. Allred followed him in.

". . . what'd I do that for?" Jackson continued to Jaeger

41

in a surprisingly serious voice. "None of that for me, mahn. Wreck you, that's what it does."

"Who's gettin' too much?" Charlie Allred was a short, blocky, corrugated-faced mulatto with the voice of a wood-rasp.

"Line here," Jaeger said, thinking quickly. He kept his eyes on the cards as he spoke. "Tells me he's putting down some of these chicks who've been stealing all his starch. So weak now, he can't blow note one."

"Hell, this mother never could," Allred laughed.

Jaeger listened to the two of them start insulting each other with foul, limitless imagination. He was glad Charlie had been thrown off the track. Two years ago the trumpetman had spent ten months in Kentucky. Heroin had brought him down to a hundred and twenty pounds. He had tried suicide twice. It didn't pay to mention any kind of habit when he was around.

Jaeger never did beat his game of solitaire.

They talked about women and professional football. Reuben came in. He had a magnificent smile. Allred and Britton un-cased their horns and started blowing soft triplets. Jackson sat backward in a cane chair and cracked his knuckles and whis-pered a scat, double-time *Lover Come Back to Me*. When Augustine arrived Jaeger jumped up. Nick took an electric razor out of his coatpocket and gave it to him. Jaeger shaved and handed the razor to Reuben.

They drank and smoked, drifted in and out, yawned, fooled with mouthpieces and valves and shirtcuffs, joked, just sat and stared at the paint-flaking walls. It was an old story to all of them. It was another nameless night of all the hundreds and thousands of nights in damp back rooms, on darkened buses roaring unnoticed and unannounced through a handful of lights in anonymous towns, in old balcony-stacked concert-

42

halls where Beethoven had thundered the night before, in hotel rooms, in the backs of cars, in hotel rooms.

The owner, Angelo, came in and wanted to know how everybody was. Jackson told him they were all going to fly, they felt sensational, cool as fools, gone, good Jesus they were going to be way out! He looked as though he could hardly keep his eyes open. Augustine blew a wet smear on his trombone as Angelo left. Jaeger did not look up from clipping his fingernails.

At nine-thirty Allred stood, fluttered the valves of his horn, and pushed open the door. It sounded like a lynching was going on in the club. He let the door swing shut.

"Wonder when the people come on down," he drawled.

The others got to their feet and sucked hungrily at cigarettes. As always, Jaeger's hands felt stiff and chilled, but he knew the feeling would pass once he was at the keys. He wondered dimly if Jones did tension exercises to keep his hands strong and supple. He ought to take care of them, he thought. The steel mills was one hell of a note for a pianist.

Britton and Reuben went out. Allred stuffed a clean handkerchief in his breastpocket.

"Bring that kazoo, Nicky boy," Jackson said from the door.

Augustine aimed a blast at him.

"Will you catch that cat get off!" Jackson said to Jaeger. "I think you ought to get that cut so's it keeps, Nicky. That's the —get *out* of there with that damn slide, you no-trombone-playin' . . . No messin', men. Let's make this scene, what you say?"

Together the three of them went into the narrow passageway and abruptly into faces like massed opals, into the sibilance, the instant hot immensity of spotlights. Jaeger stepped up, edged past a cymbal and Britton and a microphone, stepped over cords and sat loosely at the piano. He wondered if Helen would be angry, if she would be down tonight. Then

43

he stopped thinking about her and began to play quiet triads and arpeggios.

Allred spent a full half-minute twisting the microphone to the height he wanted. It buzzed like a giant insect, then lifted into an earsplitting whine. Finally it was all right. They limbered up in six directions—playing with odd, private phrases, tuning up, experimenting, not yet caring about the crowd. All of them looked bored. The audience was patient. After a short while Jaeger nodded to Allred. Charlie took his horn from his lips. The others looked at him.

" '*dido,*" he said, and turned to face the crowd.

One two three four *jump*—everybody in, get on it . . . and there it was, what they did for themselves and the zouzou and the hundred thousand nights of everyone who wanted.

It was a normal Saturday night. They were good, and the crowd always wanted more than it got. By the third set Reuben had to change clothes and Allred was blowing like a hammer. They were all heated up except Jaeger. He did enough, but no more. On other nights like this he had been brought up by the collective excitement when one of the others—Nick or Dave or Charlie—had blown things to a raging pitch that was enough to ignite the whole place. But tonight Jaeger had nothing extra to give. He did a job.

Between the first three sets he looked for Helen, but she hadn't come. He was not much worried by it. What gnawed at him, dulled him, was his nearly helpless fixation on Jones. It was as if at regular intervals a voice intruded with the command to not think of Jones, to *not* think of him, and of course for the next minute or so he could think of nothing else.

It was snowing when he left the club. He did not join Jackson and Nick when they went to eat. Silent soft paleness fell slowly and melted on his lips. It was cold and fresh. The streets were mute, peaceful, white. He covered his face with his hands. This day and this night had made him want her so badly.

He drove four blocks toward her apartment, changed his mind and headed for his own. His desire told him she had to be there.

With little surprise he heard the coda of the sextet's recording of *Indiana*. A heavy silence followed—he could hear the faint hum of the car radio. A long silence. Very impressive. A signature: Henneberry the Great.

Yes . . .

More silence.

. . . Jaeger's Indiana . . . cool as blue ice . . . crystallized and true and gem-perfect in this night's darkness. Remember it . . . as if you could forget, could not recall . . . something —like—this—

And Jaeger heard himself as Henneberry played back a section in the middle of the record. He did not share Henneberry's enthusiasm for the passage. It was nothing special. But if the jockey wanted to think it was great—well, that was all right. A man could use all the help he could get.

—that was Ross Jaeger in there . . . fine. Jaeger's men . . . as you faithful know . . . are emitting this same sort . . . of very fine sounds at the zouzou. Yes, here . . . not in Paris, faithful. They should be around for some time . . . and you, yes you, The Woman, ought to be there to get with them . . . . . . soon.

Silence again.

Jaeger thought about Henneberry. He was a monstrous balloon of words, of poses, but also, of information. Henneberry was on the inside as much as any non-musician could ever be. He was vain and false and pompous, but he had influence. He knew people all over the city, and the people could do things such as learning more about a pianist who called himself Jones. Jaeger could not forget that Henneberry had helped him once when he needed it most, at the beginning. Of course it hadn't been out of generosity, but the praise had helped. Both of them.

. . . *Let's talk* . . . *about the snow, the poetic*——

Jaeger pushed the button. One of the worst things about trying to be an artist, he reflected, was that a man had to ask so much from so many gold-plated parasites. The more he thought about it, the more depression weighed on him. It was sinking him. He was a celebrity and felt like a zero. He was still begging, still with his hand out, still asking for something to make him not worry.

His throat and eyes hurt when he found her waiting. She knew without him having to tell her. And in the dark room he fed.

4

Silk was effeminate. Against the flesh it was too perfectly cool, its slippery folds suggesting softness. And in dressing-gowns it was also contemptibly common. So nouveau riche, so Jewish.

His round pink face still disfigured by sleep, Henneberry moved among the low, smooth growths of furniture on the carved carpet. For a robe he wore a hooded monklike garment of coarse black wool drawn in at the waist by a thick rope; on his feet were fat dark leather sandals. Henneberry was secretly proud of his costume—it was simple, classically so, and somewhere in his head paraded the ideas of drama and mankind and the intellect. Every now and then the costume gave him a warm, flabby feeling toward The Masses, The Little Man who listened to his program.

At heart the little men terrified him. There were so many. On more than a few nights, alone under the toasting spread of his electric blanket, Henneberry had bulged horror-eyed at the thought of Henneberry sliding into the mewling, dazed, directionless surge of the mainstream, suffering indignities and God knows what else. But this half-dream was infrequent. It gave him mild excitement, a sense of having been in danger. He could make it go away merely by thinking of his contract, his listener-rating, the luxuries of his apartment,

47

or his bone-white Ferrari even now being given its weekly tuneup at the garage.

Door-chimes surprised him. Hurriedly he pulled the hood from his soft face and put on glasses with richly grained mahogany frames. His eyesight was perfect. As he went to the door his movements became as exquisitely deliberate as those of an underwater fern.

"Ah—The Piano," Henneberry said. His voice was strong and deep and did not betray the inferiority he felt in Jaeger's presence. He shook hands and invited Jaeger in. A bite of breakfast? No? It was simple to send out, the restaurant was —a drink, then?

Jaeger said he would settle for coffee, and Henneberry primed the percolator and plugged it in. Vaguely he wondered why Jaeger hadn't commented on his robe or sandals, or, for that matter, on the apartment. Jaeger had never been to this one.

His sharp face preoccupied, Jaeger sat on the slablike couch with his long arms extended along the top. Henneberry sank into a yellow canvas butterfly chair, lit a cigarette, and looked wisely and expectantly through the shifting layers of pale blue smoke. By saying nothing a man never exposed himself. Henneberry crossed his legs. The ash lengthened on his cigarette. Jaeger spoke just as the electric percolator began to drum furiously in the kitchen.

"I need help," Jaeger said. "Maybe this isn't the right way to go about it . . . maybe I don't need help at all. I don't know. But I've thought about it for a week now, and this seems the best way."

Henneberry listened to Jaeger describe his efforts to locate the unknown pianist. It was obvious that Jaeger had fought down pride, was still fighting it, to ask for help. And even now he seemed confused about what he wanted. Henneberry

48

experienced a rare, delicious feeling of contempt for Jaeger. He pitied Jaeger, and consequently admired himself.

"Where is this record store?" Henneberry artfully stroked his right palm along an immaculately brushed temple.

Jaeger told him, and added that the owner of the store acted as though the search was a kind of game.

"Is it?"

"Let me ask you something," Jaeger said in a deadly voice. "How long have you been playing piano?"

Henneberry shrugged, smiled, couldn't think of a single remark to get himself off the damnable hook. He was a frustrated jazzman and Jaeger knew it. Henneberry's pity shifted to anger.

"No," Jaeger said. He stood and began pacing aimlessly across the thick carpet. "It isn't a game. I want to find out more about him and hear him again. A musician doesn't plug up his ears when he's gone so far . . . if he's worth anything he keeps listening for new things, new sounds, what somebody else is trying to find. You ought to know that. Tell me when Louis stopped listening to other horns. Tell me when he said 'I've heard all there is.' No, Louis hasn't said it and he won't. He's too smart and too great to be that stupid. When a man stops listening, he's dead, buried. When a man has all the answers, he doesn't need them. He's dead."

As Jaeger spoke Henneberry's face assumed a look of profound, but cultured, sadness. It was some time before he was prepared to comment.

"Not a gift, but a curse," he murmured.

"What?"

"Nothing." Henneberry sighed, mentally reviewed the sound of the quotation, wherever it was from. Then he got up and went to the kitchen. He returned with two black coffees and set them on a low white table in the center of which was a silky, stark piece of tormented driftwood. "Ross—" he said softly "—do you read?"

"What do you think I was doing at the Conservatory?" Jaeger asked with a frown.

"No, I mean *books*. Literature." The second *t* was very clear.

"Books? I don't have time for them any more. They don't apply."

Henneberry's lips formed a wry smile as he shook his head. The comfortable feeling of pity was coming back.

"Calls himself Jones." Jaeger could not leave it alone. "From his looks I think he goes twenty, twenty-five . . . somewhere in there. White boy. I let him get away."

"And you want me to get some information on him . . ."

Jaeger's face was suddenly annoyed. He set the smoking coffeecup into its saucer with a clatter.

"No, don't get his pitch, Roger. Don't bother. You've got a lot of records to keep lint off of, you've got to keep those sandals all polished, you've got to make—"

"Ross, Ross—please." Henneberry had his hand up as if to ward off a physical blow. "Have I, now, at any time during our talk, given the impression that I won't help you get some information on this boy?"

"You could have said so. I don't need all the jive about books."

"Very well," Henneberry said easily. "Consider it undertaken. You'll have your Jones in less than two weeks." *And what will you do with him?* he wanted to add, but the tight surliness of Jaeger's mouth warned him against asking. So instead Henneberry carried in the percolator. He wanted to talk, to hear the sound of his own voice. And Jaeger had always interested him. A compulsive sort of personality that either attracted or repelled. Henneberry knew no one who was indifferent to Jaeger; there was too much intensity in him to be ignored. Jaeger had a splendid musical background and a talent greater than he himself would admit, but he was perpetually dissatisfied with himself, perpetually examining everything around his life for some clue, some indication which would bring him closer to his obsession—greatness.

They talked in casual tones about the Chicago jazz scene, a new Herman record both of them admired, the confinement of a tubercular bassist—and all the while Henneberry felt a memory growing on him. Finally he recognized it. Jaeger reminded him, as never before, of Bern DeWitt. It was strange he had not seen it before. Both had been pianists and good friends. Both had been fanatically serious, devoted to the importance of what they played. And, as near-equals, they had been friendlier than any other rivals Henneberry had known.

But there had been a difference. DeWitt hadn't excluded everything non-musical. He read and he thought and argued and worried. He did too much. And now, finally, there was another difference—now Ross Jaeger sat in this room in this December and could only remind Henneberry of Bern De-Witt, because DeWitt was dead. Dead of some rare sudden fever in some filthy foreign city nobody remembered. He had asked for it. He had always asked for it—The Answer. He had, in the end, given up music. The announcer wondered, feeling a faint pang in his bowels and a new appreciation of his apartment, if DeWitt had had time to reconsider.

"Tell me, Ross—" he intoned, rocking on his sandals li' a fat friar "—why it is that a lot of you modernists hav   talent for trouble. You engineer it. You—" he waved his hands in dramatic helplessness. He did not really want to know.

Jaeger shrugged and blew on his coffee.

"There is a pattern," Henneberry continued. "I've watched it all these years—a certain extremism, a bizarre way of living, a sort of frantic expressionism. Take clothes, for example . . .

or the heavy drinking, drug-addiction . . . perversions of all kinds, the—"

"You don't know jazzmen like you think you do." Jaeger's voice was slow and unangry, and Henneberry ignored it.

"—I was just thinking of DeWitt," Henneberry said loudly. He saw Jaeger's eyes close and remain that way. Henneberry decided he had better not talk about DeWitt. "Of course a study of the history of jazz doesn't completely exonerate its pioneers. Take Buddy Bolden, if you will. A great horn. The man couldn't read a note. Free of a good many complexities of modern jazz; simple and direct, you say. Yet Bolden blew himself insane—literally insane—leading a parade. Or Rappolo, still in his twenties, climbing telephone poles to play his clarinet . . . no, hardly in his twenties. And I confess I'm pressed to think of others among the pioneers. But you modernists? Ah—hundreds. Hundreds who've gone off the deepest end. Why? What is the reason? Tell me, you who are inside."

Jaeger sat glaring at the figure in the carpet. He had nothing to say.

Henneberry studied him. It was hard to tell whether Jaeger was silent out of boredom, anger at being lectured, or resentment at being obliged to listen because he had asked for help. Henneberry suspected this last. It was Jaeger's big weakness. He needed to be liked, and because of this he made concessions and gave in to obligations. On the surface he would seem genuinely polite, but inside, Henneberry felt, resentment smoldered. Jaeger hated the hypocrite in himself and held it against others who forced him to it. The analysis pleased Henneberry. It was fortunate that most people were like Jaeger in this way. They could be manipulated so easily.

Henneberry walked to the lemon-colored venetian blinds and stood with his back to the couch. In the lifeless winter light his face was ashen, his mouth soft and depraved. With a manicured hand he parted the cold flexible slats and looked five stories into the street. It was powdery white, and the trees were sheathed in ice. He let the blinds buckle into position.

"What about this piano, this Jones? How do you know he's worth finding out about?"

"I've heard him."

"But it's possible we're getting involved for nothing."

"Goddamn it, I told you I heard him. I know he has something."

"Everybody's got something, haven't they now? You're determined to believe that until convinced otherwise."

"It keeps me alive."

"A good answer," Henneberry said with a nod of appreciation.

"It's not original."

"Nothing is, Ross. Nothing is."

"Unless it's Jones," Jaeger said softly. "Helen—you know her—Helen and the owner of the store and myself are the only ones who've caught him, and Helen has a fine ear. She didn't say much, but I have a feeling . . ."

"Your young lady flipped," Henneberry inserted, using the jargon of which he was so conscious.

"I think so." Jaeger's eyes narrowed as he nodded. "And the owner—Schwab. He's nowhere if it isn't classical, but when I saw him again yesterday he seemed to be still pretty impressed with Jones, and, well . . . any jazzman has to have something to do that."

"And how many times has this genius been in the store?"

"Just once—no, twice." Jaeger squinted. "The last time a week ago Thursday—a week ago last night. And I let him get away."

"Mmmm." Henneberry tapped a finger against the side of his nose. "I should say all of you are assuming a great deal—far too much. You haven't the semblance of a guarantee he'll

53

return; and if he doesn't, if he never comes back, if all you have is this one night and a lot of talk—what happens? Is this enough to make you go on? How long do you search for this ghost?"

"He'll play there again."

"But if he doesn't?"

"He'll play somewhere else."

"And you'll find him."

"And he won't get away." Jaeger clapped his hands on his bony knees and stood up. His fugitive dark eyes were irritated again. "All right—I know what you're thinking. You're wondering what I'll do when I find him. Well, I don't know. I haven't got the answers. I don't sit down and figure it all out ahead of time. Probably it isn't very in*tel*ligent, I know, but I haven't got time for that. I play piano. That's what I do. That's what I've got time for."

Impassively Henneberry watched Jaeger thrust his arms into his deep blue overcoat. He knew the pianist was regretting the entire scene for having revealed too much of himself, but it was too late. And in more ways than one. It was too late for Jaeger to turn back. The higher he went, the better and more famous he became, the more he was ruled by his obsession with greatness. He admitted his inferiority to a few other jazz pianists, but they were known quantities. In time, Jaeger believed, he would surpass them. What ate at him were the unknowns, the half-knowns—all the Joneses. Again Henneberry pitied him. Now was the time for a kind word. When the announcer spoke it was in his most creamy tone.

Newborn was BP's Jones

"Ross—" he said, joining Jaeger in his walk to the door "—as I said, we'll have Jones in a week or so. I have all the necessary facts—the address and description." Behind his glasses his eyes were half-lidded, cornered at the pianist whose anger was already dissipating. "I assure you we'll find out

54

about him . . . and if he's been run over by a truck, we'll locate the grave. How is that now?"

"Good enough," Jaeger replied abstractedly. "I asked you for help because you know who's blowing what where better than anyone else in Chicago."

Henneberry almost sighed with pleasure. Gruffly, to conceal it, he said:

"It is my life." Then, feeling sad and faintly philosophical, he opened the tall oak door.

"You'll get in touch with me at the club?"

Henneberry nodded like a hinged Buddha. He was gratified to see Jaeger phrase his wants as questions. Their relationship had been expertly defined this afternoon, and Henneberry intended to keep it that way. He made it a point to shut the door before the elevator had risen; Jaeger could wait alone.

The boy who delivered the lovely hot breakfast was, Henneberry could see, somewhat frightened by the black hooded robe. It was just as well, probably better, that he was. Familiarity, to think in clichés, bred contempt. It was dangerous to be understood too soon. People had to be given something to think about; and in such an insignificant meeting as this, the robe was a most effective puzzle. Besides, the youngster would remember it and tell others what Roger Henneberry wore in his apartment. A robe, a big black hangman's robe with a hood. The listeners would tell others. It would be a good thing. Legends got started that way.

Henneberry arranged his breakfast on the beautiful white table in front of the couch. He had double orders of everything: frothy orange juice, poached eggs, link sausages, whole wheat toast and a paper nutcup of strawberry jam, his own coffee, and a longjohn with rich sweet maple frosting. The lineup was almost too pretty to eat.

As he ate he began to feel smug and accomplished. Jaeger

had come to him for help. Jaeger trusted him. And the pianist hadn't forgotten his debt of three, almost four, years.

The truth was that Henneberry himself had needed Jaeger as badly as the pianist had needed him. When Jaeger was unknown, Henneberry had already established himself but had begun to suffer intimations of a fall from favor. He had been growing stale. People had begun to be indifferent. What was needed was controversy, argument, any trick to revive interest. Henneberry had found his answer in Ross Jaeger: solidly talented and with large capacity for improvement, serious, and the kind of musician who wouldn't lose his head over sudden popularity. Jaeger had been perfect. Henneberry had held him up as a better jazzman than several top-name pianists, and Jaeger responded by nearly killing himself trying to live up to the role. And he had actually improved his work until now everything said of him in the past was true—he was a fine, imaginative, driving jazzman. He was still grateful to Henneberry, and of course the announcer was indebted to him. Without a talent he could shape to his own ends, Henneberry was nothing.

For awhile Henneberry daydreamed. It was his favorite. In it he exchanged places with Jaeger and became the center of attraction as he played magnificent, unheard-of jazz in a hushed nightclub of velvet drapes and soft-mouthed women. The spotlight sharpened his features as he bent over the keyboard, his eyes lowered and somber with the look of inner sorrow. And the women adored him as their men envied his greatness. He was Henneberry. There was no other piano in the world.

He passed his hand over his eyes. He felt almost erotic. His mind switched from himself to Jaeger, to the fruity darkness of the girl, Helen, back to himself, to Jaeger again, and finally, as though all these dreams had been preliminaries, to Jones.

Was Jones as good as Jaeger? Ross was one of the best

pianists in the country. He had proved it in New York, Philadelphia, San Francisco, Los Angeles, now here in Chicago again. He had proved it on the concert-tours and on any number of records with trios, big bands, and now his sextet. Everything considered, Jaeger was worth at least a quarter of a million dollars—much more, if he took care of himself. Henneberry's mind advanced one step. Jones was young; he had years of profit ahead. If he was as great as Jaeger seemed to fear he was . . . Again Henneberry dreamed, but this dream was not so impossible. Yes, he would find Jones.

He finished calculating and lit a cork-tipped cigarette and with feigned disinterest looked at the cover of a national entertainment magazine. Good coloring, Henneberry thought as he admired himself, but a bit too puckish. The photographer should have had more sense. Well, someday there would be time for a trip to Ottawa. Karsh had the ability to fix a man's personality.

The afternoon was dismal. Outside was the leaden cold; pellets of flying ice picked at the gray, rivulet-creased windows. He grew restless, let the magazine fall to the carpet, looked at the white-and-gold face of the electric clock, lurched to his feet and began to wander about the room picking up and examining and replacing any small objects that caught his eye. He found it hard to forget the young, unknown pianist. The good life hovered shimmering in his vision.

Even the tape-recorder failed to distract him. It was one of his latest acquisitions and the core of the custombuilt audio system which had cost him five thousand dollars. He turned it off with a sigh of ennui. The telephone burred politely.

It was the garage, and except for the transmission, the Ferrari was all right.

Well, Henneberry said blankly.

Oh, nothing to it, the garage said. Everything was taken care of. The transmission wouldn't give any more trouble.

Fine, he said, trying to remember when the transmission had given him trouble. That wasn't a bad little car, was it?

In a class by itself, said the garage. Really a pleasure to be able to work on it.

Well, he told the garage, the thrill for him was in driving it. Ticked along like a Swiss watch—that is, of course the Ferrari was Italian . . . Anyhow, it was too bad America didn't do such precision machinework.

The garage agreed. It certainly was a fine car.

Henneberry put the phone in its cradle and smiled. Once again he strolled about the darkening room. He halted before two long rows of books and put a hand to his chin. Ah, the books. Supple and warm in calfskin and morocco, brilliant-colored variety of dustjackets, thick books, thin, burnished gold-edged, so excellent. For a long time he gazed at them with devout possessiveness, and then, feeling his scalp needle slightly, walked stately and plump into the bedroom.

In the full-length mirror he saw himself: the robe, the gorgeous somber blackness of it, his face handsome in shadow, yes, heavy but nonetheless handsome, now—with his glasses off—his eyes darkly ascetic, dramatic. He gestured with left hand outstretched. He leered over his right shoulder, scowled. He folded his arms and looked slyly at his ponderous reflection, lifted his head.

"Now Paul—"

5

Holidays, especially Christmas, are black for most young men who are alone in a city. Surrounded by others who are not alone, the lonely one sees himself as unloved, without even a chance to give love, feels deep within him an awful isolation, and is afraid it will always be this way. He wants to be known to others. He wants to tell people who he thinks he is, but the very few who bother to listen have their own ideas of who he is. He cannot get through to another human being. Tortured by self-pity, he crowds to the center of the city with hopes of meeting someone like himself—and thousands there are. But his vanity makes him feel ashamed and proud, and he is afraid he will be rejected. So with his eyes he alternately fumbles and stares at the others, who alternately stare and fumble at him, and in the end his despair drives him to some professional sympathizer such as a religionist or a whore, or to a movie or a bottle, and if enraged, to a fight with a bigger man who usually shoves him down with one clumsy punch. The next day he can hardly chew his cafeteria food, but the loneliness is not so bad in daylight.

And then there are others.

It was early Christmas Eve when Virgil Jones put his face to the screened window and asked for a roundtrip ticket to Randolph Street. The flossy, henlike woman punched one magenta ticket and poked both into the metal cup with his change. Hatless and wearing a coarse overcoat, he went out on the long elevated wooden platform to wait for the IC electric train.

The night was like black crystal. Below the platform, along the tracks and curbs and lamp-posts, snow was sooty and pitted. Cars flashed by. Commanding the intersection of streets and tracks was the bright glassy clutter of Walgreen's. Newsboys garbled shouts on opposite corners. Some of the stores were open and there were a few shoppers.

On the platform fidgeted several drab men and women, two quietly drunk Marines, and a seal-coated mother who hissed sweetly through a veil at her daughter. The girl was painfully, grimly fifteen. Overweight and overdressed, she stood on her high heels as if they were ice-skates. Every few seconds she looked for the train. Out of helpless curiosity her eyes strayed to Jones. He winked. After that she looked for the train all the time.

A yellow-white bead in the distance grew larger, shimmering, and the bells began to hammer as the black-and-white crossing-gates came down like frozen fingers. Jones moved across the broad white safety line and stood almost on the edge of the platform. A sudden slugging rumble and the blunt nose of the first coach was on him, slowing with shrieks—stopped. As its doors slid open he turned and crossed the platform and after only a single glance jumped.

He landed on his feet in grayrock between the southbound tracks. Then he stepped over the outside rail, waited for a panel truck to pass, and crossed the street. He let his train tickets flutter to the pavement.

Not many people were on the street. A bird-legged man with wet red eyes came out of a tavern and blinked and focused and blinked as he searched his coatpockets for something. The closing door of the tavern chopped off an ascending string of carol-notes. Near the globe of a streetlamp a silver wreath rattled like a skeleton. It was a curiously stilled night.

Lights were on in the music store. There were no customers.

Seymour Schwab was in the back room. On the unpainted table lay a half-eaten tin of sardines, a box of soda crackers, an empty jar of instant coffee, a cup, and a can of evaporated milk. The room was hot. There was the smell of cardboard. A faucet dripped with slow regularity. When he heard the door open Schwab lifted his head from his hands and went to engage the customer.

He and Jones looked at each other. Schwab did not try to dissemble. He immediately motioned to the piano, and, as Jones sat down, locked the front door and flipped off the window lights. On his return Schwab pulled off three overhead fluorescents before boosting himself onto the counter. The store was deep in shadow. Wind pressed cracking sounds along the windows. Schwab filled his pipe, lit it. He did not want Jones to leave. Not tonight. This night would be very long, and he wanted Jones to play until the sky was gray again.

The music was everywhere, reflective and solitary. Schwab could hardly see the pianist's head and back, but he could hear. He did not interrupt. He was afraid a request or any fatuous praise might antagonize Jones, although even as he thought this he sensed that whatever he did or did not do would have little effect on the man. Jones seemed completely indifferent to everyone but himself. And he played magnificently.

But Schwab could not concentrate on listening. His mind went behind the music, to Jones, and from the pianist, to himself. In the few weeks since Jones first appeared, Schwab had begun thinking about him much of the time. And with his lonely, restless mind he had invented a relationship between them. They were alone. Both had few—if Jones had any—close friends. Both were drifters—unattached, independent, adding one day to the next, getting up and going to bed and getting up and going to bed again, executing the motions of living with no visible purpose except perhaps to keep themselves alive and occupied and in readiness for the day when they might find some direction. It was being alone that bound them together.

But there was a great difference, and Schwab could not understand it. Jones was alone without being lonely. He seemed to be actually happy.

Schwab told himself he was thinking too much. He was making a problem out of nothing . . . yet— Life was not chance or a confusion of indulged emotions. A man had to think out his problems, look at them as honestly as he knew how, find and apply the answers. At times the answers came from other men who, whether they won or lost, passed on their answers. But who had had the answer to loneliness? *It is not good that the man should be alone,* Schwab recalled. As far back as Genesis.

After this Schwab's mind veered from idea to idea until it was fixed on the music again. He knew next to nothing about jazz, but as he listened he began to feel a deep and positive appreciation of the strength, imagination and confidence of this piano. It seemed as though a man needed only to be able to hear to appreciate. No lessons were necessary. Jones was direct. He was a teacher who wasted no words. When he moved his hands he meant it. Again Schwab wondered why such a talent was unrecognized, why a man like Jaeger was a celebrity while Jones was unknown. Something was wrong.

Time passed. Schwab brought out the sardines and crackers and put them on the bench beside Jones. The pianist glanced, nodded, and continued his slow, delicate rendition of *Yester-*

days. Schwab returned to the counter. When the music stopped he could hear the dry crunch of crackers. Then the piano started again.

It was then that Schwab began to feel a certain nervousness. He did not know why, but it was there. The situation was unusual, if not almost ludicrous—a darkened store, sardines and crackers, two men who did not know each other, one playing the piano, the other waiting, yes, now waiting for him to finish so that they might talk, so that . . . Schwab knew. He had a job to do. He had promised the girl and Jaeger that he would find out more about Jones. It was an obligation he didn't trust. He wanted to know Jones for himself, not for someone else. And he had a vague suspicion that Jones would be better off if he did not get involved with Jaeger.

Abruptly he blinked, dropped from the counter and walked toward the door. Jones was waiting there, hands out of sight, the collar of his black coat framing the pale tight face. As Schwab fitted the key he expected to hear some sort of thanks from Jones. There was none. Jones was outside before Schwab realized it. The whole thing was over, and he had accomplished nothing.

He almost sprinted to the back of the store, threw himself into his coat, and on his way out yanked the strings of the lights which were still buzzing blue-white. He slammed the door, locked it.

The figure in the distance was unmistakable.

Muttering to himself for being so stupidly inept, Schwab lagged a block behind the pianist. He thought of calling out, but decided against it and instead quickened his pace to overtake Jones. His feet stung with every step. The air was becoming colder, and there was a long ghostly ribbon of clouds above the notched cornices of the roofs. The figure ahead of him was heading in the direction of the lake, and in three more blocks would reach the train station.

Schwab told himself he was not going to chase all over the city after anyone. He had no sooner thought it than the figure suddenly disappeared in the middle of the next block.

He did not know the block very well. A meatmarket, a dimestore, a Chinese restaurant, other shops, and above them, yes, dentists, a lawyer, a chiropractor . . . a hotel or rooms? He approached the point at which Jones had disappeared. There were many doorways and recessed entrances to stores, and all of them were dark. He was very close to it now. This one, he thought. This is the—

Wide eyes were not twelve inches from his.

For a timeless instant his heart stopped, he felt nothing, heard nothing, saw nothing but the eyes. Schwab backed off, his heart clubbed inside his ribs, a sound of wind was in his head.

"Well—" his lips said. His tongue protruded and wet them. Jones' eyes stared, lidless and artificial. In a matter of seconds Schwab recovered from his surprise. "I wanted to talk to you," he said.

"You want to know me." Jones' face came into the watery light. There was nothing sinister about his eyes; they had become mild and pleasant. "But don't try to know me too much. Some people have . . . well, we'll get along, and you'll be better for it. Let's have a drink over there. Is this Christmas Eve? Here—" his hand held a white card "—keep this."

It was an ordinary three-by-five card used for filing. On one side were horizontal blue lines; the other side was blank except for a single, tipped line of print. Schwab could not read it in the poor light. He held it as Jones walked with him across the heavy red bricks to a violet-lighted bar and its sign sputtering *Top Hat Top Hat Top Hat Top* like an idiot.

"My name is Schwab," he said as they reached the opposite curb. "Seymour Schwab."

"Virgil Jones. It's not on the card, but that's what it is."

As they pushed through the gouged wooden doors Schwab looked at the pianist—the entire face was bright and faintly, secretly amused at something not visible in the bar. There were few empty stools. All the booths were crammed with doughy forearms and slick, dismal blue serge. The *Top Hat Top Hat,* Schwab thought, sounded like a goose-farm. Everyone seemed to be trying to convince everyone else of whatever it was that was worth the shouting. And the jukebox was boiling.

They found two stools at the rear of the square bar. Schwab was aware that the pianist mounted as though he had been doing it all his life. The bartender was busy. While waiting, Schwab held the card to catch an amber glow from behind him. The printing had been done with a cheap rubber-alphabet-and-tweezers set. There was only one line.

I AM THE LAST INDIVIDUAL IN THE WORLD

He read it three times. Then, feeling an uneasy mixture of fear and an impulse to laugh, he noticed that Jones had been watching.

"Don't let it worry you," the voice said close to his ear. "I'm not blind or insane. You exist—all these people are real, too. It's just that nobody is an individual any more."

"Oh? Then what are we?"

"People who belong to everybody and everything else. In pieces. You don't own yourselves."

Without thinking, Schwab started to return the card.

"Keep it," Jones said. "You'll look at it again some day."

They ordered drinks. Schwab drummed his fingers on the scarred damp wood of the bar, studied the wide belt of tobacco-haze near the ceiling, then suddenly frowned. His eyes had fastened onto the pianist's left ear. It was curiously misshaped. The skin was white and swollen. It was the ear of a man who had been beaten heavily more than a few times. For the first time, then, Schwab gave close attention to the entire head and discovered that the face carried out the impression. Whatever Jones had been doing over the years, he had certainly run into violent opposition.

With this realization the whole evening began to seem dislocated; in Schwab's mind the few words spoken so far had the quality of a phonograph record played at too slow a speed, the words low and smeared like the speech of a spastic. Yet the words on the card remained clear: *I am the last individual in the world.*

"Tell me—" Schwab said "—do you really believe what's on this card?"

"What?" Jones grimaced and leaned closer.

"I said—do you really believe this?"

"I wouldn't say it if I didn't believe it." His tone of voice was patient and sincere, as if starting a lesson he had given many times before.

"Then you must feel . . . isolated."

"No. I have myself. Nobody else matters."

"Is that so?" Schwab looked intently at him. "Are you enough?"

With one motion Jones smiled and turned to face the question. His hand rested on Schwab's shoulder.

"I have to be," he said. "Everybody does. And they know it—that's the bad part. Everybody knows the biggest secret of all, and they won't use it. I suppose it's too much work." He looked around the crowded, noisy bar. "This is what I meant when I said people don't own themselves. All these people have jobs and families and ten million obligations. Inside, where it matters the most, all of them would like to be doing

66

something else, something they've always wanted to do. Maybe they'd just like to *try* another way of living. But they won't. They forget after awhile and tell themselves they really didn't want to change their lives. No, they have to 'make a living' and be a good citizen and all that. Take somebody like that old man—there, the one who's loosening his tie—think of him when he was about twenty-one. What did he want to do? Where did he want to go? When did he stop trying?"

"What have you got against the old man?"

"Nothing. Nothing at all. But look at the way he's breathing. He's sick. He's old and sick and not drunk enough, and this might be his last Christmas."

"You're a cheery philosopher."

"Ah," Jones exclaimed with a laugh. "You're like the rest of them."

"Naturally. Aren't you the only individual in here?"

"See?" Still smiling, Jones shook his head. "The bitterness comes out so easily."

"But you're not bitter."

"Why should I be? I'm not bitter at any *thing* because no *thing* is designed to make me unhappy. Things don't care. I could scream at the snow, but I don't think it would pay much attention to me—it would keep falling until it got ready to stop. And people? I don't get bitter at them. They just don't matter enough."

"You don't like people."

"I didn't say that. Ah, well . . ." he looked into space ". . . no one understands right away."

"Oh—I see now. The misunderstood young man."

Jones scratched his thin pale hair and laughed again. "You keep trying to defeat me, don't you? Well, that's the way it is all the time. Only remember: I'm not trying to beat *you* at anything. I'm not mad at you."

Schwab ordered another pair of drinks and looked around

67

the bar at all the moonish blurs of faces, at all the red mouths gabbling smoking drinking cackling. Dimly he realized the jukebox was moaning *Ave Maria*. It was a dismal way to spend Christmas Eve. He turned heated eyes at the calm, superior, untouchable, aloof, goddamnable contentment of Jones. He had an overwhelming desire to infect the pianist with his misery, to keep Jones with him. So he began buying drinks. Jones drank as fast as the glasses were set in front of him.

"What do *you* do for a living?" Schwab wanted to know.

"I do what I have to do, then what I want to do."

"A very original formula, I must say. Even the old man with the tie does that—all these 'failures' do that."

"Right," Jones answered, "more or less. But I have to do only a few things. Eat, pay for a place to sleep, have some warm clothes. It—"

"If that," Schwab broke in, "is your idea of—"

"—makes a big difference," Jones interrupted to continue. "I accept what I can't change and don't accept what I can change."

"You are simply full of formulas, aren't you?"

Jones' composure was undisturbed. "I'm working at the steel mills now. It takes care of the things I need."

"What do you do, *shovel?*"

"It depends. They tell us what we're supposed to do when we get there in the morning. Sometimes it's a shovel."

"And you like this sort of work . . ."

"When a job starts to bother me, I quit. I don't believe a job should own a man. A man gradually kills himself if he's working at something he doesn't like."

Schwab was silent for some time. "How old are you?"

"You're thinking," Jones answered with an easy grin, "that I can talk like this because I'm young and don't have any obligations or much ambition. Compared with other people, I guess you're right—but I don't care to worry about what

68

they think. The point is that I'm going to keep things this way. I don't belong to any job or any man or woman or any religion or any politics or the normal idea of success. I own myself. My name is Virgil Jones, and there's nobody like me in the whole world—there never has been and there never will be. Think about that. It's true for you too, true for everybody. Think of it. You have one life. It belongs to you." His voice had slowed to a deliberate, strong cadence.

"I'm one man," he went on, "and I'm going to own myself as long as I live. Selfish, you're thinking. All right, but remember that when people call a man selfish it's usually because he's doing what he wants to do instead of doing what they want him to do. So call me anything you like. I'll understand." The pianist half-closed his eyes and sniffled. His cold was becoming more bothersome.

Schwab did not know what to say. He had given up his intention of making Jones feel bad. Now he was partly ashamed that he had ever wanted to do such a cheap and selfish—yes, selfish—thing. Jones was not a bad sort. He wasn't arrogant in spite of his huge opinion of himself, and didn't act as though he despised everyone else for not living as he did. And, having such musical ability, he had none of the false pride which would make a laborer's job unthinkable.

"You play the piano very well, you know." As he said it Schwab noticed that Jones used both hands with equal skill in everything he did. His simplest, commonplace motions were unusually graceful.

"You've been playing for a number of years," Schwab went on.

Jones merely nodded. He seemed more interested in reading labels on faraway whiskey bottles.

"Probably intense practice," Schwab probed.

"There was a lot." And then Jones suddenly opened up. "I spent a long time with about a hundred teachers before I found out that it mattered and didn't matter. You know—it matters, but it doesn't matter—all this. It's never as important as you think it is, but still you can't say it's even close to being not important at all."

"A hundred teachers . . ." Schwab reflected. "Money can do a great deal . . ."

"Money? There wasn't much. Donations, that's what happened. I guess because they saw something in me. *'Promise,'* they used to say to me—you know how teachers are. So they passed me around, and I suppose all of them pretended they were young again, and that made them feel good for awhile."

Schwab squeezed his eyelids together. Opened them. Everything looked the same as before.

"You could probably make a lot of money playing professionally . . . or have you—"

"I've had jobs doing that," Jones said softly. "The longest one was three nights. I'm not what they call a good entertainer."

"That doesn't sound right. I'd say you're one of the very few men I've heard who make this jazz worth listening." Schwab sensed that his speech sounded blurred, incomplete. "To," he added.

"All *you* ask is to listen. Most people want to be entertained. That's what they call it. They want a puppet. But I'm not that."

"I can understand." Schwab frowned and tried to focus his eyes on the yellow plastic swizzlestick near his glass. It had been a long time since he had drunk so much so quickly. "But listen," he said in a hoarse voice, "isn't it just like another job? Don't you have to 'accept'—that's *your* word—what the job demands? Hunh?"

"No. When I'm a laborer only my hands are hired. When I play the piano it's both my hands and my head, and nobody

70

tells me what has to go on up there," Jones said, tapping his forehead with one strong finger.

The liquor began to have its effect on Schwab. He grew morose, stared glumly at the slatted floorboards behind the bar. He didn't feel too well. Glancing at Jones, he noticed that the pianist still seemed alert and clear-eyed. Jones had too many answers. Nothing so far had been able to dislodge him, even momentarily, from the mountain of his conceit. Jones was too sure of himself, and once again Schwab's loneliness goaded him on.

"Do you have a girl?" he asked.

"A girl?"

"Yes, a *girl,* a *wo*man. Here, I'll draw you a picture of one in case you meet one sometime . . ."

"I don't have a pencil," Jones said blandly.

Schwab answered between his teeth. *"Wit*-ty. Very, very *wit*-ty. You are a wag, Mister Jones. The last individual in the world . . . uncompromising is—you are . . ." His mind spiraled in confusion; he did not know where to put the words he was trying to think of. His eyes felt bleared and hot, and he thought of the black silence of his apartment. In his mind's eye the walls rose smooth and cold and windowless, and on the floor the rug grew thick and muffling. "Not funny. You're not at all," he mumbled.

"Don't let it own you."

"Let what?" He looked Jones up and down and felt himself begin to breathe more heavily.

"Being alone," Jones said. "Is your wife gone? Dead?"

Schwab could not answer.

"It's a bad thing," Jones went on, "but don't let it rule you. You've got your own life to—"

"That's enough!" Somehow he got off the stool. The ceiling the walls the shapeless faces the refracted colors through jagged glass spun crazily and melted like hot wax. He thrust his

71

face close to Jones'. The pianist's eyes showed no nervousness —they were, in fact, enragingly calm. Other faces were turned.

"Listen," Schwab hissed. "You listen . . . you—all the answers to all the questions, haven't you? Nothing bothers the great Virgil Jones, does it? Oh no, the great last individual has no problems, has he? If he doesn't like something, why, he just quits, he runs away from it. That's what he does . . . he's afraid—goddamn it, *stop leaning on your elbow!*"

A new voice said "*Gent*le-men" close to his ear. "*Gent*le-men . . ."

Schwab's mouth sagged, then shut itself loosely. He swallowed, and as he tasted the sourness in his throat, as his eyes felt like hot stones and as he lost the words of anger, his mind was suddenly illuminated by a soundless blinding spray like a rocket bursting in his skull—a mistake.

The flare died. It was dark again.

He pivoted clumsily and started to push through the jungle of shoulders and elbows and rumps along the bar. The floor seemed to be heaving. A talcumed face above emerald sequins made a smacking noise with its lips. He pushed the door, gasped with the shock of air. For a moment he let it freeze his throat and lungs and brain. Then he stumped past cold black storefronts in the direction of the music store, his car, and home.

Is your wife gone? Dead?

He passed someone—or were there two?—in a doorway. Above the thin singing wind in telephone wires the moon was like an eye. He turned and looked the length of the dark windscoured street. Should he go back? No. His vanity said no.

His Nash was paralyzingly cold inside, its windshield opaque with rime. The engine caught, died, caught again. He sat thinking as the car warmed up.

What had happened to Jones that made him so indifferent

to others? Where did he think he was going? Where *was* he going? Where was anyone going?

The windshield was clearing. He started the wipers, watched them scrape and push the softening ice. Soon the windshield sparkled like tinsel, like tinsel, and for a single razorlike second Schwab believed he was going home to a Christmas tree and his wife.

6

As Helen stepped from the elevator into the marbleized lobby her legs were suddenly wrapped in cold wind from the revolving door. After buying a pack of cigarettes at the cigar stand, she pulled her coat tight and went into the black, slushy, windswept street. The slickered crowd surged through beams of cars helpless in the rush of another Monday's end; mist slanted silver against streetlamps and headlights, became red and green and violet near neon. A traffic-whistle piped its piercing two-tone. Horns sounded and tires spun in the black wetness.

At Wabash Schwab was waiting in a drugstore. His glasses shone and his topcoat was streaked with rain. He took her arm and they went outside again.

"You'll have to tell me how to act," he shouted above the roar of an elevated train overhead.

"Don't," she said with her mouth close to his ear. "Too many people do that."

They ate dinner in a carpeted, candle-shadowy restaurant Helen hadn't noticed before. She did notice, however, that Schwab was looking around with a strained yet subdued expression. More than once she found herself glancing with him in an effort to identify that which attracted him.

"I'm sorry," he said suddenly. "It's just that I've been here before—in different circumstances." Then, without giving her a chance to interrupt, he told her about his wife. As he talked his voice gained balance, and upon finishing he hastily warned, "Look, Helen—this mustn't be a damper on the evening; I wanted to tell you merely to account for any 'moodiness' I might fall prey to now and then. And of course things aren't so bad when you're able to talk about them . . . *So!* tell me how you liked the Mozart."

"I honestly haven't listened to it." Her mind was still on his revelation. She felt sorry for him, but warned herself against a show of affectionate pity. Lonely men often thought any affection meant more than it was ever intended to be.

Schwab exhaled heavily. "You haven't listened to it. I might have known you'd forget it for this *be*bop boogiewoogie- woogie stuff, or whatever it's called . . ."

"I haven't had a chance," she said, smiling indulgently. "But suppose you tell me the news you said you had."

"Yes. Well, your boy has been in to see me a couple of times."

"Did you find out where he lives?"

Schwab blinked rapidly in mock amazement. "Just which one *is* your boy?"

"I thought you meant—"

"You're getting ahead of me." Schwab tapped his thumbnail on the stem of his goblet. "*Jaeger* has been in . . . and I must say we didn't hit it off so well—but that's past now. He's a rather—uh . . . intense fellow, isn't he?"

She nodded.

"Yes, but I think I can understand. You see, I've listened to some jazz records—his, for the most part—in the last few days, and it appears he's more of a celebrity than I thought. I guess it takes seriousness to get where he is, and more seriousness to stay up there." His forehead ridged. "But this isn't what you want to hear. About Jones—yes, he was in again,

Christmas Eve. Moreover, I had quite a talk with him . . ." His voice trailed off as he made a cage of his fingers and stared at the patterned tablecloth. "Am I entitled to one question before I begin? Good. The question: *Why?* Why does a successful musician like Jaeger spend time and energy in bothering with such an unknown as Jones? For what purpose?"

Helen moved the tip of her forefinger around the hollow of a cold spoon. She shook her head almost imperceptibly.

"I don't know if I can speak for Ross," she said. "But I've loved him long enough to try. You see, Ross has done this before; maybe he'll 'bother with unknowns' all his life. Maybe that's the thing that will keep him going. Jazz is everything with him, and he's determined to be the *best*—the best jazz pianist of all time. He needs to be reminded that he's *better* than others, and naturally he knows that he is when he hears some unknown who can't even sit in the same room with him when it comes to the piano. Jazz is his world. I tell him that he—well, that's between the two of us." She did not want to talk beyond that.

"Thank you for answering, Helen. Now for Jones . . ." He opened his billfold and gave her the card. "There he is, or who he thinks he is."

She read it, read it again. "I don't understand."

"Therein lies the tale." In a careful, reflective voice he told her what had happened, and as he finished he took back the card and slid it into his billfold.

"How did he know your wife—?"

"I guess I'm more transparent than I realized. Anyhow, the night went *poof!* because of my temper, and I'm sorry. I've been back to the tavern," he said with self-reproach. "Saturday I went in there hoping he might be a regular or that someone could tell me where he lives—I still don't know. No one remembered." He returned to his meal with a sad face.

Helen tried to form a unified picture of Jones from the story she had just heard. In her imagination, however, the pianist seemed like a jigsaw puzzle with only a few of the pieces joined. Parts, important parts, were missing.

"He sounds a little bit off, don't you think?" she asked.

"Perhaps."

"Well, that card, for instance . . ."

Schwab wiped his mouth with his napkin. "I know. I thought the same thing before he started talking. Remember, I can't give a verbatim report of what he said—but I tell you, when he explained himself he didn't sound so unreasonable. Understand me, Helen, I don't say he's found any universal truth or anything, but I *do* say he appears to live by what he believes, and that it seems to give him more calm confidence than I've seen in—than I've *ever* seen in anyone I've known. The man is unshakable."

"That's easy," she said with sudden annoyance. "Jones doesn't risk anything because he hasn't any goal, any ambition. We could all be 'unshakable' if we lived from day to day, like dogs."

Schwab smiled thinly. "But who would accept such a life?"

"Virgil Jones. The last individual dog in the world."

They finished the meal by talking about the jazz concert. She was glad she had invited Schwab. She could not tell if he was really interested or merely being polite, but it was easy to see he was enjoying not being alone. She determined to see more of him.

The air was filled with small pellets of snow which bounced and then disintegrated within seconds. Traffic was very light; they were able to cross against the light at every intersection. Schwab frequently blew into his cupped gloveless hands, and finally sunk them in his pockets. The night was growing colder.

"Do you know something?" he said, turning the upper half

77

of his body at a right angle to the wind. "I'm not too upset about losing my temper with Jones . . ."

"Why should you be?"

"Well, I know Ross wants to hear him again, and I thought I might have angered Jones into not coming back. But I think he'll come back—watch the curb. There. You see, Jones claims he 'owns' himself. Logically, then, that should mean that I have no effect on him; but I suspect he's human enough to want to prove it, and he'll prove it by coming back. He's almost forced to. He may not care what other people think, but you can be sure he cares what Jones thinks."

"Are you sure you're not thinking too much?"

"Is that bad?"

"It can be," she said, and thought of Ross.

Michigan Avenue appeared like a sudden grassy clearing among high cliffs of stone and steel. From the heights shone a stunning row of quick dazzling electric signs, changing, blinking, moving new colors with mechanical fluidity, washing the wet black street and polished cars with white and scarlet and pale blue as along the wealthy face of the city hurried hundreds against the wild rushing wind. From a block away Helen could see and almost feel the excitement building itself in the light-splashed area of Orchestra Hall. It was always exciting to her; she never tired of jazz. At the entrance crowded a mass of well-dressed, bareheaded men and women, most of them young and quiet, holding their excitement inside. There were many Negroes and Japanese. There were magnificently pale girls, dark girls, boys with hair too long and slick. Everyone seemed friendly. Cigarettes glowed, waggled with voices; there was a hoarse voice, the wet press at the door, the talk of jazz, of The Hawk of Flip of Lester of Dave and J. C. and Jackson and Safranski and Ross and Sarah, the nervous quieted impatience inside, all of it electric, crackling, contagious.

Their seats were far back and near the right wall. Surrounding them were young faces of all colors and shapes. Schwab's face came in a regular order of frowns, smiles, and blank incomprehension.

"Relax," she whispered at his ear. "The natives are friendly."

"I suppose these are the 'real' jazz-lovers back here."

"Of course." She looked around with a thin smile. "Have you ever been to a concert or play or game where you didn't hear where the real experts sat?" But she genuinely liked these cheaper seats. She had paid for them herself because she did not like to ask Ross for favors, and, more important, because the music was cleaner at a distance. Sometimes, sitting close, people did more watching than listening.

The heavy curtain drew back ten minutes late, revealing a stage empty except for a grand piano, a pearly cluster of drums, several cane chairs and three microphones. Packed into every corner of the huge hall, the audience silenced, stirred. Scattered coughs arose. Suddenly a cheer went up as a trombonist came onstage with an alto saxophonist. Next came a fawn-colored Negro with a springy stride; he climbed into the middle of his drums as a wave of applause moved backward over the crowd. It was some time before everyone came on. All of them acted loose and happy. They tuned up, paired off or in threes—their clothes draping big-shouldered as they worked with riffs and choruses, scraps of anything they had a mind to. Finally a spotlight pinned one curtained wing and followed the tall, easy grace of the promoter as he walked to the center microphone. He said a few seemingly offhand words, and bowed to let the jazz speak for itself.

Bap Bap went a heel on the boards, and they were only three notes gone before the audience roared to let the jazzmen know *it* knew—*C Jam Blues,* the driving, amazingly simple two-note blues with the strength of a locomotive. The concert was on, ready or not.

Helen looked at Schwab. He was frowning and his mouth was not fully closed. I wonder what he feels, she thought. Most likely that it's all very disorganized—very, very disorganized. Then she sat up to listen. The musicians formed one of the best groups in the country, and had been on tour for the past ten months. During that time there had been steady changes in personnel as some left to head their own combos or to join others, but replacements were made quickly, and the quality of jazz was still high. It seemed to Helen that replacements were always available. Somebody was always ready to take the place of a man who disappeared.

The first set lasted forty minutes, and closed with a languid *She's Funny That Way* featuring a fine, delicate, spiraling trumpet solo which went almost unapplauded. Helen was hard-faced as she accompanied Schwab to the lobby.

"It makes me sick," she began, making a place for herself near a sand-filled pillar for cigarettes. "That solo of West's— that was the trumpet—was the best thing so far, but just because it wasn't fast or loud . . ." She was at a loss to describe her disgust. "I thought these people would know better."

"Come on," Schwab smiled, "you take it too seriously."

"All right." She looked around at the close, elbowing mass of suits and dresses and hands with rings and watches and bracelets. "I suppose I get annoyed because I know what some musicians are trying for, how seriously *they* take it. It's a shame to see anyone go unappreciated when he's trying his best; I like to let them know they're not playing in a vacuum . . . Anyhow—how did you like it?"

"I did, for whatever that's worth. But what are the words I'm to use when I like this jazz? Isn't there some terminology . . . I've heard highschool girls say—uh . . . what is it now . . . ?"

"Just say you liked it. You'll go crazy if you start using all the hip talk."

" 'Hip'? "

"In the know. A cat who digs."

He looked at her. "I see what you mean."

"Do you really understand?"

"About going crazy," he said.

She decided not to tell him that crazy meant something else too.

Only a few in the audience knew that Jaeger was coming from the zouzou to sit in at the concert, so, when the promoter introduced him midway through the last set, the crowd erupted with a sustained explosion of surprise and delight. It was something for nothing, no extra charge, and the something was a better jazzman than anyone on stage.

She sat up straight, alerted because Jaeger did not even bow or wave in return for the applause, but instead went business-like and almost angry to the piano in the spotlight. Even from the distance she could see he was irritable. He sat and waited for the bass and drums to get ready.

Giving himself the beat with his heel, he charged into *Lover* as if he meant to pound the legs from under the piano. His attack was furious and smashing, and to those who were either untrained or had an incomplete idea of what he could do at his best, it sounded like great piano. But Helen knew it was not nearly his best. It had speed and terrific weight and the beat, but she could hear none of the clean, frozen sharp-ness for which she listened. He was sloppy. He was Nick Augustine at the piano. Big, rough, driving, driving, driving. And the audience loved it. She knew that many of them were stamping and whistling and bobbing rhythmically because they honestly liked the crude power; she knew that others shouting were shouting mainly because he was Ross Jaeger and they were afraid to suggest that he wasn't great this night. But he was not, and as she witnessed his repeated up-tempo fury on *Sweet Georgia Brown* she came to realize, slowly, unhappily, that he was blasting the piano because he had to. He could not expect appreciation of his subtle and thoughtful skill. He needed immediate shouts, immediate praise.

And he got them. The huge hall was full of thunder as he stood, and nodded now, and left, the white column of light pinning him like a thin, wound-up puppet disappearing behind the curtains. And the crowd wanted more. They stood and wanted more. He did not return. She knew he had already left for the zouzou.

After the concert Schwab drove her to the club through thick silver shafts of rain angling against the mirrorlike black street. Dark figures were everywhere ducking for shelter. Any minute, she thought, Chicago could expect a tornado. The weather was always fantastically inconsistent. She thought of Jones. Did he work in this rain? Did his hands get cracked and red and full of needles from the cold? He was a laborer, Schwab had said. Why? Couldn't he find a better job? From the little she had heard of Jones, he seemed to be far from stupid. If he was above average then, how could he be satisfied with such a punishing, futureless job? There had to be something wrong with a man like that.

She could see that Schwab was surprised by the dim, cramped and smoky nightclub. Yes, she imagined, Schwab had expected a den of gold-and-wine curtains and muted sounds, an elaborate platform on which the musicians played, and most of all, space in which to relax and listen. Instead he was forced to sit with his knees glued and drawn back, his eyes stung with smoke and his ears assaulted by a trombone that sounded like the beginning of a cavalry charge.

When the sextet left the stand she saw Jaeger go directly toward the back room. She also saw three drab, middle-aged men leave a booth. Schwab carried both drinks, and in the booth the nightclub was not such a cell. She sat where she could watch the entrance to the back room.

82

"Lee . . ." She touched Jackson's arm as he passed. Remembering, she delayed her question until she had introduced Schwab. Jackson remained standing, his habitually loose smile strangely forced.

"Does Ross know we're here?" she asked.

"I guess," Jackson said quietly. "He's on back. Be out in a bit, girl. Sure thing. Well . . . I got to pick up on some air. Nice meetin' you, daddy-o. Yeah—Ross'll be out, Helen."

She said thanks vacantly. Her mind had gone into the room where she knew Ross was drinking. For a long time her eyes fixed on nothing.

"Leonine," Schwab reflected. "An engaging fellow."

"They're all engaging. Musicians are absolutely . . . don't mind me. I'm just bitter because I never learned to play the tuba."

"Have I said something wrong? If I did, I'm—"

"No, of course not." She sighed, looked about distractedly, set her drink against the bakelite ashtray. "I don't know why I talk to you so much. Maybe it's because you're a good listener, maybe because you're not a musician—you're outside of this. Maybe that's why I tell you so much."

"I'll always listen." Schwab was grateful.

"And I'll probably always talk. That's what I'll do. Talk and hold a man's head in the right place when he's got the blues. I'm sorry," she added quickly, remembering that when Schwab felt blue he had no woman to hold his head anywhere.

"Forget it," he said with understanding. "Do you want to tell me what bothers you, Helen?"

She closed her dark-lashed eyes. "Greatness."

"Ross?"

"I don't have many illusions about myself." When she opened her eyes she saw Schwab frowning as he tapped his thumbknuckle against lower teeth. "Yes, Ross," she told him.

"He's big. He's one of the jazzmen who matters. People listen when he plays. His agency in New York listens when he talks. But it isn't enough for him . . . he wants more. He wants his own idea of greatness."

"Greatness," he repeated. "It's like 'success'—a bad word. An abstraction we try to make concrete . . . and what grief we find. All of us, yes."

"Not everyone."

"Yes, everyone—I insist on it. Everyone in his own way, in his own terms. It is all relative, of course, but nevertheless, it is in all of us. And it starts with wanting to be *better than*. There is the first step." He bit his lower lip. "And we all take it . . . musicians—creative artists, I should say—are no special breed, I think. Superiority. Yes. Look, doesn't that girl over there—the pretty Italian-looking one with big white earrings, yes, that one—don't you think she wants to be considered *better than,* say . . . that—" his heavy-lensed eyes flashed over the crowded tables "—that blonde, for instance? Of course she does, and vice-versa. If not 'better' in some vague way, then better-looking, having a better personality or figure; if none of those, then having a boyfriend who is better-looking or has a better personality, perhaps even one who has nothing but more money or a bigger, newer car. We all compare like that, one way or the other. We need to tell ourselves we're—we've got to be—better than *some*one. What a terrible state of mind we'd be in if we couldn't tell ourselves that!"

"But that isn't necessarily 'greatness.' "

"Not exactly, but remember, I said this thing was relative. The point is that each of us has a scale of values—don't ask me where we get them, although I will say most people accept their personal values with a dangerous absence of criticism— and these values give us a kind of balance, uneasy as it may be. We need this. We need to feel superior to other human beings. Without that feeling we'd be in an awful condition. Some-

84

times that happens, you know. Read the newspapers. When a man comes to see himself as the *worst* being in the world, when he's no longer able to tolerate his own existence, he loses everything. He loses respect first for himself, then for others, and finally, for life. He murders his ego, and then himself. He hangs himself, cuts his wrists, jumps out of windows, takes gas, eats poison . . . so. Yes, I see you're wondering what all this has to do with greatness. Well, in short, I think —there is no difference. God is The Devil, Love is Hate, The Greatest Sinner is The Greatest Saint."

In her mind loomed Ross: his thin, hard body grown to the piano, the lock of dark hair curved above half-fainting eyes as his hands blurred above the keys, his right heel like a piston, the beat, the beat, fused with his body to the piano, the altar, and in his eyes were dreams.

"Then," she said, "someday he might believe that he's the worst."

"Who?"

"Ross, of course."

"Oh . . . yes—yes, of course." His mind appeared to be somewhere else. "Uh . . . unlikely, though. Balance . . . um —'maturity,' so to speak. I . . . all that comes with time and experience, I suppose. If I were you I wouldn't—"

"Seymour—" she looked closely at him "—what were you thinking about?"

Schwab blinked, smiled nervously, rubbed his hands together and shook his head. He looked beyond her, signaled.

"Nothing," he said. "Nothing at all. Shall we have a drink?"

7

Paul Bauer was a clean, spare, sixty-year-old machine with aluminum hair and the patience of a guillotine. A bachelor, he wore Robert Hall suits in mealy shades, ties knotted like dried peas. One day a week, subject to change without notice, he spent eight hours at his office overlooking the greenish scum of the Chicago River. It was hard to say why he went there at all. Perhaps it was to think of what he had been, what he still was. Or perhaps it was only to wipe a film of dust from the photographs ranging the paneled wall like the trophies of a headhunter.

At the moment he was especially fond of one picture, a portrait of a round-faced man with glasses. The prizefighters and the old colored pianist were all right, but the round-faced man was best—best because he was now sitting on the other side of the applewood desk, looking like what he was, a man who was owned.

"I went there today," Henneberry said. "Of course one shouldn't expect too much from the initial attempt, Paul. You understand my position . . ."

"I understand your position." His voice, like each of his fingers, had the dry, silky quality of chalk.

". . . A stranger, as I admit I am in some quarters of Chicago, is unable to ask questions without arousing some suspicion, and I must say that the owner, a Seymour Schwab, was reluctant to answer most of them."

"You failed," Bauer said without emotion.

"Not exactly, Paul. I—"

"You found out what the store looks like inside. You also had a hot fudge sundae at the nearest drugstore and were recognized by a couple of highschool girls who asked you for your autograph and you gave it to them, and if they hadn't recognized you, you would have put hot fudge sundaes in your face all afternoon until some little girls saw who you were and wet their pants." Again his voice was flat and calm.

"Oh, hah . . ." Henneberry tried a laugh to hide his embarrassment. "You're being hard on me, Paul."

"So you don't know where he lives."

"I've told you all I know, Paul. Jaeger—"

"No you haven't." He picked up a paperweight and slowly shook it. Inside the glass ball snow swirled around a castle. "You're one of these bright young men, Henneberry. This paperweight I have here—watch it. See, the snow is slowing down, starting to fall to the bottom. In another thirty seconds this ball will be as clear as if nothing had ever happened in there. We'll be able to see the castle inside. Everything will be clear again. Transparent, like you, announcer. All I have to do is shake you up, and after a few seconds you get very clear . . ."

Henneberry did not seem to know what to do with his mouth. His fingers counted each other. He stood and walked to the window. A creamy gull floated past and after a weak cry stood on one stiff wing and vanished into the mist. On the river a boat drew a wide V in the water. Henneberry watched the traffic on the bridge.

"I know what you're thinking," Bauer said. "I knew it a minute after you started talking, announcer. I could see what

you really wanted was control of this Jones. You were thinking that I'm old and have too much money and nothing to do
but count it. You wanted my blessing, and help, if you needed
it. Here, turn around and look at me." His bloodless lips
parted to show small teeth too perfect, too shiny. "Not a very
good try. You ought to realize that nothing is greater than
its creator. I am yours."

"I dare say I am independent now, Paul."

Bauer's smile became a thin straight line. "Don't 'dare say'
too much. I warn you. And I ask you how you'd like to be
on the street in less than a week . . . Ah, your mouth opens,
but it doesn't say anything. Make it say something, announcer."

"I could—could go away. Go to California."

Bauer looked at his thumbnail. "I've been there. And I'm
remembered. Would you like to try another location? India?"

"All right, Paul." Henneberry sat down heavily. "I'm sorry."

"That isn't *nec*essary," Bauer said in the manner of addressing a child. "I understand. We all like to influence others,
to have a certain control over them. The trouble is, everyone
isn't fit to control others, everyone isn't strong enough. Those
who are weak are ruled. That is life. The weak can only
dream; it is a rag doll they like to sleep with, this idea of
ruling."

Henneberry nodded like a tired horse. "What do you want
me to do, Paul?"

"The usual. Nothing right now."

"But supposing someone else were to—"

"Let me worry about that." As the old man stood, conclud-
ing the discussion, his narrow face changed from a sudden
idea. "Wait for me to call you, announcer. I might have some
work for you, and who knows?—maybe part of this Jones.
Would you like that?"

"I would."

"Maybe a fifth, to begin with. That could mean a lot. Jones is a great pianist." No sooner had he said it than he wheeled, stared out the window.

"Have you heard him?" Henneberry asked in surprise.

"No," Bauer answered evenly, his back still toward the desk, "but Ross Jaeger is no fool about music. He's a fool about life, but not about music."

"But Ross has only heard him once."

Bauer turned around. His eyelids looked heavy. "I assume and act when the weak are still asking themselves questions. Now you can leave and ask yourself all the questions you want." Again he turned to the window, his bony hands joined behind his back.

When the door closed Paul Bauer swung around, strode across the room and locked it. He said something to himself. He struck his right fist into his other palm, began pacing like a nervous bird. After some time he stopped before one of the photographs. It was of an old Negro with a shy, wrinkled face. With both hands Bauer removed two thumbtacks, stood indecisively for a moment, and then replaced them. He stepped back and looked at his gallery. Several minutes passed before he returned to his desk and slipped a wallet from his inside breastpocket. He opened it and began unshuffling cards and folded papers. Finally he stopped and held something in his clawlike hand. It was an ordinary three-by-five card used for filing, and on it was a single line of rubber-stamp print.

When shortly past midnight he walked into the smoky hot Bar & Grill on South Park faces turned and the talking and laughter fell off. Stopped altogether. From somewhere in the underlit room came the high, sorrowful voice of Dinah Washington singing through the scratch and hiss of an old record.

> . . . . . . but I won't be blue always,
> For the sun will shine in *my* back door some day.
> Trouble in mind, that's true . . .

They looked narrow-eyed at his white skin and whitish hair and leaned together over the bar and resumed talking—now guardedly, now lifting heavy eyes toward him every few words. Several of the women looked for something in the darkness at the rear of the long room.

> . . . . . . lay my head on some lonesome railroad iron,
> Let the two-nineteen train *ease* my troubl'd mind.
> Trouble in mind, I'm . . .

Jones stood at the door-end of the bar and was instantly approached by an old arthritic Negro wearing a hotel hand-towel as an apron. In a perfectly-at-ease voice Jones asked for a bottle of Miller's.

"No Miller's," the old man said, his lips continuing to move after the words had passed. "Canadian Ace, Fox—"

"Canadian Ace."

The bartender did not move. He licked his lips and fingered the handtowel stuffed around his waist. He glanced toward the back of the room where now most of the people were looking.

"Boss," the old man said softly, "we just runned outa beer this minute. Maybe ef you come back sometime, we . . . maybe ef . . ." But he could not even convince himself. He hobbled to the cooler and came back with the bottle of beer.

Jones was just watching the foam reach its peak an inch from the top of the glass when the record ended. He did not seem to notice the gathering silence. He drank and refilled and did not bother to pick up his change. Even when a door slammed and all the dark faces wrenched toward it, and then toward him, he remained as calm and assured as if there was nothing at all unusual in drinking in a place even white policemen avoided.

From the single toilet door in the back had come a heavy-weight of a Negro whose wound-up walk suggested that he had done more than a little boxing. And when his face pushed into the faded light at the end of the bar there was no doubt. It was a flat, hard-lipped face with eyes made nearly Oriental by swellings of scar tissue at the brows. His skin was a peculiar olive color and he wore a wide-brimmed fedora so nappy that it appeared made of gray fur. He was smiling when he joined two women at the other end of the bar. But his face did not hold the smile. One of the women made a decisive motion with her head, and the deep eyes followed her indication, and there was nothing anybody could do then because he was already on his way toward the white boy.

"Now Jewel . . ." the bartender said weakly, moving along behind the bar, ". . . Jewel, you just think what you doin' now . . . you ain't got no call to get the law down on us heah . . . now that's all they is to it, I say."

The big Negro ignored the words. He continued walking until he stood close behind and a few feet to the right of where Jones now lowered his glass and slowly turned on the barstool. For a long time Jones faced him without any trace of nervousness.

"This boy ain't doin' us no harm at-all," the old man said, his words quivering with fear and anger. "He goin' suck up his beer and get out and they's no harm done you, Jewel."

The big man took his hands from the pockets of his chalk-striped suitcoat. His voice was as flat as a knife when he spoke:

"Ah don' like the color you motherfuckin' skin."

From the far end of the bar rose a shrill, delighted cry. The men seated nearby stared at Jones and were silent.

Jones continued eyeing the big brutal face.

"Damn you, Jewel!" shouted the old man. "I'm fixing to call the *po*lice, you don't leave off this talk!" No one was listening to him.

"Well—what you got to say, white boy?"

"Nothing," Jones said steadily. "I came in here to have a beer, not to talk."

"Oh, you ain' gonna talk? You too good to talk to us, huh?"

Jones raised the glass to his lips.

With one blurred open-handed sweep the big man smashed the glass from Jones' hand against the loops of a cane chair. And this time his thick voice was a scream:

"What makes you think you gotta right to come on in here for any damn thing? You think you white pimps own ALL this city?"

Jones did not answer.

"Come on," the big man said roughly, reaching for Jones' elbow, "Ah reckon you n' me go outside . . ."

"You don't have to drag me." Jones pulled his arm back so that the meaty brown fingers seized air.

"Hey!" the voice raged. "You gettin' *cute?* You want it *here?*" He did not wait for an answer. Just as Jones was getting off the stool, the Negro swung. The hammer of a fist struck with a pulpy crack against the left side of Jones' head, knocking him facefirst to the littered floor.

"Now you done it!" the old man screamed. "Now you gone and done it for sure, you big dumb nigger you!" All the while his furious anger spit out, he was coming around the end of the bar and finally bent down as best he could over the huddled motionless figure.

"Man," said an awed voice from the bar, "you sho' hit him a lick, Jewel."

"Ah teached him, all right Ah did." For a moment he rubbed his opposite thumb across the knuckles of his right hand and watched the old man laboriously drag the white boy and prop him against a stack of Coke cases. Then Jewel went muttering back to his women at the other end of the bar.

The old man straightened. "Leave me have that rag," he commanded a group of men. He caught the soggy cloth, folded it and put it to Jones' forehead. "Smart man down theah," he said to the men, his eyes snapping down the bar. "He so smart and randy we gonna make anothah war in this town like the last one. Be shootin' each othah outa streetcars agin. Wait and see. That dumb nigger—*yes, you, you big goddamn Bushman! . . . I ain't scared of you nohow!*—he knock anybody in the head for enough to buy him some pussy, and now this boy just 'cause he white. Lord God, we gonna have a war sure . . ."

"Ah," said a stocky man with dimestore glasses, "you too old, Crip, that's all I got to say. This white boy axed for it. He got no business messin' down here where *we* live."

"Now you done said it," said another.

"We gets in a war," said a drunk and happy woman, show-ing bright gold-filled teeth, "Jewel goin' be a tank and I goin' *ride*." With a whoop she led the others in laughter.

The old man's mouth curled with disgust. With a horny thumb he lifted Jones' right eyelid and then jumped when he saw that the eye was looking at him. Immediately the other eye opened.

"Boy—I . . ."

"Never mind," Jones said strengthlessly and without anger. "I'm all right now." He pressed his hand to the side of his head.

"Catch hold my hand now and—"

"Thanks, but I'll make it by myself in a minute."

"I just don't know . . . boy, you got to understand . . . this man ain't right in his *head*, he ain't. He do this all the time—whop folks bad just for nothin'." His voice fell to a whisper. "I tell you some one of these days they goin' fry his butt down to Cook County 'lectric chair, and believe me it can't be too soon for me. Jewel just does bad for all of us. But what can a old man like me do? I can't do nothin' at-all, that's what. I can just . . . dog it, I can't rightly do one damn thing I think of. You know? How you feeling? You ain't goin' get the law on me, is you boy? I just a old—"

"It wasn't your fault." He tried but stopped shaking his head to emphasize his words. His eyes squinted and then closed briefly. "No, I'm not going to make trouble for any of you."

"Get the law on Jewel."

Unaided, Jones got to his feet without answering. He looked at the line of faces watching as the old man ineffectually slapped at the dirt on his coat. Then, with the entire room frozen into place, he went to his bottle on the bar and asked for a glass. It was some time before anyone moved, and then it was as though in slow-motion. The old man brought the glass, and Jones emptied his bottle, and as he started to drink, Jewel was behind him again.

"Ah guess you mus' of liked that first one, you come back to get some more, boy."

Exactly as he had done before, Jones turned on the stool. This time, however, his voice was not mild.

"I came in here to have a bottle of beer. I'm going to have it. If it takes me two hours, I'm drinking this beer. Your move."

They stared at each other. Jewel began rubbing his knuckles; his upper lip twisted faintly. Jones held the glass in his right hand.

"Drink you beer. Go on—drink you beer."

For several seconds Jones did not move. Then he raised the glass and drank half.

Jewel laughed viciously. "Good, huh? You drink it when Ah tells—"

94

Before he could finish, Jones drank more and continued staring.

"Hah!" Jewel averted his eyes, scoffed again, and talked to the walls. "You jus' a *flea,* that's all. Ah could mash you . . . whap!—" he snapped his fingers "—if Ah want to. Easy. Sheeit, you jus' a no-count white *bug* to me. Hear?"

Jones drained the glass and set it on the bar. He got off the barstool and nodded politely to the men around him.

"Goodnight," he said to the old man, and nodded curtly to Jewel as he moved toward the door.

"You get on outta here n' stay on out now on!" Jewel shouted.

With frantic, painful haste the old man intercepted Jones near the door and clutched at his sleeve.

"You ain't goin' make a fuss with the *police?*"

"No. It wouldn't be right to take it out on all of you for what only he did. That wouldn't be right," Jones finished, clapping his hand lightly on the old man's shoulder.

"Sure glad to heah that, sure glad you feel that way. But boy —just some advice . . . ef you don' mind . . . you shouldn't *ought* to come down heah ef you want some juice. You ought to just not. You white folks got plenty places of you *own* wheah you can have a good time. You ought to keep to *them* places. They *yours.* It ain't that—"

"Hey, Crip!" a husky voice roared. *"Leave off suckin' round that ofay—you too old to try passin' any more, nigger!"* The hot shadowy room shrieked with laughter.

"O my," groaned the old man, holding the door open for Jones, "see what I puts up with? Heah that crap I get back theah? Man, I get *so* brought down these days. I got pains and bills and I got to take all this too, and I sweah it brings me down so's I believe I goin' be the most happiest man at my funeral."

95

8

At ten o'clock a white-hot strip of steel forty feet long had been all right going into the last shaping die, but when it started to come out, people began running. The strip arched searing high in the smoky air and then writhed down, oozing like toothpaste as the whistles screamed and screamed until they suddenly stopped and the mill was quiet except for the giant, twisted, reddening hissing in air. Mechanics came, swore, clambered. The mill was down. And if it hadn't been for the cobble, the laborers thought later, what went on about Jones might never have happened.

When the mill went down there was no work except for repairmen and those cranemen and cold-saw workers not directly connected with the rolling-process. It was a simple situation: no steel, no work. Nothing to clean or polish or sweep; this was a blooming mill, not a restaurant. So the laborers sat and got warm and smoked and drank coffee from milkbottles and told jokes, and if the mill was down all day, well, that was the way it was.

There had been five men in one of the roller operator shacks at the time Jones came in. An elaborate story of fornication was in progress, so the others merely nodded to him. He sat on the bench, drew up his legs so that his forearms rested on his knees, and began reading a week-old newspaper page he had got from the floor. Loud, broad laughter marked the end of the story, and, after shaking his head with complete, wordless satisfaction, the storyteller, an old Negro with whitish furze on his cheeks, turned to Jones.

"Hey, Sometimey," he said. "What you saying?"

"Nothing yet," Jones said, a smile playing at the corners of his mouth.

"Then what you reading so studious about?"

And Jones had been about to answer when the door opened. It was Matulich, a pusher none of the laborers liked. He had a square face and a prominent underjaw and was thick through the chest. His mouth worked like a pair of pliers.

"Let's go," he said to Jones, and motioned outside.

Jones looked at him questioningly and did not move.

"I said let's *go,*" Matulich repeated.

"The mill is still down."

"Look—you hear what I said? Now get up off your dead ass."

"The mill is still down," Jones said calmly.

Matulich put his hands on his hips and glared around the crowded shack. Everyone knew he was trying to get Jones to do a job—some small, meaningless, pretty-up job—he himself would get credit for.

"What's your name?" he asked roughly.

"You know what it is," Jones said.

"Why don't you leave off, Matulich?" the storyteller said. "They ain't no work to be done, and you knows it."

"You keep out of this, Johnson."

For some reason Jones started to laugh.

"Oh, it's funny, is it?"

"That's right," Jones said, still laughing softly, "it's funny." His easy, careless amusement spread to the others, and as they made big eyes and began chuckling, fury expanded Matulich's face.

97

"We'll see how funny this is," he growled at Jones. "We'll see Cas about this! And where's your *hat*? That's another thing—not paying attention to safety rules!"

"Inside my jacket," Jones said, ignoring Matulich, "is a fedora about a sixteenth of an inch thick, made of felt. This protects me from falling objects such as a thirty-pound billet. Matulich wears, as you see, a leather cap. This protects him—"

"A smart sonofabitch, ain't you?" The pusher seized Jones' arm and tried to force him off the bench.

"Take—your—hand—away." In the sudden absolute silence Jones' words clicked like the mechanism of a weapon.

Matulich withdrew his hand. "You coming to see Cas?" he said in a voice that still threatened.

"Get out of here."

Matulich tossed his head like an angered bull and charged out, heading for the tin-roofed office fifty yards away. Jones picked up the piece of newspaper and resumed reading as if nothing had happened. Someone struck a match. Another blew his nose.

"Hey, guy," a voice said. "You shouldn't of pissed him off like that. Him and Cas are—well, you know . . ."

"Yeah, man," someone else said. "I don't know what to tell you."

They all started mumbling sadly and seriously about what a bad deal it was to get any boss down on you. Jones went on reading.

"Sometimey—" the storyteller said "—none of us likes that old H.S. no better'n you does—but shoot, boy, you got to remember who he is. He got connexions. You cain't just go on and angry up the bosses like that. A man got to back off once in a while . . ."

"Damn right," another voice said. "You can't beat City Hall."

"There you go," the storyteller said in agreement. "One

man got not a snowball chance these days. The system already set up. All the big jobs is taken, and we just a bunch of sheeps."

"So they fire me," Jones said indifferently.

"So they fires him," the storyteller told the others. And then to Jones: "Mighty proud talk, boy, but I guess you ain't seen times when you belly sucking you backbone . . ."

"I make my times," Jones answered in an almost inaudible voice.

"Proud—mighty proud talk. Good to hear. But boy, I cain't see how you aim on keeping it *up*."

Jones replied with a shrug.

In less than five minutes the shack door opened. Matulich wore a heavy smirk when he spoke. Jones calmly put down the paper, got up nonchalantly, and left with him.

"That ripped it," a voice sighed.

"Know something?" said a pale, hard-eyed Pole. "I knew that kid wasn't going to be around here long. I knew it right away. He just asks for it, all the time."

"Always rockin' the boat," said another.

"Like at the canteen," the Pole said. "Remember that?"

They all remembered. On his second day at the mills Jones had made the mistake of not backing down to an open-hearth man during lunchtime at the canteen. When it was over—and it was the fastest slugging any of them had ever seen—they had led Jones, protesting, to the infirmary for five stitches where the crown of his head had struck the edge of a table. He had been in the right, all of them had agreed, but Jesus-MaryandJoseph, being right wasn't worth five stitches.

"He just don't give a damn for nothing," said the Pole.

"He'll give a damn when Cas gets him," another voice said.

"I don't know about that. There's something about this guy . . . I don't think he will. I got four-bits says he don't."

"Four-bits. You got a lotta confidence."

"Four-*bits*. Put your money where your mouth is."

The bet was made. They waited. The Pole picked up the newspaper Jones had been reading, wrinkled his nose, and let the page slide to the floor. It was the society page.

"Going to miss old Sometimey," the storyteller said aloud and to no one in particular. "Sure, sure—I tell you he gets himself let off for this. He going to be fired, all right. They been watching him all along. Works good, but you knows that ain't all they wants from a man. Man got to have the right *at*-ti-tude. And he ain't got it. No, man. Just don't take nothing from nobody . . ." For a second his lips curled back over long thin teeth. "But dogged if he ain't the *banty*est rooster I done ever worked with."

Jones was gone five minutes, then ten, fifteen, and as time went by the Pole began clearing his throat and jingling his pocket for the benefit of his betting opponent. After nearly a half-hour the door opened and Jones was smiling at all of them.

"They fired me," he announced. "But you can see I'm still alive."

And that was all.

He was gone.

"Pay me," said the Pole, standing.

"Like hell I will," the other said. "We didn't bet on if he was getting canned or not. We bet on whether Cas gave him a bad time and he took it. Didn't we, Johnson? Wasn't that the bet?"

"Ask Matulich," the storyteller said. "That was the bet, and he can tell you what happened."

The Pole and the other went outside and looked across the hotbed for Matulich. He was not in sight. A few laborers straggled along toward the canteen. A nearby cold-saw made a piercing shriek and fell off to a whine. In the distance they could see Jones walking jauntily past a salamander topped with fluttering blue flames.

"I know I win," the Pole said. "When that kid come in just now he didn't look like nobody finished eating him out. He looked like he always does, like he don't care for nothing."

"Hey Matulich!" the other called. Two figures had come out of the office. One was bareheaded and wore a checkerboard mackinaw—Cas. He was shaking his head angrily. Finally Matulich left him. The Pole and the other waited until he came up to them, then asked the question.

Matulich folded his arms across his chest and looked far away to the point where Jones, miniature in the distance, walked between a canyon of stacked steel beams toward Personnel.

"Someday," he said, "that sonofabitch is going to get killed."

The Pole made a face, turned to the other.

"I don't bet much," he said, accepting the fifty-cent piece, "but I bet on the right things."

Seymour Schwab walked back and forth behind the counter and now and then tapped a protruding record into alignment. He had an unlit pipe in his mouth and a frown above his glasses. Finally he leaned against the counter, stared at the front door, and tried to create another premonition.

In order to ease his impatience and a feeling of guilt, Schwab had taken to self-willed premonitions, at the rate of two or three a day, concerning Jones' reappearance. None of them had come true. Jones had not returned since Christmas Eve, almost two weeks ago, and Schwab blamed himself. He had lost his temper and he had lost Jones, and the unadmitted truth was that he, Schwab, was beginning to see the pianist not as someone interesting in himself, but as a kind of object whose acquisition would make the girl happy. Schwab was unconsciously counting on Jones to get him in-

volved with jazz, nightlife, and Helen, although he knew
Jaeger had to be included in their relationship. When Schwab
thought about the two of them he did not know how to feel.
He wondered if they would eventually get married. If they
were sleeping together now. And? But he could conclude
only that he wanted to do some thing which would please
her, even if it meant nothing more than helping Jaeger find
Jones, and himself. That was what he wanted, he guessed.
To do a thing which would make her happy. It was all he
had a right to want.

Now he watched the early night outside, saw seemingly dis-
embodied heads passing the windows, saw tubes of neon, reflections quick in glass, saw mirrored colors, headlights. It
was the fifth night of the year.

At six o'clock Jaeger put in his customary appearance. He
wore a gabardine raincoat and his face was as taut as a drum-
head. As he came toward the counter, shaking rain from his
coat and the ends of his fingers, Schwab let him know with
a motion of his head that no, Jones had not been in.

Jaeger said he had heard Henneberry had been in.

Schwab said he didn't know the name. Was he looking
for Jones?

Jaeger said yes, and described the announcer.

Schwab remembered.

Jaeger asked if he remembered Henneberry saying that he
wouldn't be back, that the idea of hunting the pianist was
childish.

Schwab did not remember Henneberry saying that.

Jaeger tapped a thumbnail against his teeth and swore. He
said he thought so.

Watching the man in front of him, Schwab began to fear
that the situation was more complicated and serious than he
had thought. At first there had been only the nameless vagrant
who had played the piano. Then the girl and Jaeger had

heard, had become involved. Jaeger: famous, successful, and infected with the idea of greatness. And through him a man named Henneberry, an arrogantly superior fat man who wore customtailored suits, who was undoubtedly someone of importance, and who had apparently lied to Jaeger about continuing the search for Jones.

And meanwhile the vagrant had become infinitely more. The last individual in the world, as he had described himself.

For a long time Jaeger paced the floor in a triangular pattern, his eyes alert to every sound coming from the vicinity of the front door. At last he stopped forming the triangles and asked to listen to Stravinsky for awhile.

Schwab wanted to know if he really wanted Stravinsky.

Jaeger said he did.

Schwab pouted but nevertheless handed over an album and watched Jaeger go into one of the booths.

In the next twenty minutes a few customers came in but did not stay long. Jaeger opened the door of the booth to let smoke billow out. His face did not look as if it enjoyed Stravinsky. It didn't look as if it enjoyed much of anything. Finally he handed back the album.

Prokofiev? Schwab asked.

Jaeger shook his head and said he was getting tired of waiting. The way he said it implied that he was not only tired of this night, but of all the nights he had waited in vain. He was tired and angry and ashamed that he, a celebrity, had pridelessly lowered himself by waiting in an insignificant neighborhood record store for a pianist who had the nerve to be indifferent to him. But he did not say any of these things. Instead he lit a cigarette and with one big hand massaged his throat as if trying to help the smoke pass. Then he glanced at his wrist and said he would wait for ten minutes.

After half that time Schwab looked at the figure in the doorway and told Jaeger he wouldn't have to wait any longer.

TWO

I

Months later, after the strange and terrible end, Schwab was able to remember in infinite detail the first real meeting of the pianists. Jones played and Jaeger listened, and in Schwab's mind the scene remained with the impersonal clarity of a scientific photograph.

Jones worked at the piano for over a half-hour. Jaeger looked at the wall. Schwab looked at Jaeger. There was no indication of feeling on Jaeger's face, but Schwab could not help noticing that he was chain-smoking as if each cigarette was the last he would ever have. His cheeks sucked in so that the reddish coal traveled visibly toward his lips, and he smoked each cigarette dangerously short. He did not move until Jones had finished.

Jones did not seem impressed when Jaeger told him who he was, nor did he show any modest gratitude when Jaeger praised what he had done on the piano. Jones merely nodded as if to say that he was generally accepted as a fine jazz pianist, but that it didn't matter to him if anyone thought he was the worst.

"I don't understand," Jaeger said, driven by an urgency to know everything as soon as possible. "You've been blowing piano a long time, right?"

" 'Blowing'?"

"Playing," Jaeger explained with an impatient frown.

"Oh. Yes, you could call it a long time."

"And why jazz?"

"Why? I haven't thought about it."

"That's what I mean when I say I don't understand. You don't know why you're playing? Why do you do this instead of something else?"

"I like the sounds."

Jaeger looked helplessly at Schwab, then back to Jones. "That's a hell of a reason."

Jones shrugged. "I don't care what you think of it. I don't feel obliged to justify myself to you or anyone else."

"Then how about yourself?"

"That answer," Jones said, smiling, "is for me, not you."

Jaeger did not know what to say. He had heard of the pianist's queer fascination with himself, and was now seeing it work with the blunt strength of a hammer. Even as Jones talked in a tone never close to anger or annoyance, his wide blue eyes were shifting craftily as if behind them his brain out of long practice selected answers to confound its questioners. Jones reminded him of a man on trial—a shrewd, confident man who somehow channeled questions into an area in which the answers were already prepared. Jones seemed to be in control of a situation from the moment it started.

"Tell me something—" Jaeger did not have much time; he had to drive to the club for another night's work. "I've been told you've had some piano jobs . . ." He waited for Jones to say yes or no, but the pianist silently continued watching him. "Well, *have* you?"

"Yes. And I suppose he told you." Jones pointed toward Schwab, who was clumsily busying himself behind the counter.

"Not directly."

"Oh? The dark-haired girl who was in here with you one night?"

"*Yes.*" He felt anger roiling within. Jones had a way of turning a conversation completely around. "That's beside the point! Just forget it. Now what I want to know is if you're planning to handle some piano jobs here in Chicago." Why he asked, he didn't know; it was a compulsion he had to satisfy.

"Maybe," Jones answered without enthusiasm. "I'll need money in a little while."

"And then what?"

"Then nothing, for all I know. You seem to think I have a kind of plan. No, I don't spend my time planning. If I play the piano, I play the piano. If I don't, I do something else."

"It's as simple as that, eh?"

"Sure, why shouldn't it be?"

Jaeger spread his hands in a gesture that could have meant *Of course, why shouldn't it be?* or *This idiot is hopeless.* But Jones, he knew, was not an idiot, nor was he hopeless. He was simple, too simple for comfort. He acted as though he didn't know what he was going to do from day to day, but didn't let it worry him. He was maddeningly self-contained and sure of himself.

Before leaving, Jaeger learned his address but was unable to get any guarantee on when he might find Jones in his rooms. Jones did not appear to care who wanted to know him. His way of living would not change. God Himself would have to wait in the hallway if Jones was not at home.

At the zouzou that night, Jaeger's playing was erratic, jumbled. On one number he would be brilliant; on the next, if a listener shut his eyes, it was hard to tell if the piano was there at all.

Everyone in the sextet noticed the difference. They could feel it. Still, they said nothing, not because Jaeger was too big to be criticized, but because they knew every man had a right to an off-night now and then. Nobody could be great all the time. It was too much to ask of any man.

Between the second and third sets Jaeger telephoned Helen: told her he had heard Jones again and had talked with him, told her he might see her after the—well, he might come over and might not, might be hungry for an omelet and Canadian bacon, might—he didn't know . . . but sleep warm, don't wait up for him. Then he hung up and went in the back room and with his nailfile slit the seal on a fifth of White Horse.

Alone, he fought to organize and make clear what he wanted to do, but felt his ability to think crumbling like a flood-wall. Scenes, choruses, pieces of conversation, phrasing, ideas, rhythms—all of them in the muddy waters, trickling at first, then undercutting and finally spurting through the widened gash, and as his mind rushed to stop the flow, and did, another trickle began, and another, slow seepage unstoppable. Jones. Jones. The truth. The greatest jazz pianist he had heard since one night, long ago and in a nightclub the name of which he could not even remember, an unknown battering ram named Peterson had done so many things to *Talk of the Town*. And tonight it had been an unknown who called himself Jones. Who played jazz because he liked the sounds. Who might take an engagement just because he was short of money. Who was good, so good that it was bad to think about it.

So he went back to the piano and sat and hammered his anger into it, his fingers hard and blurred, punishing the slick keys in fury as the others sensed it and jammed with him, driving him home, and for a quarter-hour the nightclub rocked double-time to *No Note, Big Blues,* but after this one burst Jaeger was nothing for the rest of the night. He did not go to see Helen.

Someone had once called his apartment The Mission, and the name stayed. Even if his neighbors didn't.

Jaeger lived on the first floor of a three-flat on the Northwest Side. When he was on the road the apartment was occupied by another jazzman, or two, or any combination of men and women willing to pay the rent and guarantee that the windows would not be cardboard when Jaeger got back. It was living jam-session style: everybody sat in.

It had taken a week and a lot of money to line the ceiling and walls with cork, but when finished and all the doors and windows were closed, great things—musically and otherwise —happened inside. Now and then the police came for a social call and to allay the fears of some nervous passerby who had reported seeing dozens of people—a lot of them colored, it seemed—carrying things into the building. The police were no trouble. After having made two unsuccessful raids for narcotics, they were more curious than antagonistic. Once they made a special call just to tell Jaeger they had heard a meeting of Communists was going on. Everyone enjoyed the joke. After sending the law on its way with a good stiff drink, Jaeger opened the windows and for more than an hour led the rest in playing *Russian Lullaby* and *The Volga Boatmen* and *Meadowland*.

Now, sitting in the frantic, disorderly collection of chairs and record albums and ashtrays with a fifth of whisky propped between his shoes, he stared at a gray and blue rep tie hanging from a brass floorlamp. He drank. The tie, still knotted, had been there for at least two months, and he didn't know whose it was. Things had a way of accumulating. Cufflinks, ties, sunglasses, packs of cigarettes, magazines and letters, cracked reeds for saxophones and clarinets, a trumpet mouthpiece, unopened cans of beer, all speeds of records and once a spool of recording tape he had never got around to hearing. In one corner stood his baby grand piano; in the other a vibraharp on which he occasionally limbered his arms and wrists. Someday, he told himself seriously, he would get around to spending more time with the vibes.

But at the moment he was telling himself to slow down, to get a grip on himself and to think things out.

He had finally heard enough of Jones. That was something. That was better than knowing so little. All right. Now the thing to do was to think it through carefully. Add and subtract. Understand what it was that Jones had and he did not have. Be honest.

One thing he had to do, Jaeger decided, was to keep his thoughts to himself. It was weak to expose himself to others. This was his affair; dragging in others wouldn't give him the answer. The whole conflict was in himself and his estimation of Jones. He repeated his resolution. It sounded right. It sounded like an answer. He poured himself another drink, but when it was only half-gone he fell asleep, alone in his soundproofed room.

The next morning he called Helen and, not quite believing the words as he spoke them, told her that Jones was a fine jazz pianist, that Jones seemed to know what he was doing every inch of the way—but hadn't he played *Waterfront* the night they had first heard him? Well, he told her, Jones had played it again last night. Oh, he had done a great job on it, but maybe he was pretty narrow. Maybe Jones didn't know much. At any rate, Jaeger said, he had found him, and everything was going to be all right.

When he replaced the telephone he felt better than he had in a long time. The idea of Jones' possible narrowness had come suddenly. A few polished numbers didn't make Jones a top-rate jazzman. A man had to prove himself over a period of time; he had to expand before deserving respect. Jones could be nothing more than a flash. It was an encouraging thought.

Jaeger lit a cigarette and dialed again.

Because Henneberry had only the voice and none of the talent for acting, Jaeger was unsettled by the way the announcer reacted to the news. The low, metallic voice tried to sound indifferent when Jaeger said he had found and had heard Virgil Jones. The announcer said with artificial limpidity that he was glad this hide-and-seek had ended. Now that it was over, could he get some sleep? He was really exhausted. His late show, plus a television appearance, you know. He invited Jaeger to call him some evening. Perhaps one of these nights they could arrange to have Ross on the show.

Jaeger hung up. He was angered and suspicious, not fooled. The announcer was anything but indifferent to Jones.

He went to the South Side in midafternoon the next day. Jones was not around, but the landlady said she was sure he hadn't packed up and left, though he didn't own but a handful of things and so he really maybe could have, you couldn't prove it by her. A peculiar young man he was, she said, never having no visitors or friends she knew of, just sticking to himself all the time like he was hiding. Come back in a couple hours, she said. He might be in then.

He did not find Virgil Jones until two days later. It was late morning of a cold, gray, growthless day, and the night before had been another continual strain at the piano. For some reason Jaeger could not yet identify clearly, he found himself unable to approach his choruses with confidence. More than once, just before the rest of the sextet broke away to leave him in the open, he had suffered a numbing fear that his fingers would freeze and he would be sitting alone and helpless in the spotlight as everybody watched.

"Come in," Jones said. His voice was cordial and had lost the nasal tone it had carried because of his headcold. He was wearing a gray sweatsuit and had a yellow towel stuffed around his neck.

"I tried to get you a couple of days ago." Jaeger noticed that the room looked worn and anonymous. It was a dismal place.

"Was that you?" Jones asked.

Jaeger frowned. "You mean there was someone else?"

"Sure. Do you know Henneberry? You're surprised—well, he was here."

"What did he say?"

"You ought to ask him that. But you won't. There really isn't any need for it now." Jones looked out the window.

"What do you mean, there isn't any need *now?*"

"I'm going to play for money," he said, still gazing down into the street. "Starting next week. I don't know where, but it doesn't make any difference as long as I get paid."

Jaeger shook his head sadly. "You say Henneberry talked you into this . . ."

"I didn't hear . . ."

"Henneberry talked you into it, didn't he?"

"No," Jones answered with shocking loudness yet without anger in his voice. "I wasn't talked into anything. I decided."

"Have it your way," Jaeger said, moving his hands in a gesture of futility. "So you're going to make money, lots of it. I suppose it says that in the contract?"

"There isn't any contract."

"There *what?*"

"Isn't any contract. We have a verbal agreement. My idea." He came away from the window and faced Jaeger. "As for making lots of money, I don't care. I've never had a lot and I'll never need too much. Only enough to buy time. That's where money is important—it buys time, it helps you do what you want when you want. So when I make enough money to buy enough time, I'll quit. Then I can have all my time to myself."

"Have you told Henneberry this?"

"No, but it doesn't matter. He hasn't got anything to say about how I run my life. Nobody has."

Jaeger pressed the tip of his tongue against an upper left molar and with his eyes tried to penetrate the calm, almost naive mask of the pianist's face. Jaeger did not like to see anyone fooled, and here in front of him stood the most trusting fool he had ever seen.

"I want to tell you something," Jaeger said. "I think you have a right to know, and if you want to know why I'm telling you, well, put it down to professional sympathy and let it go at that." Then, supercautious against revealing his own fears, he recounted to Jones the circumstances leading to the present situation. He made it a point to convince Jones that no one—neither Schwab nor the girl nor Jaeger himself—had told Henneberry that he lived in these rooms above the barbershop. And Jaeger underlined his words with the fact of Henneberry's attempted indifference.

Jones did not seem impressed. He sat in a fat chair and folded his arms and listened with blank unconcern.

"—does it mean?" Jaeger continued. "First, Henneberry isn't a booking agent, and he's never been a personal manager. That means he can't offer you anything legitimately—not by himself. He has to have help. So all this talk about getting you an engagement is just contact work that he's doing for somebody else, somebody who's got the money and know-how to take a chance on you. And second, I can make a good guess on who that somebody is—the king bloodsucker in the business. Name of Bauer, a—what's the matter?"

Jones had his knuckles to his mouth. His eyes were thinking in quick arcs. Finally he shook his head.

"You know him?" Jaeger asked.

"I guess not."

"Well, don't be in a hurry." Jaeger crossed his legs and picked at the crease in his trousers. "Bauer was retired, the last I knew, but that doesn't mean anything. If he hears of a new musician or a fighter or some new angle to own something or somebody, he 'unretires' pretty damned fast. It's kind of a hobby with him, owning people, watching them dance when he pulls the strings. And he's smart. He figures everything out to the last nickel and dime, and he's got the patience to outlast anybody I know of. So watch it."

Jones looked back as if none of the words had had any effect.

"Look, man—" Jaeger said, angered "—I'm pitching you on this for your own good. If he's behind all this, it doesn't pay to mess with him. I mean it now. If you think you can call the shots with him, I've got news for you. You're going to get introduced to some of the punchies who do his shakeups for him—that's right, some of the fighters, or the exes, I ought to say—and I'll tell you now it wouldn't be the first time they worked somebody over behind a billboard. You want your head in one piece? You want to be able to pick up a glass of water with your hands? Well, just remember, this town is full of guys who'll do anything for a buck, and Bauer has both the bucks and the guys. I'm not saying he's going to put you in cement or anything like that, but I *am* saying you'd better watch yourself about this offer Henneberry made. You'd better watch yourself from now on."

"He owned you once, didn't he? Isn't that it?"

Jaeger stood up. "Yes," he said, nodding set-jawed and with his eyes in another time. "Yes, he owned me for awhile, and it cost me too much to get away from him."

"Thanks for the advice," Jones said lazily, "but I don't think I'll need it. Bauer can't own me. Nobody can. And I'm not going to be owned by the fear of him . . . or these sluggers you talk about. If he's behind all this and is out to use me, he's in for a shock. I'll tell you that."

"Don't be so goddamned sure of yourself, man."

"I can't help it," Jones said mildly. "It's the way I am."

Jaeger grimaced. Jones' confidence was so huge that for a

fraction of a second Jaeger wanted to cross the room in one stride and into that stone-calm face shout *Keep it up! Keep playing hero and see where it gets you!* But instead he shook his head and made a bitter, silent mouth. Jones did not get up to see him out.

That night, after the show, Jaeger left the zouzou by himself and drove to several clubs on the far North Side. Nothing was doing. He returned, through the tall dark cliffs of The Loop because he did not like the Outer Drive's view of black waves, and aimed the heavy car south. Something would turn up somewhere. His eyes were hot and his skin felt pasted to his cheekbones, but he did not want to sleep. There were some nights on which sleep seemed a penalty for wanting to do too much. It was an execution. When a man slept he was dead to all the life and excitement of a city.

From habit he listened to Henneberry, finally snapped him off. Outside, wind whistled against the wing vents. Streets were chill and empty, and above them, arc-lights shone like old pearls.

He thought, and could not understand. Jones was innocent and not innocent—at the same time acting as though he could be exploited like a child and yet as though behind his façade of simplicity his mind would revolt the moment it saw itself deceived. He was going to play. He was going to play the piano and himself against Bauer and Henneberry and the jazzmen who would hear him and praise him or damn him. How far would he go?

Curiously, Jaeger thought, understanding Jones was like being lost in a house of mirrors with a twin. You saw and identified yourself; you saw and identified the twin—but after awhile, having moved around, altering the angle of vision from which you knew yourself, you saw an image that looked like you and moved like you and, yes, stared back at you, and you wondered if it was really you, not the other, but you

117

couldn't move a hand or blink an eye or make a sound because to do so would mean you were not you, but only a hand or an eye or a voice, and was this all a man could say of himself? I am hands. I am a name. I am a Cadillac going south in the city of Chicago at three o'clock in the morning. What else am I? What will I be in an hour? What tomorrow? Next week, next month, next year? What will I be in fifty years? Not even hands. Only a name. Such as DeWitt?

2

Jones began, solo, the third week of January.

There were no window signs or banners at the muted, soft-lighted cocktail lounge on Seventy-first Street. His audience was made up of salesmen and accountants and boxcar-expeditors and engineering draftsmen with their wives or perhaps neatly-turned stenographers or receptionists or unfooled divorcees, and everyone had nice times knowing one another with light organ music and no television in the background. None of them had ever really listened to the organist who had been playing for two months, so the arrival of Jones was hardly noticed. Jones was, in a way, stillborn.

And Jaeger had been right: Bauer was behind the scenes, working through Henneberry.

The announcer did what he was told and asked few questions, but in his mind they piled up and would not disengage. Bauer had never wanted to meet Jones, and had acted, at times, violently afraid of the pianist's finding out that he was involved. Further, Bauer had made unbelievable concessions.

First was the point of no contract. Then Bauer had made all the arrangements for Jones' union card, and had shown no objections to Jones' insistence that he play only three nights a week. But what was most incredible of all was that Bauer was getting nothing—not a penny of percentage. He had spent and was still spending money on Jones without a return. And he kept his motives a secret.

Knowing the agent, however, Henneberry could guess, especially if he analyzed the rigid instructions Bauer had given. Jones was to play here for two weeks. Then over on Seventy-ninth for two more weeks. After that he was scheduled to come north again, only this time at a different lounge, for three weeks, at four nights a week. And when that engagement was finished, Sixty-third Street was in line. All of this without publicity. Not a sign or a line of print in any of the trade magazines or newspapers. Henneberry had the job of seeing to that, and also to the silencing of any other disc-jockeys or *Downbeat* writers who might just happen to walk into one of the lounges some night and decide to give this new pianist a play on the air or in a column. It was all very strict, and would have been like a long-range battle plan except that there was no provision for changes. The plan was inflexible, but Henneberry was aware that since Jones knew nothing about it, it could be altered with the pianist none the wiser. The only purpose Henneberry could guess was that Paul Bauer was building Jones to a certain point at which the agent would suddenly cash in. Again, there was a chance that Bauer was simply getting old, and wanted to amuse himself. He was at any rate giving more time and thought to Jones than he had to anyone else.

On the first night, following orders, Henneberry was on the scene at eight-thirty. Under his arm he carried a wedge-shaped sign such as those on the desks of business people. He ordered a Manhattan and gave the sign to the bartender. Then Henneberry took his drink to a table near the half-curtained, half-slatted windows. He faced the bass end of the platformed Solovox at the open end of the three-quarter circle bar. Behind the instrument a mirror with a blue cast was angled so that the keyboard was visible.

The sign had been put on top of the piano. NO REQUESTS

Some of the people, he noticed, were looking at him now and then. He lifted the glass, repressed a shiver from the chill sweet strong liquid. Nervous despite his lofty superiority, he read his watch every five minutes.

Jones made him nervous. During both their meetings Henneberry had been unable to force a single hint of respect from the pianist. There had been no respect, no awe, no gratitude. Jones hadn't been rude or aggressive—he had seemed simply unimpressed by the praise lavished on him; he had given the impression that if everyone in the world were to hate him unless he changed the part of his hair, his hair would stay the same.

Henneberry turned as the door opened. A couple, neat, their hands together with the looseness of familiarity. It was not quite nine o'clock.

Supposing Jones took a notion not to come? He would be capable of it. Without a contract he could indulge any whim with no fear of having to account for it, he could come and go as he pleased, play or not play, submit to or defy any changes in location, in short, he could make a fool of everyone. Again Henneberry lipped his drink and wondered.

Why in God's name had Paul agreed to so much when he hadn't even heard Jones?

At that moment the door opened. Jones was bareheaded and wore a ratty brown overcoat. As he came to the table, Henneberry felt some relief to see that he was clean-shaven. Under the coat, however, the pianist was wearing a cheap blue suit and a brown shirt with no tie. The only good thing Henneberry could see was that Jones looked clean.

"How do you feel?" Henneberry asked.

"Good." Jones rubbed his hands together. "Where's the piano?"

Henneberry pointed. "It's a Solovox. Do you know how to operate it?"

"I'll find out. How do I get at it?"

"There's a—"

"I see. A lid in the bar. All right." He went over and ducked under the lid and came up on the inside of the bar, pushed back the bench and sat down. All his movements were extraordinarily swift and direct. With the same quick precision he reached for the sign, read it, and set it on the floor out of sight. Then he began his experiments with the keys.

Henneberry looked around the bar. Only the young couple seemed interested in Jones; the others glanced up from time to time, but acted indifferent to this new entertainer.

Hurriedly the announcer asked for another drink. His stomach was fluttering. Paul had promised him twenty per cent of Jones to start with, and right now it amounted to nothing. How much would it be? Or would Jones be a failure and shatter all his hopes?

One second, there was silence; the next, there was the piano —a slow, firm *Blue Moon,* and after only a single chorus Henneberry was certain that at last his dreams were possible.

And the piano moved, going over and over the refrain until it appeared Jones might have forgot the rest—but then he broke off and went on, far beyond the simple melody, beyond anything remembered. It was the most amazingly original interpretation the announcer had ever heard. Instead of conventionally-flattened thirds and sevenths, Jones was dropping the remaining notes a half-pitch and wrenching the blue notes to normal *Es* and *Bs,* inverting the whole pattern of the blues. And in addition he was lagging a half-beat behind the normal rhythm, moving smoothly and consistently, bouncing along in a private beat with terrific confidence and poise. Every so often he would insert several bars of the normal rhythm only to abandon it again, to lag behind the just-established pace, to stab and flicker the keys until there seemed to be nothing else he could possibly do to *Blue Moon,* and then it was the end.

There was almost no applause. Everyone in the bar was staring in the direction of the piano, but there was no applause. Several of the faces at the bar wore an expression of suspicion that the piano was out of tune.

Immediately the piano leaped into sound again—this time straight and solid into *Them There Eyes,* not flatted, not lagging, but sharp and exact. Jones romped through the whole of it once, then again, then suddenly veered off on another tangent and hammered away as if he would never stop. Henneberry was strapped erect in his chair.

After ten minutes Jones lashed a heavy chord, stopped. Silence. Someone started to applaud, but Jones rode right over it and began reworking the tune half-time. The music sounded absolutely new as he leaned to the keyboard with an intense, solitary concentration that had a kind of savagery about it. His icy eyes were never on the keys or roving the room, but were always staring straight into the wood in front of him. He showed neither excitement nor passion for what he was doing. He was like a machine geared to perfection.

For a time it seemed to Henneberry that Jones was going to play all night without a minute's rest. As it was, he went on for more than an hour before coming down from the stand. Henneberry noticed that most of the people looked relieved.

"You give them," he said as Jones sat down, "more than they are entitled to. Forty-five minutes a set is enough . . . especially when the quality is as high as yours."

Jones did not take to the advice or to the flattery. His face indicated that he thought such talk unimportant if not completely irrelevant.

"I thought I was doing you a favor," Henneberry said carefully. "Most of these habitués, you understand, regard a jazz pianist as just another entertainer. That's why I had the sign made—to keep them from making asinine requests for favorite tunes. My thinking on the matter is that an artist must be allowed to create what he wants to create, in his own fashion, without pressures. To please indiscriminating and uneducated people is to corrupt the artist, and, in the last analysis, the art itself, don't you think?"

"All this is about that sign saying no requests?"

Henneberry delayed answering, partly for effect but mostly out of a certain confusion Jones had caused him.

"Basically," he managed, "yes. But the sign is a symbol of what I've just said, and I had it made to . . . well, to protect you." The truth was that he had been amazed when Bauer ordered him to put it up wherever Jones was playing.

"I don't need protection," Jones said mildly.

"I know, yes—but I didn't mean it that way . . ." Henneberry was becoming muddled and nervous. Jones had a manner of interpreting words so that the speaker felt uncertain of what he himself meant.

"About the sign—" Jones said "—I don't need it to keep me from being corrupted."

"Of course, of course. But you'll have requests."

"I know."

"I should think it would be annoying."

"That's my affair. When they ask, they ask. Until then I don't worry about what they 'might' do."

"Very well, have it your way. I merely thought I would save you some trouble."

"No one has to save me from anything. And as for trouble, I'm used to it."

Henneberry could understand that. Although the inflection of the pianist's voice was never arrogant or superior, every one of his statements carried a massively defiant positiveness that angered the announcer to the point where making trouble for Jones became a sort of goal. Henneberry found himself plotting ways of shaking some of the insulting confidence out of Jones. But it was too early. He brushed his hand across his eyes—he would have to wait.

Jones went back to the stand too soon. He didn't seem to care for a rest. The audience, still generally indifferent, was getting far more for its money than it would have got from any other comparable musician.

As Henneberry had to leave for his broadcast, they had no more conversation that night.

Bauer sounded satisfied when the announcer told him of the first night. There were no new instructions, and the old ones remained unchanged. Henneberry was to be on hand for the first set. Seeing Jones the next time, he was to try to learn if anything unusual had happened—in other words, if anyone had discovered Jones before it was safe.

What about Jaeger? Ross was onto Jones. He might start talking it around.

Do nothing, Bauer advised. Jaeger wouldn't be trouble. And the vine had it that the sextet was breaking up after its engagement at the zouzou; Jaeger was going to single out on The Coast for awhile. He wouldn't be trouble.

Late one morning Jaeger was locking his car when someone shouted at him from across the South Side street. It was Jones, dressed in his motley and big-fitting clothes as usual, who even as he called started across the brick street without looking for cars. For some reason Jones seemed genuinely glad to see him.

As the two of them sat drinking coffee in Walgreen's, however, Jones gave no particular indication of why he had called to Jaeger like an old friend and had hurried to see him. The expression in his wide eyes was strangely bright and animalistic, but his mouth talked about commonplace things such

125

as the coffee itself, about how the two-mile-out pumping crib looked so close on cold days when the lake was calm, about any number of irrelevant matters.

Jaeger could not understand why Jones said nothing about music. Here they were—probably the two best jazz pianists in Chicago—and all Jones could find to talk about had nothing to do with jazz, or with anything important, for that matter.

Finally he had to force it.

Jones was willing to answer. The job, he said, was an easy one, and he was making twice the money he had at the steel mills. After a few months he could afford to quit.

"Can you?" Jaeger looked at him sideways.

"Not now. I can't quit now because I haven't got enough money."

"How much is 'enough'?"

"I don't know. Haven't thought a lot about it. But some morning I'll wake up and look outside and say 'That's enough.' And it will be."

"Do you really believe that, man?" Jaeger had seen people who talked like this before, but he had never known any of them to make good on their promise. "Do you think you can stop as easy as that?"

"Sure. I don't need a lot of money. And I'm not going to be one of those people who spend more time making it than they do enjoying it."

"So when you get enough, you're going to sit back and spend it."

Jones nodded at a display of sweetrolls.

"And when it runs out?" Jaeger asked.

"I'll make some more . . . say, you're just like the rest. Everybody wants to know how I'm going to spend my life. Hell, I don't know for sure, except that I'm always going to do what I want to do. I don't see why everybody is so interested in everybody else. Taking care of yourself is a big enough job, I think. And from the faces of people I see every day, I don't think many of them are doing a good job." He leaned closer. "Do you know what they do to horses that have to turn a wheel for power? They blind them. They put out their eyes so they'll think they're going somewhere, but all they do is go around and around until one day they drop dead in the traces. Then they get another horse and blind him too. That's why I like talking to old failures."

Bewildered, Jaeger stared. "Old failures?"

"People," Jones explained, sipping his coffee. "Not the ones who have a lot of money. All they talk about is how smart they were to make it and how they wouldn't do anything different if they had their lives to live over. And not old women. They aren't good for anything except cooking, and then they expect you to eat a ton of it. No, I like to talk to the old men. You can learn a lot. That's why I'm so smart."

"You're smart, eh?"

"Sure. You'll see." Jones acted completely unaware that he had sounded conceited—and if he was aware of it, he didn't seem to give it a second thought. "Talk to the old men. They have the answers."

Before the morning ended Jaeger worked the conversation back to jazz and learned where and when Jones was at the piano. Because of his commitment at the zouzou, it was impossible for him to get out south to hear Jones. It was altogether frustrating.

And, later in the week, it was surprising to Henneberry that Jones proved punctual, honest, and not at all erratic. Jones came on time and continued playing more piano than he had to. He was always in a calm, contented mood, although there was about him a certain coldness, a kind of unwillingness to be too friendly with anyone. Often, carrying a tall golden bottle of Miller's High Life and dressed in his neat but shabby blue suit, Jones managed to talk to three or four different people during his intermission. He never forced himself upon them. A musician just off the stand has no trouble finding someone who wants to talk to him. Usually the patron is not so honored as he is proud of an association he wears for his own glory, but most musicians understand this too.

Henneberry's pride took a whipping in the first week. No one recognized who he was, and Jones treated him with no more attention than if the announcer had been a shipping clerk who had dropped in for a quick beer.

In one way Henneberry consoled himself. It had to be. If some young jazz-addict were to recognize Roger Henneberry listening to an unknown, unpublicized pianist, and if this recognition were to happen more than once, by implication this pianist Jones would be someone worth hearing. The information would spread until half the aficionados in the city were swarming into every hole-in-the-wall at which Jones played. Jones would look over the crowd and realize they had come to hear him. He might get dangerous ideas. And he had too many of those already.

On Monday night of the second and final week Henneberry was just leaving when Helen entered with Seymour Schwab. Only a few casual, incomplete sentences were exchanged before the announcer left.

He jammed himself into the first phonebooth he found. Bauer was crisply authoritative. Forget about the girl and whoever was with her. Forget about Jaeger. Stop panicking or else. Don't be afraid of losing what they could make from Jones.

Again, the last night of Jones' engagement, Henneberry met Helen and Schwab. This time not even sentences passed between them. A nod, that was all. The girl had never been diplomatic in relations with Henneberry. And Schwab was sharp-sighted enough to see behind the announcer's impressive but shallow façade.

None of the three knew what was going on in the minds of the other two concerning Jones, but it was just as well. Each knew that at times it was better to keep ideas to oneself until they were clear.

Both Helen and Schwab were flattered. Once more Jones spent at least two of his intermissions with them. Still, there was about him a guardedness that seemed to say *We are talking like friends, I know, but it doesn't mean I am obligated to you in any way.* Schwab had never seen anyone who insisted on being so alone.

More than once Schwab tried to maneuver Jones into talking about his past, but the pianist would answer questions just so far before breaking off into either dead silence or a completely new subject. Usually Jones had plenty to say about himself. Himself, however, seemed to be some person who existed only at this moment—not in the past, not in the future. He had no regrets and no clear plans. And what was most impressive of all was that he was never depressed or morbidly uncertain.

At first there was nothing different about the cocktail lounge on Seventy-ninth near Stony Island. It looked like the twin of the first, and the people were not vastly different. They liked hearing live music instead of the usual jukebox fare, though from the faces they made after Jones had been playing for a few minutes indicated that this music was not what could be called easy listening. This led some of them to lean over the bar and, in the brief rest between numbers, ask Jones to play a favorite tune.

He would never ignore them. From beneath his flat, whitish hair his pale eyes would look at them with an unoffended, steady gaze; then his mouth would move, shaping: *No.* That answered requests.

Some customers tried buying him a bottle of beer or a high-ball, telling the bartender to set it within reach of the piano. Jones would see it placed, would follow the bartender's finger to the one who had bought the drink, and then would smile his thanks. When he got a chance, Jones drank. But if the one who had bought the drink then requested a certain tune, the answer was the same: *No.* Always in a kindly way. Always the same answer.

The three—Henneberry, the girl and Schwab—still crossed paths. The announcer could only guess that Jaeger had asked her to listen to Jones because he himself could never make it as long as he had to play downtown. Schwab, Henneberry imagined, tagged along as a kind of insurance against the usual approaches made to lone women in a bar.

In the second week, however, Jaeger came in with the girl, and it was that night when the trouble started.

Seeing Jaeger, wondering why he wasn't at the zouzou, and angered because the pianist gave him only a perfunctory greeting, Henneberry decided to stay around. He called the studio and instructed them to have an emergency tape ready, he might be late. The tape would carry him for an hour, after which he would take over and finish the program.

But the trouble had nothing to do with Jaeger.

The trouble came from a bird-faced young man sitting at the bar exactly opposite Henneberry. The announcer noticed the glittering eyes staring at him. He tried to ignore them. He concentrated on the piano, on the moody, turned-in re-flectiveness of *I Don't Stand a Ghost of a Chance,* on the statuelike figure of Jones bent to the music. His glance snapped across the bar again, and in an instant Henneberry saw that it was too late. He had been recognized. The eyes were even now making the inference. Roger Henneberry had come all the way out south to hear a pianoman. If this Jones drew a man like Henneberry, he must be great.

Between sets the angular young man slipped off his stool and, on his way to the phonebooth, almost stumbled over Ross Jaeger's feet.

By the time Jones went on the stand again there were at least a half-dozen people crowded with the one who had spotted Henneberry. All of them had the serious, attentive faces of those who know they are hearing something worthwhile. Every so often one or more of them would glance back in the direction of Jaeger, who was himself oblivious to everything but what Jones was doing to *Blue Lou*. And after every number the cluster across the bar applauded wildly.

There was no hiding Jones.

Henneberry did not have a chance to contact Bauer until nearly two-thirty in the morning. He explained as best he could.

The silent receiver was like a barbell in his hand.

Finally Bauer said that it had to happen sometime. He did not sound upset.

Henneberry wanted to know what they should do now. They had to get Jones on a contract, he said. A free man couldn't be trusted. Any day he could agree to work for someone else, could cut them off without warning.

Bauer said to relax.

Henneberry said within a month Jones would be known all over the city. Word-of-mouth was something that couldn't be stopped. Every agent and promoter would be after Jones. And what if they made him better offers?

Bauer said to be patient. He said he knew what he was doing.

3

"That's just the way he is, girl . . ."

She watched Jackson's dark bearded mouth moving behind the steam from his coffeecup.

". . . always pushin' it. He been a long time with it now—he just tired, all beat-out, that's all. You see if I ain't right. After he picks up on a week in the pad he'll be great. A mahn got to get a break once in a while."

She wished it could be as simple as that. A miracle cure. One week away from the piano and Ross would be completely recovered—having found the answer by lying on his back and taking milk orange juice fresh vegetables as if his body was the thing that was sick. Well, in five more days he would have that week before leaving for San Francisco, and perhaps, after seeing and hearing Jones as she knew Ross would, he might calm down and realize that his ideas of success made him his own worst enemy. Perhaps he would learn that from the young, confident pianist who played only for himself and didn't care what anyone else thought.

She looked out the window of the B/G cafeteria. Lunch hour. A conveyor belt of cold-bleached faces. February wind glueing coats to bodies, blearing eyes, ripping at corners of mouths. Someday she would go to California with Ross—she would go everywhere with him. Someday because he was not ready yet.

"And what about you, Lee?"

"Me?" Jackson put a huge slick fingernail in the middle of his black knit tie. "Gig around here for awhile . . . maybe get with some cats passin' through, maybe head East or somewhere. I ain't in no hurry right now, girl. You hear Nicky's goin' to ElAy to be in some movie?"

She shook her head, and as it moved to the left she noticed two men in workclothes staring at her with disgust in their eyes. It had happened before. Let them think what they wanted—they would do it anyway.

Jackson's laugh wheezed across the table. "A gasser, it's goin' to be! Nicky supposed to be a *drummer* in some murder picture. Now that I got to see."

She shuddered as he drank off his scalding coffee with four big quick swallows. His throat was asbestos, his heart a turbine. He never paid any attention to his machinery. He simply let it drive him.

For another half-hour they talked loosely of music. The sextet was splitting in all directions. Britton had been putting off a decision on an offer from a big band and had finally accepted; now Allred had lined up Reuben and a local alto saxman for a combo he was forming; Nick to Hollywood; Jackson still in Chicago; Ross to The Coast for three weeks or more. That was what happened. Form a fine group of musicians, hold them together as long as possible, and then watch them disintegrate, go their separate ways.

That was what happened to everything you wanted to keep —it was changed by the precipitate of Time. Nothing stayed the same. Time had no stop. That was a truth you could not fight.

All right, she told herself, accept what you cannot change.

As she thought it, the words were suddenly superimposed on the image of Virgil Jones.

She was at the zouzou every night of the final week.

Listening, watching, thinking, she could see that what Jackson had only dared imply was true. Ross was like a watchspring wound to refusal. He could not, would not, back off and give himself any rest from the tension. During Allred's or Britton's or Jackson's breaks he could have done enough with simple, relaxed chords behind them—but no, he went at the keys as if every chord had to be true and perfect and completely original, as if everyone listening had ears for only the piano. Every chord exact, flawless. He tried so hard that when he had his own break, stripped and alone, he had to be superperfect. Which was impossible.

But he tried, and tried so hard that he wound himself tighter, wound the piano into a thing too tense and brittle to carry the free and easy beat. And it was then that they began cutting into his breaks, blowing in and taking the lead from him just as they always did with Nick Augustine.

What was worst of all was that she could see Ross knew what they were doing, and why. They were trying to help him. Helping hands to a cripple.

Between sets, however, they were pretty fair actors, letting the conversation drift as if nothing were really important or worth worrying about. And of course none of them ever mentioned the one night Jaeger hadn't even shown up for work. If a man ran into something that brought him down, their actions seemed to say, well, that was his business, and the best thing to do was to let him work it out for himself. You helped him when he asked for it, but you didn't mess with him when he wanted to keep it to himself. What the hell, a man had enough troubles of his own without looking for more.

During the final week Jaeger was not much good for anything. He drank a great deal and said very little. He said nothing at all about Jones.

Studying his drawn, furiously intense face, Helen began to see that his going away to be by himself was not only the wisest but the only step toward a solution. He would gain perspective from the two thousand miles. He could look across the distance and see things as they really were—that is, if first he looked at himself.

At times, giving herself a sense of remoteness by an effort of the will, she found herself almost disgusted with the near-neurotic fears he had. But the disgust and disillusionment did not last long. She saw them for what they were: luxuries. It was smugly easy for her to criticize him for making such a mountain of Jones. She did not play the piano. She had never studied, she reminded herself, for sixteen hours while working six more. She had never known and would never know what it felt like to find someone who was able to do, almost without effort, that which she had devoted her life to for so many years. All the work erased. Traceless. It was what he believed, and believing made it a reality.

the zouzou was dismantled on the last night. The wrecking crew was Ross Jaeger & Company, aided and abetted by five strong-lunged fellow-tradesmen who wandered in from the north. After one o'clock all eleven jammed onto the stand and for the next two hours hammered the place apart beam by beam and chair by chair. They used all the tools they could carry, and when the job was done they sat around and had one last drink on it before packing up and going off into the night, into the city, into wherever they were going for another job, another time of smoke and faces and sounds and jazz.

Jaeger did exactly what she thought he would do. The next night he came to her apartment and told her they were going south to hear Jones.

Beside him as he drove, hearing the regular, airy pulse-beat of the wipers, she kept her teeth hard on her lower lip. She hadn't felt so relieved in months. For some reason—perhaps the brilliant piano Ross had played on his last night, proving to himself that he still had it in him—he now drove and talked and acted stable and no longer afraid. His confidence was returning.

Don't wonder why, she told herself. If it was because he'd had a pint of scotch, it was because he'd had a pint of scotch. Don't ask too many questions when things are going good. Don't bring him down when he feels confident. Give him time to work it out. Just be there, always, when he needs you.

Jones was playing at a noisy, cheap cocktail lounge buried under the elevated tracks on Sixty-third Street. Only half-full because it was too big, too purple and too tough, the lounge featured a rhythm trio whose repertoire consisted of jump tunes and slow blues padded with worn lyrics about pulling down the shades and boogiein' all night, love that chick 'cause she fits so tight. There was a cold smell of metal. Every so often the thunderous rattle of the El seemed to shake the bottles behind the bar. The waitresses were bigbutted in slacks as they went lumpily from table to table with brown bottles and not even an attempt at a smile.

Jones was not in sight.

Normally she and Jaeger would have sat far back rather than near the stand and the inevitable drink-buyers and autograph-hounds, but in this place Jaeger was unrecognized and safe. The main reason he now sat close, however, was because it was the only way the piano would be audible above the rough, smoke-filled clatter.

"This is Bauer, all right." Jaeger swung his head around, then up toward the trio with a sour expression. "An intermission man to these dogs . . . and look at the crowd, will you?"

"Yes." Her eyes took in several tables, saw with some surprise a few faces she had seen at the lounge on Seventy-ninth.

Jones had a following. Not many, but it was a beginning. She decided nothing would be accomplished by telling Ross that Jones had already won a few disciples.

"I can't understand," Jaeger said, putting his right hand over an ear to shut out the trio, "why Paul is doing it this way. You know—keeping him down like this. Usually he gives a big buildup and tries to make as much as he can before pulling out. That's the deal he worked on Bontemps, and that was only a couple of years ago. He's handling Jones—and I know Henneberry isn't anything but the front—as if he's got a long-range plan worked out."

"Bauer probably has, Ross. Remember who Jones is—with all his talk about being the last individual in the world, about how nobody owns him and how he won't compromise with anyone or anything. When he was out at the Moritz I got a chance to talk, or better yet, to listen to him . . . and I can see why Bauer might have to take it easy. Jones is the kind of boy you have to make new rules for." *When he was out at the Moritz,* she remembered. Jones had been like steel. She had never met a man like him. The most stubbornly selfish and egoistic person in the world—yet strangely enough, never mean or vicious, somehow never really inconsiderate as were other selfish people. She could not understand. More than once, at sudden and unwarned moments, Jones had been incongruously polite with the outmoded, formal gentleness of an old man. She could not understand. The last individual in the world? He was not that simple. He was more than a printed card or a group of words, more than a piano and a staggering talent. He was something that always escaped knowing.

"I think . . . are you listening?" Jaeger's sinewy face was puzzled and not far from annoyance.

"Of course. You think . . ."

"I just wanted to say that maybe this intermission arrangement is Bauer's way of taking some of the bighead out of Jones. Jesus, these guys are from Nowhere City—listen to them . . . they're not even *try*ing, damn it. Drive a man out of his skull, getting hit with that all night."

"Maybe Jones is across the street lushing it up and trying to forget."

"Uh-uh." Jaeger shook his head. "Here he comes now."

Dreamily unconcerned and aloof as always, Jones strolled in as though he just happened to be passing by, and that he would, if the mood came upon him, stroll right out again. He completely ignored the few who called to him.

Jaeger reached out and touched Jones' elbow as he passed.

"Oh." He stopped and gave his usual restrained, enigmatic smile. "I didn't expect to see you people here. Some place, eh?"

She saw that his hair was scrubby and his clothes still looked as if he had bought them at a rummage sale. He was clean enough, but wore clothes like a color-blind man in a hurry.

"A pit," Jaeger said. "How long is the sentence?"

"What?" Jones bent and cupped hand behind ear. "I didn't hear."

"How long is this date?"

"Two more weeks."

"Then where?"

Jones made his mouth indifferent. "Some place else. Henneberry arranges all that. It doesn't make any difference where it is."

"It would to me," Jaeger said abrasively. "I don't see how you can take it." He jerked his head toward the noise of the trio.

She cornered her eyes at Jaeger.

"I don't mind," Jones said. "They've got a right to play the way they want to."

"Sure they have—everybody has. But I don't have to like it. And how does it feel to be only a fill-in for them?"

138

Again Jones shaped his expression to one of unconcern. "I don't worry about that. It doesn't change my playing. What I do is just the same no matter who's filling in for who."

"You could be doing better," Jaeger insisted as he crushed out a cigarette.

"Could be. But the sounds would be the same—so you see, 'doing better' would mean only more money, or words like colossal in front of my name, and I've already got a name. It's Virgil."

The trio toyed with a fast little riff, tagged it with a flatted chord, and relaxed, finished. The bassman and pianist stepped off the stand as the guitarist put his lips to the microphone.

"At this time it gives us great pleasure to introduce to all of you for your listening pleasure that sensational swinging pianist making such a great name on the street that can't be beat, I mean none other than Virgil Jones . . ." He smacked his palms together to stimulate applause, but not much came. He took off his guitar and went for a drink.

Then a strange thing happened. Just as Jones had taken off his coat and was settling it into a vacant chair at Jaeger's table, he began to blink rapidly. He turned his face away and closed his eyes and seized the back of the chair and leaned on the support. In a matter of seconds he straightened, set his shoulders, and then went businesslike to the piano.

No one took particular notice of what had gone on.

He began with *Talk of the Town*. He played it as he played all his selections—as if he had written both the music and the lyrics, and as if he meant, from deep within, each note and every word. On his face there was nothing. He was ice. He was cold and perfect.

Perfect?

Too perfect for two, she could see. For Jaeger, his eyes focused on nothing so that he might hear better. For the trio's pianist, slumped at the bar and staring at Jones as though hypnotized. And herself? She did not know other than that Jones played beyond the words she had for it.

After *Talk of the Town* she watched Jones throw his head back and shake it as if freeing himself from a harness, then, as quickly as a stab-thrust, lean forward and strike with both big hands *Tea for Two*—the same, belting attack he had used the first night in Schwab's store.

And Jones kept it up. He never seemed to tire.

What I do is just the same no matter who's filling in for who. She could see and hear the truth of what he had said. He did not care about comparisons and opinions and ideas of success—he played for himself and himself alone. Success doesn't matter. Jaeger and the audience don't matter. Talk as much as you want to when I'm playing. Sing songs, shoot guns, start a riot—it doesn't matter. I'll go on at the piano whatever you do, and if you don't like my playing, leave. Just leave. I don't need an audience. I could be in here all alone and I would still be the same. All I need is the piano and myself, and if I had to, I could get along without the piano.

Jones put away six numbers during his set. Two of them, she learned from Jaeger, were undoubtedly originals; and all six, she saw from his expression, were as good as or better than anything he had ever heard.

When Jones came off the stand he sat with them and had a double whiskey and water. It did not seem to bother him that the trio was getting more attention than he had got.

Conversation was a struggle. Jones talked about everything but music, and Jaeger kept trying to work music into the butterflying pattern of Jones' observations on liquor February shoes roast beef laundromats Gary old men in the park and why Social Security wasn't very secure.

"Say—" Jaeger finally wedged "—how would you like to come with us when you're through tonight? We're—"

"I'd like to."

"You don't even know where we're going," Jaeger said irritably.

"That's all right. It doesn't make any difference. Yes, I'd be happy to go with you, wherever you're going."

Jaeger's coal-like eyes turned toward the ceiling. From then on he was a man who had given up trying to learn a foreign language—not angered, but only withdrawn in ineptitude.

So she sat with him, and Jones went on the stand again to blaze away, and after the next set he did not join them but instead went along the bar and was picked up by a hard-packed blonde who bought him one drink and put her thigh against his and bought him another drink before he left her to play his third set. And after he ended that he came back to the table as if he had never been away and as if the blonde hadn't looked at him with eyes that promised the next drink she bought for him would be poisoned.

Helen was not to forget that night nor the following nights of Jaeger's last week. After Jones had finished they got in the car and made the rounds. They drove to Wilson Avenue and to West Side cellar-clubs, to records at The Mission and, once, at her apartment; they toured South into any number of black-and-tans or solid blacks; they went everywhere and heard all the jazz there was to hear in Chicago.

Jaeger was the master key. He opened any door to any basement or bar or apartment where jazz was going on. Faces at doors said Well goddamn me if it ain't Pops, now we gonna get some piano for a change, well fall on in, man, fall right on in! And so she went in close to Ross and behind them was the strange rough face no one knew yet, Virgil Jones, and the three of them sat and listened and drank and talked as Jones, the outsider, sat perfectly at ease and unawed by anything that happened. He was always introduced by Ross as a "great pianoman"—but whenever asked to sit in, he refused. Courteously but flatly. And if they insisted further, he ignored them. Once he had taken a stand, there was no changing him.

There was no changing Jaeger, either. He too refused to sit in at the piano, but unlike Jones, always pleaded an excuse. No, she would hear Ross say, I'm not going near one for a week. Promised myself a rest. Been hitting it too hard. Hands tired. Next time I come through I'll blow the place out. But not now, thanks.

She wished he would say No and let it go at that. Ross Jaeger, deferred to and fawned over and exalted by all the jazzmen wanting to learn from him, making excuses, being too considerate. Needing to be liked.

Or was it, she wondered, out of fear?

Normally he would have needed no excuses. He would have got up and gone to the piano and turned out something like *Tenderly* or *Lullaby* or *Under My Skin* and everybody would have been knocked out from hearing him. He would have played anything he had a mind to, knowing he was at least four hands better than anyone in the place.

But not now. Now he said No, I'm not going near one for a week.

While Virgil Jones watched with pale, wide-set eyes that showed nothing of what he might be thinking, except perhaps that he didn't care whether Jaeger got on the piano for three hours or whether he didn't go near one for the rest of his life.

It took Seymour Schwab to draw him out about Jaeger. Blunt Schwab, the one who seemed the only person able to approach the pianist.

On a Thursday night Schwab had been in the cocktail lounge when she and Ross arrived to hear Jones. And because Schwab was lonely and unashamedly eager to go with them on their all night tour, he got in the back seat with Jones as Ross barreled the Cadillac for a roadhouse halfway to Joliet.

The combo was nothing. Its drummer couldn't keep his sticks off the cymbals, the pianist had no drive and no ideas, whereas those of the tenor saxophonist had been heard before, note-for-note, from the horns of Phillips and Cobb and Illinois Jacquet. There was also too much dancing which looked too much like upright fornication.

The expedition was a failure, and she could see that Ross would settle down to serious drinking if the four of them didn't get out soon.

Gussie's, I'll drive, she was about to suggest, when Schwab put a question she had thought he had the sense to avoid.

"What do you think of Jaeger here, Virgil?"

"As a person," Jones answered calmly, for some reason looking at her, "I would tell him before I told you or anyone else."

"No," Schwab said, "I don't mean that. As a musician."

"He hasn't heard me," Jaeger said.

"Yes I have—on records. And you're a fine musician, one of the best I've heard."

"Who else do you like?" Jaeger said in a tone that did not hide his pleasure yet the annoyance he felt from the awkwardness of the situation she knew had eaten at him for a long time. Jones had shown no interest in what Jaeger played. It had been deadly indifference that seemed implied disapproval. Now that it was out in the open and was praise, she knew Jaeger was inwardly humiliated.

"I don't know much about jazz," Jones answered the question. "I can't remember many names, but it really doesn't matter—my opinion of other musicians. They are what they are, and have to keep being that whether I like them or not. My ideas of what is good mightn't agree with theirs, so who am I to say they haven't got a right to theirs?"

"Anarchy," Schwab said.

"You've got to have some standards," Jaeger said.

"Talk," Jones said easily. "All theory and no practice. What difference does it make what standards I have as long as I don't use them to hurt other people?"

"But you don't care about others," Schwab said.

Jones gave a half-nod.

"And indifference hurts," Schwab concluded.

"That's their doing, not mine. If somebody tells me his feelings will be hurt if I don't pay attention to him, it's blackmail. And I won't buy. And I won't feel guilty. Nobody in the world has any right to make you feel guilty because you won't do what they want you to do. That's all I've got to say. The rest is what ifs and but ifs and supposing thises—all talk. Let's drink whiskey."

And that was that. His words were unequivocal. They reverberated in her mind as though amplified and echoed. If a man was what he believed, she thought, then Jones was the loneliest, proudest man in the world. Alone and independent and assured.

She was not able to find out how Jaeger had taken everything he had heard. He was quiet and too busy to talk much. He packed as if he would be away for a long time. Watching him, feeling a weak draining sensation inside, she still said nothing that might give him an extra burden. She told herself that going away was always like this. Time passed, things were left unsaid.

Unsaid into morning, into afternoon, into the final cold smoky dusk hung like a vast fabric above white and red and green lights and metal-colored glare of the airport and the distant featureless face of Ross turning to look at her for a final remembrance before disappearing into the black square of the huge shuddering silver plane.

4

Under the massive vaulted roof of the Stadium hung an un-
stirring pall of chill smoke. Suspended in diffused light were
impersonal and musty odors of sawdust and cold steel. Shrill
whistle. The DePaul guards brought the slick orange-brown
ball upcourt—*bump bump bump*—to the edge of the purple-
jerseyed defense—*bumpbump bump.* Pass. Pass. *Bump.* Pass.
Pass, quick hook-pass under the backboard, jump like a
sprung toy, ball arching, off the rim, tip, another tip, veered
in air, a twisting leap and a purple jersey free with the ball,
bump, pass, *bumpbumpbump,* a long lobbing pass and flat
hammering of feet and ball on gleaming wood, driving under
the glass board, UP, and a roar of ten thousand as the white
net surged. The giant black scoreboard blinked NU 39 D 36.

Henneberry sauntered along the wide cement aisle behind
the red slatted seats. His big face was studiedly indifferent.
There was another roar, but he did not turn his head. A blue-
and-white usher adjusted a deferential smile. Henneberry
turned into the box-seats near midcourt and descended the
shallow stone steps.

"Paul . . ."

Bauer's delicate face turned to reveal teeth that seemed made
of semi-transparent plastic. His eyes were the color of ice, as
with a chalky hand he pulled down the seat beside him and

indicated that Henneberry was to wait until he, Bauer, had the time to speak. He then leaned away to talk to a black-coated, gray-hatted man having the profile of a toad.

A DePaul player was at the free-throw line. Henneberry followed the ball as it looped in without touching the rim. He noticed the toad put a mark in a small brown spiral note-book. The toad did not appear very happy.

"I'd like to talk to you, Paul . . ."

Bauer's eyes pinched, following the action.

"It's important." The crowd-roar forced him to bend close to the silvery head. "We're going to have trouble with Jones."

Bauer's face constricted. Without excusing himself or look-ing back at the game, he stood and climbed the steps with Henneberry.

They went through a short tunnel and came out near a refreshment stand decorated with red and white corrugated paper. There was the mixed smell of beer, steam, mustard and wet oilcloth. Bauer paid for the two lukewarm hotdogs and the big waxed containers of beer. Several yards to the left of the stand was a secluded space backed by tall Xs of tubular steel.

" 'Trouble.' " Bauer drank and licked the thread of foam from his upper lip.

"It's really Jaeger's doing." Henneberry bit into his hotdog. It did not look right with his expensive face; he manipulated it as though it were an animal that did not want to be eaten. And the mustard-blotched tissuepaper gave him no end of trouble. "Mgwmmf mhnn *snac*—" chewed his mouth "—all last week Ross took him around to clubs and showed him off, as it were."

"You went with them?"

"No."

"Then you're assuming again, announcer."

"No, Paul. Tance told me. Tance and Trinidad were gigging out on Ashland when Ross came in with Jones and advertised him as a new piano who would hit the top someday. Naturally that isn't such an advantageous move at this stage of the game. What I mean to say is that Jones has found out how good he is. Dangerous, Paul. He'll be in a position to make more demands—" Henneberry sighed weakly with a trace of desperation "—as if he doesn't make enough already."

"He's making trouble?" For some reason a faint brief flame of something that could have been satisfaction lit Bauer's eyes. It was almost as if he not only expected Jones to make trouble, but welcomed its coming.

"The usual," Henneberry said. "No requests, generally doesn't even allow time for applause, accepts every drink bought for him and then ignores the person who has bought it —and lately he's played classical works—straight classical, mind you—that have succeeded only in angering that rough crowd he's playing for. He is a living insult, Paul. He respects nothing and no one but himself, and the people sense it. I've observed more than a few who would have shot him if they'd had a gun. And now you can imagine how difficult he will be after learning that one of the best musicians around thinks so highly of him. He'll be impossible . . ."

"Is this what you came to tell me?" the agent asked over the rim of his cup.

"I suppose it doesn't worry you."

"No." Bauer threw the cup behind a steel beam. "Remember what I told you when you wet your pants about the people Jones was starting to draw? Patience, I told you."

"But Jones is still pulling them in."

"Don't interrupt. As I said, I know what I'm doing when I tell you to relax. I know, I know—you want to make a big, quick piece of change off Jones. You want to make him overnight, pick up your money, and then get out. The only trouble is, announcer, *I* don't want it that way—understand? It's going to be *my* way, and my way is patience."

"Of course," Henneberry said sourly. "Patience, it seems to me, is comparatively easy when one is able to afford it."

"Exactly."

"But that applies to you, Paul, not to me."

"Exactly again," Bauer said in his brittle bonelike voice. His eyes were heavy with disdainful superiority. "And that, announcer, is the point. You don't matter. Jones belongs to me, not you. I will reward you from time to time for your work—and maybe, at the end, you can have Jones for yourself."

"Providing he isn't used up."

"Oh," Bauer said, smiling, "you can have him then, too."

Henneberry did not know an answer. To Bauer's last statement or to any fragment of the secretive, inexplicable way he was acting. Of late Henneberry had had recurring impulses to abandon the whole affair and let Bauer handle it himself. Nothing definite had been accomplished, and Jones had been playing nearly three months. He was now working five nights a week, but only as an intermission pianist in a cheap, anonymous bar on the South Side. Not a thing was being done about the fair number of followers he had won, and Henneberry knew from experience that popularity withered and dried and was dust if left unattended. Yet was Jones ready for all the independence of fame and money? No, Henneberry concluded angrily. Jones was already too damned independent.

His beer smelled like horsepiss. He dropped the cup in a metal can and wiped his lips with a handkerchief monogrammed by whirling script.

"Then," he said to Bauer, "we're to do nothing."

Bauer nodded once.

"Nothing about a contract," the announcer went on. "We're to continue risking the chance that he may sign with someone else."

148

"No risk." Bauer took a step toward the tunnel leading back to the box-seats. He carried himself like a man who had just performed a trick of magic that had baffled his audience.

For a few minutes they stood behind the last row of boxes and directed their faces toward the basketball game. Henneberry had a sudden impression that when he left the Stadium the snow would have disappeared from the streets and the trees would be fat with sticky buds. Time was passing. Everything would be coming to life.

"Paul," he said, "I'm not doubting your methods—obviously you have thought this out thoroughly—but don't you think it would be wise if you were to meet Jones? Perhaps in that way you—"

"I've thought it out, all right, and I'm not going to meet Jones yet. Now you can think what you want, announcer, but I've done a lot of things nobody understood till later . . . and I haven't done too bad for a country boy, have I? So—" a roar shook loose from the crowd and buffeted the stairwall "—you just follow my orders and you'll make out all right, announcer. You'll get what you've got coming. We'll both get all we need."

Henneberry sagged against the cold railing and watched the thin figure pick its way down the steps and resume its perch like some ancient, gritty bird. Henneberry remained standing there for some time, pretending to watch the game while his mind doubled back in uncertainties. Dimly but with an incontrovertible finality it came to him that he had made a mistake in thinking he could have Jones to himself. Bauer was in the way. He would always be in the way. Well, he told himself, Bauer's talent was management. Bauer would be behind the scenes; Henneberry would be onstage.

He smiled, and, as he descended the steps and began a ponderously slow and proud exit along the giant oval path, he had the tremendous impression that faces shrank back at his approach.

Sixty-third Street in Chicago is like a fighter who has taken too many punches for too many years. It wears old clothes and has a loud rough voice that is sometimes an entirely new language. It is always moving with a nervous little half-shuffling, half-jerking purposefulness that makes it seem like a fighter coming out for the final round knowing he is far behind on points. It has to win by a knockout. What it will win, it does not know. It is not even sure who it is fighting. But one thing it does know: Keep Moving.

And it moves in a sunless world. Above whine and growl swaying elevated trains which seem about to topple into the street at any second; below lurch buses and drunks of all colors wrapped in last week's newspapers. While at night this world flashes and screeches in a spectrum of neon and noise and smells of brick and beer and lust. Keep Moving.

Geographically, this is a mile closer to the big time.

Jones was improving beyond any talking of it. He needed only himself to convince those who came to listen. He needed no drums or bass to give him the deep surging beat, no harmony or counterpoint with guitar or bass—nothing but his two big hands and what he had in his head.

Almost always he came alone and left alone. He could have had a woman as often as he needed one, but he did not appear to need even that. Nor did he take up with any of the musicians—all of them competent but unoriginal neighborhood entertainers—who started coming in to hear him. He was never loftily superior as he talked with them, but acted as though the thing they shared, music, was an irrelevance much like the relationship of sixth cousins meeting in middleage.

Everyone who met him—and there were many because he would listen or talk to anyone—had the impression that he would never be attached to anything except the piano, and it often seemed as though he had no real love for that. He played passionless and powerful, exact and untiring.

There were some in the audience who saw an emptiness in him. He was adrift, without any real friends and without any purpose, and they felt sorry for him out of that timeless practice of projecting their own loneliness into him. It had to be their loneliness. It certainly wasn't his.

But, inevitably, along with those who admired or pitied him were those who hated him. Right down the line they were people so weak and unsure of themselves that they were loud, dogmatic, viciously and constantly critical of anyone who not only had different values, but who twisted the knife by being satisfied and successful. They hated him for his confidence, his strength, and for his indifference to them. Night after night a morbid fascination drew them into the bar with the hope that somehow, some night, they might force him to compromise.

It was hard to say whether Jones lacked the sense to understand their hatred or whether he actually didn't care how many hated him. He did as he had always done. He was prompt, gave the people more than an honest amount of jazz piano, accepted drinks graciously, and refused to play for anyone but himself. God Himself would not have got an answer to a request.

Among the haters were three South Siders in their late twenties who wore Can't Bust 'Em overalls in the daytime and at night togged themselves out in one-button-roll sportcoats and crocheted ties with knots the size of their fists. They pretended to an appreciation of jazz, but this was only because jazz-spots, like churches, were good places to pick up women. And of course if they got a woman it made an impression if the entertainer, like the preacher, knew you and called you by your first name.

The only trouble was that Jones drank all the drinks they bought him and still acted as though he owed them nothing.

One Friday night the three came in with girls they had met at a Legion dance the Saturday before. They could have gone to another nightclub or even downtown to a movie, but to each of them Jones had become a kind of habit and a challenge. Their vanity insisted that he would not ignore them forever and would finally, certainly break down some night and treat them with special consideration.

As the night progressed they listened to him play and watched as he drained the glass they had bought him; they tried to catch his attention as he came off the stand and instead of coming to their booth went to talk to an elderly man and then to a fine-looking Greek girl sitting with a Jew wearing thick glasses and then to a colored couple and then to somebody else—but not to them, never to them during all the times he came off the stand, not once admitting their existence as they crouched infuriated and frustrated and did not impress the girls with their worldliness and friendship with a jazz musician.

Finally, along about midnight, the one wearing a handpainted silk tie went to the washroom, and when he came back Jones was with him.

"I'd like you to meet Virgil Jones," said Handpainted Tie. His mouth was as smug as a snake's.

Jones remained standing and repeated the names of the girls—Jo, Mary, Ginny . . . or Ginger—as they were introduced. Then he tipped his head but did not shake hands to acknowledge George and Eddie.

"Sit down and have a drink." Handpainted Tie was expansive.

"Yeah, have a drink," said Eddie. He grappled with a chair and set it to the booth.

152

"No," Jones said. He made a curiously formal bow to the girls. "Goodbye." Then he left them: Jo and Ginger shaping soundless *It was nice meeting yous*, Mary looking stupidly at Tie and Eddie and George, and they looking at Jones with eyes that could have burned holes in brick.

"I can't dope it out," muttered Tie. "The bastard is a regular joe when I ask him to come over and meet some people, and then he just takes off . . ."

"He's a big deal," said Eddie.

"I got his deal," said George. "Come on, I don't like it here no more."

And so they left and ate at a Peter Pan and complained about the bigheaded Jones and kept complaining for three miles in the Buick before Tie decided they had better get off the subject and see what was up with the girls. But nothing was up. The girls were rigid, and concerned about their clothes and hair, and Ginny even brought up Jones again and asked Tie if he didn't think Jones was kind of goodlooking.

Tie said he wouldn't know. Did she think he was fruit or something that he cared how men looked?

Ginny said she didn't like that kind of talk.

Tie said he didn't like her kind of talk much, either.

George said he heard a lot of musicians were queer. And they took the needle, too. All you had to do was look in their eyes, if the pupil was real big that meant they were taking dope.

Jo said she hadn't got a good look at Jones' pupils.

Tie stared out the window and counted streetlamps. Nothing was up, all right.

Even before they dropped the girls off, Tie and Eddie and George had it in their heads that Jones had ruined the night, that he had made them look like clods, and that they would go back to the club and wait for him to finish. What they would do then, they didn't know. But it would be something.

And when they had done it, Jones would know that he couldn't go around making people look bad.

Parked directly across the street from the entrance, the three of them sat in the darkened car and waited. Smoke was thick in the car. They had plenty of time to work themselves up. Tie felt like a gangster. Eddie and George concocted images of violence in which their punches were sledgehammers. They wished the girls, any girls, were around to see.

People began coming out of the club. Some walked, others drove off. In less than five minutes the street was deserted. No sign of Jones.

Just when they began to suspect that he had eluded them, out he came—but he was not alone. A girl and another man were with him.

Tie said "Now" from the side of his mouth, and the three of them got out of the car and crossed the street. They still had no clear idea of what they would do.

Helen was the first to notice their approach. For a second she looked up and down the street, then said something that caused both Schwab and Jones to turn toward the tight phalanx nearing them.

"What's the story?" Tie had stopped on the sidewalk only a few paces from Jones. Everyone was looking at everyone else. Schwab nervously put one hand to his glasses.

"I don't know what story you're talking about." Jones did not appear interested.

"Yes you do."

"You know what story, all right," George said menacingly.

"Did you three," Jones said in a cool tone, "walk over here just to play guessing games?"

There was no answer. Feet scraped on cement. Tie ran the tip of his tongue across his lips. Noises of night and the street were distant and unreal.

"You're pretty fuckin' good, aren't—"

"Watch your mouth," Jones said. Suddenly he was cocked like the hammer of a gun. "A lady is here."

"Fuck her," Tie said, and then gave a dazed little grunt as his head snapped brokenly from the impact of Jones' right fist. With catlike speed Jones pivoted and powered a ramrod left into Eddie's charging, hating face, but even as he went down, George had swung into clumsy action and Tie was pounding Jones from behind. Schwab pulled off his glasses and then didn't know where to put them. He finally pushed them at Helen and ran forward to scramble like some gradeschooler. There were grunts and curses and a sob. Schwab sat on the pavement and stared at his shoes as though trying to understand how to tie them.

It was not long before Jones was lying face down and the three were thumping him with fists and feet. Tie was crying and kicking at the same time.

Helen flung herself against legs and arms and fists and covered Jones' head with her arms and screamed for them to stop kicking or they would kill him. In an instant the scene froze: Eddie and Tie and George standing club-armed and panting; Schwab putting a hand to his mouth like a child; Jones unconscious and the girl kneeling over him. Then, as quickly as it had started, it disintegrated as the three plunged and staggered across the cobblestoned street and jumped in the car and with the squeal of rubber shot away.

There was nothing to do for Jones. She could only turn him over and prop his bloody head on her purse and wait. Schwab was still dazed, although he had regained his feet and his glasses.

"I'm going to call the police," he said.

"No," she said, one hand automatically and helplessly stroking Jones' forehead. "This isn't the place or the time to leave a girl alone. Those three were mild—they used only fists. This street has worse at this time of night."

155

Schwab sank to one knee and looked into the bruised and sliced face. Jones' breathing was steady but ragged and liquid.

"Why?" Schwab let his mouth sag after the question. He shook his head and then touched his right temple as though trying to keep something in place. "Why did they do it? What did they have against him?"

"I don't know." She continued moving her shapely fingers over his forehead. "Probably nothing important. People always fight for the little reasons."

Presently Jones came to. His eyes opened quickly, but without the ability to focus. He did not try to get up. For a minute he lay motionless as Helen told him he was going to be all right. His large eyes were soft as they searched every feature of her face.

"Now," he said at last. "I'm going to stand up, and I don't want any help or any argument. Get away now. There. If I start to fall, I don't want you to help me. I'll get up by myself and stand by myself and walk by myself. I don't want any help."

And he got up awkwardly, reeled once, steadied himself, and then dropped to his left knee and hand.

"Get—your—hands—away," he warned as they reached for him. "I don't need any help." Immediately he jerked himself up and took a wide, squared-off stance. This time he did not go down again. He simply refused to. "Now—" he said, surprisingly poised "—shall we go?"

"We'll drive you over to the IC Hospital . . ." Helen said. "Just for a checkup. They kicked you awfully hard, Virgil."

"No hospital," he said. "And no police, either. If you want to, drive me home. Otherwise, I'll take a bus."

They tried to argue with him, to convince him that his face and hands—especially his hands—needed looking after.

"No. My hands are all right. They're strong." He appeared to be absolutely unconcerned about his face and the ribs which

156

had been kicked so savagely. Anyone who had witnessed the beating he had taken would have known that he was in pain, but his face said nothing—no pain, no anger, no shame.

"Why did they do it?" Schwab asked as he started the Nash.

"Because I wouldn't let them use me," Jones said in a controlled and revengeless voice.

" 'Use' you?" Helen asked.

"Yes. They tried to use me to impress the girls they were with. As soon as I saw it, of course, I left them. That's why they beat me up. They came back to teach me a lesson. I'm not supposed to forget it." He laughed and slipped his tongue between swollen lips. His left eye was sheathed and shiny.

"You act," Helen said, "like you'll forget it by tomorrow."

"Oh, no. I won't forget it. I've had a whole lot of lessons from a lot of teachers, and I've never forgotten any of them. The thing is—" he added, smiling at the windshield "—I always come out with the wrong answer."

Together they looked at him. Ten minutes ago he had been beaten and kicked unconscious, and only now was his body beginning to come alive with pain; yet he still wore a warped smile and lifted head as if to proclaim to the world that the deepest satisfaction would always belong to him.

5

They blind them. They put out their eyes so they'll think they're going somewhere, but all they do is go around and around until one day they drop dead in the traces.

Jaeger remembered. It had become a chorus he could not shake from his mind. Always it was there: poised and shapeless in dark recesses, waiting for the splintered second when his mind was open between thoughts. Then *all they do is go around and around until* he snapped his brain to the keyboard or a gleam of brass, or to an odor of sea or the mauve fog of the Golden Gate or the steep slick fall of Powell Street or perhaps only to a Mennen matchbook pulpy in a gutter.

Were his eyes out? He was uncertain. There were times when he thought so. At times he could not see for looking.

His contract at Fack's was for three weeks, but from the crowds he drew with his playing Jaeger could have stayed three years. He was working with four local musicians who were blowing over their heads in order to keep up with him. From the first and only time they had got together before opening night—the session had been in Fack's while outside sang a gray afternoon filled with shining wires of rain—Jaeger had shown them more piano than they had ever heard before. Wearing a black jersey poloshirt and an old pair of peach-colored flannel slacks, he had been stripped for action—and had given it to them. Chain-smoking, his frowning forehead stippled with perspiration, he had blasted the coda to one number, looked up briefly, called out another tune, stomped, and led them off again. By four o'clock the trumpetman could only kiss out his choruses and the drummer was brushing with one hand at a time. At four-thirty Jaeger had said that was it, not too bad, be back no later than a quarter to nine.

That was the pattern. He was in charge. And within three days everyone in and around San Francisco who knew the meaning of jazz had found out that one hell of a piano had come to town.

The only trouble was that Jaeger himself did not believe it.

He wished . . . yes, he wished that Jones was not. Not a pianoman. Not anything. Only a name like the thousands of Joneses you could find in any city telephone directory. Only a man like everyone else: working at a job, hoping for promotions, worried about taking on weight and losing his hair, getting pleasure out of watching a football game or drinking beer with friends or playing cards. A man like everyone else.

But wishing could not make it true. Jones was. He was unlike anyone Jaeger had ever known. He worked at a job, it was true, but he did not worry about promotions or weight or hair or anything, for that matter. And he did not get pleasure out of football or friends because the only thing that gave him pleasure was himself.

I am the last individual in the world. His claim was no longer hard to understand, but behind it lay the unanswered question: How could a man be so alone and unambitious and still be so confident and content? There was a secret somewhere within him. There had to be.

Between sets at Fack's Jaeger found himself alone. Coming out of the back room after a drink and standing in the shadows along one wall, he could see and feel countless eyes watching him. They wanted to meet him, buy him a drink, talk to him about jazz, find out how he liked San Francisco and what he thought about Chet and Brubeck and Shorty. They wanted to know him so that later, over campus coffee, they could say, casually, that they were talking to Ross Jaeger the other night and he said San Francisco was a great town, he would like to live here someday, and that Brubeck was way the hell out as far as piano went. Jaeger knew what was hidden in the glances because the eyes had been the same at the zouzou, at Berg's, at Birdland and the Deuces and The Silhouette, at every place small enough to bring him close to the audience. Sometimes one of them would drift over and ask for his autograph, and when he had signed, every now and then they would be encouraged into inviting him to join their table. And in places like this, where he knew no one, he accepted gratefully but did not dare show it. He had his pride. It would not do to impose himself on anyone who looked at him as a celebrity.

So, inevitably, there were times when they stared at him but did not ask, while he noticed them but could not ask, and presently he would climb to the piano and play for them again.

All the first week it was the same at closing time. The others in the quintet were fifth-raters who had so much respect for him that he was never asked to join them; they assumed that Jaeger had his own life to lead, and that after playing with them all night he had had enough of them. And, just as he felt toward the audience, Jaeger secreted his isolation and made no attempt to impose himself on them.

So he would leave Fack's alone and drive his Hertz Cadillac to an all-night chophouse or across the Bay Bridge to Oakland or else halfway down the Peninsula along its El Camino Real, where, still brilliantly awake, he smoked over bottomless black coffee and ate cheese or bacon omelets. Then he would go back to his hotel, take a scalding shower, and fall asleep with The Sporting Green of *The Chronicle* folded on his chest.

The second week brought relief. It started with a guest-spot on an afternoon record program, and the same night he got a call from Flip Phillips, who was opening at The Blackhawk. San Francisco was opening like a night-blossoming flower.

Phillips knew good people in the city. Together Jaeger and he would meet at either one of the clubs after their shows and head out for apartments on Russian Hill or ranch-low homes across the Bay. Only twice did the sleepy-eyed tenorman pack his saxophone for a night of extra-curricular jamming with Jaeger on piano. For the most part their hosts let them relax and treated them like any normal friends. Jazz conversation was not compulsory, and it was a tonic to be able to sound off about politics and advertising and winter baseball trades and the shortsightedness of the tract-home building boom in California and why Los Angeles should be expelled from the state for giving it such a bad name.

But the evenings always ended. The fog rolled from the sea like a glacier of wool, muffling the sun and orange bridge-girders and pastel-sided houses, mirroring asphalt with dampness, making blurs of faces and headlights and morning neon, and finally, as always, bringing with it another day and the time when Jaeger was again in his room alone.

Dressed in a white terrycloth robe and with slippered feet braced against the windowsill, he wore memory in his eyes and cigarettes in his mouth. The cigarettes were from the carton Helen had given him before leaving. She had opened each package and one by one had put every cigarette between heavy red lips. The oil of her lipstick had dried and was now tasteless, but he felt the touch of her each time he bit the darkened end.

He remembered too much, felt the touch of too many things. Helen and himself. Jones. He conjured the face of

Jones, and it loomed just to the left of the framed koda-chrome of Lake Tahoe, unruffled and crystalline, on the wall above his bed.

He remembered DeWitt. Incandescent-eyed, his brows a thick dark bar across the sunken face, Bern DeWitt had read books, attended a thousand lectures, and had argued, argued, argued. The Wild Man. His speech crowded with expressions like capitalistic perpetuity, moral obligations, technological unemployment, parasitic citizens, you're simply exhibiting bourgeois sentimentality, economic slavery, of course—what did you expect? Old CTR, as Line Jackson had got to calling him. Comes The Revolution DeWitt.

Now dead. Now never the revolution.

Now never again a night like the one on which, both being free, they had gone to the Blue Note to hear Tatum's piano. DeWitt had listened impassively and had spent most of his time in looking into the audience.

They had walked away from the club in a warm, soft driz-zle that lacquered Randolph Street to a glare. A beacon wheeled across the depthless spring sky.

"So—" Bern had said at last, the fingers of his big right hand curling as if he were gathering up a length of rope "—a year ago Art would have gassed me, man." The hand kept pulling. "But not now, Ross . . . never again. Neither Art, nor you, nor anyone else—no matter what kind of piano you have."

"Let's grab something to eat."

"Sure. Feed the flesh." DeWitt's smile was a thread. "But jazz is nothing, do you know that? What all of us are doing—what this man isn't going to do much longer—is trivial. Even vicious. We amuse the people so they'll forget that not one of their lives is worth a curse in hell. We make them happy on weekends so they can go back on Monday and file papers and punch machines and collect a miserable check on Friday so they can spend it hearing us get them ready for Monday again. We are a kind of sugar-tit, you know. We are musical tits covered with a layer of opium. Kind of a bizarre image, I know, but it's the truth. Music soothes, etcetera. The breasts would be mighty savage if we weren't employed to keep them gurgling, I'll tell you."

"Ah, put it down, dad," Jaeger had said, shaking his head. "You can't expect all of us to stop what we're doing just to help a few million people we've never seen."

"I have every right to expect it. It's an obligation supported by every major moral code of mankind."

"And how many live up to it?"

"Here's one who will."

"You say that now."

"I say it now. Come around in ten years and I'll still be saying it."

"Be yourself, Bern." Jaeger had felt an unnamable foreboding of disaster brush his eyes like the swift frantic beat of moth-wings.

"For the first time," DeWitt had insisted, still using his hands in accompaniment, "I'm really myself—Bernard De-Witt. This is who I am. This is what I have to do."

The drizzle had increased to a soggy spray in their faces. They passed a pair of young couples who with surprise parted to allow them an avenue.

And DeWitt had smiled sardonically after a few paces. "Did that make you feel good?"

Jaeger had pretended he didn't understand.

"Those kids," DeWitt had said. "Turn around now and you'll see them looking back at us—their heroes. It makes a man feel great to see a crowd break ground ahead of him, doesn't it, Ross?"

"They don't matter," he had lied. Then, however, feeling

cheap, he added: "The music matters. That's what I think is important."

"Of course. That's what we have to tell ourselves. Everything for the music. But is it enough, Ross? Can you get everything you want out of eighty-eight keys? How about it?"

"It starts there. That's where it starts—with the keys."

"Agreed, man, agreed generally. But where does it end?"

Now, watching a cablecar gamely pulling itself up the arcaded street below his window, Jaeger was impaled on the question DeWitt had thrust that night. *Where does it end?*

For DeWitt it had ended not ten months later. The news had been, like Bern himself, vague and incomplete. An inch in the morning papers. In the trade magazines, more. A photograph. DeWitt and who he had been, what he had been, what he had played, how good he had been. Had been. Was not now.

Mercury had asked him, then, to record a memorial album, and he had finished the eight sides with a feeling of desolation he could not explain. He felt a void, a trackless emptiness within him.

The critics, Henneberry most of all, had considered three of the numbers in the album the best Ross had ever done. But all of their words had missed the most important point: the mechanical perfection. That had been what Jaeger was trying to achieve. Flawless precision so impressive and compelling that it concealed the absence of feeling. "In the true spirit of Bern DeWitt," Henneberry had said. A glib phrase he himself didn't understand. But Jaeger knew. He knew as a musician and as Bern's closest friend. The true spirit of DeWitt was hollow. In the end he had hated jazz. In the end the crowds had still come to hear his delicate, singing piano while he played martyrlike for enough money with which he could begin to save the world.

And how had he felt before he died? Had he thought Yes,

164

dying like this is better than living like that? Had there been time to ask any questions before the fever had shaken him to death? What had he asked, and what had he answered?

Jaeger went to his portable phonograph and carefully handled a red-labeled record. Scarred and scratched, it was worth a gang of money to some people. DeWitt's *Sunny Side of the Street*—the first thing he had ever recorded. He had believed in jazz then.

. . . leave your worries on the doorstep, . . .

Now he was gone. And Fats, too. Both of them gone, nothing but a disc of wax spinning slowly in a hot room. Fats, Bern . . . Jaeger. Yes, it would be the same with everyone. Remembered for a little while.

I used to walk in the shade . . .

And there was Bern, actually there on that record, his fingers pumping out the notes. With practice, Jaeger knew, a man could play this note-for-note, but it would not be the same. The fingers would not be the same.

He played the record again. Morning shadows came into the room and empurpled chairs and empty glasses. He put another cigarette in his mouth. And looked at Tahoe and thought of Jones.

There was an answer there, something that seemed to take care of all the questions. Jones was the most satisfied man he had ever seen. Jones knew something that enabled him to go on day after day and night after night with no visible worries, no arguments, not a sign of doubt. But that something, Jaeger told himself, didn't lie in the music. Jones seemed to have no love for jazz; he played like a man solving an equation. But how could he not feel and still be able to put feeling in the music?

165

Somewhere there was an answer.

The more he thought about it, the more he believed he had once known it. There had been a time, in New York, when like now, his whole life was the piano, but unlike now, it had given him the same strength and satisfaction he saw in Jones. Back in the time of his first important job on Fifty-second Street, playing intermissions and listening to Pres and Norvo nearby during his breaks. In the days of Juilliard. It had put him in contact with a symposium of ideas and techniques, and by recognizing jazz as a legitimate form of music it had given him the encouragement he needed.

Then there had been Chicago—a two-week run that had stretched into a month, then two months, and finally three when Henneberry had begun backing him on the air.

After that had come the first unmistakable signs of success: a contract with Bauer, a recording contract, jobs with combos, with big bands, jobs everywhere in halls and cellars and clubs and once in an armory where the band played in the boxing ring while nine thousand people blocked off the exits and Joe Priest kept worrying about a fire, ROSS JAEGER on banners, in lights, his pictures in *Downbeat* expanding from half-columns to one-columns to twos, his picture on the cover, and the ultimate tribute—younger pianists copying his style.

Success. The stature he had always wanted. But something was wrong. Instead of happiness he found only more complications, new and unexpected things to worry about. What had he lost? Where could he find it again?

When anyone lost something, the best procedure was to re-trace every step and start at the beginning. Go back to where you had started from, look slowly and thoroughly, and somewhere along the path you would find what you had lost.

His eyelids were hot sheaths. He pulled the shades and slept. When he woke the late sun had glazed gold walls of buildings on Market and shaded blue-black the deep sidestreets. Above the Bay a Constellation silvered for an instant against pale sky. He could smell the sea—slow green surge, in and out of the windows, shoring and receding.

He raked fingers through his hair and stared dully into space. Sleep was selfish. It solved the need for itself. That was all it solved.

The afternoons grew long. Several days, nagged sleepless by the suspicion that he would miss a vital clue, he went to Union Square. But all he found were whirling pigeons and gulls. All he saw were old men too cold and damp and turned in upon themselves to tell him what they saw.

So Jaeger would walk away. He would walk south and east and then north, looking at everything and at nothing, west, and north again, and at times, being in a place he did not know too well, it was not strange that he had lost his sense of direction.

6

The wind was always. By day there was no sun and by night no stars. For an hour hail broke branches, bounced like quicksilver on black streets. Nothing else happened except the cold.

Schwab's life had become more bearable. It was still parceled out in a lonely apartment and in morning openings to customers who caused inventories of endless records before evening closings, but because of Virgil Jones he was learning to live with himself and to accept routine. There was no trick to it. What had to be done was simply done, finished, and out of the way. Whenever Schwab sensed bitterness coming upon him he would stop and meticulously load his pipe and light it. Then he would remind himself that all work was a job—Job: covered with boils, but enduring—and that he was free to quit this job and try something else. A man could never allow a job to own him. It killed him. He walked and talked and every so often forgot himself and laughed, but he was really dead. The city was full of these men. They were "making a living," but they were dead.

And again because of Jones, he had found an escape from long and lonely nights. Three and sometimes four nights a week he and Helen would drive out to Sixty-third to hear the pianist, and every time Schwab saw Jones it was with a sense of shame. Jones was far more alone than anyone else in the city, it seemed, yet he appeared just as contented and unembittered as if he had had hundreds of genuine friends and enough money for ten lifetimes.

So Jones had become his silent critic as well as the excuse with which he could be with Helen.

Who was lonely too, Schwab could tell as he covertly watched her dark passionate eyes trifling with various faces and objects in the nightclub. Lonely not because Jaeger was in San Francisco. Lonely because she knew he was lonely and needed help and she was not with him. Her life was empty without him. It was the kind of devotion that was always dangerous, Schwab felt, but then again, who was he to call her emotions unwise when his own were not flawless? Schwab said nothing. He sat and drank and chatted and listened to Jones. He observed the way her hair grew along her temples. He saw that for the time being she was making Jones into Jaeger.

How odd it was, he thought. How curious that Jones should be the one person who could make both of them less lonely.

Because the young pianist was still the same. He was unshakably confident and self-subsistent, and continued to act as though he didn't care how anyone else might feel or say. Grief or happiness or frustration or success were private affairs. He wasn't about to become involved in anything that didn't concern him.

The first night after the beating had been a good example of his quiet, immense strength. He had taken the stand, and the hard white spotlight had snapped on, and he had looked horrible. His right eye was swollen shut and the left half of his upper lip hung over the lower. His left jaw was skinned and bruised. Schwab had not been able to make sure until later that Jones' hair had been simply disarrayed and not rough with dried blood.

And Jones had begun playing the piano not with an attitude that nothing had happened and that everyone should still look at him as unchanged, but with a certain defiant angle to his head, admitting that his face was disfigured, yes, and that was all there was to it. Not even to imply that his ugliness was only temporary.

Schwab had been indelibly impressed, for it seemed to him that Jones' whole being had spoken for more than himself and the beating he had taken. *If I have an ugly face,* Jones had said without words, *or if I had only one eye or one arm or leg, or if I couldn't walk like the rest of you, I am what I am, and I do not have to explain or justify or alter my life in any way in order to make peace with you.*

Now, nights later, bruises yellowing on his face, Jones was the same as always: defiantly individual and uncompromising. He played what he wanted to play the way he wanted to play it. He followed no fashions, bowed to no authorities, and listened to no applause. Nothing shook him. It was he who, night by night, was beginning to shake everything else.

Helen knew more about the workings of the jazz-scene than Schwab had first thought. She was outspoken, and honest enough to admit ignorance of some of the questions put to her.

From her Schwab learned—and was able, later, to corroborate it by visible evidence—that Jones was being controlled by an unseen figure named Bauer, who for some reason no one knew preferred to have no contact with Jones, but instead used the poseur Henneberry as a kind of front. There was every indication, moreover, that the announcer himself didn't know what Bauer was really up to. During their several meetings at various clubs Schwab had come away feeling as if he had been talking to a critically sick man; Henneberry was full of wanting to hope, but also of fear because he had no idea of what was going on. He was cooperating desperately.

If Jones knew anything of all the wire-pulling going on behind him, he gave no sign. He revolted against none of the unexplained, sudden directives which had moved him from one piano to another on the South Side.

"Why should I mind?" he had said to Schwab and Helen one night between appearances. "The pianos are the same. Some could use a tuning, I guess, but they're all close enough."

"That isn't what I mean," she had said. "You could be doing a lot better."

"Better? Oh, probably . . . but I'm doing what I like to do and I'm making more money than I've ever had before. I don't care to make all the money in the world."

"She's talking about fame, too," Schwab had inserted.

Jones gave a short laugh. "That's something I don't think about. Fame."

"Then you feel it's stupid," Helen said, "for people to want it?"

"Not always. Sometimes it's the one thing that keeps people up, the idea that they might be famous. If it helps them, okay. But fame just doesn't matter to me. It can't matter. If I started to worry about being famous I'd be handing out pieces of myself."

"And you," Schwab said, "are the last individual in the world." The words had slipped out before he could stop them.

In the muffled light Jones' face had an indeterminate expression. With three fingers of his right hand he touched the bridge of his nose and shook his head almost imperceptibly.

"Sorry," Schwab had said.

"Oh, that's all right—I wasn't bothered by that. You've got a right to think what you want to. Only remember—" his wide-set eyes aimed steadily but without anger "—I've got a right too. And I believe it. And that's enough."

There it was again. The same inviolable sureness, the same calm poise that seemed impossible to upset.

The following Monday, a week before Jaeger was to come

back to Chicago, Jones was shifted to an even less appetizing nightclub on Sixty-third Street. The Leopard Lounge was more of a pit. It was dirty and threatening and in ambush behind girders of the Elevated. Many more Negroes were in the audience. Nearly all of them, Schwab was surprised to find, were acting roles of people whose race gave them an inherent understanding and appreciation of jazz. He knew they were acting because of the things they said and the types of music they wildly applauded. They did not know jazz from noise, and that was a fact. Even he had learned to listen and distinguish good from bad, though he still had little sympathy with the music.

For the first two nights Jones played against the babble of the mob that seldom stopped to hear him. He did not seem to mind. He asked nothing from them. They were to ask nothing from him.

But The Leopard Lounge was deceptive. It looked like a cell in which a musician could languish forgotten for years, but it proved to be the place from which Jones' piano reached every corner of the city.

It might have been that Bauer had designed it, or that jazz fans had special tuners in their heads, or that spring was coming and more people were on the streets at night, or that it was a sheerly accidental, untraceable discovery, but there was no mistaking the result: The Leopard Lounge became, overnight, the place for great jazz piano. The name: *Jones*. By word-of-mouth it passed. *Catch this Jones*. It passed over cigarettes and coffee in steamy Loop restaurants; it passed at parties, at nightclubs and drugstores and fountains, at magazine racks; in the Union Hall it passed; it moved through nameless streets of the city in darkness and in new spring light. *Jones. The Greatest. Just Too Much Piano. Out South.*

After the telegram from Jaeger, Helen went five nights a week with Schwab. Ross was not coming back soon enough.

In a week, perhaps two, he would be in Chicago again. The telegram had come from Palm Springs.

Schwab had read it, returned it, and suggested that they listen to Jones again. The next afternoon he called her again, heard her say she would be happy to have dinner downtown. Automatically, it seemed to Schwab, the evening ended with Jones.

Schwab told himself he knew why he was seeing her and thinking of her so often. He wanted to occupy her time, to make her forget her troubles with Jaeger. Helen was a warm, honest woman. Schwab liked her. He knew how it felt to be lonely. He liked her, he did not love her.

By the second Friday there were people standing in the doorway of The Leopard Lounge. Inside hovered haze and unusual silence as Jones went to the piano. He still wore an old unpressed blue suit and no tie. There was a flurry of quieting. Ice rattled nervously in a glass. Jones sat down and spread his hands and played.

There were times when he got going and wouldn't stop. His sets would last two hours then—all jazz, solid jazz, rambling through all the standards, introducing new strange melodies that belonged to him from the opening chord. A few nights he played Mozart with an ability that made Schwab shake his head because he could find no words for his amazement. He was looking on genius, Schwab realized, but the genius was not what he had expected to find it. It was a cold thing. It had no heart. It was all mind and control. But, inexplicably, the music itself was not without emotion. Through all its chord progressions and arpeggios and counterpointed complexities there was as much emotion as any man could wish for, yet in Jones himself there was only cold skill.

Musicians began coming in to hear Jones. Not only the musicians from the neighborhood, but jazzmen from all over the city. To hear Jones, this fine piano, this man who played just for himself and didn't care about being big-time or whether anyone liked him or not.

Critics from magazines and newspapers came in. Some took notes, others merely closed their eyes and listened, and all of them, at one time or another, tried to get Jones to their tables.

On a few occasions he accepted their invitations, but even as he sat with them he treated them as any other human beings and not as people who were in a position to bring him fame and success. His combative face never showed that he was impressed or flattered. Nor did it show hurt or anger when they took offense to the way he was acting toward them. Unmoved by innuendoes and elliptical phrases of criticism, he obviously didn't care what people said or thought about him.

Since the first—Christmas Eve and the card he still carried in his billfold—Schwab had seen Jones as indecipherable. Every now and then there would be a flash like the brief ghostly illumination of lightning, and a fragment of Jones would stand clear; but these flashes were too rare and irregularly spaced. Each one revealed something, but as yet they could not be pieced together to form a whole. Of course it would have been easy to accept the statement on the card as the whole and to explain Jones by that, yet it would still not explain the card itself. Jones was not the result of the card. The card was the result of him. And what had happened that had made him first think of the words, that had made it necessary for him to buy the rubber alphabet and cheap cards, that now moved him to distribute these cards sparingly but with the conviction of a religionist? Something had happened to Jones. Something huge. A profound and painful experience that had driven him deeply into himself, away from the world.

Yet, Schwab asked himself, what evidence was there that Jones had been hurt, and that that experience had made him withdraw from society? None. At least the normal reaction was absent. When a man was wounded he drew back from the cause and usually hated it. In order he became self-pitying, then cynical, and finally full of self-righteous bitterness. But even if he went through the stages he could never remove the marks each had made on him. He might be beyond cynicism, but its trace would be on him. He might be past self-pity, but it too would disclose itself in unguarded moments.

And Jones showed nothing. It was true that he had approached cynicism on that dreamlike night at the Top Hat, but, Schwab had to consider, cynics sneered and made a virtue of disbelief, while the pianist had only observed dispassionately and without any personal anger at what he saw. He had seemed to look around and admit the world as it was —turning sluggishly in a beginningless and endless circle of hope, fear, satisfaction, frustration, worry, happiness, life and death, purposeless living and premature dying, its people diseased with doubt yet turning with the turn, stuck insecurely in this city and that town, hoping for the hope to hope for success, people everywhere trying to make the best of what little time they had—and he had looked at all of it and had come up with an answer that said that he, Virgil Jones, one man, was nothing, but yet was everything. He was one man and this was the world. That was the nature of things. The world went on without him, and he would go on without the world.

Was Jones so wrong? Schwab asked himself.

He could not answer for sure. One thing he did know, however, and that was that Jones was the most independent and unfrightened man he had ever met.

With a half-smile he turned toward Helen and saw that she was listening intently to the piano. Her fine clean dark face gave no hint of what she was thinking. For a moment Schwab studied the heavy black ring on her left hand. Jaeger. She was thinking of him, wondering if in the hazy, ovenlike heat of

Palm Springs Ross would be able to relax and to appraise himself for what he had been and what he inescapably had to be.

It was no surprise to anyone, least of all Helen, to learn that Henneberry had given his endorsement to Jones on the air. Inasmuch as the announcer was network size, Jones was instantly a celebrity to jazz-fans who lived in other cities and could only hope to hear him on records or at a touring concert.

"He had to," Helen said. She looked across the table-cluttered room to where Henneberry was posing with expert disdain among a pack of whinnying admirers. "*Downbeat* comes out the day after tomorrow, and I've heard they've got a page-one story on Jones. Just a few inches, but enough to let people know Old Butterlips isn't the only one who can 'discover' a jazzman around here. So he had to do it to protect himself . . . and naturally, he took all the credit."

"I thought," Schwab said, "this Bauer exercised some control in this matter of publicity."

"He does. Not as much as he used to, though."

"Don't you think the article could be his doing? You know, what they call a 'plant' . . ."

She shook her head. "I really doubt it, Seymour. '*Beat* has enough of a reputation to be its own boss. Then again—" she put her hands palm-up on the table "—somebody can control things if he simply knows what's going to happen a few days before it does. I know some people who'd sell their souls to have that kind of power for just one week."

"I read a story like that a long time ago. It was about horse-racing—this fellow managed to get a newspaper a day ahead of time. Won a lot of money."

"I saw the movie, I think," she said. "Didn't he read his own obituary at the end?"

"Uh—yes, that was it. He saw his own death-notice."

"What happened after that? I don't remember it too well."

Schwab frowned and thought and shook his head.

"He probably didn't die," she said. "Dick Powell was the lead, and they wouldn't let him die."

And so night after night Schwab sat with her and talked on the edges of subjects at which they could only guess: Bauer's role in the sudden publicity given the pianist, Henneberry's interest in the success for which Jones appeared certain to reach, Jaeger's reaction to the change when he would return, and most of all, Jones himself.

For all the talking Jones did, Schwab was never able to feel that he really knew the pianist. Each time Schwab sensed an emptiness, a vague and undefined blank which if filled in would give him some basis for understanding. But the void remained. Jones talked and talked and seemed to have an opinion on every subject, yet when he had finished there was only the mass of words and the impression in Schwab that the pianist was a kind of magician—keeping all eyes on cards and balls and handkerchiefs while the truly important action was going on elsewhere. And even when Schwab saw and memorized all the paraphernalia, he knew it was wrong to think that all the cards and handkerchiefs and balls equaled the magician himself. No, the man was something else, something more, but what he was Schwab could not say.

There were certain undeniable facts. Jones had not changed his way of life. He still lived in the same miserable overheated rooms on the same rundown street. He still wore cheap clothes and spent money freely but not lavishly. He could never throw money around. There simply weren't many things he wanted to buy. Whiskey, food, carfare and an occasional pack of four-for-a-dollar cotton socks—these were the only things he appeared to need. He had no affairs with banks or other investments; his wealth was growing somewhere in his rooms.

Toward his audience Jones was indifferent to the point of insult. He certainly didn't act as though he considered himself a celebrity. Every night he was prompt and unswaggering, and when asked to give an autograph he acted more embarrassed than annoyed when he refused. No one got his autograph. He gave no one special attention.

Except Helen, Schwab noticed with surprise the night before Ross Jaeger was due.

Hints—nothing more—faint, unprovable hints made with his eyes at unexpected moments. He would be playing and perhaps they would be at a table facing his cropped white head above the piano-top, and for an instant the wide blue eyes would narrow and shift coldly and secretly in Helen's direction. He would be drinking with them and as he raised his glass those same ice-blue eyes would stare at her over the edge. He would walk into the club at the beginning of an evening, his head straight ahead but his eyes sweeping over all the faces and suddenly stopping, then moving on after they had found her.

The discovery made Schwab wonder why he had never thought along these lines before. What about Jones and women? How could he be sexually normal—and there had never been any indication that he wasn't—yet do without a woman? It was not that a man needed to sleep with a woman regularly in order to prove his masculinity; he could be a celibate with firm willpower, but even celibates took notice of women. Unless they were afraid to notice.

And Jones? The self-styled last individual in the world? How did he account for women?

Alone in his apartment, Schwab reflected. He was very nervous. The question was like the night outside. Now it was dark. Only a few scattered squares of yellow light shone above dim streetlamps. The sky was opaque, without height. But in a few hours the lights would multiply and the sky would lift like silk, and there would be purple and finally white-gold. In time everything would be clear.

Jones was . . . What? Schwab now viewed him as having

been more reserved than usual in the presence of Helen. Jones had been polite with the exquisite formal precision of an old man. And the fight. Schwab smiled, shook his head in the darkness. Jones had rushed to defend her sensibilities when she had been exposed to obscenity. Schwab put his thumbnail in a space between two teeth. And shook his head again. It had been a long time since he had seen anyone defend the capitalized Virtue of A Woman. Quite Victorian, really. Or else lower-class. Certainly not the upper-class or intellectual thing to do. Virtue there consisted of displaying none.

"So!" Schwab said to a shadowed Degas on one wall. He went to the kitchen and flipped the light-switch. His mind told him that he had discovered something of great importance about Jones. Well, he would have to wait and see.

He fried himself three eggs and slid them on a plate and jogged ketchup on them. Why not? It tasted good in his mouth, didn't it? And who was to tell him that he was not to put ketchup on sunnyside eggs at three-thirty in the morning?

7

Jaeger came back to the city with a coppery tan and a trunkful of Egyptian-cotton sportshirts and suede. His eyes were startlingly white and clear set against the color of his skin. Outwardly he was strong and certain.

During the days Leonine Jackson was the only person to see him regularly. They played golf at Jackson Park. If they were early enough the grass would be smoky with mist and dew, and they would sometimes get in as many as thirty-six holes on the smooth emerald hills. Jackson would press a tee, set his ball, and address it as if he aimed to pound it a good way toward Iowa. More than once he stopped his vibrating windup to ask Jaeger if he didn't think he looked like Ezzard Charles. Jaeger would say More and more every day—now hit the ball.

From the moment he would watch Jackson's first drive curve like a scythe into the tall thickening trees, Jaeger was absorbed in what he had to do: hit the ball on the green, tap the ball in the hole. He and Jackson would talk about everything but jazz as they crossed the spongy grass and breathed cool yellow-green air. Budding trees were loud with sparrows. On several holes Jaeger held his putts to watch steaming, lather-mouthed horses jittering along nearby cinder paths.

It gave him no special satisfaction that he always won by

ten or more strokes. Golfing was enough. Hitting the ball on the green and tapping the ball in the cup kept his mind from other things.

The sextet was regrouping under Allred. Charlie had made a fair go of the one formed after the first breakup, but now that Britton had decided that blowing in a big band was like being buried alive and Jackson was getting restless for some steady work, Allred had called them back. Reuben was still on drums. Nick Augustine was in Hollywood waiting for someone to do something about the movie, and had been replaced by a capable, imaginative alto saxman named Buddy Tance. J. R. Guthrie was on piano. Jaeger had intended to refuse when asked to join, but no one had asked him.

Plans were that in two weeks the sextet would ferry new cars to San Diego, after which they were to open in Los Angeles. Meanwhile they were getting together in a studio every afternoon and blowing through a sheaf of arrangements. Tance and J. R. were fitting in pretty well.

At night most of them were gigging around Chicago, picking up a few dollars to keep themselves honest and to avoid going stale on ideas. Some nights they sat in with another combo, just for kicks, or else drifted around to the clubs and listened from the other side of the bar. Allred was the only one working steady, and then it was filling in for a man who was getting lip-sores cured. J. R. was working steady too. But in another way. He spent most of his nights at the Nob Hill on Lake Park, listening to Jones.

Jaeger saw a lot of his replacement because he too went south to hear this man who was teaching more piano than that street had ever learned before.

Helen went along. Jaeger would pick her up at work and drive to an expensive restaurant where he would order expensive dinners and pretend that he enjoyed them. He would also pretend interest in her clothes or earrings or handbag, and in her vivid, almost frantic enthusiasm for something she had read or someone she had seen. He believed he was playing a convincing role.

Afterward they would go to Nob Hill. It was big and outdated and its poor acoustics were worse for the steady buzz and hiss and tinkle and rattle of the crowd that jammed nearly every available foot of space to hear Virgil Jones. The pianist was no longer an intermissionist to any group. He was the feature. The thick blue letters outside said so. The faces of the crowd said so. And his piano closed any argument.

Now when Jones would come to join them he had to force his way through the hands, arms and faces of the crowd that wanted him to stop, to talk, to autograph, to be someone special to each of them. At no time, however, did his face show either annoyance or pleasure at all the attention he was getting. He was independent of all the pressures and beginning evidences of fame. And he was, when he got to their table, just as bland and aloof toward them—so much so that it would have been hard to say why he had even bothered to sit with them in the first place.

Jaeger tried to draw him out about Henneberry and Bauer, but had no luck. Jones seemed completely ignorant of the plotting going on behind his back. More surprising, he did not appear to care. He talked—and did not talk—as though it was unthinkable to him that anyone would try to play him for a fool.

Jaeger knew better. As a matter of fact, nearly every musician knew better. A man with talent could be bled dry and picked apart bone by bone if he carried his trust in others too far. A man with talent was surrounded by other people who fed on him.

Driving home at night, alone or with Helen, Jaeger would listen as Henneberry claimed credit for discovering Jones. For a reason everyone knew by now, Henneberry played no records of Jones. The pianist had flatly refused to make records. It seemed as though he was doing everything possible to avoid success; but the more Jones shunned publicity and fame, the more he got. No records meant that anyone who wanted to hear him was obliged to travel out to Nob Hill. The crowds were capacity.

Understanding Bauer's connection was impossible. From all past experience Jaeger knew that the chalky old man was as remorseless and cold as a rifle. Aim. Aim carefully. Fire. Pick up what is left. That was the way Bauer worked. Even now, Jaeger was sure, Bauer was taking aim on Jones . . . but how? He could not say.

And there was Jones, the target, innocently confident and strong in himself, playing the piano, becoming a legendary and solitary figure, going on and up with an almost childlike faith that no one could ever hurt him.

It was not long before Jaeger grew nervous with inactivity. He could not stand to listen to a piano and not play himself. So he wired New York, and after a week of phone calls and telegrams took a two-week job at a matchbox of a nightclub on Chicago's Near North. He was given a banner above the entrance and a one-column box in all the newspapers. On both sides of the door were glossy portraits of him with and without the piano as a prop. He played solo.

Weeknights gave him what he wanted. There was never much of a crowd. In a bright corner a 26-girl clup-clumped dice for a bald man; along the bar slouched several richly-dressed men and women who seemed to have their minds on something else. The bar was spare and clean and dark. Colors and sounds were subdued.

He played from an elevated stand behind the bar and near the door. A few nights were unseasonably warm, even sultry, and the doors were wedged open so that he could see the torsos of people passing on the pavement. He heard the unintelligible fragments of talk, sounds of cars and of Rush Street making money, and had the sensation of a washed-out rainbow brilliance from all the clubs and restaurants.

What gave him the most pleasure was knowing that he could halt the truncated bodies passing the door, could turn the feet to bring them in until the faces appeared, until there they were—drawn into the club, coming in to hear who played this piano. He controlled them with his music just as surely as if he had settled a noose over their bodies and had pulled. And not once did they leave in less than an hour.

There were times—between numbers, when he would be rambling on the upper keys, fluttering trills and runs, poking chords, just messing around to keep his fingers loose—when he could hear the shuffling and scraping outside, and then the talk as whoever it was had stopped to look at his pictures. He could hear his name in what he imagined to be an awed tone. Soon the faces would come in. He would go on rambling, his eyes vague and without focus, his fingers quick, light, experimental, expert.

He would play requests. Giving his audience what it wanted had never been a crucial decision for him. As long, of course, as they knew enough not to request the dog tunes or syrupy ballads that had come out a month ago or less. Whenever Hit Parade addicts put in their bids for such numbers he would pretend not to hear. And if they persisted, he stayed deaf. It was not long before they stopped asking. Then he could turn his hearing back on, and he was never deaf to the jazz-fans. He liked playing for them. They knew the score, most of them. They understood that although he was there to entertain them it did not mean he was only an entertainer. He had a right to feelings of his own. Jazz was primarily a feeling for and with the music, they knew, and the best way to get true jazz was to let the musician have his feeling. Let him play what was inside him. Give him the freedom to be himself.

And if you really had to request something, ask for a good solid standard like *If I Had You* or *Body and Soul* or *She's Funny That Way* or *Sweet Lorraine,* a fine, meaningful tune a man can play with his heart as well as his hands.

So Jaeger spent his nights, pressing himself into the piano, his eyes somewhere lost, sometimes found on Helen as she sat against the opposite wall and was there, simply there, for whatever he wanted her to be.

After a night's closing they would get something to eat and they would not talk about Jones.

In each of their minds was what was happening. Jones was knocking the South Side to pieces with his piano. Six nights a week he was drawing capacity crowds. His picture—a flash-shot taken at Nob Hill, since he had refused to sit for a portrait—had dominated a recent page in *Downbeat* along with liberal and superlative quotes from critics and jazzmen who had heard him. *Ross Jaeger: "A lot of power. One of the strongest pianomen I've heard in the last ten years."* Already there was talk that Jones would soon be headlining at his first top spot—either the Blue Note or the zouzou.

During the afternoons Jaeger could find nothing to do. The wet, unpredictable spring weather had set in, and he did not feel like playing golf so late in the day. Helen was at work. Idly he thought of marriage, decided to put it off again until he was more organized and sure of himself. That was a hell of a thing to do—get married when you were still going around in circles. Drag the woman along. Start hating yourself for your failures. And blaming her.

He pounded his fists once on the arms of the chair and with the same motion got to his feet. Outside gathered clouds. There was a rushing sound in the trees. Spring again. Everybody was getting on the move. Tuesday, tomorrow, was his night off.

Usually the impromptu sessions at Jaeger's place were casual and relaxed codas to long nights under a spotlight. Everybody came to relax. They just brought along whatever they happened to have in their hands and followed the crowd to The Mission. When they woke the next afternoon—sometimes still there, sometimes not—their heads felt like snare drums full of marbles, but they sure had relaxed.

But when he asked for a get-together it was not the same. There was not much relaxing. When Jaeger set up a party they all knew he needed one.

Drinking had got underway around midnight, and now, past three, everyone was fairly well settled. Jackson perched on the arm of a chair and joked with Helen. Dave Britton sat on the floor with one ear to a soft, limpid tenor sax coming from the phonograph. Buddy Tance sat at the piano and looked at a magazine and drank. Over in one corner was Ivy Davis, a young moon-faced brunette who played enough guitar to attract good jazzmen wherever she jobbed. She had just closed a long run at a New York supper club and was working her trio west. Sitting around her were two NBC staff trumpetmen and her husband Norman, who played discreet harmonic chords on the piano of the trio. They were talking about Denmark.

On the couch, with Jaeger and J. R., sat The Wig. Wray Carter was her name. She was one of the finest female jazz vocalists in the country, and wasn't called The Wig because of her brown frizzly hair. Her temperament had earned her the title. Seeing her in a rage made a man wonder if the pressure would literally blow the whole top of her head through the ceiling. And no one in his right mind ever called her The Wig to her face. It was like looking for gasoline with a match. Now, however, soothed by expensive bourbon and knowing that Jaeger and Guthrie hung on her words because they admired her whiplike singing, Wray was content to merely monopolize the conversation without challenging the men to either a fight or the bedroom.

"—wouldn't want him," she was saying. "He may be the most by himself, but I wouldn't have him behind me. Not this girl. Ain't going to belt myself blind blowing against that cat. Hell no. I'm the hero, and anybody who wants to get with me better remember it. Jones wouldn't make it. He's too much of a goddamned hero himself. Too many heroes is nowhere. Right, pops?"

"Jones wouldn't be your piano anyway," Jaeger said.

"I haven't asked him yet."

"Then take a rest—you couldn't get him." His sharply-chiseled face frowned at her. "You've been away, Wray. You don't know this Jones—I do. He won't go with anybody else, that's all. Why, just last week I heard he turned down three big bids to blow with bands. He just won't play with or for anybody but himself . . ."

"He's awful fine," Guthrie put in.

"Sure he is," Jaeger said to both of them. "But he's going to make it his way or not at all. It's as simple as that." His eyes had grown bright.

"Mama's got news for that boy," Wray said. "He sticks around and he ain't going to have his way very long. Not in this screwed-up business. Who the hell does he think he is, a human being? My God, I got over that jive a long time ago."

"He'll start digging it pretty soon," Guthrie said.

Jaeger's voice was a whisper. "I'd like to see that . . ."

"You will, daddy," she said, patting his knee, "you will."

"He's awful good," Guthrie said. "Christ-awful good."

Wray squinted at him. "Oh, bite me. 'He's good, he's good.' That all you can say? We're all good, goddamn it. We're all the greatest, so stop creaming over Jones, will you? Look at the Ross here if you want to flip over a piano, why don't you?

Here's the man who can do more with one finger and a hard on than Jones can do with an armful of hands."

"Put it down," Jaeger said. "I've got a pressagent." From his face it was evident that her praise had worked the opposite effect intended. When people praised so lavishly and clumsily it was to him a sure sign that they thought he needed it; and if they thought that, they were feeling sorry for him.

Which was true.

Wray knew. Jackson knew. And Dave Britton. Ivy Davis and her husband knew. Most of all, Helen knew.

They knew that Jaeger was developing and trying to perfect a bare and forceful style of piano. Listening to the classics had given him the belief that truly great music had a clean, simple quality which rendered everything else worthless confusion. Superficially the great music might appear complex and even obscure, but at its core it was constructed along firm, positive, even logical lines, and these lines were all arranged in perfect progression to their conclusion. He had come to believe this as an absolute truth—but like any absolutist he had forced himself into a corner, and like any true believer he stood there in the pride of knowing what was denied to others.

And now two very bad things had happened.

First, he suffered the common curse. Fame had robbed him of the freedom to experiment. His style was recognized, established. It made him Ross Jaeger and not Erroll Garner or Nat Cole. It made him the one people listened to and paid to hear. It had become him. He could not change it. He would not be himself if he did. People would not recognize him. He would have trouble recognizing himself.

And second, he had told himself that Virgil Jones was within an inch of the true music.

Jaeger went over to Britton and sat on the floor beside the lazy unspooling music from the phonograph.

You seeee Lauurra . . .

New York. Summer, only last summer. Leaves limp, the sky white with the heat, buildings shimmering as though reflected in water—a day like that. In the studio. Young wearing a black flowered sportshirt with silver buttons the size of half-dollars, and just grinning at all the jive about it. Tance was there then. Yes he was. And Burnis on guitar. Stuck on a high stool, his thin orange shoes hooked in its rungs. Allred was thinner and needed a shave. With a mute in his horn, bopping away on *Blue Lou*. Jackson picked it up and pretty soon everybody was pushing it along quick and soft. The engineers trying to get them going on *Laura*, cut it and get it done and go home. Jackson wanting to send out for some iced tea; had to have it, couldn't blow go without it. *All right, all—Ross, could you . . . how about it, fellas? How about cutting it and all of us cutting out of this hotbox?* No, this was going fine now. Cool in here, man. Loose as a snake, just playing around with *Lou,* just easy listening. Why not do this instead of *Laura?* Oh, no no no no, some other time, Freddie Ford had said. So they had finally made it, finally knocked it out after three false starts, which wasn't bad, everything considered. And then another to make sure.

. . . for she's only a dream

So now here it was, spinning out at him with all the slow loose freedom of that day in New York. Only last summer.

Trying to attract as little attention as possible, Jaeger got up unsteadily and went to the piano. For a long time he did not touch the keys. The blacks smeared into the whites. Slippery. With his eyes he counted octaves and tried to stop the swinging in his head swaying back and forth, white, white and black, white, black, black and white, black, white like an arclamp on a wire in the wind.

From one corner Helen and Jackson watched him.

"Cruel and stupid," she whispered.

"Now look—" Jackson shielded his mouth with his cigarette-hand as if fearing his lips might be read "—just slow down, girl. I'm only one—"

"I don't care whose fault it is. The fact is, it's done, over with, finished, and it was a stupid thing to do." Her lips thinned and trembled. "Look at him sitting there. Who do you think he is, man? God Himself? Do you think Ross is so big that he can't feel unwanted when you get together again and not ask him? He's human, Line. He may be a great jazzman, a real giant, a celebrity, but he's still human."

"Sure, sure," Jackson pacified, still behind his hand, "but he's going to pick up one of these days, girl. Right now this Jones boy got him bugged a little. Ross just needs a little time to get with hisself, figure things out, go away for a rest . . ."

"He just came back from one. I'm tired of him having to go away for a rest."

Jackson dropped his hand. "What you sayin'—*you* tired?"

"Sorry. I didn't mean it. Forget—"

"All you chicks alike that way. Always askin' too much, always gettin' *tired* when a mahn maybe ain't got all the answers . . ."

"I said I didn't mean it."

". . . maybe you ought to find youself some mahn works downtown in a office punchin' a machine where it gives him all the answers."

"Please."

"Sure, that's what to do. Get *tired* of him, just cut out, leave him by hisself."

"Please." She reached and gripped his hand. Her eyes were shut and the lids fluttered. "Stop it stop it." Her throat spasmed as she pleaded.

Jackson's hand hardened. He did not say anything.

190

"You're right," she said at last. "He has to find it his own way and in his own time, I know. I've always known that, Line."

"It ain't easy, girl." He looked at her with terrific affection.

"Don't remind me." She smiled weakly. "I start feeling sorry for myself, like I was just now. Line . . . I won't quit. If all I can do is *be,* I'll be that. He needs me and I need him. He'll find the answer some day, and I'll be with him when he does."

"Ooo my," Jackson said, grinning lazily, "I wish I was mixed-up, little girl. These mixed-up cats get the *gon*est chicks, I swear."

Jaeger struck a few light chords. Then with one finger he tapped out *Margie,* slow and choppy. After that, arpeggios. He wandered around on the keys for awhile, spread another chord, poured himself a drink, scratched his thick dark hair.

"How about it, daddy-o?" The Wig got up and walked over to him. Leaning in the curve of the grand piano, she turned and asked Ivy Davis if she had brought her guitar. Ivy hadn't. Jackson said he would get some newspapers and sit in on drums.

Soon the three of them took off on a number they fell into almost automatically—*I Only Have Eyes for You.*

The Wig took it through once, straight, nothing spectacular, her fine creamy voice quietly letting the rhythm carry it as Jackson's supple hands fanned and swirled, softly hissing on the newspapers, sliding the beat with the piano. After Jaeger had counted out a stilted thirty-two bars The Wig upped the beat with sharp flawless quick snaps of her fingers and took off again with a bop. Sounds, no words, but the meaningless syllables had a rhythm that struck the upbeat like so many small mallets, picking up the spirit with her fluid phrasing and infallible, infectious sense of rhythm.

When that was finished they ran through *All of Me* while

everyone leaned into the listening and Norman Davis watched Jaeger with an envious childlike half-smile. The NBC staffers sat back and let their heels stomp lightly on the rug; Guthrie and Tance sat loosely and moved their eyebrows.

Another drink, just before she started *I Got It Bad,* moved The Wig over the threshold of sleepy stupefaction. She managed to get to the part where Monday rolls around, but that was all. She was asleep the moment she reached the couch.

Jaeger and Jackson floated through *Just You, Just Me,* tagged it with a flourish, and called it a night.

Shortly after that the party broke up. They got their coats and wondered what time it was and looked out the window and said that it would probably be a fine day. They shook hands with Ross and thanked him and wished him a ball in New York. When The Wig woke up she didn't know where she was, but then, suddenly recovering in a frantic kind of confusion, threw her arm around Jaeger's neck as if she would never see him again.

Jackson pulled her off and got her out the door. She braced her legs and called Good Night, Sweet Prince to Jaeger. Then she began weaving in high-heeled, ermine-coated recklessness along the empty street as the party ended with sounds of Negro voices and slammings of car doors and the clear tones of Wray Carter singing to the gray spring dawn of when the fisssh are jumping and Monday rollls . . .

On the last night, afterward, they lay close and were conscious of time.

Through the darkness Helen could see that his mouth looked soft and thick but that his face was stone. She reached to brush back a lock of hair curving over his damp forehead, then let him take her hand and bite the tip of one finger.

"Do you want it this way?" she asked.

"Yes."

"The plane might be grounded. Have to wait. I could wait with you, darling."

"No. Stay here and get some sleep."

"You know I won't be able to."

"Try."

"I won't be able to." She rubbed her left eye against the tight thin flesh of his shoulder. "O Ross . . ."

"Stop it, stop it," he whispered into her hair. "I'll be back."

Her voice broke and she let herself go and her face was smashed weeping uncontrollably in his neck. "O God I'll miss you so."

"Don't make it harder for—"

"I—can't—c-can't—" And then she felt his powerful fingers behind her head and pressing, and she did not fight it any longer and heard her grief wailing like a lost child who finds everyone in the world a stranger.

In time exhaustion subdued her to an occasional fitful, muffled sob of protest. Through silvery eyes she memorized his profile and told herself that he would come back, would come back, and then he would not have to go away again.

"—and I know why." His voice was quietly deep and came to her from far off. Staring at nothing, she listened.

"I'm not blaming anyone. I've had a lot of time to think about it, and I'm not blaming anyone. I'm not saying I was brought up this way and can't help it if I want to be the *'best'* —all I know is that this wanting to be the best is built into me. Competition. That's what I remember. Be better than the next man, don't let him get ahead of you. Practice, study, practice all day so you'll be the best in the world. Be the best. Be a success. That's all I can remember . . . they didn't want me to be like them. They wanted me to be a success." He leaned on one elbow. In the yellow flare of the match his eyes were without focus. His hand was unsteady with the flame to the cigarette.

193

"So I believed them." He lay back and exhaled. "I guess maybe I believed them more than I should have. Anyhow, you know how I've been—listening to every new piano, every new idea, trying to find out this and that and everything I could to make me better, make me a success. And it wasn't so easy at first . . . for a long time, to be honest. *Every*body was better. I was doing things they had done five years before. I'd do something and think it was new, really my own, and then sometime later I'd find out it was so old nobody was doing it anymore. *They Didn't Believe Me* was like that. Not a new idea in it, and I wanted to quit. I wanted to give up a lot of times. I'd say to myself *Who cares? Why not forget about jazz and what you want to play?* I'd tell myself to sign up with a big band and give the squares what they want. I'd tell myself to get a job selling used-cars and make a fortune and forget about playing what I thought I wanted to play. I'd look around and see lots of money just waiting to be picked up. Then I'd see all these jazzmen doing anything to make a living—selling insurance, selling television, running around tracking down guys who goofed on car payments, doing gigs for Elks Clubs and Legion Posts if they were lucky enough to get a job blowing. I saw them doing everything except the thing they really wanted to do. And I wanted to quit before I got sour like they were. But then I'd remember—" the coal-point brightened yellow-green and lit a dim circle on his face "—I'd remember what he kept telling me. *I would have made it if I hadn't given up too soon.* That's what he used to say to me. *Don't ever give up,* he'd say. *You'll have the rest of your life to remember that you quit.* He never got over that, you know. I think it was the thing that killed him, that he gave up too soon." There was silence. Heavy. "I kind of liked the old guy," Jaeger said.

"AnyhowIrememberedallthat and kept going. And made it. I made it where a lot of others didn't. So I suppose I should be happy. I've got everything I thought I wanted—money, a beautiful woman, people mobbing me for autographs, everything I wanted. But now I don't know . . . I wonder if there isn't something else. Not something more, like more money, or anything like that. Something different. A better thing. Maybe it's just called happiness, I don't know. Do you know what I mean?"

"I think so. You mean Virgil Jones."

He made a sound of agreement. "You know, when I first met him I thought of him only as a great pianoman, nothing else. I thought he was ten times the jazzman I was, and I was afraid of him. I got to thinking he would make everybody forget me. But it's funny . . . I don't think of him that way anymore. It doesn't bother me like it used to, honestly.

"What bothers me—" his voice drifted in the darkness "—is the way he lives, this being the 'last individual in the world.' He's happy, you know that?"

"He seems to be."

"He *is*. I know it. I've never seen him any other way."

"It's hard to tell. He keeps things to himself."

"No he doesn't. He only seems to. The trouble with us is that we can't understand how he can be so happy, and so we think he must be keeping his unhappiness inside. No, he's not unhappy. I know it. He's found the answer—the one I want."

She put her mouth to his ear. For a long time she held back the words, hoping that he would understand before she had to say them. But he did not speak.

"Darling," she whispered, "it's impossible. The answer is his. It belongs to him, to everything he has been and is and will be."

"I can have it too."

"You're not *him*. You're *you*—you'll always be you. You can't live someone else's life."

"Everybody can have his answer. Why not? Why can't we

195

use his answers if they help us? I believed in success and being rich and famous, and now I have it and I've found out it's nothing. Look at Jones. He doesn't believe in anything like that, and he's found the way to live."

"Alone?"

"No, I don't mean that. Something else. I don't know what."

"Why don't you ask him?"

"I have." He sat up, shook his head tiredly, and mumbled toward the windows. "All he talks about are old men and blind horses."

She looked at his gradually deepening silhouette staring like a statue into the paling light. It was nearly time for him to leave.

She was not as depressed as she had been. Ross seemed to know himself better than she had thought, and if he believed he would find an answer in New York she would not discourage him. Answers were for different people and were found in many places. She would not presume to say that New York would be a dead-end. Only Jaeger could say that, and then only after he had searched there.

He got out of bed and stood lighting another cigarette.

"Put it out." Her fingers clenched in the pillow and her voice was strange in her ears. "And don't dress. Don't dress. Not yet not yet not yet not yet . . ."

And he came to her then and there was nothing but him and when it was over her senses were veiled and blurred so that sounds held no meaning and the growing light, the morning, the day spreading on her soft dark hair seemed a dream she could dispel if only she could, if only she could stretch out her hand, if only she could stretch out her hand and feel him still there.

8

The days of spring were gold and green and blue, and he was still alone and, apparently, content.

Never later than eight-fifteen in the morning he would come down from his rooms above the barbershop and cross the cool street for breakfast. The waitress now gave him little of her mind. He was only another name and face, only another regular who didn't try to get familiar or let his checks stack in the register. She had given up caring about his making tomato juice with ketchup. Some morning, she thought, this Jones would not show up, or else she would be on her way to Denver, and she would never see him again, but that was life.

He was not a celebrity because to the neighborhood celebrities were either dead or lived in New York or Hollywood or stayed at The Pump Room between planes. And if someone had announced Jones as a man worth noticing because he played great jazz, the people would have noticed him, all right, but with the same expressions they wore when reading of a crime, because they knew enough about this *jazz* and these musicians. A lot of noise, that's all it is. Loud and fast, trumpets, and somebody beating on drums, it all sounds the same, and all these little highschool sluts dance to it. And the men who play it. The musicians are the ones. Most of them are coloreds who can't even read or write let alone read music, and if that isn't bad enough, they take dope to keep going. They make a pile, all right, but not many of them live very long because of all the drinking and marijuana. There's just no accounting for whites who play this jazz. They're either geniuses and that's next door to the nuthouse or they're men who were never built to hold a steady job and settle down.

So it was better that the neighborhood did not know Jones played jazz, and that the people looked on him as merely a harmless drifter who talked with everyone and made friends with no one.

He was a drifter. After breakfast he would stretch himself and blink his wide blue eyes and walk out into the sights and sounds of spring—cars beaded with last night's shower, leaf-droppings on the sidewalks beside which dull-breasted robins tugged and listened at the weak wet grass, sun-spangled metal and glass, the fecund smell of trees and bushed lawns. He ranged up and down the streets and talked of small things. Unimportant things. The kind of talk that passes the time of day on a porch in Iowa, on a street in Texas, at a California drive-in, over marble-topped tables in countless towns and cities on washed-air mornings of spring. Small talk. Weather, a baseball game, past Presidents, a movie star, business, a Jewish joke, a television program, what the Russians were up to, what the United States Congress was up to.

The lake was not far away. White-laced surf scoured the yellow velvet sand. Stuck in the vast shimmering expanse of beach were a few dumpy women sunning their calves and shading their eyes with one hand or a newspaper. Two young girls lay like thin straight branches soaking the sun. The water plashed, hissed, withdrew. The water was gray-green and paralyzingly cold.

It was not like winter. Then the water had been only a line just below the horizon. As far as the eye could see was a giant field of dirty white ice and snow; the shoreline was piled with an endless series of huge heaved-up mounds of ice. Then there had been no old women sunning themselves. Then there had been no one but himself.

Now he stood at the water's edge for a long time before turning to walk back to where the grass began.

On the blistered green benches old men sat like sparrows on a fence. Their eyes followed him. None of them called to him, but all of them watched him. He walked lazily toward the benches as if he would sit down, but then, unpredictably, continued walking away from them. The old men put pipes back between their lips. Crossed and recrossed their brittle legs. That was the way the boy was—a strange one, he was. He didn't want to talk today. Tomorrow the boy might talk for an hour straight, but today his mind wasn't set to it, and one thing you couldn't do with him was to get him to do something he was set against. Pigheaded that way. A nice enough boy, never mean or making fun of people, but awful pigheaded.

And his ideas. He was too young to have ideas like he had. About God, for instance:

"No, I don't believe. Not in the way you do. Not that we have another life coming after this one. But it's your right to believe what you want to—I'm not going to sit here and tell you that what you believe in is wrong or ignorant just because it doesn't agree with my beliefs. You aren't going to make me believe in God merely by talking to me, and I'm not going to convince you there isn't by just talking to you. We all have to find things by ourselves. I haven't found your God yet. Maybe someday I will. But if I do, it will be by myself. It won't be because I'm doing what somebody else has told me I ought to believe. Hell? Why should I be afraid of that? I'll worry about it when the time comes. I don't see many people letting the idea of it get in their way when they commit a crime or cheat somebody out of a few dollars. But Hell is a good place you think about when you go to church. So go right ahead and believe in God. If there is one I think he's glad to have you . . . and if there isn't one and we just die and that's all, you won't be able to be sorry for believing in something that never was. You'll be dead, and you won't feel anything then. Good luck!"

Or, the very next day, his clean snowy head uplifted and talking to the sun, about politics:

"Yes, I vote. If the one I pick wins, that's good; if he isn't elected I have to accept that too. But once the election is over I forget about it until the next time. Hoover? That was a long time ago. I don't get excited about things like that. The past is past. Done with. It can't be changed. No use getting bitter over something you can't change. Politics isn't for me. It's for the people I vote for and don't vote for. If I got to the point where I got upset or angry about politics, I'd do something about it. It would be necessary then. Otherwise I wouldn't let it upset me if I wasn't actually going to do something about it. Anger is vicious if a man doesn't aim it at the object that angers him. He aims it at something else, which usually doesn't deserve it. Communism? I don't believe in it. You can if you want to, but I don't. Because it seems to me that it tries to make a political animal out of man. He's an animal, I'll agree with that, but no man or group or ruler can tell me that man has got to be political and social. He can be something else, and he doesn't 'have to be' anything but a man. I think that is the only proven right. A man is a man. Nobody owns the right to tell him what he has to be. He is an individual, more or less . . . mostly less. Would I help a starving man? Where is he? Not around, eh? Well then, bring one here and I'll do what I can for him. Otherwise don't talk about starving men. You only excite yourself with wondering. It's only talk. There ought to be a lot more doing and not so much talk about doing. Listen to us. See? Jaw-exercise. Let's talk about the sky. That's a nice big topic."

That was the way he was. He opened his mouth and let it come out, and the way he talked, crazy-fast, gave a man the idea that this boy just didn't care how he sounded or whether his ideas were put together right. There they were, the ideas. Take them or leave them—it didn't seem to make any difference. And not afraid to have an opinion. The boy had an opinion on everything. The System, for example, or That's The Way Things Are:

"The 'system' is an excuse for not trying to do what you want to do. Look around . . . where's the system? All I see is confusion and people who're afraid. Of what, it depends. But mostly themselves, I guess. Afraid of being failures. Wanting to get along with 'the way things are.' Well, they *aren't,* that's all. You don't have to give in. You don't have to compromise the important things. Fight them and you'll win every time. Why? Because one man who believes in himself is stronger than a million who don't. The only system I see is being born and living and dying. That's the system to think about. Birth, life, death. You don't remember being afraid of the first one, do you? Well then, why be afraid of the other two? You got through being born. You'll get through living and dying, too. Just don't be afraid. Stand up straight. You won't live forever, but you won't have a dull life."

Virgil Jones didn't talk all the time, however. On some days he said only a few words of greeting and sat down to listen. And what a listener he was. You could not find listeners like that unless you paid them. When he was listening he never interrupted. He sat very still and looked directly into your eyes and made a man feel as though the things he was saying were the most important things in the world.

So the old men told him. They talked of where they had been born and of what they had done and of the things they believed in long ago. They told him that the world was going to hell fast, and now and then they misquoted passages from the Bible. They had regrets, not for the world especially, but for the things they themselves hadn't done. Women they hadn't known, places they hadn't got around to getting to, jobs they wanted to try but hadn't, women they hadn't known, fellows they hadn't given what had been coming to them, the times they'd wanted to tell off the boss but hadn't, old pals they wished they had kept track of, women they wondered about. Regrets. Rarely were they sorry for the things they had done. It was what they had not done that made them unhappy in their age.

Twice a week Jones would go to a matinee. Without consulting a newspaper or calling the theater to find out what pictures were on, he would sometimes walk more than four miles to a show. He always went in no matter what was playing. Among housewives and skittish arrogant children and rustlings of popcorn bags his darkened face was never disappointed or bored with the action on the screen. He appeared interested in everything.

On other days he would go to museums or to the bleachers of Sox Park or simply to a green, tree-cool park where he spread a morning paper and slept out the afternoons. He never hurried. Unlike the normal man who orients free time and even his entire life around the work that pays him, Jones' habits seemed to say that this, his free time, not the piano or the money, was his main concern. The days were becoming beautiful, the grass was soft, the sun warm and deep, sounds of traffic were gentle and dreamlike when heard with eyes closed. There were no appointments to be made. No promises to keep. No obligations to anyone but himself.

He never sought out the company of musicians. And it was

neither right nor wrong to say that he practiced. It was just that he made it look like something else. At least three times a week, during the day, he would be passing a tavern, and would look in the door, and when there was a piano he would be playing it within two minutes. Sometimes he would be told to stop after not very long; other times he would play for as much as an hour. He was always experimenting, and his ideas were limitless.

When he played at night his piano was always new, always daring yet never tangled with badly conceived innovations, always a special brand of jazz that no one could imitate. Nob Hill was his. He owned it when he played.

There:

Suddenly through the doorway at five minutes to nine, hatless, the collar of his cheap coat turned up and framing his face, white and relaxed and sometimes unshaven, looking not at all as a famous jazzman should, looking careless to the point of indifference as he walked down the lane opened by the crowd along the bar, disappeared into the back room and came out almost immediately, his coat gone, ducked under the bar and came up on the stage and went directly to the piano as the audience flurried whispers glasses chairs readying to listen.

Lights dimmed.

He would squeeze each hand, stare at the middle of the keyboard, and begin with something that seemed to have just entered his mind.

> The leaves of brown
> came tumb—ling down
>
>   remember?

He played everything. Ballads, jump tunes, original numbers he carried in his head, and occasionally even a classical composition played exactly as written by Chopin or Mozart or Rachmaninoff. Not often enough for the crowd's liking would he play the blues. Once or twice in twelve nights— that was all. But when he did, they were really the blues. Huge and sad and hammering, twenty years and a lot of lives ago, blues so deep and true that it was hard to admit that any white man could know such things.

It was not long before he had the reputation of a brilliant but eccentric jazzman who played what he felt like playing and refused to honor requests. The audience told itself that it was accepting and respecting his rights. Exactly what rights they were was never clear, but Jones' whole being seemed to insist on respect. He had been right when he had told Henneberry that he needed no help from any sign or from anyone else.

One night, however, he appeared to go too far. And he did the same thing three times in that week.

He had been playing *Body and Soul*. Slowly, perfectly, building it to the climax of emotion. Mounting, spiraling closer and closer to the finale.

When he stopped.

Simply took his hands off the keys.

With face frowning, jaw tight.

The entire audience was silent. Involuntarily they were leaning toward the piano, waiting for the music that had yet to come.

But when it did they could hardly hear it. When his hands went to the keys he turned and lowered his head, and his powerful fingers barely touched the keys. He played so softly that a baffled and outraged murmur traveled across and out from those listeners in the rear. The end brought grudging applause.

For a moment he sat with the fingers of his left hand behind his ear. Then he took them away, set, and plunged into *Air Mail Special*. And this time everyone could hear.

But the next night the same thing happened, and this time midway through *'A' Train,* and those who had been in the audience the night before decided that if this was something new he was trying for effect, it didn't come off at all.

And the third night he stopped in the middle of Bach, frowned once more, and finished the selection almost inaudibly.

It was insulting.

Those among the audience who had admired his stubborn, uncompromising individuality now growled among themselves that Jones could not do this to them. It was unheard of. He would find himself in an empty night club if he kept this up. Confidence was one thing—arrogance was another.

And the others, those who envied and in turn hated him for his egotism, congratulated themselves for having known Jones all along for what he was: a selfish, spoiled, near-madman possessed with a freak of talent. Of course he would stop in the middle of a number and finish so that no one else could hear it. It was inevitable he would come to this. Where this sort of thing would end there was no foretelling, but it couldn't possibly be good.

The musicians who had come to listen were puzzled and annoyed at first, then finally concluded that Jones was beginning to be like a lot of jazzmen whose every move was an occasion of note. Biggity. The real Big Head. And that was a little bit flipped, thrown out of balance.

The critics did not know what to think. They resented such a display, but there was no arguing that when Jones didn't trail into near-soundlessness the piano they heard was still astonishingly good. Was it right to bring the man to judgment along with his work? Did a jazzman have to be a decent human being as well as a great artist? Or was the work itself enough? Was Jones, was anyone who created genuine art, obliged to do it and at the same time bind himself to the rules and opinions of his audience?

If Jones imagined what an impact his practices had, he showed no sign of knowing or even caring about what others might be thinking.

Between sets he would most often sit with Seymour Schwab. There were times when not more than a dozen words were exchanged between them before Jones had to play again, yet neither seemed discontent. Jones would resume playing; Schwab would resume drinking, watching, and keeping his thoughts to himself.

When Helen Kostakos was with Schwab Jones would drink three whiskey highballs and talk a great deal. Then he would go to the piano and make his next set long and violent.

If neither of the two were in the nightclub Jones would go off by himself or sit with anyone who happened to strike his fancy, or, once or twice, with Roger Henneberry. The announcer was extremely nervous whenever this happened. He was obviously worrying before, during, and after any encounter with Jones. It was true that Jones had consistently rejected all offers from other agents and agencies. And at no time had he gone back on his verbal agreements. He never tried to deceive. He was maddeningly blunt and honest.

They would drink, and Henneberry would relay the latest plan of Paul Bauer, and Jones would refuse to follow it. He refused to do a two-week job in Milwaukee, turned down a guest-appearance on both radio and television, refused to make recordings or to play with any other musicians, would not go to parties to meet important people, said that he would buy a new suit when he decided he needed one, and refused to sign anything. He was being offered opportunities every young jazzman would give half a soul for, and he did not take them. He was satisfied with what he was doing. He was not in a famous club drawing the fabulous salary he could have had, but apparently he did not care.

When his nights were over Jones usually went home alone on a bus. On warm nights he walked. It would take him more than an hour, and he did not walk slowly. The streets were dim, empty. Alley-mouths were black. The only sounds were his soft, mechanical footsteps as he walked alone.

One Wednesday night he was in the middle of a block when a shape detached itself from the shadows ahead. Jones did not slow down, and the woman did not move. When he passed her she said something that made him stop. Soon she was guiding him by his left bicep up the worn carpeted stairway. Her hair was the color of beer and she had dry skin. She said her name was Mavis.

The apartment was cheap but virtuously prim. In one corner was a television set with fingerprints on its dead gray glass. Gazing at it from an end-table was a man whose out-of-focus face had been handpainted and framed in tiny gold leaves. He looked as though he had tasted something bitter. And when Jones went into the bedroom with the woman, the man in the photograph still stared ahead with brown oily eyes and a wry vermilion mouth.

Jones saw her regularly.

She told him that her husband had been killed flying P-23's in the war and that she was beginning to get over him. Of course it wasn't easy, but she had to make the best of things. She also told Jones that Chicago was the best town for work but the climate had its drawbacks, especially if you had a sinus like she had. One of these days she was going to go to Miami and lay in the sun for a month.

It was not long before she stopped talking about P-23's and the medals she had put someplace. She told Jones that she liked him; he was awfully good. Kind of funny, she said, but sweet. Was his name really Virgil? She liked Babylamb better. That was what she got to calling him at certain times—Babylamb. But he still got none of it as a gift.

9

For two years Bauer had carried the card, and remembered:

"You've got to meet this boy, Paul." Voorhies hovered beside him like a giant white moth in the dusk. "Stay here in Philly for a week—no more. You really can't afford to leave without meeting him."

"I am retired, and—" The nudge stopped him.

"So am I," Voorhies laughed. "But somehow I manage to come out of retirement every time there's a choice piece of property."

"This what's-his-name isn't a building." He climbed in the long powderblue Lincoln and waited for Voorhies to get behind the wheel. "I have all the money I need," he said as the car moved elegantly north on Broad Street.

"Oh, I realize that, Paul—but it's not a question of that. You and I don't have to think of money anymore. We're liberated, free, so to speak. Money is for the sheep to think about. We don't have to waste our energies on it . . . but I don't have to tell *you* this."

"Then why all this talk about him?"

"Because he's someone special."

"So he plays piano. That's nothing new to me."

"No," Voorhies said. "But let's you and I understand each other, Paul. We can admit it now. We're not interested in real estate or musicians or fighters for the money they can bring us. What we own and control are simply the means to an end, and the end is power—sheer, pure and simple power. Control. Ownership. Am I right?"

Bauer watched him with a noncommittal stare, and was silent.

"Well, you might not admit it, Paul, but it's true. Both of us have come a long, hard way up the ladder, and now we own more than we'll ever be able to use. We're past wanting to get rich . . . that is, as far as material wealth goes. Do I care about the thousand I lost on Navy today? No, I just wanted to amuse myself by betting. The game was more interesting that way. And you? You bet for the same reason— to amuse yourself, that was all. So here we are, with more money than we know what to do with, and we're bored. Yes, you and I are getting old and bored, and the only things left for us to own are people, other human beings. I've got a nephew I've given more than three thousand to, just so he can have an education. I own him, Paul. I own the whole family. They're like puppies when Uncle Ed comes around. So I give them another milkbone and watch them wag their tails and look up at me with big thank yous in their eyes. But don't think that Uncle Ed doesn't know they're waiting for him to die. Oh, yes. That's what they want. They want to be able to stop wagging their tails and licking my hand, because they hate themselves when they do it. Think of it, Paul, over in Camden there's a houseful of people hating me and being afraid of me and waiting for me to visit them, spending half their damned lives just thinking about me." As he turned left on Walnut Street his deerskin gloves made little sucking noises on the wheel.

Bauer smiled thinly and directed his eyes toward the overcoated masses pushing like faceless animals in the frozen darkness.

"And *you*—" he heard Voorhies say "—I know you're laughing at me, Paul. You've got a right to. I'm spouting about one miserable house over in Jersey, and you're the fagan who owns more souls than the devil himself."

"That's just it." He put fingertips to his eyelids and massaged them gently. "I don't want any more." When he opened his eyes he saw Voorhies nodding at the windshield and wearing smugness on his mouth.

"And *that*," said the mouth, "is 'just it.' That's why you have to meet this boy—because he doesn't care whether you want to stay retired or not, because he doesn't give a damn about you, because he doesn't want to join you or anybody else. Paul, this is one boy you couldn't own if you tried."

Slowly, like a smooth precision machine, Bauer's head turned and stared until it got attention.

"Name," he said.

"Calls himself Jones."

"Address."

"That's a long story, Paul. Let's have something to eat and—"

"I don't want stories. Address," he repeated.

"Don't get excited, Paul."

"Where does he live?"

Voorhies sighed, whipped the car into a parking space in front of a restaurant with a black-and-gold façade. He switched off the throbbing. Blinked. Tasted his lips.

"In a boilerroom," he said. "He lives in a basement over near Germantown. Now, do you want to hear more about him? All right—we'll get some food and I'll tell you . . ."

There was no one, it seemed, who could claim to really know the boy named Jones. No one could say where he was from or when he had come to Philadelphia. They were able to trace him only as far back as July, when he had taken up living next to the boilers, but even then he had given the impression of knowing the city as no stranger ever could.

At first he had worked as a dishwasher in an all-night diner, but one day it was revealed that he had quit two days previously and was now doing something else. The new job turned out to be playing the piano in a cheap tavern near the Schuylkill River, but the owners when questioned wore sour faces and said that they had fired him on the second night. A nut, they said he was. No, they didn't know what he was doing now, and what was more, they didn't care. A week later the trail started again at a box-factory. It disappeared in four days. He had been fired again. No, he had been a good enough worker, but he had never shown proper respect for the rules set up by management. And again the trail led to a tavern. And again he had not lasted very long. He played "weird" music, things nobody had ever heard before. And he wouldn't play any of the tunes that people asked for. He was a foul ball from the word go, the waitress said. The screwiest character she had ever seen.

It was always like that. Jones worked at everything, but none of the jobs lasted more than a week. With the exception of the piano engagements, the work was invariably simple and unthinking and of the sort requiring the least intelligence. Dishwashing, stacking boxes, shoveling coal, loading boxcars, jackhammer work, stockroom piling—and from all of them he had been fired. Strangely enough, only a few of his former employers showed any vehemence when they remembered him. The great majority recalled him with a shrug and an expression of puzzlement indicating that it was too bad any man as quick and bright and strong as that had to be such a misfit and a hardhead.

But his jobs were not the worst of it.

The police knew him by his first name, and it was not out of any friendship.

Virgil Jones was a habitual troublemaker. If his crimes had been larcenous he would have been spending his entire life in prison.

His record, however, as long as it was, was more exasperating than dangerous. The record showed that he had been arrested in St. Louis, Kansas City, Tampa, Boston, Chicago, Salt Lake City, Fort Worth, Abilene, New Orleans and Savannah. And it was always for the same offense: Disturbing the Peace.

It had been August in the boilerroom when he had first introduced himself to the Philadelphia police. In September he had disturbed the peace on two occasions. In October, once. November had been remarkable—he had not been inside the station all month. But with December not half-gone, he had been picked up twice already. Every time it was the same story. He was not drunk and he did not resist arrest. He was simply taken in because when the squad arrived at the scene of the fight they found Jones in the middle of it, and when they asked bystanders how it had started, fingers pointed to him. Something he had said, they said. Something someone else had said to him. His attitude, they said. His attitude.

So away he went, showing neither anger at the people who had hit him, nor remorse for having hit them, nor fear of the police who roughed him into the squadcar and took him to the station where, because he would not pay bribe or fine, he spent a night or even two or three in the tank. And on good authority it was said that he was almost always more bruised and swollen by the time the police were finished. There was a story that two detectives had once sent him to the hospital with a near-fractured skull. But this had not caused him to change his ways.

Now, in December, he was still living in the boilerroom in the vicinity of Germantown. The building housed a While-U-Wait tailor, a gift shop and a store selling religious objects, and, upstairs, a lawyer of sorts and the main office of a hair-growing specialist. A few doors down the street lived three prostitutes who were not high-priced. They were, in fact, virtually free. What attraction Jones had for them was not clear, but they had been known to buy him food and invite him to their apartment and even to spend hours talking and drinking beer with him amid piles of newspapers and the smell of cinders in the boilerroom. It was said that Jones would do odd jobs around their apartment, such as repairing a lamp or a leaky faucet or putting a bedspring back in place. A great many things were said about his association with them, but he had never been known to confirm or deny any of the talk. He acted as though nothing anyone said would have the slightest effect on the way he chose to lead his life.

"And that, Paul," Voorhies mumbled past a cigar, "is the point I'm making. This Jones does just what he wants to do, all the time; he doesn't care what everybody else does or thinks. He runs his own life and won't let anybody have part of it. That's why I say you couldn't own him if you tried . . . and I've got a grand that says I'm right."

Bauer closed his eyes. "No bet," he said wearily. "Your Jones is half-cracked, and I'm not so stupid as to risk anything on him. Especially the time."

"I seem to remember—" Voorhies said with a smile that became a challenging frown "—you claiming that you could own anybody if you really wanted to."

"That's right."

"And you still claim that?"

"Anyone," Bauer affirmed. "It's only a question of time. That, and finding their weakness. Everyone has a vulnerable spot. It's just a matter of time before I find it, and when I do, the game is over."

"And you haven't got the time . . ."

"Or the interest." He gazed at the ragged cluster of tiny

silver bubbles in his waterglass. There was what seemed a long silence.

"Paul—I don't think you understand. You don't realize what I'm saying. *I'm saying that this Jones is the only person you won't be able to control.* Do you know what that means? It means that he's the one who can ruin your theory—everything you believe in. He's dangerous, Paul . . . . . . or are you already aware of that?"

"What're you trying to prove?"

"Nothing—nothing in particular." The thick, hairy-backed hands flattened in a gesture of defensive innocence. "Except— except for the sake of . . . should we call it curiosity? An experiment. To see if you still have your fantastic touch. To see if Uncle Ed is right when he says it's impossible to compromise *every*body. Oh, I agree that most of these drones come cheap, but I don't think you can buy all of them. Some of them, like Jones, aren't for sale."

"I can buy anyone."

"You just said that, Paul."

"I say it again." Anger was expanding in his throat. His stomach roiled with the warning that he would need some capsules as soon as he got back to his hotel. "Double the bet," he said.

"Well . . ." Voorhies leaned back and smiled. "But no violence, no strongarming, you understand."

"Double the bet," Bauer said.

A week was not much time, but he calculated that it would prove enough for what he had to do. Voorhies had made it easy by letting his confidence betray him into agreeing that a single compromise by Jones would decide the bet. It did not have to be anything major; a simple but unmistakable concession would do.

Within two hours on Monday morning it had been arranged. Bauer had talked to the owner of an obscure tavern

215

and had promised to pay the full salary of the pianist who would be there that night. The pay was to be one hundred dollars a night for twelve nights, and Jones was to receive a hundred the first time, five hundred on the sixth night, and the final six hundred his last night. The owner was instructed to give only vague answers if Jones happened to ask who was behind the hiring.

Voorhies wondered if it was ethical to try to buy the outcome by paying Jones out of Bauer's own pocket.

Bauer answered that ethical was only a word, and that plans had to be modified according to the time-element—one week.

Then why, Voorhies wanted to know, had he offered twelve nights?

Bauer chose not to answer.

After having talked Voorhies into contacting Jones through one of the prostitutes, Bauer napped away the afternoon untroubled by doubt. He was certain that Jones would accept the offer. Money, and the promise of more, never failed.

That night, when he walked in purposely late, Bauer knew he had been right. Jones was at the piano. Furthermore, he looked like an easy mark. It was hard to believe that he could be the violent nonconformist Voorhies had described. He looked too young and too satisfied to be dangerous.

But as they sat at one of the square wooden tables facing the piano Bauer realized almost at once that he was listening to jazz so original that it was frightening. At the moment Jones was cool and deft and bouncing through *No Moon at All* in a way Bauer knew would make any jazz audience hold its breath. He looked around at the putty-colored faces in the tavern. They were not listening, not even admitting with their eyes that there was any music in the place. He looked back to Jones and saw that the young towhead did not seem to care if anyone was listening or not. The piano never faltered or exploded in an attempt to force attention; it went on and on, independent of everything and everyone.

"The boy has no pride," he whispered with an artificial smile.

Voorhies shook his head. "I told you—he just doesn't care how other people act. He doesn't bother with them."

"Plays only for himself, eh?"

"Always."

"We'll see."

"If you're thinking of testing him, I'm going to enjoy the sight of him turning down your request, Paul."

"He'll play for me. Not tonight, but he'll play a request in less than a week."

"Do you want to make that the compromise?"

Bauer raised his thin-lidded eyes. "Are you serious?"

"Of course."

"For God's sake, make a decent bet. Getting him to play a measly request is too simple."

"Don't be so sure, Paul. Remember—the act itself isn't all of it. It's the attitude that I'm betting on. What I mean by making a compromise is that if and when Jones does what you ask, he'll show me that he's doing it *because* you asked. There's a difference—a big difference—and I'm betting that no matter what he does, he'll do it in a way that will show that he's doing it for himself. You and I won't matter. He'll do it for himself. That's what I'm sure of—" he tipped back in his chair and spread a smile over his thick fat face "—and I think I'll order a few suits made up in advance. Then, I'll—"

Bauer stopped listening to the boast-threats of money. Voorhies had been right about money being little more than an amusement and a topic of conversation; it really did not matter any longer. What was a thousand dollars? Five thousand? Nothing. How could money matter when it increased itself faster than it was spent? No, the important issue was beyond baubles and leisure. Control, power—those were the riches. The ability to order something done and see it done. The position from which you could say to a man that you were not concerned with what he stood for, that he would do what you stood for simply because it was in your power to make him do it.

Nothing gave the satisfaction of power. The end was power. The means were unimportant. Power was enough. It was everything.

The night was long, but he did not tire of hearing Jones. The pianist was unmistakably brilliant, a near-genius, and there was a secret exultation in Bauer as he watched the man he would control playing on and on without knowing what lay ahead of him.

He made no attempt to meet Jones. The time would come, and it had to be done properly.

On Thursday night Bauer did not go to the tavern. He telephoned the owner and instructed him to tell Jones that he would not have to play the following night. Of course he would still be paid, but instead of going to the tavern he was to be at a certain address at ten o'clock.

Jones was on time. His clothes were old, he was wearing a faded blue shirt open at the neck, and his hair looked as though it had been combed by fingers. He came into the luxurious apartment with no trace of embarrassment or shyness in the presence of the dozen spectacular young women and the few expensively dressed men Voorhies had rounded up. Near the windows stood a gleaming Baldwin grand piano, but Jones took no particular notice of it.

"I suppose," Voorhies began, clearly enjoying the role he had been quite willing to accept, "you're wondering why you're here."

Jones merely looked at him as if he didn't suppose anything and hadn't even bothered to wonder.

"Well, we'll come to that," Voorhies said. "First . . ." And he began introducing the shabby pianist around the gathering. Jones startled the first few women by offering to shake hands with them, but outside of that there was nothing unusual in his behavior—though his bearing could have been more humble and less nonchalant, considering the beauty of the women.

The last introduction was to Paul Bauer himself, who was sitting in a throne of a purple brocaded chair near the piano. Jones said "Hello" in the same dull voice, shook hands, and then turned away as if expecting more introductions.

Bauer eyed him as Voorhies began explaining that his brilliance had made everyone want to meet him. It was a lie, of course. The opening lie of flattery—strong flattery because it came from these women and these powerful, successful men. Jones was not impressed. He made his face to say that it was all right if anyone wanted to be interested in him, but also that he didn't care if they ignored him or actually disliked his piano. He listened politely. He was patient but indifferent.

Then why had he come? Watching, thinking for a lever, Bauer was momentarily thwarted. Jones had been surprisingly tractable, almost weak in agreeing first to play at the tavern and now to come to the apartment. There had to be a reason behind such willingness. Was his solitariness an act? It was possible. It could be that he was doing nothing more than making a virtue of necessity. It was clear that Jones was neither rich nor handsome nor a brilliant thinker or conversationalist. The only ability he had was with the piano; it was his crutch. Without it, he was crippled. Without it, he lived in a boilerroom and associated with whores and got into trouble as soon as he went into normal society. He hated society because it pointed up his own deficiencies, but at the same time was drawn to it because of the need to prove himself. That was why he had come. And he would play the piano. They would have to beg him, but he would play. It was the only way he could gain equality.

For nearly an hour Jones was permitted to relax and mingle with the others. He did not have much to say, and drank as fast as his glass was refilled.

Bauer felt himself growing tired and impatient. He motioned to Voorhies. *And bring him,* he signaled with his fingers.

"Jones," he said when the pianist was standing in front of him, "not everybody here has heard your work. Most of them have taken my word for it."

"Who are you?"

Bauer pressed his lips together and stared at the pianist.

"He's had experience," Voorhies said.

"Oh."

"Never mind about that . . . I was saying that these people are anxious to hear what you can do. Here's a piano, right here . . ."

Jones raised and lowered his eyebrows. "Then this is why I've been brought here—to play the piano, to satisfy the curiosity of your friends."

"No," Bauer said easily. He was conscious that faces had turned and were watching him. They were not interested in hearing Jones. They had been bought for the evening solely to provide surroundings for his bet. "You were invited because I wanted you here. And you came, didn't you?"

"Because I wanted to." His face was bland, his voice calm with sureness. "But that's quibbling. Looking around, though—" and he did, his pale eyes sweeping over the faces "—I feel that what you are trying to get me to do is to play the piano. After I do that for awhile, you'll try to get me to play a request. Then you'll be satisfied."

Bauer felt his intestines coil and knot. It was all he could do

220

to rivet his eyes on Jones and avoid the faces watching Bauer being outguessed and anticipated as never before.

"Do you know who I *am?*"

The pianist opened his mouth with a warped smile, but apparently thought better of what he had been about to say and instead stayed silent and unruffled.

"Obviously you don't," Bauer said between his teeth. "So I'll tell you that people aren't in the habit of telling me what ideas and plans I have or should have. Furthermore, people don't tell me what *they* want to do or don't want to do. They do what I say."

"I am not people," Jones said. "I am not 'they.'"

"And I'm not impressed with that. To me you're just another human being who happens to play the piano . . ." His voice dwindled, died. He did not know how to go on. By anticipating exactly what had been planned, Jones had thrown him off-balance and had robbed him of the freedom to use a carefully developed persuasion. Jones had been far more perceptive than imagined. Even now, Bauer thought, he seemed to sense that he had the upper hand and could retain it by simply remaining silent and stubborn.

"You don't want to play?" Voorhies asked.

"No. Not tonight. I'll play tomorrow night. I'm down at The Spa six nights a week, if anyone really wants to listen."

"Why weren't you there tonight?" Bauer asked.

"Because I was given the night off to come here."

Bauer nodded with a sly smile. "Doesn't that mean anything to you?"

"Yes." Jones thought for a second. "You must be the person who got me the job."

"Very good. Very good deduction, young man. Now tell me who is paying you . . . . . . ah, I see you understand. Fine. Then you've begun to see who I am and what I can do, haven't you?"

"I see who you are, and what you are."

"Then do us the honor." He emphasized the final word. Palm-up, he moved his bony right hand toward the piano which was now hemmed in by the women and men who waited.

"Goodnight," Jones said to one wall, and started for the door.

Bauer half-rose from his chair. "You refuse?"

Jones turned to face the crowd. "I refuse. If this party was a job and I came here to work, I would play. But I wasn't hired for this. I was invited to amuse you. How did I realize it so soon? It wasn't hard. I've had a lot of practice. People have tried to use me before. After awhile I can spot it pretty quick. You want to make me your puppet, Mister Bauer. But you can't. Nobody can. You might impress these people, but you don't bother me. You can buy these people, but I'm not for sale—at any price."

"You are a stupid and stubborn young man," Bauer said. He felt his face coloring with anger and shame. Everyone was watching.

"And you, sir, are old. Very old. That is all I have to say."

In the silence after the door closed there were muffled coughs and brushings of nervous shoes on the carpet. Bauer pushed himself erect and concentrated on looking directly ahead. He muttered a few words and waited for his overcoat and then shuffled to the door.

"Everyone go home," Voorhies called.

"No." He edged his body around to confront them. His silvery head shook as though palsied. "Stay. Drink all the whiskey, have a good time. And remember tonight. You might think I was a fool to expose myself the way I did, but I wasn't. If you doubt me, remember what I say now, all of you. Remember the name of this pianist: Jones. You will hear

222

of him again. And when you do, watch him. Follow his career and see what happens to him. Watch and wait, and see what happens to him. Then—then come to me . . . and tell me who was the fool."

He went back to his hotel alone and for a long time did not try to sleep. In his mind hung the face, the remembered words *And you, sir, are old are old very old are old,* the defiance. For two hours he lay fully dressed on the bed, his hands locked beneath his head, and looked unseeing at the ceiling. From somewhere came the sound of water rushing through pipes. *You don't bother me. You are old. You want to make me your puppet, but you can't.*

Late the next morning he sent the two thousand by messenger to Voorhies' apartment. He did not want to deliver it personally; it would be minimized and refused out of the embarrassment Voorhies felt for what had happened. And no one was allowed to feel sorry for Paul Bauer.

Immediately afterward he contacted the owner of the tavern and gave the necessary orders. If Jones showed up to play— and it was probable that he would—he was to be paid in full for the week, but after the second week he was to get nothing. Yes, nothing. Not a cent of the last six hundred. No, there would be no trouble. And on that Bauer was secretly willing to bet everything he owned.

There was one more thing he had to do before leaving for Chicago. He had to see Jones again.

It was as Voorhies had described. The neighborhood was squalid and bleak and cold with winter-beaten brick. Grimy automobiles and dark-clothed people moved with the same sluggish quality along the littered streets. After several tries he found the paneless half-door to the low squarish tunnel leading to the grooved wooden steps descending to the basement. There were no lights, and even in the middle of the day it was oppressively dark.

The door was open. From inside came a steady hissing.

He called hello: strong, demanding, not admitting the unease he felt in the darkened, hissing room.

"Is anyone here!"

Something rustled a newspaper. There was no answer.

He struck a match. In the uneven pulsing yellow light he could see an army cot flanked by two upended orange-crates. A few feet from the boiler stood an angry brown dressing table with a perfectly clean mirror. Above it hung a shadeless lightbulb. He pulled it on and touched his index finger to the mirror. There was no dust. He shook his head and blew out the match. Then he sat down on the hard cot to wait. The air was thick and motionless. His eyelids felt weighted.

Through the filmy half-opening of his sight he saw the light go out. With a gasp he sat up. Then relaxed and composed himself.

"What did you want to see me about?" As Jones spoke his head moved and the bulb appeared again.

"Curiosity," he muttered. It had been stupid to fall asleep as he had. It had been stupid to come at all. Everything had been a mistake from the very beginning. But as he gradually regained his senses his antagonism and purpose returned. "About last night," he added in a tone of inflexible superiority.

"That's over with," Jones said, still standing.

"You think so, eh?"

"Yesterday ended at midnight."

"For you, perhaps."

"And that's enough. No one else matters."

Bauer lifted his eyes and watched the lithe figure pacing back and forth in front of him. Trouble. He was trouble to the police and to everyone he met. No one could own him, he had said. And no one but himself mattered. He was very young and full of illusions. He would learn. Illusions could

224

be made terribly expensive. He was tough and confident, but he could be made to pay.

"Tell me, young man—have you ever thought of making a career of music?"

"What I think isn't your concern."

"Too bad." He made an ugly face and looked around at the dull deadness of the room. "I could do things for you . . . or do you like to live in this kind of filth?"

"Where I live my life and how I live my life is my choice. Oh, I know about last night. The women. The expensive place. Aimed at making me want that kind of life. But you made a mistake. I'm Virgil Jones. I'm not hungry for the things I don't have. When I want something, I get it."

"So do I, son. So do I."

"Then good hunting. Now go home and count the people you own . . . but—" he reached in a sidepocket and pulled out an untidy wad of paper fastened with a rubberband "—here. Take this. I give these to people who can use them."

Bauer held the card close and read it. Suddenly he wanted to be away from the hissing and the heat and the strong dangerous deadly gaze of this lunatic. He fumbled the card into his pocket and got up with nervous haste. Words would not fit in his mouth. When he reached the door he felt safe enough to throw Jones a penetrating, prolonged look.

"We'll probably meet again," Jones said from the depths of the basement. "People usually meet me again."

Bauer pulled the door shut. The tunnel walls were cold brick, textured like sandpaper. It seemed to him that he had never really known what a brick was.

It had been a dream from the beginning—the bet, the lengths to which he had gone in an effort to win, the total loss, the failure, the failure, and he had been called old, and now this: emerging old from the bottom of a building, the laughter in his ears, and he was not able to say who it was who was laughing.

When he reached the street, however, he knew it could not have been a dream. It was still Philadelphia, still winter. And when he put his hand in his pocket the card was still there.

On the bright flickering pavement outside the zouzou milled all the latecomers. They looked at their watches and talked and had to be satisfied with the scratchy blare of the loud-speaker hooked up to the microphones inside. At the moment a good eight-man Dixieland outfit was chopping out *That's A-Plenty*. The trumpet came out of the fat speaker and took quick bites of warm spring air. Every now and then passers-by would slow or stop to listen and stare before shrugging with half-amused, half-baffled disapproval and continuing along the street. Nine-thirty, only an hour into a normally dull Thursday night, their expressions seemed to say, and already there was an overflow crowd. What in God's name did that music have that it could draw so many people?

Shortly before ten o'clock Virgil Jones got off a streetcar and walked toward the entrance. His hands were in the pock-ets of an age-limp raincoat and he wore no hat.

"It's him There he is Jones Yes, it's him What do you say, man?" And with the spontaneous awe that is so tremendously flattering to a celebrity, they all shrank back to form an aisle. But he did not act flattered. He did not even act disdainful. He simply passed through them as if they were not there.

A heavyset Italian opened the inner door. By the time Jones had gone twenty feet along the body-packed bar, faces began to turn and talking increased and the Dixielanders were hammering away alone.

In the back room Jones hung up his coat and sat at the table. A game of 13-solitaire was unfinished before him. He looked at the walls and then at his left thumbnail.

Angelo pranced in and said it would be about ten minutes. How did he feel?

Jones' pale eyes studied him. "Cut off that loudspeaker on the street when I start."

"You object to it?"

"You know I'm not playing for the street."

"Well . . ." Angelo's mouth was inverted with helpless discomfort. "It attracts the people and keeps the others waiting until they can get in. It's business, Jones. Very valuable."

"I don't want to argue with you."

"It's nice to let everybody hear the music. Don't you think it makes them happier out there?"

"I don't care. And you can think what you want to about me—I don't care about that either. But remember, I'm not obliged to make them happy, just as they're not obliged to listen to me. They can all go home if they want to. I don't care."

"Don't you want to make people happy?"

"People make themselves happy or unhappy. That's their business. Don't go obliging me."

Angelo folded his arms, raised his round eyes to the low ceiling. "You know something?" He wrinkled his mouth. "I've had a bunch of good what you call musicians in this here room over the years, but I'm telling you you are the worst businessman I ever seen. Not an ounce of the sense. *But—*" he slapped the sides of his legs "—you are supposed to be one hell of a piano player, they tell me. So I give in on this loudspeaker thing. You get your way." He stopped at the door. "You know something else? I don't like you. I'm not so dumb that I tell you your business, and I know you got some big backing behind you in this, but I don't like you. You always make too much trouble."

When the Dixieland crew slammed through *Panama* to end the first set, Angelo cut off the loudspeaker and went over to the big table where Henneberry was sitting with a band-leader and a critic. There were handshakes all around. Henneberry nodded, stood and followed the owner toward the stand. Angelo bent and flipped switches. A spotlight on the piano was the only illumination. The crowd became mute as the announcer portentously entered the core of light.

"Tonight—" He waited for further silence. He let his glassed eyes pass casually over the audience. When there was absolutely no sound he let the silence gather for a moment.

"Tonight is, simply, Virgil Jones . . . a piano . . . sounds of brilliant imagination . . . flawless execution. Virgil Jones. A new personality, a name you will remember." He waited again. "I give him to you."

He smiled and descended from the stand as the crowd burst into furious applause, applause that meant they knew they were seeing the debut of a great jazzman.

Fingers closed on Henneberry's elbow. Jones' face came close.

"That's the last of that talk," the mouth whispered. "You don't 'give' me to anybody." Ungripped, the hand clenched in air, dropped to the pianist's side. He went up on the stand.

The silence had all the overgrown, unnerving weight of a crowd acting as a single huge body. It was the crucial and unreal moment when any sound can seem a terrific violence. The tension reached the breaking-point.

But Jones had no nerves. He stabbed the keys once, twice, three times—and began with a nameless blues, a big powerful thing with a four-four beat so solid that it could have supported a house. He went straight through the blues, looked

229

up as the applause cascaded out of the dimness, and cut it off with *Sweet Georgia Brown.*

The people looked at each other, asked themselves what was going on, craned toward the critics. Jones was not waiting for applause. He was playing as if he and the piano were in an empty room. The music had an aggressive, almost frenzied drive, but he himself was icy, his young face frozen with no emotion.

And he forced them into silence. No chatter competed with him, and during the few-second breaks between numbers the whispers were hurried and the applause staggered before he was at the keys again.

He played for exactly forty minutes, and when he wound it up the audience sagged as though deflated. As he came down from the stand the gathered applause found itself with a long, swelling rush of many hands and voices and shrill whistles. A dozen people stood to shout and beat their palms together. The musicians nodded, nodded, and stared into their glasses. The critics shook their heads with slow admiration. There was no doubt about it. Eccentric as he was, annoyingly self-possessed as he was, Virgil Jones was a fantastic newcomer to modern jazz.

The audience was divided almost equally—half had come to hear Jones, the other half to listen to the Dixieland alternates.

Of the Dixieland school was a ferretlike man named Greene Todd. By day he was an associate professor of anthropology at Roosevelt College and by night the most respected critic of jazz in Chicago. He had none of Henneberry's fame or power, but was intelligent and honest and admired for his fairness. Now, as usual, he sat hidden like a bright-eyed rat amid the tumult and resisted the impulse to leap forward with a squeal of his own. He had been witness, he told himself, to something great. True, Jones was not a Dixielander—the chord progressions, fugue derivations and phrasings were all of a modern conception—but Jones was someone more than merely another exciting modern jazz pianist. The weakness of pianists such as Ross Jaeger, Todd considered, was in relying on right hand work. Their treble was dazzling, but the bass drive mediocre to flimsy. They lacked solidity. The ideas were there, worlds of them, but seldom rested on a firm foundation. Not so Jones. Jones had everything. His right hand was blazing and his left was like the working end of a triphammer. He played a big stride piano Todd had not heard since the days of Fats Waller. When Jones started moving that left hand the walls of the zouzou seemed to breathe like a giant bellows. He was, in short, a pianist with all of the strengths and none of the weaknesses of jazz. Todd resolved to meet him and to find out how and where he had learned his genius.

But when Jones descended from the stand he did a curious thing. As everyone watched—Todd and Henneberry and a dozen musicians all wanting him to recognize them and knowing that the audience would be impressed with whomever he joined—Jones walked through the maze of tables and suddenly sat at one occupied by two young couples who were more astonished than anyone else. He smiled at them, talked to them, ordered a drink, and began an aimless conversation as if he were no one special, just another one of the crowd.

That was the way he was. For the few he pleased he angered ten times as many. He never did what was expected. He refused to act like a professional musician by associating with others of his kind. He rejected the idea of posturing like a celebrity. Still wearing cheap clothes and riding public transportation to and from the club, he continued to talk with all sorts of people and to make friends with none of them. He would not give his autograph, and it wasn't long before everyone had been forced to accept the fact that he was not going to play requests for anyone. That was the way he was. He forced people to accept him. He was not going to change.

Inside of two weeks Virgil Jones was known to jazz-initiates as the brightest and most promising new pianoman in jazz. Henneberrys in New York and California and on nearly all the stations between repeated his name, quoted what was being written about him in the trade magazines, and organized petitions asking him to record "for the development of our great, indigenous art form—Jazz." Some of the correspondence came to the zouzou, most of it to Henneberry.

The announcer tried flattery. Promises. Flattery. He culled praisewords and was sly. But the answer was the same: No. Jones was not interested in any of the offers, any of the pleas. Nothing written, or said, or grown powerful through tradition, could induce him to change his ways. And what ways they were.

Like the time he had been introduced to the great blind pianist whose presence usually froze fingers and numbed brains of jazzmen all over the country. Jones hadn't been impressed. He sat awhile and chatted and persistently worked the conversation far afield of jazz. Talking with the most famous jazz pianist and honored by a deep and sincere interest of someone so great, Jones behaved as if he was listening to just another ordinary pianist. Moreover, he showed absolutely no special consideration or admiration for a man who had conquered such a handicap as blindness. But then, before leaving the table for his next set, Jones had extended both hands and rested them on those of the blind man. For two seconds. That was the only tribute he had paid.

Or like another time when he had been discovered on his night off lumpily pounding an out-of-tune piano in a burlesque pit on South State. The incident would have never got out if it hadn't been that the regular pianist had called the union and that somewhere in the evening there had been a fistfight.

Or the story, never confirmed or denied, of a college student who some years ago had gone to the Railroad Fair. A jazz enthusiast, he had seen Jones there, but not in the audience. Jones had been an Indian. Wearing full headdress and with his stained face disfigured by paint, he had been tomahawking settlers on the lakefront every afternoon for a week.

Or like the time he had been seen in serious conversation with a female lion at Brookfield Zoo.

There were other stories, but it was becoming more difficult to separate the possible from the impossible. Jones seemed capable of anything. Why he did the things he did, no one could say. The fact was that he did them and never apologized or tried to justify his actions afterward. His life was apparently guided by a primitive rule stating that anything a man did was good provided it was not aimed at injuring others.

Strangely enough, in the face of his independence and insulting lack of consideration for anyone but himself, within two weeks he had become a minor god of the very people he rebuffed and angered. It was as if he had come to expiate the sins of their weaknesses. In him his followers found vicarious realization of an individuality they did not have the strength to maintain. He stood alone where they could not.

Paul Bauer liked the sound of rain. On hot days he wore shorts and lived in his manicured lawn behind the imperial white house in Park Forest. With a pitcher of grapejuice he would sink himself into a chaise lounge beneath a canvas awning, twist a small wheel in the grass, and listen to the silver-foil patter from the garden hose aimed to arch its spray on the canvas above. It was a lulling sound. Peaceful. Curved like talons, his fingers slowly stopped thrumming on the flat painted arms of the lounge. The pattering was endless. His eyelids would close like small silk curtains.

When he woke it would be late afternoon. Sun still seared

the air. Leaves hung. Above limp heavy trees the sky was smoky blue with heat. Birdcalls rasped. Midsummer was such dry death.

He would finish the gourd-shaped pitcher of grapejuice and then go in the house for his shower and talcum. There was no hurry. He had patience now.

Not so Henneberry, he thought. Hen Henneberry. Three times a week he would come, clucking and looking into the grass, cackling this, questioning that, imagining everything. Fretting, unable to feed his hunger, finding only pebbles in the grass.

"Patience," Bauer would say.

But still Henneberry came squawking on the lawn. Why not soon? Jones was ready. His reputation was growing daily. Why persist in keeping him buried in Chicago? There was a fortune to be made from a tour. The Coast, New York—in either Jones would draw tremendous crowds. What was the good of having him unless he was being used?

"Patience."

" 'Patience.' " Henneberry scowled at the ice in his Tom Collins, shook his jowls angrily. "I dare say you can afford to say that—inasmuch as this entire affair seems to be sort of a game with you. I confess I don't understand your attitude, Paul. You continually refuse to meet Jones, and just as continually make concessions to him. Look at what you've done—you keep him in good standing with the local, you place him in clubs musicians work years to reach, you take none of his earnings and give me a pittance, you give in to him on any number of things such as recordings and endorsements and the out-of-town offers. I simply don't understand."

"That's not your business, announcer. Remember what I said at the beginning—I'm the one who decides what's to be done with Jones. Don't forget that." Carefully he drew on

234

thin ivory-colored linen trousers. "Hand me that belt. The alligator. Directly in front of you, stupid."

Henneberry complied and exhaled with exasperation. "I remember what you said, Paul, and I won't forget it. But I am still human. Naturally I think about things I don't understand, especially when they concern me—and this does, I hope you realize. There I am, on the air night after night, publicizing Jones, praising him, telling my audience that he is the greatest new pianist in jazz. And what do I get in return? A few dollars. Not even recognition from him. Do you know what that means? Can you understand how I feel when he ignores me in front of everyone?"

"All your adorers . . ."

"Yes! if you insist—my adorers. The people who regard me as an authority and a power. What do you think they must think when they see Jones treating me like any common idiot who likes jazz?"

"Probably that you're an idiot."

Henneberry grunted and made jumbled figures in the air with his hands and strode back and forth like a man in a cage. He was sick with frustration. He could not accept what was.

"Really—" he began again, pivoting clumsily "—I thought I would never see such an extraordinary situation. Here we are: Paul Bauer, a man who has always dictated his own terms, who has always been on the offensive, who has ruled instead of being ruled; and myself, a personality accustomed to being respected and obeyed—here we are, the two men who control jazz in this city, who shape opinion, make men famous or forgotten, and what are we doing? Yes, that is the question, Paul. And the answer? We're being dictated to, forced on the defensive, ignored, reduced to impotence, made fools of—and by whom? A stubborn nobody from the gutter.

235

That's who. A stubborn nobody with delusions of grandeur . . ."

"Give me that handkerchief, announcer." He pressed it to his throat twice and then slipped it in a hip pocket.

"I trust I've made my position clear, Paul."

Bauer nodded and then shrugged.

"I don't enjoy," Henneberry went on, "the prospect of continued subservience to Jones' whims. There—that is my position."

"Ready?"

Henneberry looked blank. "For what?"

"To drive me into the city. I have an appointment with a man about a welterweight, and I like riding in your shiny snob car. Jaguar, isn't it?"

Indulging the announcer's periodic outbursts was the only course to take. Henneberry's "position" had no more strength than a house of cards, but it did his ego good, Bauer knew, to protest the way he was being mistreated and thwarted in his impatience to bleed the pianst. And it was sad, in a way, because if everything developed as planned, Henneberry would never get what he wanted from Jones.

During the long stifling days and airless nights Bauer considered the latest news of Jones and concluded that his plan was working as well as possible. It was moving slowly, of course, but the end was worth waiting for.

So Bauer waited while Henneberry shrank and Jones grew. And he did not lose sight of his purpose as Jones moved into the Blue Note and brought with him hundreds of followers. He watched and saw that Jones was becoming far more than merely a celebrated jazz pianist. Jones was growing into a symbol. *Live for yourself.* That was what his actions said. *Account to no one for what you believe. Have confidence in what you feel is right for you. Compromise with nothing.*

Bauer smiled: dry, cynical. Standing unnoticed in the crowd

near the door one night, he could see that Jones meant this to the faces. There they were: faces of musicians and students, faces of salesmen, of actresses visiting on an off night, young faces and old faces, uninterpretable faces in the anonymity of diffused light and mass-production clothing, faces ageing— and all of them turned toward the piano and the strong young head illuminated like a shape of stone, the hands playing jazz, the notes announcing themselves with a bold finality that ignored both criticism and praise.

He smiled again. Yes, that was what he meant to most of these faces. They could understand what he was preaching with his hands and with all his actions, but not one of the audience would ever act upon it. They were weak. They were human and weak. Jones was a curiosity. He was something to see and listen to and read about. That was who he was— someone else.

In the shade again, with the artifice of rain hypnotically cool and steady above his head, Bauer toyed with the faces he had seen the night before. They were all the same. All masks of subdued desperation, all uncertain, all gazing with dulling hope for some answer to some question for some day. Gazing. What did they want? Something they did not have. It was always the idea of something they did not have that kept people alive. It kept them working and worrying and hoping and working. Until one day, too soon, not at all right because they hadn't been given time to get ready and so many things were still to be had and said and done and tried and so much had to be undone and tried again, until one day too soon they found themselves out of time, out of all time, dead.

He laughed softly. His thin old head moved from side to side.

Like a pendulum.
Like a pendulum.
Like a pendulum.

The smile vanished. His mouth did not close fully. He looked toward the tall green cones of trees brushing whispers through the hot yellow air. He looked at the sky and then at the grass. From somewhere a breeze lifted and chilled him. His flesh stippled as he shivered in the shade suddenly grown cold.

His mouth still open, he lurched to his feet and into the feeble sun. Everything was becoming colder. With one hand he stooped and wrenched a fistful of bright grass. He studied it, smelled it and crushed it and flung it away. When he looked into his palm it was stained and there was a dark green blade stuck near the base of his thumb. From the wrought-iron-and-glass table he took a cigarette lighter. Holding the thin blade of grass between his fingers, he set fire to it. It did not want to burn. He put it on the edge of the table and gave it to the flame again. It was a long time before the blade of grass shriveled and was dead.

II

Of late, especially this night, she could detect in his phrases a
tone of unhappy resignation. It was unaccountable, but there.

"Of course I don't mind," Schwab was saying above the
humming of the engine. "I'm rather honored that you feel
free to tell me all these things—so go right ahead."

"I feel like a weakling."

"Nonsense, girl. Your real concern is that others will consider you weak, isn't that so? Well, agreed or not, you
shouldn't feel guilty for having aired your worries about Ross.
Every one of us needs someone to talk to."

"Unless we're Jones."

He smiled frozenly. "Perhaps. But—" he dismissed the pianist for the time being "—naturally you're worried about Ross.
So am I, and look at me—I'm only remotely involved with
him and haven't an ounce of sympathy for what he does . . .
that is, jazz. Still, he interests me. Because of you, for one
thing, and perhaps because he's . . . well, a celebrity."

"And what else?"

"Nothing."

"You were going to say something else."

He drove silently for a block. "All right. Ross seems to me
a type—an archetype, if you will. To me he's the model for
our time, the success-worshipper and seeker, the man who

spends all his life and a tremendous amount of energy looking for 'The Answer.' That was what I was about to say."

She thought of the night Ross had gone to New York. Then
he had seemed to realize why he wanted success and how hollow and wrong it was to believe it could be everything. Yes,
he had realized it, but did he believe it enough to act upon it?
From his infrequent, brief, vague phonecalls and letters it did
not seem as though he had changed. He was still looking for
the same things in the same places.

"I hope I haven't offended you, Helen."

She shook her head and slowly blinked.

"You know," Schwab said quietly, "a trip east isn't expensive, and I'd be happy to—"

"Thanks, no." She straightened herself, revived. "Ross
hasn't asked me to come, and anyway, I think we all know
that he's got to find himself by himself. The mirrors are the
same no matter where you are. But thanks again." She put
her hand on his shoulder.

His head turned with a forced smile. "Hell, ain't it?"

"It sure is," she said.

And it was. For that night, the next night, all the nights
with no Ross and no knowing. But, she lectured herself, things
had to be lived with, and this was one of them. When you
couldn't live with something, give it up. But if you had already tried to give it up and found you couldn't, then you had
to live with it.

Why Ross? Why not someone more normal, more solid and
average? A nice-looking young man who worked from nine
to five and polished his car on weekends. Pleasant, diplomatic.
One who made friends easily and generously, had a fair repertoire of jokes, bowled one night a week, and talked about
owning a home someday. Who worried mildly about business
and Russia and seriously about lung-cancer from cigarettes. A
perfunctory young citizen who perfunctorily got up and went

off to perfunctory work and came home to eat and watch flawless television detectives and afterward perfunctorily created children saddled with rashes and heartbreakingly unintelligible with earaches and in what seemed less than a moonphase became young men and young women perfunctorily going out and coming in while this thinning-haired citizen nodded and smiled at the flawless detectives who perfunctorily smoked cigarettes and did not seem to worry about cancer.

Why Ross? She had given herself the answer. It was because he was not these things, and because since knowing him she would never be able to look at these things and see herself a part of them.

And yet Schwab had called Ross a type, a "model for our time"—and Schwab was not blind. He watched. He was always watching. He saw a lot more than he would admit to. What did he see in Jones? Another type? Or did he see, as she did, a question-mark of a man who had happened into all their lives and was by his unchangeable personality dominating everyone he met? That was what he was doing—he was dominating them. He was declaring himself as an individual, the last in the world, and everyone who met him seemed to come away changed.

Ross had started all over again in New York.

She had begun to increase her worries of how their relationship would end.

Schwab seemed almost indifferent to his business. He spent his nights like a man with only a few months to live.

Henneberry was being revealed as pompous and inept, powerless to impress anyone who simply refused to be impressed.

Critics were revising their opinions of pianists, and musicians of all instruments were copying the inventions of Jones.

And Jones was still the same.

Curiously enough, for all the confusion and doubt he was causing her, she enjoyed talking with him. Hardly a week would pass but he would join her for a drink between sets. Most often they talked of commonplace things, but there was a certain quality to his language that made the most ordinary discussion something special. It was hard for her to say why this was. Perhaps, she thought, Jones was so positive about his ideas that the smallest of them appeared the size of a major conviction of any normal person. Jones was certain of everything he said.

Yet for all his absolutism he was openly tolerant of any and all other viewpoints. Not once did she hear him criticize someone for an idea contrary to his. He would make it clear that he could not believe it, but that any other idea had just as much right to exist as his did. His words seemed to add up to the attitude that every man had personal ideas of right and wrong. Sometimes these ideas were identical with those of other men, but when they differed no man had the right to claim his ideas as true for the other man. A man was a man. He was not two men, or three, or a dozen, or a city or a state or a nation. He was a man. One.

Jones did not talk all the time, however. When she would bring Ross into the conversation Jones suddenly became close-tongued and let his eyes wander as though seeking a path of escape. In a short while he would finish his drink and leave.

She did not understand. The only way she could explain it was that Jones was simply unpredictable; if any single prediction could be made of Jones, it was that he was unpredictable.

The summer nights were hot and lonely for her. Schwab would call on the telephone. He would ask if she had heard from Ross. Most often she said no. Then he would ask her how work was. As usual, she would answer. With requirements out of the way, he would next ask if she would like to hear some music. See a movie? A play, or just a drive along the lake for some cool night air? Thanks, but no, not tonight, she would answer. Maybe Friday or Saturday. Now please don't think I don't enjoy your company. It's simply that this heat makes me limp and not interested in doing much of anything.

Not even the big dull books she had taken to reading.

Not even the thought of Jones and what a giant he was getting to be.

Not even answering letters. Not when his thick, splashy script covered only one side of a page and said nothing. Not when it took Ross so long to write and say nothing.

Now was the dangerous time.

In her mind lived the dark images: father, mother, two brothers, sister. At first it had been only in their eyes. *This man is not for you. He is not Greek. He is too old. He is in a bad business.* Then it had been in their mouths. *This man is not for you.* Sullen, hurt resentment at her silent defiance. Their mouths promising *You will see. This is not right. It cannot go on. Do you understand?* It had been their wills against hers. *We know these musicians. This will end in a bad way if you do not stop.* Pressures. The slow steady force from all sides compressing. Aunts and uncles and cousins—everyone of the same mind. *This will end in a bad way if you do not stop.* She had been forced to choose. She had not wanted to. She had wanted to keep both, but they had never been willing to let her. They had pushed her to a decision. And they had lost. Why had they had to lose? Or was it she who had really lost?

Now was the time of questioning.

In the hot Chicago kitchen she thought of the hot St. Louis kitchen and the hot New York room. This was what it had come to after all the words. Three rooms in three cities. The airless dark of a summer night. And none of the rooms knowing where it would end.

She could not go back. It was not a matter of pride. It was a matter of need. Ross needed her and she needed him. Love was not a thing of convenience.

There could have been others, she knew. There could still be a handsome young man of the right family and with a future that was charted and sober and pleasant. Together—all of them—they would sit in the hot St. Louis kitchen and talk and drink coffee and eat lamb on Sundays and afterward the men would play poker while the women spoke the language and dried silverware.

She did not hate the scene. It had the warm, secure feeling of routine, of a planned and orderly life among stable elements. But she did not want to stand in that kitchen and see herself standing there at thirty and at thirty-five and forty, at fifty speaking the language and still drying silverware, at fifty-five, at sixty, the taste of lamb and Retsina in her mouth and the memory of Ross in her eyes. She did not want to grow old in regret.

So it had to be this:

Waiting.

Reading in the trade magazines that Ross was playing here with a quintet, there as a single, sitting in on a recording-date, still searching in New York.

Waiting.

Writing him only those things he wanted to hear—that she loved him, that she missed him, that Henneberry was still praising his records nightly and that musicians were asking about him.

Telling herself that before the summer was over his answer would be hers and that then she would know she had never been wrong in giving herself to him.

12

With his back to the spiked iron fence Jaeger sat in the clinging heat of summer. At his feet an ancient shoeshiner slapped
oxblood polish onto the sides of his shoes. Afternoon hung.
Broadway was a languid procession of seersucker and cotton
and Navy whites. A red light became green and cars moved
forward like tired beetles.

Stubbled by three days of neglect, his chin was sunk onto
his shirtfront. He raised only his eyes to the passing faces.
Nearly all the faces were damp and strangely bloated, mouths
opening and closing like those of fishes. He took no particular
notice of any single face. They glided into his vision, passed
through, and were gone.

When the job was done Jaeger stepped down and handed
a dollar to the shoeshiner and walked away. His tailored
clothes were still in impeccable condition. Except for his face
he looked like a man with all the self-assurance of wealth.

For the rest of the afternoon he dawdled along Broadway
from the Battery to the hot green triangle of City Hall Park.
The delicate hands of his watch barely moved. He sighted a
distant drugstore and thought of ice-slivers in lemonade. His
tongue licked the roof of his mouth. He looked at a bench.
He could not decide. He did not want to make so many
decisions. Finally he sank onto the thin, weathered bench and

stretched his arms along its top. Deciding not to decide was the easiest thing to do.

Since coming to the city he had lived like a vagrant. From time to time he had taken odd piano jobs around Manhattan and twice out on Long Island. He had made a brief radio appearance and had been on a recording-date. But most of his time was spent in drifting.

His third-floor room overlooked a square of cement. Below, in the dark, damp well, nothing stirred except scraps of newspaper and throwaways and an occasional torn envelope. It was like living on the edge of a pit.

Against one wall of the room stood a brass bed and a closet of cardboard stained like cedarwood. Opposite the bed crouched a washstand, the pipes of which had been recently painted a bright silver. The bureau was big and baroque and its ivory enamel looked as though it had been buttered on. The rug was of an indistinguishable color and had the texture of a gunnysack. Under the washstand, where the rug had worn through, silverfish flickered across the boards.

The room was where he wanted to live. It was as if he had taken it to satisfy a feeling that he needed to punish himself.

He had gone to Birdland the first week. He had said hello, given his hand all around, answered questions, told the men who was doing what and where, said Chi was beginning to wake up with jazz again. Yes, he had answered, this Jones was laying down some great piano. Jones, Jones, everyone had wanted to know. Did he really have it? And Jaeger had told them that Jones had the ideas and the hands—yes, he had it as far as Jaeger was concerned.

He did not go beyond that because he had never practiced putting down another musician. As long as a man was trying and doing his best, Jaeger would not criticize. The only jazzmen who brought his disapproval into the open were those who gave jazz a bad name—the lushes and snowbirds who were always getting picked up on either narcotics or on morals charges, the juiceheads who got so fractured that they wouldn't show up for a date and couldn't be located for a week. They had a right to live their own lives, of course, but not when the way they lived them made people look at every jazzman like some kind of a freak. He would never forget the time when in Copenhagen a Dane had confessed to him that he had come to the jazz concert only to see how a "real dopefiend" acted. The musician in question was the drummer, and the truth was that he had been on the needle off and on for over two years. But that was beside the point. The point was that it was a hell of a note when jazz got to be more sideshow than music.

So he couldn't honestly criticize Jones. The young pianist was a sort of weird one, all right, but when he did something, no one came away with the idea that all jazzmen acted like that. Jones had a way of making everything he did seem as though it belonged to him and to nobody else.

The entire night at Birdland had been awkward. After answering the questions there had not been much to say. He had known what they were thinking. They had heard that he was slipping, that he was all knotted up for some reason or the other. That night they had asked him to sit in, he had said no, and they had not insisted. Afterward they had wanted to know if he felt like coming along for a few hours out on The Island—he didn't have to blow at all. And he had declined that too. They had asked him to fall in again and not to be a stranger. All right, he had said. He would see them.

The first week had been like that. Dropping in, shaking hands, answering questions, saying thanks but no, he didn't feel like any piano just then. He had got sick of questions, of requests, of all the pressures. He knew that everyone was trying to help, but he hated being treated like a cripple.

During the second week he said all right to Ned at GAC

and had hooked with a quintet blowing in the Village. He was not sure why he agreed. Probably out of restlessness, he thought.

At the first rehearsal Jaeger wasn't sure how the young quintet regarded him; their expressions could have meant they admired him as a genius or as a relic. They made him nervous.

But in the beginning the group had been all right. He led them and they knew where he was going and stayed with him. His hands fashioned light, bouncing passages punching out the rhythm. His hands hammered sharp and savage. His tone was perfect. More than once he thought he had seen the others glancing wisely at each other as if to say that any man who said Jaeger was through was out of his skull.

You're damned right, he had exulted to himself. I'm getting it back again, and this time I'll hang onto it. I will. This is the way it started, right here in New York, and I'm finding it again. Get with me, you guys, and I'll bring you the moon.

But his elation hadn't lasted, and it was his own fault. He had come to distrust optimism. Doubt infected him, and festered.

On the third night, after the first set, he had accused the tenor saxman and guitarist of getting sloppy. He had told them they ought to go big band if they wanted to get by with that kind of work. He stomped out of the back room and went to the bar.

After the second set he read them off again. The guitarist was surly but said nothing. The tenorman said sarcastically that they couldn't be expected to satisfy someone the size of Jaeger. We do our best, he said. Jaeger told him that if that was the best he could do he ought to turn in his card and give somebody else a job.

Hung over the bar, waiting for the third set to begin, he had fought to hold himself together. There was still a job to

248

be done. Walking out would be doing the same thing he could not tolerate in other jazzmen. He had another drink. Sometimes it helped a man reach a point where he was able to accept what he didn't like when sober.

Drink, however, hadn't helped him this night. Midway through the third set the quintet submitted to the mounting cries requesting *How High the Moon.*

Automatically, as he had done hundreds and hundreds of times before, Jaeger kicked off the beat and started in. He felt like a machine. The melody itself was still one he liked more than most others, but he had played it too much. It was worn out. He was worn out. Sounds grinding out of a machine, paid for, played for, mechanical and changeless—all for the college boys with crewcuts and white shoes, tapping red rubber soles in time out of time offbeat to the limping tenor and staggering guitar, the drummer clubbing brass brass brass, smoke suddenly stinging in his own nostrils and his hands wet and wanting to make fists to smash all the stupid faces into splinters.

He did not remember playing his break. He did not really recall playing two numbers afterward.

It was true, however. If he had cracked there would have been faces staring at him as he walked to the back room, and the tenorman wouldn't have come in and offered him a cigarette. Jaeger inhaled and let the smoke drift thickly from his mouth.

"Sorry, man," he said.

The tenorman hadn't answered.

"About those words," Jaeger said to one cuff of his pants. "I guess I'm not ready to work with anybody else yet. You know, man. I guess I'm asking too much."

"So—I'm an idealist too." The tenorman was young and blond and had a forehead that looked as though he had gone through the windshield in an accident.

"I'm cutting out," Jaeger had told him. "Don't worry, I'll get a good man to fill in—you won't be hung up on my account. He'll get in touch with you tomorrow. This is my last night."

The tenorman had protested at length, but Jaeger did not weaken to the flattery. It was his last night, he repeated. He did not want to talk about it anymore.

From that night on he had played only as a favor for a friend or as a self-trial of one night. None of the affairs had gone very well. The recording-date had been only passable, and then, he was convinced, only because there had been twelve men blowing and his piano hadn't been out in the open.

He had hardly anything to do. By day he wandered around and by night he wandered around. And all the time his mind was a sluggish confusion of chords and phrasing and Virgil Jones and of Helen.

Now, his pants plucking at the bench as he stood up, he rubbed a hand over his rough jaw and watched the distant chaos as buildings emptied their workers at the end of another day. He felt a certain pleasure in being unshaven and having wasted the afternoon in a park with all the other do-nothings. If he wanted to spend an afternoon with the sun on his face and his shoes in the grass, he could. He had just done it, and he could do it again tomorrow.

But yet, when he began walking and encountered his reflection in a store window, he hoped that he would get back to his room without being recognized.

That night he took the subway to the Polo Grounds and sat in the bleachers for a twelve-inning game. Afterward he had a drink at a bar, bought a pint of Old Taylor, and returned to his room.

The adjoining building stood so that from a certain position at his window he could look down the street for almost a block. He opened the bottle and put his feet on the sill. Warm air touched his face; the dingy curtains breathed once. Beyond the edge of the next building he followed the probing headlights of a car. Every so often—not this night as yet—he would see a lone man walking the street. The times and direction varied, but it was always the same man. Jaeger had taken to watching for the man. The small, clicking man passing into and out of the soft spread pool of the streetlamp, going somewhere, coming from somewhere else. Into and out of the light. Clicking through the darkness on some private mission. There were times when Jaeger wanted to leave his room and follow the man who clicked like some wound-up toy. He wanted to walk the streets, follow to the door, see the room, the woman, the place where the clicking man found his answers.

Jaeger did not see him until three-thirty that night. He knew it was the same man. But the figure was not clicking. It made no sound as it ran.

The man was running in the darkness. Swift and silent, running as though in terror of something pursuing in the night. Puny fists pumping like pistons at his chest, his head twice wrenching to see behind. Then he ran out of view. Nothing followed. The street lay quiet again. Nothing followed.

Jaeger passed a wide hand over his eyes. Somewhere in the city, at three-thirty of a summer morning, the man was running. Like a fugitive. From where to where, and why? The street lay silent in dark heat.

He was never to see the clicking man again.

That night, and the next and the next, Jaeger pushed himself to the bed, collapsed, and slept on his back. He woke in a furnace. His shoulders itched. He made a flabby noise with his lips. His hot eyes tried to draw into his head away from the light. Every step brought a gigantic ache to his brain. He fell back onto the bed and tried to sleep away the misery. It was no use. With his teeth sunk into his lower lip, he got up again and cupped water to his eyes and finally all over his face and neck and roughed a coarse towel on his skin. When he had finished he stood in the center of the furnace and blinked at all four walls. Now that he had met the day—was it morning or afternoon?—he did not know what to do with it.

It was early afternoon, white-gold with heat, and in his mailbox there was a letter from Helen. He read it over a Bromo-Seltzer and iced black coffee and toast.

She shamed him. She was so strong in her patience, in her faith in him. He could not bring himself to read the letter again.

That was what happened, he thought. You met a thousand women and treated them decently, and not one of them was worth it. Then you met one who mattered more than all the others, and you treated her like something worse than common. That was what happened. It was stupid and wrong, but that was the way it was. When you messed with the others you didn't have a problem in the world. The cards were turning up right, one after the other, you could see what was ahead of you and you knew your piano would get better and it was only a matter of time before you'd be at the top. You believed in yourself; you had direction. But as soon as you met the one worth more than all the other women, you started doubting. She wasn't to blame. You were the one. You began looking ahead and seeing a lot of things: mistakes, bad breaks, failure. And all of them seemed worse because now you had someone worth succeeding for. Mistakes, failure, losing your direction and dragging her down with you. And you didn't want to hurt her that way. You wanted to be to her all the things you felt you could be, so you kept trying to find yourself again. If she was hurt it was only because it was better that way, the early and sudden way, than to lie to yourself and spread the hurt over her lifetime. Yes, he supposed, life was like that. The decent people were always getting hurt one way or another.

He had to stop thinking. He needed to feel, to relax and rest his mind. His kind of jazz was not what he wanted. The jazz that allowed him to feel, simply to soak it up without worrying about competition or new phrasings, was down at the Village.

When he pushed into the sudden smoke and dimness that night he heard the horn. A big, pure horn blowing *Dawn at Marblehead* in a way that had never changed. From a table he looked toward the stand where Romeo stood, old and black and as straight as a pipe, blowing sounds no one ever forgot. Jaeger recognized only Eddie Henry on clarinet and Heavy Baker on trombone—the other three, two of them white, were young and not well-known. But there was old Romeo Turner leading all of them into the music, and it didn't take an expert to know that this was the genuine article.

He was trying, later, to count the bubbles on the surface of his highball when the hand clapped on his shoulder.

"Romeo," he said, finding that he could still smile.

"My O My. It is little old Ross come home." Romeo let his arm slide all the way around Jaeger's neck.

"Sit down," Jaeger said, "and I'll buy you a jug."

Romeo sat. He was wearing a banana-colored suit. His old face tapered from an extraordinarily wide forehead to a sharp chin so that he looked like an ebony top. He lit a black cigarette with a gold tip and lolled in the flimsy chair. His eyes gleamed.

"I hear you was in town somewheres," he said. "What you doing down here? You give up on that bebop slop? Damn me, man, tell me everything you been up to since I seen you last."

"Well—" Jaeger halted. He could not go on with the farce

of a two-year résumé with this as its ending. "You know all there is to know, I guess."

"Now that's something," Romeo said. "You know I don't hold with all that jive in them magazines, so how'm I supposed to keep up on what you been doing and where?"

"You hear the talk."

"Unhunh. I listens only to Romeo's big fat horn."

"Sure." Suddenly Jaeger felt a swarming compulsion to tell Romeo everything. He had to tell someone, and Romeo was just old and wise enough to be the man. "Look at me, man," he said to the glossily dark eyes. "Tell me what you see."

Romeo looked in the air. "This damn heat brings a man down, it does."

"All right, sure—go ahead and be easy with me. Don't say what I know, what you know, what everybody knows. I'm beat. Jaeger is all beat out. He's nowhere on piano and he can't stand the sight of himself. That's what I've been doing—getting beat down. Just because—" He stopped again. As a Dixieland horn man Romeo would have little interest in Jones. Besides, what Jones meant to him was still unclear in his own mind. "No," he concluded, "it isn't the heat, man."

Romeo smoked. He took the cigarette from his lips and admired the gold tip. He moved his tongue over his teeth. With a strong square hand he waved away an autograph-seeker.

"I always says," he finally began, "a man don't have to be what folks says about him. Seem to me a man don't have to put up with that. Know what I mean?"

"That's if what they say isn't true . . ."

"Hell. What you got to watch is letting them make you think so. You got to be the one who makes it true or not, Ross. Nobody can bring you down if you don't want none of it."

"What you're saying," Jaeger said guardedly after finishing his drink, "is that I'm my own worst enemy. Right?"

254

"One way to put it. But I likes to think of myself being my best friend. Depends, man."

Jaeger turned it over in his mind for a short while. He ordered another drink for both. Romeo was old and sharp enough—that much was clear. He had been in the middle of everything, had seen war and boom and bootlegging and depression and war again, had played for sandwiches and gin and a place to sleep, for a king and a whole city of people, had been idolized and copied, sworn at, shot at and knocked around, and yet here he was, still going strong, still the unkillable Romeo.

"Tell me," Jaeger said thickly. "What's with this mess? What do you get out of it?"

"Which mess you talking about? Lots of messes around."

"This—*this,* six a week as a trained seal blowing a horn for all the squares."

"Ross—" the ebony face was puckered, serious "—you ought to put that kind of talk down. That ain't like you."

"We're not seals?"

"We ain't no seals and you knows it. If we was seals we'd be making money for blowing a ramble only once a night. You shouldn't ought to talk like that, Ross. You gets bitter and you ain't worth nothing no more."

"You get bitter, all right. What other way is there? Just look around and ask yourself if you can be happy in a world like this . . . ask yourself where this rat-race is going to end. Where does it get you?"

Romeo wrinkled his mouth like a prune. He held a yellow shred of flame to another black cigarette. Exhaled. Rolled his eyes and rested his elbows on the table.

"I tell you, boy. Where it gets you is where it gets everybody—six feet down, and no coming up for no more choruses, leastwise in this town. Now you can't go on and get bittery about that. That is just the way it is. So you does what you can before you got to go under.

"Now why does I blow this horn? Gabriel ain't about to need no extra hep when he gets of a mind to blow. So this old horn ain't going be much hep to me. But right now, I likes it. It makes me feel good in the gut when I blows it. I can't think of anything I want to do more than blow this horn. Boy, let me tell you it is the only thing in this world for Romeo.

"And I give you something else, too. Think on it. Remember we all going end up the same place, leastwise the first stop. None of us wants to take up with this old being dead thing, but we ain't got no say about that. Well, comes ten, maybe twenty years, and old Romeo ain't rambling no more. Gone under, he is. Now it is summer and he ain't getting none of that sun, that real warm feel to his bones. But up in the sun peoples is eating and swimming and drinking and just walking around to get cool. New York and ElAy and KayCee and Memphis and Chi are still the same as always. It is hot and they's mopping their heads and saying how they wished it breezed up a bit.

"Now in them cities it gets on to evening of a Saturday, and all the young cats is going to have theyselves a ball. Fine chicks and sharp cats—all of them getting ready to juice and put down a great time and maybe screw a little, who knows?" His face lengthened, a sadness shadowed it for only an instant.

"But old Romeo is dead," he went on. "He ain't around to get in on that living. But that's what you thinks, man. Listen:

"This party gets cutting, and they all having one hell of a fine time that hot Saturday night. Gals dancing and winking, shaking a butt, and the cats giving them the big *hel*lo and I'm great and all that jive, you know. Pretty soon somebody puts on a record, and they listen and by and by ask *Who that on that horn?* Well, if they don't know they just put a finger down and stop that record and read that label. And who you think is playing that horn? *Romeo!* they says. *Romeo Turner playing that lovely horn.*

"Now, man—that is what I means. You believe I'm dug out there at that old graveyard? Naw sir, Romeo ain't there at all. Know where he is? At that ball with all them chicks, that's where. He having the damndest time of his life in all them cities at the same time, and that's one thing he never was able to do when he was up and walking around.

"And that ain't all of it, Ross. Look here: Monday morning and it's raining and cold and nobody wants to put a leg outside, it's so bad. So they stays in and listens, or if they's downtown they cut in a music store and in a booth and start hearing records. And where is Romeo? He ain't cold and getting rained on, that's a fact. He's right in that warm little booth blowing that horn of his. Yes sir. You believe me. That what it's coming to for me . . . and *you,* Ross, you *too,* man. You and me going be background to all kinds of loving and fighting and juicing, and all over the place, too. Man, you'n me *never* going die. We got the greatest end in the world, that's what. Now how can you be bitter about that, boy?"

Jaeger flattened his lips in a grimace. "Sounds nice," he said. "But I can't get worked up about what might happen in fifty years."

"Natural," Romeo said. He glared over his shoulder, frustrated. The group was already forming on the stand and waiting for him. A few patrons were eyeing him with a mixture of worship and impatience. He stood, dropped his hand on Jaeger's shoulder. "See me, Ross . . . come down and see me. We got to talk some more on this. But in the meanwhile don't bring yourself down. You plays piano so good I almost can stand listening to you. Come see me, will you now?"

Jaeger nodded, said that he would. But the motion and the word were automatic. Romeo had not helped. Of course he had an answer, but it was for him, Jaeger thought, not me.

What did Jones think of? Himself. The last individual. Doing exactly what he wanted to do. Not competing, not scrambling for success, not worried about what people thought of him. At times it seemed as though Jones thought about absolutely nothing but eating and sleeping and breathing. He too had an answer. But it was for him, Jaeger thought, not me. Or was it? Was it an answer unlike Romeo's wild dreams of the future when he would be a statue in Central Park, a plaque in Grant Park, a name in books and record catalogues? Yes, Jones' answer was different. It was for now.

Cymbal, smoke and horn beating the attack. Heels thumping under tables. Walls beginning to pulse as the whiskey coursed through his brain and smeared his vision. Through the shaking film he squinted toward the piano and the bobbing, hunched-over figure laying down the heavy four-four for Romeo's horn.

He peered at the vague blocky shape of the piano. It was the only thing he had. That, and Helen.

When he had thought about her and what she had done for him and what he had not done for her, and about how empty, barren and vain all his worries were, he drank more. And saw nothing ahead of him. It was as if he had drawn back a curtain and found nothing. Not even darkness. Nothing, simply a vast and colorless space. That was what terrified him.

By the time Jaeger left he was senseless with drink.

There was a jarring, chilled memory of a taxicab ride, streamers of neon, pavement, and finally, grass. Grass cool and wet on the palms of his hands.

He went to the bench in the park and sat down. In a short while his chin dropped on his chest and he slept.

13

It had to happen. The dull South Side neighborhood could not go on seeing things without asking questions. Every day, it seemed, the curb below Jones' rooms had Cadillacs and Lincolns and sports cars; every day people, some of them Negroes, would go up to see him. In most instances they came back down the stairs in less than a minute, looking angry about something as they drove away in their big slick cars. Young people, too, began to be seen on the street. Some of them came in groups and others came alone. The neighborhood found itself infiltrated by strangers.

The answer was not hard to learn. Jones was a musician, a great pianist who was playing jazz downtown and making a lot of money.

From then on, attitudes changed. Jones was no longer the simple fool people had thought. He was a musician, a successful one. He was earning more money than was possible. What did it matter that his habits weren't exactly normal? He was entitled to be that way. He was entitled to anything. He was a success.

Like leeches his neighbors tried to fasten onto him. Young and old, men and women—they thirsted for him. Some for the money they knew he must have had, others only for an association with success. They tried to stop him with a smile,

259

to stand being seen with him, to talk about what success was like, about the city and the weather and life in general, about him, about themselves.

Jones never seemed to take offense at such obviousness. Daily he would listen to anyone who approached him. He made it a point, however, to avoid talking to the same person at the same time each day. He refused to be party to a routine involving other people.

Suddenly, in the second week, he disappeared.

He did not eat his usual breakfast at the restaurant. He wasn't seen either on the street or at the benches near the beach.

His visitors came and went, and could not supply an answer.

That evening, with a senile gentleman from down the hall as her protector, the landlady entered Jones' room.

He was not there. Nothing he owned was there.

On the bureau was an envelope, and in it were bills and silver amounting to the exact rent up to the night on which he had left. There was no explanation and no forwarding address.

The next morning the landlady protested ignorance and innocence as to why he had left so suddenly. He might have been in some kind of trouble, someone said. There was agreement. Musicians were like that, someone else said. It was the kind of life they led. Nightwork made for trouble, especially in show business. You met a lot of people you wouldn't put anything past.

The landlady did not say anything against Jones. She continued her silent bewilderment. Others did all the guessing.

The truth, however, was simple. When she had found out how much money Jones was earning, the landlady had immediately tried to hike the rent fifty dollars a month. He had not protested. Nor had he accused her of such an obvious attempt to exploit him. But that same night he had left, and the neighborhood was never to see him again.

He next appeared, still with the same cardboard suitcase holding all his belongings, on the Northwest Side. And, just as he had done before, Jones took cheap furnished rooms and kept to himself.

But he was not wholly the same. If anyone could have known him intimately it would have been clear that day by day he was becoming more involved with an inner struggle for which he sought no help.

Outwardly he was almost unchanged. His days were spent in the usual free and irresponsible way. He wandered about the city as if it and all its variety of experiences belonged to him, as if not one single piece of existence was beneath his enjoyment.

There was no change in his ability with the piano. He was still as brilliantly inventive and strong as he had always been. He went on attacking the keys with the same unshakable confidence, daring everything and seemingly totally unafraid of mistakes or of anyone's criticism.

Yet, with increasing frequency, he was behaving strangely at the piano. As he had before, he would sometimes suddenly begin barely touching the keys, so that the tune he was playing could hardly be heard. There were times when he played so softly that even all the listeners sitting close claimed they could hear nothing. At other times Jones would finish a number, sit quietly until the applause was exhausted, and then continue to sit in silence, making no move to begin again. The audience would exchange uneasy glances, shift in its chairs, cough, look at Jones, wait, wait. And Jones would sit like a rock. The whole nightclub would wait. And he would sit. He would not even bother to appear to be thinking. Finally he would play again.

One night, with no warning whatever, Jones came down

and walked to the table where Henneberry was impressing two blonde models with talk of Acapulco. Jones did not interrupt. He let the conversation die of its own weight and his presence.

"A tour," he said simply when the announcer looked up. "You've been talking to me about a tour. All right. I'll go. How soon?"

There it was. In less than ten seconds everything Henneberry had tried so long to gain. After all the weeks and months of blunting himself against the iron contrariness of Jones—now, now the money would come in a flood.

Henneberry stammered, stalled, promised, and left inside of ten minutes to contact Paul Bauer.

So it was arranged. Bauer decided on ten men for an ensemble to offset Jones as a soloist. The musicians would not be hard to get. They knew that a tour featuring Virgil Jones would go over the top in every city scheduled. After only fourteen telegrams Bauer had signed the ten he wanted.

It wasn't necessary to wonder what had made Jones decide to go on tour. The fact was that he was going, he was doing something he had persistently refused before.

To Bauer it was unmistakable evidence that his plan was working.

To Henneberry it was his opportunity at last.

To Schwab, to Helen, and to musicians and the jazz-addicts of the city, it was another question they could not answer. Jones was an enigma. They had to be content with assuming that he had a good reason for wanting to go on tour; no one dared even approach him to ask the question.

The itinerary called for a westward swing to San Francisco, then down to Los Angeles and back through The South and up to Chicago. Jones vetoed Henneberry's suggestion of New York and other eastern cities as taking too much time. He said he did not want to spend all year traveling. And once again Bauer, through the announcer, backed down and gave Jones his way. But Bauer noted that Jones, who had previously lived from day to day and place to place as if resisting attachments, was now becoming involved both with time and one city.

Bauer lived with a telephone in his hand. Bandboys, press-agents and technicians swarmed over the rehearsal hall. Prestige and the usual facile promises enabled Henneberry to arrange a leave as MC for the tour.

Jones, meanwhile, had ended his engagement at the zouzou and had all his time to himself. He continued going to the movies and the park. He seemed neither discontent nor anxious about the tour. While the others rehearsed, he practiced in his usual way at any piano which was not being used at the time.

After St. Louis and Kansas City came Denver: gold and purple and cool at the mountains, the air clean, fresh with pine and sage, a city that could look down. And there, as in other cities, there was a stampede to hear him. And as in other cities he remained an uncompromising individualist.

He would not have anything to do with the press of crowds that reached for his signature, his smile, a brush of his hand or arm. He granted no interviews and played no benefits. Attempts to get him to make personal appearances met with failure. He acted in no way like a celebrity. His audience did not seem to matter or even to be related to the jazz he played. The public, his actions said, exists for itself and because it wants to exist. I have nothing to do with it. If the public didn't have me it would have some other person. So it takes me as I am or it rejects me. But it makes no difference either way. The important thing is to be what I am.

At the concerts he would come onstage in a dark suit and a white shirt without a tie. Even from the first row he looked very small. When he stopped, just before sitting at the piano, he stood with a peculiarly combative balance—the level-hipped, slightly up on toes, loose-armed stance of a fighter who carries his hands low and has shattering power in either fist.

He would look at the keys only briefly, and then strike.

It might be *Just Friends* or *I Don't Stand a Ghost of a Chance* or *Blues in E Flat* or *Lullaby of the Leaves* or *Northwest Passage* or some original, unheard-of melody he seemed to create as he went on. Often he played in several keys at once, and one night he changed the chords thirty-two times in the bridge. When he finished a number it was as if he had just performed the definitive version. Any pianist who followed would have to use Jones as the basis for all ideas.

Crowded backstage in the wings, the other musicians were openly puzzled. They had never known Jones to have any of their interest in jazz, that is, to listen to other jazzmen either on record or in person. Then too, he never talked like a pianist with all the background he was supposed to have; and as for practicing, there was just no accounting for how the way he practiced could make him so great. Yet there he was—blazing through a whole catalogue of jazz standards, new and old, inventing his own melodies with unmistakable signs of knowing the latest trends in technique, going beyond those trends into ideas of harmony entirely his own. Where he had learned so much was a secret they could never pry from him. Where he was still learning so much, they never pretended to guess.

In Salt Lake City it was the same. The concert was sold out in three days. Those who had missed out petitioned unsuccessfully for an extra performance. Jones, however, was the only obstacle. He did not care to appease those who could not attend the one scheduled performance. He played to a standing-room crowd and gave an unsurpassed hour of jazz piano, and when the one night was over the tour left town.

All the while, Paul Bauer was timing his moves to stay one stop ahead. From his advance posts he communicated with Henneberry and another hireling, and it was gratifying to hear that Jones was not being overly difficult. The pianist was accepting his role with the tour. He was becoming accustomed to it. And that was exactly what Bauer wanted.

In San Francisco Jones' picture, a drawing that made his eyes look like those of a madman, appeared in all the newspapers, and in the entertainment section of the Sunday *Chronicle* there was a short adulatory profile of his musical history and his impact on the jazz world. A half-dozen free-lance photographers loitered in the lobby of his hotel, another two watched and waited from a parked car. A few women bothered the desk-clerk.

But when Jones did come down, early on the morning of the show, he amiably allowed the photographers to shoot all they wanted just as long as he didn't have to stop walking to pose. The women he ignored. He walked up and down and across and up and over the city and seemed to enjoy it more than any other place the tour had been until then. And it was not surprising that in the afternoon he was seen among old men and fluttering gulls in the sun of Union Square. Nor was it unexpected that after the concert that night more than a few local jazz pianists stopped wearing ties and began to act as if they didn't care what people thought or said about anything.

By the time the tour reached Los Angeles two new developments had risen to view.

First there was the magazine. It was not a trade journal such as *Downbeat* or *Metronome*, but a national publication of ostensibly impartial news-coverage. In its music section, under the simple title "Solo," there was a photograph and an article on him. The author presented Jones as a kind of phenomenon: a solidly selfish musician whose followers only increased their admiration the more he ignored them. Here was an entertainer—and a truly giant-sized jazz pianist, the writer judged—who gained more popularity the less he tried. His manners were insulting in their self-centeredness, yet the more autographs he refused to give and the more people he dismissed without the smallest, least costly act of courtesy, the more his admirers grew like disciples of a religion. In short, he was becoming a cult. He did nothing to encourage it, but neither did he speak out against it. Virgil Jones was either one of the most extraordinarily and consistently indifferent men in America, or one of the cleverest frauds the entertainment world had seen in years. The upshot of the article was that his popularity multiplied by the thousands, while he himself did not even bother to read it. He simply raised his eyebrows at the photograph of himself when the magazine was thrust at him, mumbled an unintelligible fragment of a sentence, and walked off across the hotel lobby leaving Henneberry with no place to hide.

Second were the rumors. Jones was a perfect subject. Since hardly anything was known about his past, there were no facts to restrict speculation. And since Jones never denied anything that was said about him, the rumor-mongers felt completely free to invent stories without fear of being discredited. It was incredible that any man could endure so many fictions. But Jones did. He did not object when it was said that his original compositions were the work of an old musician he subsidized with narcotics. Nor did he refute the rumor that he himself was on heroin. He had nothing to say to the rumors that he was homosexual. He had nothing to say about any of the stories that reached him through the stupid curiosities of jazz-addicts and bellhops and other musicians. He seemed to exist on another plane—a level at which he could not be reached by any of the stones hurled at him.

266

"Get him involved," Bauer had told Henneberry before the tour had left Chicago. "Get him into things. Have him meet people who make him see himself as a great piano player. Just get him to do that."

And in Los Angeles, as in the other cities, Henneberry followed orders. Always diplomatically, he tried to get Jones to attend a party here and a meeting there, to talk with his admirers and hear their praise, to enter a room and stop the conversation and turn it, merely by his presence, to jazz, the piano, himself. At times the pianist was surprisingly willing to go along to the gatherings, but once there would stand against a wall and act totally indifferent to the gushings of female and male idolaters.

In Beverly Hills he was worse. On the second night of a three-day stand the troupe was invited to one of the small palaces after the concert. Jones went, and stood, and drank, and listened, drank some more, and was insultingly unimpressed with the celebrities who moved about him like so many fine flamingos and tapirs. It was not long before antagonism toward him was running close to the surface. And it was then that Henneberry could not help noticing a strange thing. In the antagonism was fear.

They were afraid of Jones. They were all together, at ease in familiar surroundings, and a stranger, only one man, stood against a stuccoed wall and by some silent alchemy made them all act as if he understood them better than they wanted to understand themselves. For the last hour of the evening they avoided him. He seemed to be undisturbed. He sat in a chair and continued drinking.

But Roger, a flamingo said, I cannot for the life of me see how you can *tol*erate such a man. Really, I must say he's in*suf*ferable. Why *is* he that way? Withdrawn, I mean. Look at him standing there watching everything. I could forgive him if it were out of shyness, but somehow I don't *feel* shyness in him. Why *is* he that way?

Henneberry answered that he had a theory.

Do please tell me, she said. Please.

Henneberry said that until he got more evidence to substantiate it he would rather remain silent.

The truth was that Henneberry had no theory. His mind wasn't capable of one when Jones was around. In the pianist's presence Henneberry could feel all his composure disintegrating, his mouth becoming clumsy, his brain running about looking for something to say or do.

As far as anyone could see, Jones never actually tried to unnerve others. He did it without trying.

The wind was from the north by the time the chartered bus nosed eastward across mountains and flatland. By day was the weakening sun and by night the dark balconied halls expanding like bellows with applause. The concert was playing to standing audiences. No collection of all-star jazzmen could have been more successful.

When the star of the show was not actually performing he was in his hotel room. When he wasn't there he would be walking around the cities and towns. And on the bus he would sit by himself near a rear window, his curious, wide-set eyes fixed far in the distance. At first the other musicians had tried to get to know him. And at first he had been pleasant though still reserved, not giving himself to them. But now he was becoming different. He was unapproachable. He sat by himself and lived within himself and gave no part of himself. His eyes were secret. The former easy smile was gone. Now it was warped. Part of two side teeth showed briefly between thin pale lips. Then the smile was gone. It was as if he had tasted something bitter he could not spit out but had to get used to.

In early autumn they pulled into Chicago. With the long

rough riding behind them and with thick bankrolls and clippings of praise in their pockets, the musicians stamped their shoes on the cement and looked at the skyline and were glad to be back. In two weeks they would head east, but until then there was nothing to do except spend their bread and time doing what they wanted. They were high with the feeling as they began hauling their instruments from the bus—and stopped.

Jones was standing with his back to a rear wheel. His hands were in his pockets and as he looked at the city his face seemed to have lost itself in the seeing.

He was looking at only a commonplace modern bus terminal: silent vague faces watching clocks, timetables, luggage strapped and wired and bulky and reflecting highlights of fluorescent above smooth gray cement and tile; bodies moving, legs moving, hurrying, the nameless travelers drinking rootbeer and orange or reading magazines, eyes loose in their heads as strangers regarded strangers, regarded the musicians, forgot, passed on through the station. It was impossible to say what Jones was thinking as he stood by himself and watched, but from the expression on his face it seemed as though he was grateful that he had survived.

14

Schwab turned the key. Shaking rain from his coat, he passed the racks of music and went into the back room. Some animal had been at his Saltines during the night. It took him a couple of minutes to separate the nibbled from the unnibbled. He came out into the store and went behind the counter to prepare for another day.

There was no use in pretending to himself that he hadn't changed. Business no longer meant what it once had. As he moved sluggishly around the store pulling on lights he counted *seven hundred ninety-two, ninety-three, ninety-four,* at the same time wondering if some morning he would reach a thousand. One thousand lights pulled on. Hundreds of keys turned. Thousands of records shelved. Countless crackers thrown away. *Seven ninety-five.*

Outside were straight silver lines of rain against gray sky and red brick. He stood at the window and smoked his pipe.

Was this what he wanted? Really wanted, not something he had to settle for. That was a great trouble. Men settled for life. They wanted "security." They traded their lives for it, and the Hell of it was that the most they accomplished was an uneasy peace with themselves. They calculated: Security = Success; Success = Security. And so few, so pathetically few, realized that genuine security had to be based upon being honest with themselves.

Aha, he thought, coming away from the window and kicking limply at a ball of dust, *I'm being quite smug this morning. Of course I haven't succumbed to the great delusion. I am honest with myself. O yes.*

There was work to be done. He went through the motions. It was, he thought, like reviving a . . . no, it wasn't like that . . . yes it was, it was—like reviving someone who had drowned, had drowned. Like that. That was the way it was. Like reviving someone. You had to keep working at it. You had to go through the prescribed motions because they were traditionally the right motions, and if you kept faith in those motions everything would be all right. Balance the figures, be alert to signs, keep up the motions.

But of late Schwab had found himself increasingly careless about the business. He could not keep his mind on it. At times he had even been tempted to sell out and give it all over. It wasn't that he was simply bored. He had begun to ask himself questions, and all of them, he knew, were because of Jones.

Jones had started everything. From that first night, Jones had altered all of their lives. He had come into their existences and started them doubting—first themselves, then others. It was a dangerous talent he had. Without trying, and certainly not changing his own life, he changed the lives of others. It was as if he were a carrier of a communicable disease.

The morning passed slowly. A ritual. Check listening-booths in order. Dust displays and the piano. Make instant coffee. Select record—today: Chopin—and set it in motion on the console. Drink coffee, refill. Wave to Jerry Murray. Anticipate a customer, watch her move cowlike down the street. Watch for mailman. Listen to Chopin and observe that rain is letting up. Take care of customers—two—ring up a sale, talk baffle to the other and tell her you'd be happy to help if she does decide. Find coffee grown cold. Pour fresh cup. Hello to Arnie, ask him how the Cubs are doing, laugh. Watch for mailman. Light pipe, get busy with paperwork. Wait on customers. Be disappointed with mail.

When the part-time girl came in at eleven-thirty Schwab called Farewell, Lita, and went to lunch. He was not hungry.

He did not want to do this for the rest of his life.

There it was. Sometimes the realization of great things came at strange times. Right now, he noticed, he was reading COLD SLAW and thinking *I wonder how often this happens* when all at once he knew he did not want to do this for the rest of his life.

What he *did* want, he could not say. But perhaps, he considered, it was good enough for a man to know what he *didn't* want. It was a negative way of going about it, of course, but far better than no action at all. And infinitely better than a positive acceptance of something he was in reality only settling for.

On his way back to the store along the damp street Schwab let his mind turn until it came to Jaeger. An archetype, he had once called the pianist. Now, however, that did not seem right. Jaeger was different. He was still gigantically discontent. The moment he gave up trying so hard would be when he would be of the pattern.

A metallic male voice growled that Helen was not in the office today. Schwab dialed her apartment. After five rings she answered with a clogged, sick voice. Nothing was wrong, she said. Just her period.

Schwab asked himself who he was that she should be telling him that. Then he asked her if she had heard from Ross.

Yes, she said, her voice lifting. He had called last night and said that he was hoping to get back to Chicago inside of a month or so. He had sounded better than he had in a long time. New York had been the right thing for him; he had needed the perspective of distance. No, he wasn't working regularly. Gigs, a record-date now and then—that was all. But he had sounded good. He hadn't said anything, or even asked, about Virgil Jones. She had expected him to, but he hadn't.

As Schwab hung up after a minute of small talk he felt dull anger spread in his stomach. Helen was having to pay too much for too brief a happiness. She was too decent and faithful to be subjected to the treatment she was being given. First from Ross. Confused and floundering one minute, absolutely confident the next. Up and down. Full of the sense of his own drama. Indulging it. While she waited with no real assurance. And then there was her family. It required no great perception to see that Helen had to endure their unrelenting opposition to Jaeger. In admitted self-defense she had cut herself off from them. Not completely. Breaks like that were rarely complete. Their jagged edges touched at points, and where they touched was pain. So that was her role: waiting, victimized by the ones she loved.

Now it was evening of a soggy gray day, and he had done nothing but think himself into ennui. He got into his coat and approached the plaster bust on the counter. Blind and deaf and mute, it was a rock to his touch. He could think of nothing to say to it.

He drove badly and impulsively, and inside of an hour discovered himself within a few blocks of the rooms Jones reportedly now lived in. Schwab had never been there. As a matter of fact, he thought, it had been some time since he had even seen the pianist. From a compulsion he deliberately refused to analyze, Schwab parked near the weathered, dingy

273

brick building and pushed the button above the only mail-box without a nameplate. That would be Jones. The buzzer released the door, Schwab went up, and he had been right.

Jones looked as though he hadn't shaved in a month. His white shirt was tucked into the waistband of black corduroy pants, and the shirt had only one button. His cheap black shoes were untied. He closed the door behind Schwab. Then, without an excuse, he left the room.

Schwab stood first on one foot and then the other. He inventoried the room. Chairs, a couch, lamps, a year-old magazine. Everything bare and cold. A cell in a monastery. He sat on the couch, felt its matted horsehair prod his buttocks. From another room, the bathroom, he guessed, came a sloshing sound. Jones was washing clothes. It was a long time before the faucet ran into an empty sink. Then Jones reappeared, sat in a tortuously straight chair. Crossed one leg over the other and actually smiled.

"Do you still have that card?" His face was bone-colored and his hands, lifeless in his lap, seemed to have doubled in size.

"The card you gave me last Christmas? Yes. Why—do you want it back?"

Jones shook his head. After that he merely sat and looked. It was unnerving. He seemed to feel in no way obliged to support his part of a conversation.

"I suppose—" Schwab stopped. He had been about to say *I suppose you're wondering what brings me here,* but first, he knew that Jones wasn't wondering anything of the sort, and second, he himself didn't know why he had come. He decided to tack. "I've been reading of your success."

Still the pianist made no answer. He was either at a complete loss for words or was sadistically enjoying the discomfort caused by his lack of cooperation. His face, however, revealed neither—it was a mask.

274

"From what I've gathered about you," Schwab tried again, feeling more secure when he did not have to bear dead silence, "you should be fairly close to your goal—that is, making enough money on which to retire . . ."

"Yes, I'm pretty close." There was a noticeable absence of satisfaction in his tone.

"Amazing," Schwab said with honesty. "You really intend to quit, don't you? Just as you've said you would. I admire you. Really, I've never met anyone your age who's known so . . . who's exhibited the strength of purpose that you seem to have."

"It's not as hard as all that."

"No? What of the distractions, the million and one things that throw a man off course? Just a little, mind you, just a little off course—but as you know, the error widens the farther a man goes."

Jones shrugged. "Distractions. You make them. They don't have to be distractions if you don't let them be. The only person you can blame is yourself."

Schwab suddenly sharpened his vision. The pianist's hands were no longer calm. Their movements were almost convulsive.

"Yes, yes," he said absently, his eyes still on the hands. With a series of blinks he regained the conversation. "But what are you going to do when you give up the piano? Have you decided where and how you'll live on this money you've saved?"

"No. I'll think of something when the time comes."

"Will you live in a place like this?"

Jones looked around the room. "Probably. It's cheap."

"You wouldn't care to live in your own home?"

"They cost too much."

"Oh, come on now—they cost less than you think, and besides, you'll have plenty of money."

275

"I don't mean that when I say they cost too much."

After a moment of reflection Schwab understood. Jones was not going to share his life with any*thing,* much less anyone. He wanted no responsibilities, no obligations. He was aiming for an impossible goal: 24 hours to himself. Complete, uncompromising independence. It was impossible, as fantastically unattainable as the words on the card Jones had given him that night long ago. Still, he really believed he could do it, and wasn't the conviction half the battle? Would anyone have thought it possible that a young man could walk in off the street, play a piano in some obscure music shop, and in less than a year become one of the most fabulous musicians Chicago—for that matter, the entire country—had ever known? No, it would have been fiction, yet here he sat—still believing in his ability to do anything, believing in himself because he stubbornly refused to not believe in himself.

"Do you know something?" Schwab asked, his words lip-heavy as he sucked on his pipe. "You've affected a great many people since the night you first came into my shop." He waited for a reaction. A pipe was a weapon that way. You held it between your teeth, waited. The man without a pipe was at a disadvantage.

Unless the other man was Virgil Jones. He needed no armament, and when, as now, he did not choose to react, he remained encased in his impenetrable armor of patience.

"A great many people," Schwab repeated, accepting. "This doesn't interest you?"

"Not much. It's happened before. Do you want a glass of water?"

"No—no, thank you." Irritated, he wondered what in the hell had prompted Jones to make such an offer. He shook the curiosity from his mind as a distraction. "You say it's happened before—that is, this affecting people."

"Almost always."

"In what way, may I ask? I'm extremely interested."

"They don't like me. You could even say they hate me."

"Oh, now," Schwab scoffed.

"It's true," Jones said calmly, "but don't think you have to say it isn't to make me feel good. I don't care if people don't like me. Extortion!" With a springlike movement he was on his feet. He rested his hands on top of his light hair. "That's what it is. All the time. People threaten each other. 'Don't do that,' they say. 'I don't approve, and if you keep on doing what you want to do instead of what I want you to do, I won't like you. I might even hate you if you insult me by ignoring this threat.' "

"Do you really believe that?"

"Sure I do. And you probably do too, in your own way, but you don't have to agree with the way I think. That's your business."

Through the sheen of his lenses Schwab saw the wide cold eyes on him. There was no anger, but the face was set hard. Its pale skin was tight over bone. It was the face of a prize-fighter trained to slug to the finish without taking a backward step.

"This doesn't bother you?" Schwab asked.

"What?"

"That people don't like you."

Jones shrugged.

"That they *hate* you?"

Jones moved his mouth indifferently. "I wouldn't own myself if I let people's hate bother me. They'd own me then. That's no way for a man to live—ruled by what other people think."

"I'm surprised." He knew that his short laugh was uneasy. "I can't see how you've managed to get this far. I'd think you would have collided with society at every turn."

277

The pianist smiled faintly. "I've had my crashes." Something in his voice suggested a trace of regret, but he immediately recovered and went on strongly. "Look—I want you to understand this: I'm not running at society all the time. I'm not out looking for fights with people. I'm not saying 'To hell with all you people.' I just don't feel that way. All I'm doing is what I think is the best for me, and I want to be left alone so I can do it. It's the people who won't let me alone who make all the trouble."

Schwab did not know what to answer. He twisted his left thumb and looked vaguely at the yellowed walls.

"You think it's something," Jones said, smiling mysteriously, "that I've been able to go this far, that I can make a thousand dollars a week playing the piano. That I can still be myself, too. It's not so hard. Believe me. You could do it."

"It seems to me that there's the matter of talent involved." He was somewhat surprised to find himself annoyed.

"Talent," Jones said. "That's nothing. Everybody has talent —only they don't use it. The brain is the laziest part of the body. People can do anything if they really try."

"Anything."

Jones extended his underlip, blinked.

"Flying, for instance," Schwab said. "I suppose you could, with this theory of yours, simply flap your arms and fly."

The pianist closed his eyes and held them shut and finally opened them again. His teeth were very white.

"I'm not insane," he said quietly. "Some things are possible and some aren't. All I'm saying is—" Suddenly his face became ashen and contorted; he seized his head in his hands as if to steady it.

Quickly Schwab straightened on the couch. Involuntarily his left hand reached in air.

"What's the matter?"

Jones did not answer. His lips trembled, but he did not answer.

"Is anything wrong?" Schwab called, getting to his feet. "Can I do anything to help? What's wrong?"

Again Jones did not answer. His big strong hands remained wrapped about his head and his eyes were dark pockets.

Helplessly Schwab stared. He tried again to get some response from the pianist, but it was as though an impenetrable wall had been dropped between them. There was no evidence that Jones was able even to hear what was being said to him.

Schwab could do nothing but wait. He was not conscious that his senses were absorbing anything except the sight of the pianist rigid and silent before him. Finally he saw the shoulders relax. With a slow and weak movement Jones' hands came down from his head. The wide eyes were glazed when they opened.

"Can I do anything?" Schwab asked unsteadily.

Jones looked at him. There was no comprehension.

"Can I get a doctor?"

"What?" The word was drained of strength.

"I'll call a doctor if you want, Virgil. Or I can take—"

"No," Jones broke in, "don't bother. It's all over now. Thanks anyway."

"But if there's something wrong you ought to—"

Jones waved his hand in dismissal. "Anything that's wrong is my doing. I can't blame anybody else, and I'm past having some doctor waste his time with me. Besides, he'd need cooperation—" he smiled as if genuinely enjoying the thought "—and you know I'm not so good in that department." He stood, wavered for an instant, and was then his same strong self again except that his eyes were now focused on Schwab's lips.

"Do you mind," Schwab said tentatively, "telling me what's wrong with you?"

"No, I don't mind, but I won't tell you. I guess I ought to be grateful or something for your interest, but as I said before, it's all my doing, this thing, and it wouldn't be right to involve you or anybody else in it. You'd probably start feeling responsible in a way, and that wouldn't be fair because you're really not. So I think now I'll go to bed and you'll go home, and you shouldn't give this another thought, although I suppose you will. Goodnight," he said, and opened the door.

It was later than Schwab had thought when he reached the street. The rain had begun again. The pavement was spangled with striking silver in reflections of lights. He felt sodden, unalert, stupid. He drove straight home and drank two whiskies, and the last thing he remembered was the cool clean pillow under his crowded head.

At four o'clock the next afternoon Jones came into the store.

He had shaved and made himself unusually presentable. He wore a neat blue topcoat, and what could be seen of his pants showed a sharp crease which broke above polished tan shoes.

But he had no apparent interest either in the piano or in any conversation. Acting as though everything worth saying had been disposed of the evening before, he spent a half-hour in desultory attention to pamphlets and views of the street and to answering in a friendly voice the few token courtesies Schwab felt obliged to speak. Then the pianist went out into the dusk.

He was back the next night. And behaved the same way, hoarding his reasons, uninterested in conversation, passing a half-hour.

On the third night he came over to the counter after waiting the thirty minutes. He licked his lips once, brushed an eyebrow with the heel of one hand.

"I'm leaving for New York tomorrow," he told Schwab. "I'll be gone for about two weeks on a tour. Tell that girl Helen to treat herself right."

There was nothing Schwab could do, or say, except that he would tell her, except that he wished Jones good luck in New York, except add a last lame hope that things in general would go well. Beyond that there was nothing to say. No one could invent the words which could get through the armor of this man who was so self-contained that another man could be moved to fear that the same armor might one day prove to be a prison.

15

"I will not be hurried," he said. "The time is coming."

"I'm not trying to press you, Paul—but my God, you understand my position, don't you?"

Paul Bauer's chalky old face stared stubbornly out the window of the hotel suite. The glass looked oily with beads of rain. Below, ten stories down, traffic inched in the wet dusk of New York. The height was terrible. A distant clock wore its orange hands straight up and down. Behind him he heard the announcer fuming and sighing and pacing.

"Sit down," he commanded, turning. "There is nothing you can do. This doesn't concern you until I say so."

"And when will that be?"

"Soon."

" 'Soon.' Splendid. *Soon.* How long can I live on that? In the meantime Jones continues dictating to us, making a fortune, making more money than he's ever seen before . . . while I get nothing but the scraps. Oh yes, yes, I know— you're not making any money, but you can afford to play the game, whatever it is. But think of me, will you? How long can I maintain my reputation and position when every jazz fan, the stupid asses, sees that I have no control over Jones? What did they think last night when the lunatic walked onstage in the middle of my introduction and began playing before I could even get offstage?"

Bauer would be silent. He would let Henneberry rave. The smooth fat face belonged to a fool. What did the fool want? It was clear that he did not really know. Delusions of grandeur. A half-formed notion that he, Roger Henneberry, could be another Paul Bauer. One who was above mere wealth of paper and silver. One who controlled living human beings. That was what he thought he wanted. People, Jones, buckling before him. What a joke. Given the chance—right now, suddenly, this night—Henneberry wouldn't have the sense to do one thing right. He would puff himself up and tell Jones now that he, Henneberry, was organizing everything, there would be some changes made. Signed agreements. Recording contracts. Personal appearances. Contracts. And inside of five minutes Henneberry would be shattered.

"—when he refuses, openly, everything I—"

"Oh shut up, announcer. I'm sick of your whining. Hand me last night's sheets."

As he read the figures he heard the door close roughly. He was relieved to be alone. It was much easier to calculate when fools weren't around to interrupt.

Yes, the time was coming. The plan was exhausting and devious, but there was the satisfaction of knowing that no one, not even the announcer, could guess it. Secretly, painstakingly, giving ground here, altering defenses there, Bauer had led Jones closer and closer to the point at which he wanted him. It would not be long now. A month, perhaps two; it depended on how soon the pianist's behavior indicated that success had made a deep change in him.

Bauer let the papers scale to the rug. With thin fingers he felt his jawbones, temples, the crown of his skull. Suddenly he had an idea that his eyes were dark sockets. He leaped up, kicked at the papers, hurried to the window and read the orange clock again.

There had been bad moments. Like the afternoon he had burned the blades of grass from his back lawn. That had been nerve-tearing.

But even now it was with him. Supposing he should fail? What if the trap would spring and Jones would leap clear just in time? Or if he would be caught in it but would still have the strength to pry it open and emerge as strong and defiant as ever? The triumph was not in catching him in the trap. It was in crushing him so that he could not escape.

His lips thinned in a taut smile. How easy the others had been. For them there had been no need of elaborate plans. Their defeats had been certainties from the beginning.

Bontemps: the old Negro he had exhumed four years ago: pay in cash. Watch him come alive again on the stage of the jazz-festival, on the stands of intimate, expensive clubs where jeweled women and gold-cuffed men came to hear an authentic piano of early jazz. Give Bontemps everything his simple cannibal soul hungered for. Pay in cash and watch him drape himself in bright colors, see him smile showing two white stars in shining gold, see him so drunk that he giggled when told he would get no more money, he was through.

Like all the others—like Jaeger. Easy. Encourage his disease; spread the infection with praise. See his need take it like food. Watch him struggle with the fever of greatness. Count the money he brought in. It had not mattered that he had ended the contract of his own accord. Bauer had been past caring. He had established his superiority. Jaeger had begun to bore him.

Idly he recalled from somewhere that Jaeger was even now here in New York. Probably pitying himself, and, most likely, worrying too much about Jones. It was strange that

Jaeger hadn't contacted any of the concert troupe either backstage after last night's performance or at the hotel.

Without fully knowing why he was doing it, Bauer uncradled the telephone and began calling booking agents and other informants. A few of them reported having seen Jaeger only recently. That he had been "not so high" was pretty well agreed on, but what he was really doing with himself now was anybody's guess. He wasn't working steadily; that much was certain. He seemed to be going with the directions of the wind.

Why the interest? they wanted to know. If they should see Ross should they tell him Bauer was asking about him?

Bauer answered that he did not care what they told him.

He lowered the phone. His curiosity had been satisfied. It made no difference that Jaeger would learn of his interest and might try to get help from him again. He would get none. Only a fool would waste himself in giving help when there was no chance of a return.

Self-approval hardened him as he dressed to go out. He would go to the concert and sit in the balcony and return to the hotel when Jones finished. He did not wish to be staying at the same hotel as the pianist. Only a juvenile would be attracted to living such a risk of exposure. Bauer was not so stupid. He was old, and his life had been right, was right, and the time was coming when he would show the pianist that one man could never stand alone.

It was the same as the previous night. At eight o'clock aisles were swarming. By eight-fifteen both balconies were filled and but a few gaps showed on the main floor. Some of the faces had been in the huge hall the night before. One of them was Ross Jaeger's.

At the rear on the main floor he slouched in his seat as if he did not want to be seen. With his elbows on both armrests, he had both hands joined and held in front of his face with the ends of his thumbs against his lips. Every so often he changed the cross of his legs and shifted nervously in the seat, but he did not once take his hands away from his face.

He watched the people crowding in. To see Jones. To see if he was as great as they had heard and read.

It used to be for me, he thought. *I used to stand back there and go through half a pack listening to them come in. I even remember wishing I didn't have to get out there at all.*

And now he was on the other side of the curtain, sitting far back and concealing his face with his hands, half-pretending to himself that it was really a more restful position. Now Jones was behind the curtain, and all the wish-I-weres were out here. The has-beens, too. He parted his teeth and bit the tip of his right thumb. The has-beens. Like Ross Jaeger. Remembered just as much as DeWitt, only the difference was that DeWitt had more of a right to be forgot. He was dead.

When the lights dimmed he sat up and let his hands drop into his lap and cocked his head slightly to the right in order to miss none of the sounds. He could hear the flutter of a trumpet—that would be Allred . . . no, it was Marshall —and the delicate, exercising runs on the piano and soft drum-rolls tagged with a kick-off on the bass. His trained ear listened to everything filtering through the curtain, and he knew at least five seconds before any in the crowd that the concert was ready to go.

But when the first absolute melody broke the curtains and pulled the sudden gathering wave of applause and whistles from the audience, Jaeger sat back and made no effort to listen. He had not come this second night to hear the stageful of them, even if they were doing a fine job on *Jumping With.* Jones was the one he had come to hear.

During the first set he longed to go out in the lobby for

a smoke or across the street for a good drink, but he knew that if he pushed past the half-row of knees he would be recognized. So he sat through the long session without any real interest or appreciation, and went along with the crowd in their applause only to avoid being noticed and identified.

At the intermission he hurried out and continued all the way into the hot clinging night air in which he stood in a shadow and smoked two cigarettes end-to-end. There was no taste to the cigarettes; he looked down at the crushed and blackened stubs and wondered why he had even bothered. *I'm getting so nothing's any good any more,* he told himself. *I've got to get off this kick.* But even as he thought it he knew that they were only words, and that it was a lot easier to say them than to make them work.

Waiting inside again, Jaeger could only stare sightlessly toward the curtained stage and hope that Jones would not be like he'd been the night before. He had been too good. It had not been only his piano artistry that had sent the audience away talking with hands because they could not find words to describe what they had heard—it had been Jones' whole being. From the minute he had walked into the middle of Henneberry's usual pretentious, self-indulgent introduction, Jones had announced with every move he made that he was not awed by New York or by its imposing audience or by the critics who were supposedly so powerful. And when Henneberry had awkwardly retreated toward the wings Jones had sat at the piano with no trace of nervousness, or even of interest in the audience, and had given New York forty minutes of one of the best jazz pianos it had ever witnessed.

Jaeger shook his head as the hall darkened. There was no use competing with a man a whole city couldn't beat.

When the curtains parted the spotlight blazed not on centerstage but on the piano, and there was Jones, already into the opening bars of a melody no one could hear for the sudden rolling applause. Jaeger smiled crookedly. Henneberry was not even in sight for the introduction. Jones had done something in a single night that no jazzman had been able to do in years: show Henneberry up for the phoney he was.

But for the rest of Jones' performance Jaeger did no more smiling. He watched and listened, and what he heard crushed him. Jones was every bit as great as he had been the night before. He played a completely different program than he had the first night, and, try as he could, Jaeger was not able to hear either a mistake or any other hint that Jones was unsure of what he was doing.

When it was over Jaeger again pushed through the pack milling for the exits and night air and smokes, but he did not intend to stay for the last set. He had heard Jones—that was enough. He poked a cigarette into his mouth and tried irritably to circle a group of loud young couples. It took him what seemed ten minutes to force his way through the lobby and onto the street, and then he found that his cigarette had gone out.

Lighting it, he looked back toward the swarming entrance, and in the hot brief matchflare came the realization that no one had called out to him, no one had asked for his autograph, no one had stepped back to let him pass.

He let the match fall. It would go out, he thought, when it struck the pavement.

16

What you say, man? said some mouths. Other mouths stayed on reeds and mouthpieces, and eyes shifted.

Jaeger edged through the clutter on the sound-stage and slapped a pack of cigarettes on top of the piano. He pulled off his white trenchcoat and threw it onto an empty tubular chair and rubbed the chill from his hands. His face was pale. The uneven light made dark hollows of his eyes. After lighting a cigarette he strayed to the drums and began talking with Heard.

It was early afternoon and they had all got together to cut four sides. Two were to be vocals. A few of the men said they'd heard Billie was supposed to do them; others said no, The Wig would show up any minute. None of them seemed to care very much. It was all jazz. Four takes was a good afternoon's work, but blowing with an outfit like this was painless. That is, if everybody held up.

After about five minutes Jaeger went back to the piano and began exercising with block chords and riffs and triads. He touched the stub of his cigarette to a fresh one and smoked without using his hands. His eyes pinched against the smoke. Somebody blasted three fast shocks on a trumpet. A smooth, breathy tenor started gliding into *Lester Leaps In*. The bass came in, and Heard flashed out his brushes and sifted in the beat. In less than two choruses all of them were working it over. The recording director despaired. Time cost money, and here they were fooling around with *Lester* when it wasn't scheduled at all. Everything was very disorganized.

"All right, all right," he called, forcing his way to the center of the pack. He looked like a worried bulldog. "That's enough—there. Hey! Let's go now, fellows. Let's get some work done—we haven't got all day with this. Come on, come on . . . . ."

"Well shoot, Jim," said the alto man, "we just messin' till you give us a notion what we gonna blow. Can't spect a—"

"Okay, okay. All right, here's the pitch—I don't care which one you fellows cut first, but we're going to do *If I Had You* and *Love Is Just Around the Corner.* All right . . . sure, I know—" he pushed placating hands in the smoky air "—you've all done them before . . . but this Jones has dusted them off again and they're going to get a big play. So let's make it now, men. How about it?"

When Jones had been mentioned several pairs of eyes had cornered to the piano where Jaeger sat with a fixed half-smile and his hands dead on the keys. He did not say anything. After a minute or so he looked up with an expression that said he wanted to get going and get it over with. The rest of them gave him the choice. He tapped out a slow, firm beat with his heel and led them into *If I Had You.*

They went through once, twice, stopping for suggestions, going back to test a passage, experimenting, altering and trying phrasings until they lost count of the versions.

After a long while they had pretty well homed in on it, and then they made a test and listened to the playback. They heard Jaeger lagging badly behind the trombone break, and the alto came in rough and too soon on the final chorus.

They tried again. This time the alto was all right, but

Jaeger was still missing. As he listened to his mistakes his face knotted with concentration and embarrassment. The others glanced at him. The director whispered to one of the technicians.

The booth gave them the go ahead again. Jaeger laid down the beat and lashed at the keys in an icy, controlled fury as he tried for perfection.

And he found it. They all listened to the playback and when it was over they shouted at him and grinned and said Jesus Christ, man, you blew a hell of a lot of piano in there. There was a long huddle in the booth and the director came out and announced that that had been it. A good side. The tension lifted as surely as if it could have been measured by a needle.

But still Jaeger sat hard-faced and scowling at the keyboard. He seemed to disbelieve their praise and to be half-angry that they had given it.

They were taking a break during versions of *Love Is Just Around the Corner* when Wray Carter came in, all hips and hair and wild hot eyes, her spike heels like malletblows on the asphalt tile and her mouth thrilled wide as she saw Jaeger. Behind her trailed Sol, her manager, grimly proud like a pet trained to carry papers—in this case, arrangements for which he had paid a total in four figures. She wrenched the sheaf from his hands and dropped it on top of the piano.

"Well here's my daddy," she said, reaching down to fondle the crisp hairs on the back of Jaeger's neck. "I didn't think the bit would be *this* good, baby. Why didn't somebody tell me?" she ended with a shout.

The other musicians simply looked back at her. A fine swinging chick, their faces said, but she sure could bug a session with all the noise she was always putting down.

"Listen, Wray—" the director said as though trying to

touch a snake "—we've almost got it made with the second side . . ."

"Give the girl some room," her manager said.

"I am, Sol, but remember—this is my show and what I say—"

"O my ass," Wray broke in. "I can't say hello to a man without you two getting all charged up."

"She's going," Jaeger said, and then to her: "Sit down and be a good girl and when we're through with this we'll make some music. Go on, sit over there and shut up for five minutes."

She did. Everybody stopped arguing. The break ended with all of them looking at Jaeger as if he had suddenly become ten feet tall and had all the answers.

And that was the way the second side was made. Jaeger led and the others followed. He inspired them to a performance they found hard to believe even when they heard it played back to them. None of them could guess what had happened inside Ross, but whatever it had been had made him the closest thing to perfection they had ever heard.

But again, just as before, Jaeger did not seem impressed with his achievement. He did not relax or smile. He ate cigarettes and sat waiting impatiently for Wray Carter to get on with her vocals.

The Wig was chastised. She stood near the piano and listened as Jaeger pressed out her arrangement of *A Foggy Day*. Not once did she criticize. He went through it once more, and then the whole group took it on. They blew it very soft and slow and beautiful.

"All right," Jaeger said, holding the final chord, "take it."

She got into position at the microphone, watched the signal from the director, unclenched her hands and began to sing.

She did not get far. On the second chorus her voice slipped

and she swore and backed away from the mike. The accompaniment dragged on for a few bars and then died. The control booth exchanged hand signals with the director. None of the musicians acted upset. And Jaeger waited cold and nerveless for her to begin again.

This time she got all the way through it, but stepped back from the microphone and said she wasn't satisfied. No, she did not even want to hear the playback. She wanted to try again.

Few of the musicians had ever seen her like this. Usually she had such a high opinion of herself that she wouldn't admit being so far from perfection. Usually she belted out a vocal once or twice and said The hell with it, I was great. What's next now? Now, however, her arrogance was gone. Even the way she stood seemed to admit that she knew she had to do better to be worthy of the group accompanying her.

She tried again, and again, and after each try her eyes drifted to Jaeger, and he would look back at her, and then she would frown and say she would like to give it another go.

After the eighth complete effort Jaeger did not return her look. He rubbed his eyes with his knuckles and began searching for her next arrangement.

By the time *Lover* was finished mouths and shirt collars were wet and hanging open. Dully the jazzmen lounged in their chairs. Wray sat with her elbows on her knees and listened with her eyes blank in order to hear better. *Lover* was all right. The director smiled weakly and reached for another carton of coffee. Wray's manager, as haggard as if he himself had done the vocals, brought her coat and shook his head slowly in grudging admiration. There was nothing left for the musicians to do but pack their instruments and go home for a nap before starting their jobs.

Jaeger had nothing to pack. With his trenchcoat like a cape over his shoulders he was already making for the door.

"Ross—"

He stopped, waited for her.

"Man . . . I just don't know what to say. You were the most today."

He nodded his thanks. His bony face was still haggard, serious.

"You getting something to eat?" Wray wanted to know. "Let's you and me put away a steak and some Scotch, what do you say? You can come up—"

"No thanks. I couldn't eat an egg."

"Something wrong, man?"

He shook his head, started to leave again. But this time he was blocked off by the other jazzmen. They held out their hands, gave him broad smiles, told him they'd never heard him blow better. He had been real great, they told him. What was next? Did he want to start up a combo again?

Jaeger told them he was thinking about it but that nothing was set yet. He didn't have any plans.

They did not want him to leave. They wanted to be around this man they had just heard do great things to a piano. They wanted to put their hands on him and remember.

Watching him leave alone with his coat still thrown carelessly over his square shoulders, Wray Carter cleaned her teeth with her tongue and made her eyes surly. She was thinking. With the hand that was not carrying the arrangements Sol coaxed her elbow.

As they stepped out into the chill, bare street she squinted in vain for the white trenchcoat. She shook her frizzled head.

"Something's wrong with him."

"Who?" her manager asked.

"Ross, you schmuck."

"It didn't sound like it today," he said without interest.

"I don't mean that. Something else." She was talking to squares of pavement. "Maybe I ought to call that girl of his in Chicago."

"Listen, hon—let me give you a little advice . . ."

"Go to hell, will you? This is my business."

"Is it?"

"You're damned right it is. Bad enough to see a man like Ross be brought down like he's been for the past few months, but when he starts playing great again and *still* isn't out of it—well . . ."

"Jaeger's always been that way."

"That's how much you know." Her heels tapped angrily on cement.

"I know enough to keep my nose where it belongs."

"Sure, and I know where that is . . ."

"Don't be funny, Wray. And don't forget—everybody knows Jaeger for what he is. A great pianoman who wants to be so great that any other piano'll be illegal. Jelly Roll and James P. and Fats and Tatum and Garner and Jones all rolled into one. That's what Jaeger wants to be. You can't do anything for him. A man like that needs a head-doctor."

They walked in silence until they reached Sol's Cadillac. Wray made no motion to get in.

"I thought we were going to have dinner, Wray."

"Changed my mind. Food. Jesus, that's all you think about, you blimp." Her painted face contorted with disgust.

Sol endured like a martyr long-used to suffering. "Can I drop you anywhere then?"

"Right here. See you tonight," she growled, and wheeled like an angry little animal and walked off.

"Nine-thirty!" he called after her.

But she did not receipt his reminder. With short, choppy

steps she pounded along the sidewalk and when within a block two men spoke to her she fried their ears without the slightest break in stride.

He paced the rug where reflected light formed a depthless square. He tried to work his mind.

This was success. In the day you stood on a pedestal and looked down on the shy, fawning, flattering crowd, but at night, alone, you had a headache and your fingers ached and outside a voice called in the darkness, but not for you, and the insects under the washbasin were not impressed with you.

Strange—when you wanted something so much, and got it, it became ashes in your hands. Grayness blown away with the first wind. And outside a voice called in the darkness, but not for you.

Recrossing the dank and disordered room, Jaeger caught sight of himself in the cloudy mirror. He stopped, stared, let his breath escape between his teeth. Then he resumed pacing. From somewhere behind the wall came the trickling sound of plaster. He sat on the bed, then slumped and put his hands over his eyes.

And what if it hadn't really been success? What if all of them had agreed beforehand to feed him praise? What if what they'd done was only a gigantic lie born out of pity for him? Yes, that could have been behind this afternoon. They could have been lying to him when he had actually been no better than he had before. Of course—give Jaeger a hand; he needs it in the worst way. He ran out of Chicago because Jones was too much for him. He's been living in a fleapit for months, afraid to come out, afraid to go back. Lie to him. Tell him he's better than he ever was. Give the poor son of a bitch a hand. He needs it.

He lurched from the bed and smashed his right fist into

296

his palm. Then he sloshed another three fingers of whiskey into the glass and went to the window.

Below was the cement. Three floors down. To one side glittered the fragment of the street. A couple walked languidly, arm-in-arm. All of them, everybody, stamped from the same mold—same eyes, same teeth, stomachs, feet, brains —six million in the city, and not two different. An arrangement that never changed.

He looked three floors down and began sweating profusely.

Breathing openmouthed, he came away from the window. He pulled at his left ear for no reason at all.

As long as he played the piano, Jones would block his path. Meanwhile he would grow older, less able to experiment, to dare, less able to absorb new ideas and to spend ten hours a day perfecting them.

He thought of Bern DeWitt. He was gone. He might as well have never been. And Romeo? Would he be remembered on those Saturday nights he dreamed of? No. He would be a name—nothing more, and in time all the labels would peel from all the records.

That was what happened. You were born, and lived, and died, and that was the end. You did not even leave a scratch on a wall to say *I was here*.

For a long time he sat on the bed and stared at his hands. Then he went to the bureau and with shaking fingers found a large manila envelope. He rummaged for a pencil. There was none. He searched the pockets of all his tailored suits and still found nothing with which he could write. It was fifteen minutes before he gave up and let the envelope fall to the floor.

Then he went to the window and opened it and carefully crawled out on the sill. He sat there, his feet hanging in space, his eyes shut tight and his brain swollen against his skull. He did not know who he was. His brain would not tell him all the things he wanted to think about. Ross Jaeger was not sitting here. He was not out on this ledge in the darkness. Jaeger was somewhere else—somewhere where people fought to touch him.

One motion. A sudden kick of his heels against the bricks below and he would catapult into space. Space   PAIN   Nothing.

The night air became strangely warm.

Became hot.

So hot that there was no breathing.

He felt himself going, fainting forward, his head submerged in a soaking roar, and with a sudden terrific awakening he twisted and clawed brick and wood and pulled in pain and fell facedown on the thin, filthy rug. His left hand, beginning to bleed from two torn fingernails, lay in the bare space under the basin where a panicked silverfish flickered and disappeared.

THREE

THREE

I

On a soft and vaporous night Jones returned to the city. This time he was not alone. Now he was surrounded by musicians and reporters and pressagents and besieged by hundreds of eyes that recognized him in the train station. This time he was not wearing a leather jacket and carrying a cardboard suitcase. Now he wore an expensive black topcoat and gripped an alligator case, both of which, along with two suits and a pair of shoes, he had accepted from a woman who had denounced him in the lobby of the Hotel Commodore his last night in New York.

He stayed in his cheap, sealed room on the Northwest Side for only one night. The next morning he moved into an apartment-hotel just out of the high rent district on the North Side. When he paid for the key he had instructed the manager to admit no one to his rooms either in person or by telephone. Even the maid was to have advance permission to change his linen.

But it was no use. He could not stay in his rooms forever, and when he went out the sidewalks were free and in the lobby were those whom the manager did not dare defy. Out of chairs and cars slid a television producer, agents, recording directors, photographers and writers, piano salesmen seeking a testimonial, promoters, musicians trying to get

Jones to front their combos, nightclub-owners, people who simply wanted his money, and the never-discouraged pack asking his autograph, his touch, a piece of his clothing. There were times when he nearly had to punch his way free.

No matter where he went it was almost always the same. Since his conquest-by-concert of New York he had been publicized as a genius who made himself inaccessible to everyone. He wanted to be alone. Therefore people did not want him to be alone. They insisted upon knowing him. He could not walk the streets or eat a meal in peace. Perhaps only one person in a crowd would recognize him, but that was enough.

The more he tried to be free, the more it was a challenge to all of them. Each in the crowd wanted to be the one who would finally break down his barricade.

He remained massively indifferent. His eyes were nearly always unfocused, ignoring the hands and arms and shouted offers and words of praise. He was deaf and blind and dumb. His actions seemed to say that no matter how thoughtless, inconsiderate and selfish these people might be, he would never lower himself to let them have any part of his right to be himself.

On the sixth day he accepted Henneberry's offer. The Place, a new jazz-spot in the heart of The Loop, was guaranteeing him three hundred dollars a night to follow Shearing for two weeks. Of course, the announcer said, this was an Extraordinary Thing inasmuch as usual booking procedures had been abandoned. It was a Real Tribute that Jones' popularity was such that it could violate all the stringent rules. And, naturally, the next time Jones returned to Chicago the salary would be doubled if not increased still more.

The pianist listened with his usual bland, careless, unimpressed mask of a face. From his expression it seemed that he had assumed all along that rules would be changed for him.

Unexpectedly, however, without any warning, his first night at The Place had its manager and just about everyone else running in circles.

At nine-thirty he was not there. The jammed, overflow crowd did not take to the idea of paying eighty-five cents for beer without getting Jones in return. As jazzmen in the crowd observed: the natives were getting restless.

At ten o'clock he had still not appeared. Telephone calls were made, other nightclubs were searched, threats were muttered. The crowd had given up all pretense of patient tolerance.

When he finally came in at twenty after ten the crowd parted as though he was carrying a bomb. He made no sign to show that he heard any of the things said to him in passing. He went directly to the stand, flopped his coat across the pianotop, and sat down. In the sudden brighter lights his face looked as if all the blood had drained from it. The crowd whispered uneasily.

He played *Lover Come Back to Me.* Brilliantly. Staggering with its power and invention, stunning everyone. But when he struck the final chord he closed his eyes and put his left hand to the side of his head. Then he walked off the stand and went into the back room.

After five minutes, in the middle of the wondering, dumbfounded wave of whispers, he came back.

And this time he started a marathon.

At eleven-thirty the manager was speechless. The crowd outside could not get in to spend its money because the crowd inside would not leave as long as Jones was playing. Those inside, afraid of drinking themselves beyond paying for this great night, drank as though their glasses were nippled. The Place was paralyzed.

Several attempts were made to get him away from the

piano. Each time there was no response. He seemed to have gone deaf.

The manager stalked back and huddled over the telephone behind the bar. He dialed so viciously that he got the wrong number. He swore and tried to calm himself, but when he heard Henneberry's silvery *Henneberry* his composure flew to pieces.

"This is what you give me!" he sputtered into the mouth-piece.

"Please be brief, Solly. I am on the air."

"I don't give a good goddamn where you are. I'm here, and I've got this Jones on my hands." He told Henneberry what was going on.

"Of course," the voice said loftily.

"Of course, hell! What kind of a business do I got—damn it—what kind of business do I have when I don't have any turnover?"

"You're not the—hang on, Solly, I have to dispense wisdom to my admirers . . ."

The manager gripped the dead phone and glared back to the piano. Jones was still there, still playing, still holding all the people in their chairs. A sabotager, the manager thought wildly. That's what he was. A sabotager.

". . . As I was saying—"

"That don't interest me right now. I've had more clubs in this town than you can count, Henneberry, and this is the first time I've been hosed with a guy like this Jones. What'm I supposed to do? I have to close up at three, and the way he's going it looks like he's going to be going till Christmas."

"*As I was saying*—you're not the businessman I thought you were, Solly. The publicity—"

"I'm paying him four hundred a—"

"Three hundred," Henneberry said quickly.

"Okay, so he doesn't know . . ."

"It would not be wise for him to find out."

"Okay, okay—quit changing the subject. So if I was paying him a hundred I couldn't see a take, the way he's acting."

The earpiece sighed. "I told you, Solly, you couldn't buy this kind of publicity if you wanted to. Why, I'll even mention it on my show tonight . . ."

"Thanks," the manager said sourly. "So I get all the people in the town and no place to put them. They start lining up in front in the morning, like it was a World Series or something. By eight the place is filled and there's a thousand on the sidewalk who can't get in. So great. So this Jones shows up and plays all night and none of them leave here inside. Now what kind of—"

"Talk to Paul, Sol. I have to leave. Talk to Paul." There was a metallic click.

The manager let the phone drop hard in its cradle. He compressed his lips and spread his hands helplessly. All the talk was true: Bauer was behind Jones. It explained a lot of things. But he did not want to talk to Paul Bauer. Bauer was one man you didn't tell what you wanted or didn't want.

Yet even as the manager admitted his helplessness in such a vise, he could not help wondering why Bauer was letting the pianist get away with so much. There had to be a reason. All along—from the time Jones had first made himself known until now—everyone in the business looked at this pianoman as a double-Bromo headache. Not that he was one of the usual prima donnas swaggering and posing as if he'd just been elected God. That would have been simple. There were a lot of those around, and they were easy to handle. All you had to do was remember to pretend they were impressing you. Then they gave you about as much trouble as white mice.

305

But this Jones was different. Nothing worked with him. He did things in his own way, and if you wanted him to do them your way, he still did them his way. And what could you do with a man like that?

Nearly a week later, Henneberry was still breathing curses into his cupped hand. Vaguely his senses absorbed the dials, toggle-switches, soundproofed walls, the honeycombed microphone before him, the face of his engineer behind glass, an unplaced odor of shellac, the filtered voice of Anita O'Day even now flowing out of radiospeakers all over the city this night.

This was what he was, also. Only a voice—altered, impersonal—killed by a twist of a dial. Not even that. Not even on a record. Not hardened, permanent.

He had been played for a fool. Both Paul and the pianist were making a fool of him. Paul had promised to give Jones to him, but even after almost a year all it had come to was a promise. *Soon. Be patient.* Yes, patience in the face of such a loss. Thousands of dollars to be made from the pianist, and still he, Henneberry, had to be content with hundreds. Bones to the dog.

He had thought that the tour was going to give him the chance to get a grip on Jones and to use him, but the pianist had refused to be held. He had gone on in his own quietly stubborn way, and had made a fool of everyone who had tried to control him. He had made caricatures of them all.

And Jones was still doing it, only more so, at The Place. No one challenged him.

Why?

Between pronouncements on records and commercials read with the disdainful apathy he thought they deserved, Henneberry fondled the question like a fragile vase.

Why? Why had Paul done nothing? Why had he given

in, and given in, and given in still more to the pianist? Why had he refused to meet Jones face-to-face? And, most of all, why was Jones allowed to continue in his untouchable independence?

There was a reason. There had to be. It was not senility that made Paul appear helpless to shackle the pianist. It was something else.

Later that night, wandering offended and petulant over the soft crush of his carpet, Henneberry resolved to force the issue. This absurdity could not go on forever. One man—an unknown vagrant who had walked in off the street—dictating to every critic and agent and promoter as if he considered them not an ounce more important and powerful than himself. Jones. A million Joneses, and one of them had the nerve to upset the entire order of things. It wasn't safe to let a man like that go unchecked.

Savagely Henneberry seized the telephone. In a minute he hung up and shaped his mouth into bitterness. Well, he would call again in the morning, the afternoon, at night, if he had to. Paul would answer sooner or later. This time, however, promises would not be accepted. Roger Henneberry would demand satisfaction.

He was totally unprepared for the telephone jangling him from a sleep of spiraling dreams. His vision seemed masked by gauze as he grumbled lumpily into the livingroom pale with morning. He fumbled the telephone to his ear.

"You are an idiot."

Shocked, his eyes popped, saw: morning, couch, driftwood on the table, his toenails foully yellow on thick feet. He wrinkled his lips in distaste at his dishevelment.

"Paul—I was about to call you," he said, angry with his voice that it was not yet awake and imposing.

"I'm not interested in what you were getting ready to do. I want to know what you've been doing . . ."

"Why, I've—"

"You were supposed to keep me posted on Jones."

The announcer felt his stomach turn. He sat down heavily in a wrought-iron-and-canvas chair. His mouth managed to ask what had happened.

"Last night," said the hard, flat voice, "Jones got himself in a fine fix at the club. He's over in Cook County now."

"In *jail?*" He was violently awake.

"That's right." Strangely enough, Bauer's voice had toned down and did not sound upset. It seemed almost satisfied. "Nothing to strain yourself about—you wouldn't be able to do anything anyway. I've taken care of everything already. He'll be out in an hour or two."

"My God, Paul, what did he do?"

"Walked out, that's all. When he finished his set about eleven-thirty he went outside. Everybody figured he was getting some air, but he didn't come back."

"At *all?*"

"I said he didn't come back, didn't I? Well, your bright friend Solly is about as bad as you. When the crowd kept giving him hell because Jones wasn't there to play, he lost his head. Took two of his boys and started looking."

"And where did they find him?" He was too fearful to object to the insult Bauer had flung at him.

"They didn't. They spent a couple of hours looking all over the city and ended up waiting outside that place he lives in. When he finally showed up—I don't care how it started—there was a fight."

Henneberry moaned.

"You're damned right," the voice snapped. "And both this Solly and you are lucky nobody got hurt. I've had to buy some people to put the fix in—what happened is dead and is going to stay dead and Jones is going back in Solly's place as if nothing's happened—and it's going to be worth it. In about two weeks it'll pay off."

"Two weeks?"

"You heard me, announcer. Two weeks. Now listen: I don't want one single slip-up. Drop the ball just once and you're through. I mean it, and you know it. After last night I've decided I've got our brave Mister Jones just about where he ought to be. I'm not waiting any more. So here's what you're going to do. Line him up for a concert here two weeks from now."

"Paul, I can't make—"

"You're not going to have any trouble," the voice knifed in. "I take care of that. All you have to do is make the noise for this show. It's going to be the biggest thing this town's ever seen, and Jones is Number One, understand? He's the hero—nobody else matters. I'll get the biggest names around for the card, but Jones gets all the play. That clear?"

"But you can't—"

"Don't tell *me* I can't! I can do anything, and that's the way it's going to be. Then, the morning after the show, the three of us are going to have a business meeting . . ."

Henneberry stood with so much excitement that he nearly dropped the telephone.

"Good!" he shouted into the mouthpiece. "Excellent, Paul —just excellent! This meeting . . . after it . . . I can have him then?"

"Yes." There was a silence. "I'll be through with him then."

2

When her eyes first opened she did not know what year it was. Pale gold of the cold morning fell in horizontal lines across the peach-colored blanket, drew broken lines on the dark dresser, the heap of clothing draped on a chair, the walls. In shadows she saw a large photograph of herself. She moved her hand into a stripe of light which had no warmth.

As her eyes unveiled she lay motionless, thinking. This was a morning in his bed. She could feel the heat of him sleeping beside her. He was happening again to her. Everything was the same as it had always been.

But when she moved her head softly to one side and looked at him she knew it was a lie.

Ross was dead. His thick dark hair was tangled and unclean, his face the color of bones. From his lips came the shallow breathing of exhausted sleep. He was weak. He was dead.

She was not conscious of time as she lay attempting to decide to decide. And as she thought she challenged herself with the memory that her past decisions had really been avoidances, escapes, delays and compromises. She had actually done nothing to help Ross. She had existed—that was all. She had slept with him and listened to his fears and had consoled and encouraged him, and even now, as she remembered, part of her insisted that she had done all she could, all any woman could be expected to do. A woman was designed to be absorbed by a man. She was made to be submerged, to give up her self to the man.

Again she looked at his sleeping face. And this time the other part of her said that perhaps she had lied to herself again, she had failed, she had failed both herself and him by passivity, by enduring his weaknesses instead of demanding his strengths.

After a long while she slipped out of the bed, wound one of his Sulka robes about her, and went into the kitchen. It looked like a garden of bottles, and he had been back only one week.

When she had cleaned the sink and set the table she made coffee and had her first cigarette with it. She felt strangely at peace, sitting in the embrace of cashmere, feeling erotic and potent from the sensual pleasures of this warming kitchen and its brown, steamy odor of coffee curling inside glistening windowpanes. She smoked another cigarette. There was still no sound out of the bedroom.

Next she made a huge breakfast of bacon and eggs and raisin toast limp with butter, arranged it all neatly on the table, and went to Ross and kissed him awake. He mumbled, smiled, agreed and tasted his mouth, smiled again, but when his eyes came open they would not hold to hers. Even when he entered the kitchen and admired all the food, his eyes were vague and shifting. It was a habit he had had before, but not nearly as evident as now.

He had another habit, and all during breakfast it hurt her.

It reminded her of men on West Madison Street, the ragged men of Skid Row. Every time Ross had driven her along that street she had not been able to forget. With almost total recall she saw the dull hopeless faces either stubbled or too raw and blotched, the pack of dirt-colored bodies crowded in storefronts, in hallways, around a lifted bottle, the scarecrow bodies propped against green boxes for garbage disposal. She could see again windrows of filth and paper, stores of whiskey, stores of Jesus. Glass bandaged with fluttering signs of homestyle soup. Sunken mouths of hags needing teeth. The crutches, pinned pantslegs, pinned sleeves. But most of all she saw the way old men, young men, the hags, everyone, cringed before the Cadillac. Before every car. Even when the car was making a turn and the stoplight had given them the right-of-way, they cringed and tottered back to the curb. They did not defer, nor was it a simple retreat. They cringed. And she would see them and stifle the cry, *Hate us! Spit on this Cadillac! Swear at us and fight us— please do something!* But she had never called out, and they had not cursed or defied. They had never shown the strength or the will. It was not humility. It was not gratitude for being ignored. It was not any way to be. It was being crushed.

And Ross gave in, stepped back, ate his breakfast as though he did not really deserve it, as though he was unfit to eat with someone so much better than himself.

She did not know how to tell him. It seemed as if everything, all her words and actions in the past, had been futile. For here he was—back again from his search, crushed like the ragged men on West Madison Street.

The Saturday was lazy and directionless. He put an album on the phonograph and thumbed photography magazines as the Goodman sextet fled through *Grand Slam*. She did not try to intrude. At breakfast she had finally decided what she was going to do.

After lunch they drove to Lincoln Park and walked around for an hour or so in the crisp hazy air. From a distance drifted the smell of leafsmoke. Winter was coming on. Neither of them said much. As soon as they got back to his apartment Ross turned the radio to the Illinois-Ohio State game, and that was the afternoon.

She avoided mentioning, and he did not suggest, The Place for the evening. Since coming back Ross hadn't said one word about Virgil Jones. It worried her—especially in that she felt Jones held the answer, especially since she'd decided she would ask him for help.

Ross answered her question by saying that he didn't care, Schwab could come over and the three of them could go out for dinner. It wouldn't be a bad idea, he added. Schwab just wasn't with it when it came to jazz, but otherwise he was all right. Pretty intelligent, wasn't he?

She said she guessed so.

He said something into his knuckes and went back to the football game.

When they met Schwab at Riccardo's that night she noticed almost immediately that a change had taken place in him. He came smiling to their table and confidently shook hands with Ross and acted, in general, as if he was completely at peace with himself. He did not talk as much as she had remembered, and his hands were not nervous. He did not absently touch his thick spectacles or rake his fingers through his burry hair. From martinis to demitasse he was impressively calm, poised and observant. Too observant. He seemed to be trying to look behind their eyes and between their words.

Afterward she could not recall a quarter of what they had talked about, but she did know that her nerves were frayed like twine from fearing Schwab might suddenly bring Virgil Jones into conversation. He never did, however. Not once did he say anything even hinting at a reference to Jones. It was almost as if Schwab did not trust himself with the subject.

The next day, clay-colored and filled with sheets of rain-spray, was much the same as Saturday. Ross did not go near the piano. He listened to records and parts of the Cardinals-Rams game, and she busied herself with motions of cleaning the apartment. More than once she felt repelled by the perfect domesticity of the scene: the man dull and turned-in and indifferent, the woman the resentful martyr with no hope of canonization. But her bitterness did not last long. Since she had made the decision there was expanding inside her an absolute conviction that everything was going to be all right.

Jaeger had long since lost his argument that she should quit her job and let him support her. Nevertheless he tried again that night, and lost. She was not going to be kept. That was that. So in the morning she kissed him goodbye and said she was off to work.

But she did not go there. She drove north and walked into the gaunt, false-fronted apartment-hotel and asked to see Virgil Jones.

The clerk said he was sorry, young woman, but Mister Jones made it a practice to avoid visitors. The manner in which the speech was delivered made it clear that the clerk had said this before to many young women.

For some reason she discovered herself not caring what the clerk thought of her. He could think anything he wanted. He wasn't worth rage or resentment. He wasn't even worth a reply.

Just as she posted herself in a chair near a ragged plant and with disdain watched the clerk pick up the telephone threateningly, Jones walked into the lobby.

He had come in off the street. After playing until three in the morning he had either got up after only a few hours' sleep or had not been to bed at all, yet he showed no signs of being tired. His unnaturally wide eyes were bright with energy and he walked with the fluidity of a basketball player.

As he turned at her call she saw for the first time since

knowing him a look of childish, embarrassed pleasure on his face. He said hello awkwardly and did not seem to know what to do next. At her suggestion they went out into the street again, and she did not look back at the clerk.

The cafeteria reminded her of the one in which she and Leonine Jackson had tried to talk clear the trouble with Ross. That had been a long time ago, she thought, and nothing had been cleared. Perhaps this time and this place would be different.

She did not know how to begin; Jones had always made her unsure of herself. Polite and tolerant, he had nevertheless made her feel as if all her words were wrong. By just sitting quietly, as he was doing now, he unnerved her. As she waited for her toast and coffee she studied him through her shifting defenses of cigarette-smoke. She had heard of the things he had done at The Place. This calm but tough face—she suddenly noticed a discoloration on his left cheek—was trouble. At the moment it seemed as innocent as any face in the world, but it had done things. It had demolished rules and was still taking them apart. In less than a year this face had come from the oblivion of the steel mills to one of the few true peaks in the entertainment world. And here he was now: almost shy, patient and ready to listen, having breakfast with her.

"I wanted to talk to you, Virgil," she began confidently, yet at the instant annoyed that she had started with such an empty phrase.

Jones was looking directly at her lips.

"It's not an easy thing to do . . ." flustered by his stare, she hurried on ". . . because—well, I don't like to involve other people with my problems. Especially someone like you."

Jones shrugged as if he did not understand what kind of a person he was thought to be.

"I suppose—it's about Ross—" she said, rapidly now that she had seen Jones was not likely to interrupt "—I suppose it's foolish for someone like me to speak for someone like him. People look at him and think just because he's a celebrity he doesn't have any problems. But he needs help, Virgil. Believe me. You can say he's weak—in some ways I guess he is . . . but, well, if that's the way he is, he *is,* but he's still Ross, and I'm trying to help him."

His cold blue eyes leveled over the edge of his raised cup. He was actually watching her speak more than he was listening.

"I think you can help him," she said. "You see, Ross—whether he admits it or not—measures himself against you. That's true. I saw it happening and couldn't stop it, and now it's gone too far. It's gone too far now. Ross is letting it kill him. Since he came back from New York he hasn't done a thing. He draws into a shell and does nothing, he won't even touch a piano. He doesn't want to even talk about it. He doesn't make any plans." As the words came out her mind took them up and pounded *He doesn't make plans doesn't make any plans* into her again and again until she had to close her eyes and then open them to passing faces and cars and trucks before she could go on.

"He won't listen to anyone. Nobody. But he'll listen to you, Virgil—I know he'll listen to you. You're the cause of him being this way, and you're the only—"

"Helen," he interrupted earnestly, "he'll be all right."

"All *right?*" Her cup rattled onto its saucer.

"I know, I know—you're thinking it's easy for me to say." His face seemed barely in control of an emotion she could not identify.

"It's exactly what I was thinking," she said caustically.

Jones rumpled his thin whitish hair with a rake of huge fingers. He brought his hand down and pulled it across his mouth. For a long moment his eyes went unfocused with thought. Finally he shook his head slowly.

"Believe me when I say he'll be all right. Now, this morning, you might not understand—but you will. Pretty soon." Suddenly brooding, his eyes lowered.

"What are you going to give me," she asked, "one of these It'll-all-work-out-for-the-best sermons?"

He did not answer.

Frowning, she waited. Just as she was about to repeat herself, his eyes came up and watched her mouth again. But still he did not answer.

"Didn't you hear me?" she asked irritably.

"Sorry. I was—thinking. I wasn't paying attention."

"That's nice." Her voice was icy and furious; she made a motion to get up. "Don't pay any attention. It isn't *your* problem. Oh, no, not The Great *Jones'* problem. He has *all* the answers for his *own* problems . . . he—"

"Stop talking." His hand closed around her wrist and held her helpless. "You've already said things you'll be sorry for. Don't say any more. You'll just feel worse." His grip relaxed. "Listen now—you know it as well as I do—nothing I can say is going to help Jaeger. It's something—"

"You could tell him you're *human,*" she broke in, but her words were lost as if they had not even been heard.

"—he's got to do himself."

"So you won't help him," she said.

"A long time ago," Jones continued, and again it seemed as if he had not heard, "I got talking with Jaeger. I told him how not to get the way you say he is now. I told him it wasn't the way to live—worrying about success and what other people think of you, selling yourself out like that. I told him that you have to be yourself, you have to do whatever you think is right. If everybody says your way of living is wrong, you still have to do it if you think it's right for you. But Jaeger didn't listen, I guess. Or else he just wanted to keep making his life like you say it is. And if he wants to live like that, that's his business. It wouldn't be right if I tried to change his life. If he *really* wants to get rid of being afraid and jealous and looking at me as if I'm the one who's keeping him from getting what he wants, then he's got to change himself. I can't do it. You can't. Nobody can. Except him. He's the one." He sank back in his chair and blinked rapidly as if to awaken his eyes.

"Are you through?" She did not know how she had meant the question to sound.

"Yes." His chair scraped on the tile floor. "I'm sorry if you feel bad about all this, but it wouldn't do anybody any good if I wasn't honest with you."

She crumpled the paper napkin and dropped it in her cup and did not speak as she stood to leave. Jones was right, she knew. She would have to try some other way. Exciting herself to an impulsive and emotional meeting like this had been wholly wrong. Jones could not help Ross by assuming a role. In that was the truth he had given her: pretending was not an answer. The answer for each of them was in admitting the truth and standing up to it. And perhaps for the first time in her life she really began to see, through the positiveness of Jones, that the truth was never quite as terrible as it was imagined to be.

"You're going to work now?" He held open the glass door.

"I'm late already," she said, facing him again on the sidewalk.

"Don't let them make any speeches to you," he said with a soft smile. "People work too many hours a week as it is. Not enough time for living. Well—" Awkwardly he extended his hand.

She took it and felt the restrained corded strength and all

at once felt an almost overpowering sense of warmth and sadness. She had never seen him so profoundly human as at this instant.

"—remember—" he said "—one way or the other, Jaeger will be all right. You can depend on that."

"Thanks." She noticed again that his eyes were on her lips; she looked quickly at a passerby out of embarrassment. "Thanks again," she said weakly. "I hope I'll see you again soon, Virgil."

"I won't be there much longer," he said, referring to the club downtown. "Come down. It would be good seeing you again."

When she had said goodbye she crossed the streetcar tracks and walked toward her unwashed Ford. As she fitted the key she glanced back to where she had left him.

He was still standing there. His white hair was a marker. All around him people passed, stepped aside, hurried on their separate ways. No one had recognized him yet. He stood there as if he did not know which way to turn.

"My God," she whispered, remembering how his deep eyes had clung to her lips when she spoke, "I hope he isn't falling in love with me. I hope he doesn't make that mistake."

When he had decided, he turned on the corner and began walking back to his rooms. He put his hands in his pockets, took notice of an enormous churning garbage-truck blocking traffic, smiled without interest at a goitrous hag distinguished for spitting in the slot of a mailbox at two-thirty every afternoon, walked on slowly, and just before entering the building stooped to scratch a vigorous knuckle between the ears of an orange alleycat whose tail erected with pleasure.

He did not return the greeting of the clerk, nor did he bother to take the elevator. Methodically he climbed the stone steps to the third floor, walked silently down the hall, and opened the door to his rooms. He immediately locked it behind him and crossed to the bed and lay down with his hands behind his head. For ten minutes or more he stared at the ceiling. Then he got up and from the outdate bureau took a round mirror which he propped on the edge of the bed.

Pulling up a chair, he sat and adjusted the angle of the mirror so that the reflection of his face filled the entire area. For a quiet moment he looked at himself.

Then, as he had done alone in his rooms all these months since knowing the truth, he began slowly and exaggeratedly shaping words and studying the soundless movement of his lips.

3

He had come a long way, he reflected. A year ago he was sulking in his back room like a hermit, chewing fish and crackers, dramatically strapping himself with loneliness and self-pity and wondering what he had done to deserve such grief. A year ago there had been hope for everyone but him. Present and future had been one: a wasteland. And now—now all that was changed. Now, tonight, the hermit drank Five Star and sat at ease among lovely young bodies and added his pipesmoke to the thick warm haze of The Place. Now, to be honest with himself, he did not yet know where he was going. But now it didn't seem to matter. He was enjoying himself. Why ruin it with questions? Why live in the future so much that you gradually lost your capacity to enjoy the present? People planned themselves to death. That was what they did. They joined life's AAA and got a pile of maps with charted courses, the best recommendations, and when the trip was over they showed many photographs but nothing in their heads.

From his seat at the bar Schwab reviewed the faces in the crowd. Still he saw neither Helen nor Jaeger. Part of his mind told him that he would never see them listening to Jones again, but since he could not justify the idea, he continued scanning mechanically.

He had no doubt that Jaeger was in a bad way. At Riccardo's it had been as unmistakable as if he had worn rattling shackles on his wrists and ankles. He had imprisoned himself with an idea of Jones. Foolish and impossible, Schwab thought, that any man could make so much of another. Yet it was the only answer that accounted for the progressive disintegration Jaeger had suffered in the past year.

There were times—such as now—when he despised Jaeger for being so spinelessly defeatist. Here was a pianist whose skill and worth could not be argued with, an established jazz musician who seemed to have met all the requirements of deserved fame—yet here he was, going to pieces because of a young rival whose only interest in the piano seemed to be one of self-enjoyment. A psychiatrist, Schwab considered as he sucked at his cold pipe, could in time pry loose a briefcase full of explanations, but psychiatrists were convenient gods of people with as much money as Jaeger. Convenient gods were not what was needed. What was needed most were clean mirrors and good eyesight.

He could not, however, disgust himself with Jaeger all the time. It was too easy to think another man weak when you did not actually know his soul. You could call him spineless, but you had to keep in mind that his problems might have melted your spine long ago.

For some time, waiting with all the others, he sat and drank and thought about Helen, and finally The Place suddenly charged itself as Jones came in. Ten minutes late, and looking very tired.

As usual, he went directly to the piano, granting recognition to no one on the way. He pulled off his topcoat and draped it across the chair used by the trombonist of the intermission sextet.

Heads turned, whispered, shook. There were grins. By now

there were many in the audience who knew little and cared less about jazz, who came only to amuse themselves with the sight of this eccentric everyone was talking about. From the distance Schwab watched their faces with distaste. *It's so embarrassing,* he imagined them thinking, *to not be able to say you've* seen *him.*

Yes, Schwab told them silently as the opening chord plunged the entire darkened room into quiet, *take a good look at him. Remember him so you can be a success at the next cocktail party.*

Then he passed his hand over his eyes and lost himself with the memory of what had happened the night he had visited Jones. He had not mentioned the pianist's seizure to anyone—why, he was unable to say. Every time he had considered telling Helen he had arrested the impulse. Perhaps it had been that he had not wanted her to bear the weight of the disclosure, perhaps he had not wanted Jaeger to know or even to be liable to know. Too many people were involved. And, Schwab reflected dismally, he did not know what was wrong with Jones. He could guess any number of things, but that was useless. All he could do was wait, and wonder, and wait. Meanwhile he was not even sure of how he felt about the pianist.

The last individual in the world. A brave phrase. Foolish, too, had it been mouthed by anyone else. But it belonged to Virgil Jones, and it was not foolish because he believed in it and had not denied it even for a second during his suffering that night.

It was also a terrible phrase. Behind it were implications few men, if any, would be willing to endure. There was the gigantic, never-ending aloneness against all the pressures of those who were not alone. Small pressures, petty pressures, but when like drops of water they struck again, and again, and again, and again, slowly again, steadily again, and again,

323

more water than a man had mind, again, and again, and again . . . the only escape was surrender. Give up. Renounce individuality. Join, be a part of all the rest. Be at peace with the others. Declare your individuality in colors of automobiles, in your silverware and furniture, in proud rare roses on windowsills or along walks, in ties and earrings and bracelets, in tablets of stone reading when you were, and were not.

Or, if you still refused to submit, you could find others like yourself and form a Society of Individuals. It had been done. It had been a fairly popular idea, the newspapers had said. But where did the individuals go, Schwab wondered, once they belonged to the society? With a smile he thought that if all the members had been really consistent, the meetings must have been indescribable chaos.

Abruptly he shook his head and returned his attention to Jones: now bent and secret in the spotlight, playing another private and complex melody as if he had no audience at all, as if he played for himself and refused to share the real, inner pleasure with anyone.

Schwab did not move from the bar when Jones had finnished and was walking off the stand. He watched the pianist pass between tables and go through the door. The audience seemed undecided whether or not he would come back to play again that night, but only very few rose to leave.

After a half-hour Schwab grew bored with The Place without Jones. When he was outside he looked up and down the crowded street. The unkempt, white-haired figure was not in sight. His disappearance had been like everything else about him of late: sudden, mysterious, and edged with defiance.

Back in his apartment Schwab did not even attempt to sleep for a long time. Every five minutes he changed the course of his pacing to enter the kitchen for a fresh cup of coffee. He sat down and got up again. Methodically and thoroughly he polished his glasses, put them on and blinked rapidly with satisfaction.

Well, he lectured himself, the only thing to do was to be honest about it. His restlessness could not justifiably be blamed on any of the others involved. Of course, Jones had something to do with it—so did Helen and Jaeger, for that matter. But it was one thing to admit influence, and another, quite another thing, to blame. If the situation deserved blame at all.

After thinking through another cup of coffee he decided that it did.

Blame was deserved, and he was at fault. He stood up again as if a weight had been lifted from his shoulders. The truth was not as hopeless as he had thought. The truth was that he had submitted all these years.

He had never honestly tried to find himself. He had never taken the risk of trying to discover what it was he really wanted to do. Looking back into his life it seemed that he had regarded college as an approved period of floundering, but when he had graduated he felt a sudden obligation to decide, to have security without further delay, to make for himself a responsible, pillar-of-the-community existence, to stop all this nonsense and start making money. And where had it brought him? To a wretched record shop on the wretched South Side of Chicago. To not enough profit, not enough loss. To a pale, flaccid existence in which he had grown indolent, and from which he could not escape because it was safer and more comfortable to languish within four walls that he knew. Security—that was the abstraction he was supposed to have had. That was what everybody was supposed to have. But still, a man had to remember that what he thought of as security did not apply to all men. And it was also necessary to remember that when an animal was roped and caged it was said to be secure.

So he slept and had black-and-white dreams of clay and strings, and when he woke it was Saturday, and cold.

He was busy all day. There were customers, incoming shipments, receipts to sign, boxes to unpack and records to be filed, bills to be paid, reorders to be telephoned, ashtrays emptied, coffee made and then forgotten, customers, more customers who didn't know what they wanted but were willing to be indulged.

Snow fell in the afternoon. Shaggy and fitful, and just enough to make the street seem more decayed than ever. Along about three-thirty he had half a mind to close at four, buy a bottle and every girlie magazine in Walgreen's, and go home and forget his name.

But of course he did not. He stayed on his feet, smiled, advised politely, deferred, was patient. And all the while that other half of his mind considered burning the store to the ground.

When he finally did close he was too tired for arson. He lacked the strength for any revolt. He did not even dream.

On Sunday, however, looking back at the day and to his thoughts the night before, he knew that he had not been wrong. This was not the life he wanted. It was not so much the physical effort or the marginal level of his life that was draining him. It was the idea that he was letting life slip through his fingers.

What was he doing? When he put the question to himself he heard the answer fall like a hammer and its echo. Working. If it hadn't been for Jones and the others, how would he be spending most of his evenings? Working. What was he doing with all the cool blue days of spring and summer, with all the autumns and winters? Working.

Neatly, then, with the elaborate care of a person doing

something he enjoys deep inside, Schwab took pen and paper and began to write. On one side of the paper he made a list of all the things he wanted to do but had somehow never found time for. On the other side he began listing all the places he wanted to go. Puerile, he thought even as he wrote. Anyone looking at this would think me childish.

He looked up and told a bronzed lamp to go to hell. He did not have to account himself to anyone.

Yosemite, he wrote. Not on a tour, not with a mob of Easterners during the summer. Alone, perhaps with a friend, perhaps a woman who still knew how to walk in low heels. *New Orleans.* Why not? A few weeks there, and not during Mardi Gras.

He wrote for nearly a half-hour. He put down that he would like to go to the Art Institute and Field Museum and enjoy them as much as he had when he was a boy. He wrote of Wrigley Field for a Sunday afternoon doubleheader, a good stage-play, a boat ride far out on the lake, concerts, operas, an afternoon of barbarism up at Dyche Stadium, lectures, a hundred things.

Juvenile, he thought, reviewing the list. But again, immediately, he set his jaw and cursed himself for caring too much about what he would be thought of by others. Juvenile? All right, let them go ahead and call it that. Call it anything—it was not aimed to hurt anyone, and besides, it concerned only himself now.

With his last thought he suddenly understood why he had been on the defensive, why he had continually sought to justify himself to "them" when no one had even accused him of anything. Rachel was one of the reasons. If she were alive he would not be free to act and think like this. He would be obligated to the responsibility of a family. He would have to answer to them, and to society, if he did not provide for them. Now, however, his happiness with being free implied that he was glad to have no such responsibilities, that he was glad Rachel was dead. Not true! his mind shouted, striking at the thought. Yet the other part of his mind said that this was true, unalterably true, at least in part. His contentment with freedom was not actually *because* she was dead, but he could not say her death had nothing to do with it. He had not wanted her to die. The life had seemed to run out of him there on that hot white strip of sand when he turned and did not see her far out in the water.

But she had died, and he had not been able to save her, and she would never come back. It was ended. Finally, irrecoverably. He had loved her—a part of him would always love her—but Rachel was in the past. He could not live there with her. He had to forget. No, not forget, but act as though he did. He had to meet people and go places and fall in love again, just as completely as he had with Rachel, to keep living for today and tomorrow and not yesterday.

This suspicion of self-guilt was one of the reasons. The other, he perceived, was because that for too long he had been sensitive to what others thought. He had molded himself to their opinions and prejudices and pressures so that now, when he was thinking purely of his own desires, he did not know what to do with such a luxury. He told himself that if a man kept up that kind of life it wouldn't be long before he might start forgetting to feed himself.

On Monday night, his brain still whirling with plans and excuses and indecisions, Schwab went to The Place again. He could not have said why he was being drawn there so often. Perhaps it was because the nightlife had come to represent his first step toward the life he thought he would enjoy. Perhaps it was with the fading, almost discarded hope of meeting the girl Helen. Perhaps it was because of Jones, the only man Schwab had ever known who could honestly say that he was living his life as he wanted.

328

Not until he reached the entrance and saw the signs did he know it was the pianist's closing night. Luckily he got inside. There was a larger, more unruly crowd than he had ever seen there before. By eight-thirty there was not even standing room.

Crossing one leg clumsily and propping his elbows against the bar, his mind returned to the signs outside. *Final Appearance of America's No. 1 Jazz Pianist. Last Night.* From the conversations he had overheard at the bar, Schwab guessed that posting the signs had given the manager great satisfaction. Jones had been trouble. He had drawn record crowds, but he had been trouble. It wasn't that he had deliberately stirred it up; he simply seemed to carry it with him. The only thing he could be depended on to do was the thing he wanted to do, no matter what anyone else said.

Unpredictably, Jones was prompt to the minute. And again, to the surprise of everyone, he was wearing a neat, conservative gray suit with a rich blue wool tie. But, as usual, he approached the piano without greeting any of the musicians, any of the critics, or any of the audience. He sat down and first took hold of one wrist and then the other. Waited. Almost instantly there was silence. His hands flashed down in the bright isolated whiteness.

He began with *Yesterdays,* but when he reached the bridge in the second chorus he abruptly and harshly changed keys and began a weird, winding melody no one could even pretend to recognize. For nearly five minutes he continued before suddenly reversing himself into *Just Friends,* playing that for a long time, and then swinging into an up-tempo blues which went on and on with increasing power and invention until a voice, then two, and three, and more, and in no time almost all in the audience had come alive and were calling out with wild cries of encouragement.

None of his audiences had ever been pulled along so spontaneously as this one.

His performance was like that for forty-five minutes, and when he had finished he did not leave. Instead he drifted back toward the bar and ignored all the clutching praises as if he had no use for anything but a drink. Briefly, as he made his way through the hands and faces reaching out to ask him this, tell him that, make some impression on him, be noticed, remembered, his wide pale eyes lifted and met Schwab's. He came over.

"How are you?" Jones asked, surprisingly offering his hand.

"Fine—just fine." He shook hands without being conscious of it.

"That's good." Jones ordered a bottle of beer and did not move away.

Schwab glanced, felt that others were looking at him with a mixture of envy and respect. Out of everyone in the club, including celebrated musicians and other entertainers, Jones had spoken to him. And was obviously about to say more.

"I don't think I've ever heard you better," Schwab said, feeling awkward in the silence as Jones filled his glass. Jones' eyes did not move from the flowing amber spout. Finally he looked up.

"They make a lot of money here," he said irrelevantly. "I guess they'll make more this Saturday. Are you coming?"

"To what?" He was unable to keep from staring at something he could not define in the expression in the pianist's eyes.

"A concert. At the Opera House—or somewhere. You ought to be there." He looked vaguely about the nightclub. "Tell the girl and Jaeger they ought to come too. They aren't here tonight?"

330

"Not yet, at least." He frowned. "Are you playing Saturday?"

Jones, staring back at him, nodded.

"Then I *will* come. And where after that?"

"What?"

"Where are you going after this concert? Another tour?"

"No." Jones set his half-finished glass on the bar and took his hand away. "If you see them—" his voice was not commanding "—tell them to come Saturday night. It would be— well . . ." And with an uncertain motion of his right hand he ended the conversation where it hung suspended for a moment before he turned his back and once more went toward the piano in its cold white light.

4

Almost fifteen minutes late came the first hesitant, experimentally subdued sounds of saxophone, trumpet and string bass from behind the heavy curtain. There was a press roll from the drums followed by clubbing bumps as the pedal pounded the bass. The piano came in and worked to get the string bass on pitch. The air fluttered with sounds. Lights faded, muting the audience, bringing bodies erect. Then there was silence behind the curtain.

And suddenly there was jazz as the curtain raised and in the light they were already jamming well into *Rosetta* against the quick enormous applause lifting in the hall. After an easy riding chorus the noise subsided and the men blew down as onstage strolled Roger Henneberry: bespectacled, ponderously casual, proud, smiling to the applause that greeted him, finally stopping with hands in pockets, finally intimate with the microphone and saying *Rosetta* was too fine to interrupt with introductions just yet . . . let's listen for awhile, shall we, faithful?

So he stood aside and cast his face in rapture and the jazzmen exchanged private glances which said that well, man, there were some things you just had to put up with in this job. No use in letting them bug you. Just pay them no mind and keep on blowing strong.

After judging that the appreciation-period had had its effect, Henneberry returned to the microphone and began introducing the ten musicians one by one as the others rode low in the background.

In the wings again, tingling with the thrill of having done an impressive job, the announcer slouched artfully against a backprop of a gate of scenery and lit a cigarette. Thank God the beginning had gone well. There had been times . . . The area of his mouth was damp. He hoped Jones would behave like a normal human being for at least this night. After all, he fretted, personalities such as himself couldn't be ridiculed in front of an audience without losing a lot of prestige.

Jones. Goddamn him. Goddamn his obstinacy. Goddamn his doing exactly what he wanted to do without showing the proper respect for others. Well, that would soon be changed. Tomorrow morning. In a little more than twelve hours, in Bauer's office, Jones would be his. And handling him wasn't going to be like Paul's namby-pamby tactics; things would be understood right from the start—with no arguments, either.

Henneberry pushed his body away from the prop and went over to a group of earphoned men watching meters and adjusting dials on the big square Ampex and its two slowly spinning reels. The concert was being taped for possible issue as an album. He confronted a young Chinese who was wearing his earphones like a collar.

"Now remember—" Henneberry said, warming up for the authority he would have the next day "—this pianist is not to be recorded."

"You mean Jones," the technician said matter-of-factly.

"Correct." Then, suddenly annoyed at the lack of deference shown him: "Until I say so."

"What?"

"You heard me."

"Until *you* say so? Mister Henneberry, I only work here, as they say, but I know my jazz, too. I know that Virgil Jones is one man who doesn't get taped."

"And that's as much as you know," he said with contempt.

"All right—that's all I know—but that's the deal. Now I don't know if it's strictly personal with him or whether the union is in back of him some way, but I can tell you now— I'm not putting my head on the block. No sir, these spools stop when he goes onstage. You think I wouldn't like to take some of his stuff? You bet I'd like to. But I won't. When I get the light from Petrillo or Jones himself, then I'll go ahead—not until then."

"Obviously you don't know who I am."

"Oh, I know, all right. But I only work here."

"Supposing I told you that *I* control Jones . . ."

The young Chinese looked extremely embarrassed. He lifted the left rubber cup and listened and watched a swinging needle.

"Yes, *I* control Virgil Jones," Henneberry said, his voice hoarse with frustration over the inner admission of the truth. "Keeping his works off the market is part of a plan you wouldn't understand. Do you hear me?"

The Chinese raised his head and seemed to look behind the lofty stare of the announcer. A smile brushed his lips. He bent to the machine again. From the stage honked the opening bars of *You Can Depend on Me*.

"Smart punk." Henneberry folded and unfolded his arms in anger. "Re*mem*ber that. Don't be so stupidly diligent in executing orders until you know who you're taking them from—understand? I don't expect to have to repeat that." His mouth ran away out of control. *"So when Jones goes on I want this machine going. Do you hear that?"*

The technician looked up. "You want me to tape him tonight?"

"I just said that."

"You want me to have this going?"

Perhaps it was something in the repeated question or in the hint of amusement in the Chinese's eyes . . . Henneberry turned.

Jones was standing a few yards away. He did not look angry.

"Virgil—I—we were engaged in a—"

"Eleven tomorrow morning?" Jones asked, stepping closer.

"What?"

"This talk you want to have with me—I just want to make sure of the time . . ."

"Yes. Eleven—yes." His astonished relief pitched his voice to a strange sound in his ears. Jones acted as if he hadn't heard or didn't care about the talk of pirating his piano. "You have the address?"

Jones nodded. Then he walked off toward the stage and stood in the shadows watching the musicians.

"I've changed my mind," Henneberry said curtly to the technician. "Hold the tape when he goes on." What a terrible thing to happen, he thought. Jones standing there all the time. Had he heard, and would he bring it up tomorrow morning? What would Paul say? With a feeling of having committed an irrevocable blunder he snapped flame to another cigarette and at the same time felt that his skull was beginning to split up the middle. From the ticket-pocket of his coat he took a small brushed-aluminum box and picked out two olive-colored tablets. Phenobarbital and atropine. They would fix him. Beautifully they would slow him. He would be calm and would not concern himself

335

over what had just happened or might happen. Let Jones do what he would. Henneberry gulped the pills without water. Almost instantly he told himself that he felt better. But, he asked himself with the old helpless desperation, how much longer would he have to swallow them?

At the intermission most of the jazzmen went outside for air and cigarettes. A few cut back to the dressingroom to lie down with a pocket mystery or a bottle. The drummer and guitarist sidled over to the Ampex and began asking questions of the technicians.

No one bothered Jones. Alone, as always, he paced backstage and kept his thoughts to himself. His face appeared unnaturally tired, but other than that there was no sign that he might be troubled.

When the massive storied hall was dark again, quiet again, tense with choked coughs, strained faces, Henneberry suddenly walked into the cone of light and spoke two words and backed out of sight as if fearing to expose himself any longer than was necessary.

And even before the curtain lifted, Jones was playing, and when finally he was in the spotlight and the applause he did not look up. Bent at the wide ebony grand piano, he looked very small and weak. He was playing *If I Had You,* and when he struck the final, lingering chord the audience came to its feet to let him know that everything that had been written and said of his greatness was true.

He played *Poor Butterfly* and the wildness came again.

He played something nameless, and then Ellington's *Blues,* and *I Cover the Waterfront,* and after that *More Than You Know* and *Lover* and *Laura* and *Don't Be That Way,* and at the end of an hour his hands were still moving tirelessly as the crowd began exchanging dazed, half-frightened glances.

Henneberry and the top names in jazz watched bristling from the wings. Jones was not only playing straight through the intermission but seemed intent on taking up their set-time as well. He had to stop—and soon. He couldn't make them wait all night.

But he did not stop.

He was as strong as ever after two hours.

There had never been a concert like it. At midnight he was still at the piano. He played Chopin and more jazz and Chopin again; he played a Bach fugue and then his own brilliantly simple compositions; he played *Blues* again.

The man had gone mad, sputtered the manager. The only thing to do was to drop the curtain.

But the moment it blotted out the stage there was a giant roar of protest from the audience, a roar that mounted until once more the curtain was raised and he could be seen again, sitting there as if strapped to the bench.

At twelve-fifteen the microphones were cut off. It did not do much good—his hands were strong enough to carry the music to every corner of the hall.

Henneberry came onstage and said something into his ear. There was no response. Henneberry walked off again.

At twelve-thirty the curtain came once more, and, over the solid blast of protest from the crowd, the firescreen followed. Next, the lights went up in the hall. Gradually, sullenly, the people in the rear began moving toward the exits. Those in front were still able to hear him playing behind the screen, but after some difficulty the ushers persuaded them to leave. The hall darkened at last. It was over; something not one of them would have believed if they hadn't seen it.

Backstage it was not over.

Jones was oblivious to cajolery, to outright threats by every-one from the manager down. No one could do anything with him. There was talk of a hospital. There was talk of a good many things, but no agreement could be reached.

It was decided to let him go on until he became exhausted. Jones was not dangerous. It would be all right to leave him there with the janitor. The old German asked if they were sure he wasn't dangerous.

Henneberry said of course.

The janitor wanted more of a guarantee than that. A young stagehand said he would stick around. The pianist, he said, might be a little off, but a man didn't get a chance to hear this kind of music very often, and he couldn't see why *any-*one wanted to go home.

But those involved were angered past endurance, and so they left, all of them, and in the mammoth hall were the janitor and stagehand and Virgil Jones.

The two of them left backstage brightly lit as they drew up cane chairs and listened. After a half-hour or so the stagehand walked off and came back with a pint of Four Roses. He edged to the bass end of the piano and offered the bottle to Jones in much the same way as a man trying to make friends with a vicious animal.

Jones nodded, stopped in the middle of a passage, and drank. He nodded again and impeccably picked up where he had left off.

By the time it got to be four o'clock only a lone naked 100-watt burned fiercely through the darkness. A pint of Southern Comfort had joined the empty Four Roses. The janitor was spitting thickly on the boards whenever he felt like it, and he felt like it often. All three of them took time-outs between each number and talked of Baldwins and Steinways and about how Chicago was no place to be with winter coming on.

His eyes glazed, lips twisted in a queer smile, Jones played on and on, and drank, and asked the two of them if they had a favorite song, and the concert finally came to a close with Jones fingering *Falling in Love Again* and *Dear Old Girl* as the old janitor and the stagehand sang passionately to the empty hall and wondered how such a great musician couldn't even find the tune with his voice.

5

For the fourth time in ten minutes he took out his pocket-watch and held it in his thin, blanched hand. Then he replaced it and went to the window of his office. In the cold light he looked younger than he had any right to be; his hair shone like polished silver and the skin near his mouth was like veined marble.

After a short while he turned and spoke to the door.

Roger Henneberry came in shivering affectedly from the cold. He spoke too much and too rapidly and drew designs in the air with his fat fingers.

"What time is it?" Bauer interrupted, having resumed his stance at the window.

"Five of."

"That's your chair," Bauer said, motioning.

The announcer shed his black overcoat and plumped into the shiny leather chair beneath the neat slick rows of photographs. With a great deal of care he extracted and put on a pair of heavy-rimmed glasses. His fine English shoes shuffled gently back and forth over the rug as if he was trying to charge himself with electricity.

"He'd better be here," Henneberry threatened an ashtray. "And *I'm* not going to tolerate anything like last night . . ." He watched for a response: there was none. Bauer had not

340

even appeared upset when telephoned about Jones' marathon, though it had been evident that the call had found him still awake at one-thirty. Henneberry scowled purposelessly at various objects in the room.

Suddenly from the hall sounded the clatter of the elevator-cage. Bauer left the window at once and sat behind the massive desk with folded hands arranged as if concealing something.

Footsteps approached, scraped, stopped. There was a single rap against the frosted glass.

"Come in," Bauer said, loudly but with a slight uneven quality.

Jones entered and carefully closed the door behind him. First his strong blue eyes fastened on Bauer, then switched to Henneberry, then finally to space. His face was haggard but unsurprised. His cropped white hair grew wild from the wind and his hands were quiet at his sides.

"Sit down," Bauer said cordially, indicating the chair across the desk.

Henneberry stood. "I don't believe—"

"Never mind," Bauer cut in, "we've met. Isn't that right, Jones?"

"That's right," Jones said easily, addressing Henneberry before returning his eyes to Bauer.

"So you can sit down again, announcer. I'll tell you when." As he leaned back in the big chair his head seemed to sink into his scrawny shoulders. "Yes—we've met. In Philadelphia . . . about three years ago, right?"

"Three or four," Jones said. "I don't remember."

"It was three."

The pianist shrugged.

"Our friend Virgil Jones was very young and brave then," Bauer said, speaking to Henneberry but watching Jones, "but also stupid. Young and stupid. I can remember him

341

making speeches about how no one would ever 'own' him. That's what he said, exactly. Full of high ideas about his 'rights' and 'integrity' and all that kind of idealistic garbage. Nobody, not even a man who'd pay him enough to stay alive, could ever control him. *That* was the kind of talk he passed around. Isn't that right, Jones?"

Jones angled his head. "I don't understand. I came up—"

"You will," Henneberry said, but was instantly overridden by the agent's crisp insistence:

"You came up because you were told to."

"No," Jones said mildly. "I wanted to."

"Well—" Bauer spread his fingers and smiled indulgently "—have it your way. I can see that you have to tell yourself that."

Jones started to reply but stopped with seeming resignation.

Bauer leaned back in the chair. His elbows rested on its arms and his hands were joined to form a rest for his chin. He looked toward the announcer, who was in an ineffective posture of dignity and authority.

"Very well," Bauer said measuredly, "the point of this meeting. Henneberry, over here, found out from Ross Jaeger that you'd been playing the piano in some store out South. Just like your days in Philadelphia, right? Well, Henneberry naturally came to me. . ." He retraced step-by-step what he had effected with the union, with the owners of cocktail lounges and nightclubs, and with agencies which had tried to interfere. It was an imposing summary of work; he did not reach the conclusion for some time. "So you see, Jones, you've been about as wrong as anybody can be. All along. Your hero-ideas about this 'individualism' haven't worked for ten minutes. Without me you would've been nothing—not a thing. Did you actually think you were so great that you *had* to be allowed to play? Really, did you think you were

342

hired and publicized and paid so much just because people demanded you? What did you think—that you could get away with anything you wanted because nobody was big enough to stand up to you?"

The pianist did not answer. He seemed neither shocked nor angry.

"Yes," Bauer said confidently, "I see you've been thinking that. Your ideas have worked, and now you're great, and you're great because these ideas have worked. You're untouchable now, aren't you? A big man. Life is perfect, isn't it? All that money, the easy life, all those people treating you like a king—you've got used to it. It's *always* going to be that way. Isn't that what you're thinking?"

"That's what I wanted to talk—"

"*Lis*ten." Bauer pointed his forefinger like a stiletto. "This meeting wasn't called so I could listen to another speech of yours."

Henneberry's noise of agreement was cut short.

"I'm not making a speech," Jones said. "But it seems to me that you're wasting a lot of words. This news of yours isn't new . . ."

"What?" Bauer fired his eyes at Henneberry as he spoke.

"That's right," Jones said, leveling his words at both of them. "I knew about all this backstage stuff a long time ago."

Henneberry's jaw worked as though it was broken. "Paul, believe me, I had noth—"

"Who told you?" Bauer snapped at the pianist.

"Jaeger," Jones said calmly. "Or maybe I ought to say he warned me you were probably behind all the attention I was getting."

"Jaeger," the old man muttered to the knuckles of his right fist. "What did he tell you?"

"About the way you operate—that sort of thing."

343

"And what 'sort of thing' is that?"

"Using people. Living off them and then throwing them away. A roughing-up if they—well, you know better than I do what you do."

Bauer could not control the muscles of his face. They jerked and twitched under skin that had gone dead white. His fingers picked at each other.

"How long ago did Jaeger tell you this?" he asked.

"When I first started."

"But you didn't believe him, did you?"

"It didn't make any difference to me," Jones replied, moving his eyebrows nervously. "The day he told me—and I wouldn't give him a bad time if I were you . . . he was just trying to help—when he told me, I wasn't sure I knew you."

"And you found out."

"The next day. I thought about it and finally decided you were the same one."

"And what did you think then?"

"Nothing. It still didn't make any difference to me."

An expression of incredulity seamed Bauer's face. His lips made a dry circle. He appeared to be trying to remember how to pronounce the words he was about to say.

"Do you remember," he said at last, "what happened when we met in Philadelphia?"

Jones said yes with his head.

"And you say it *still* made no difference to you that Paul Bauer, the same Paul Bauer, was behind your career in Chicago?"

Again Jones nodded.

"You're lying."

"What you think is your business."

"You're afraid to admit it," Bauer said, his dry voice shaking with anger. His eyes shone like small polished stones, yet in the infuriated glittering there was a trace of something which might have been satisfaction. "I don't believe it. You're sitting there and telling me you can't add two-and-two."

"I can add, all right. You're the one who's getting five for an answer. The trouble is, you don't know what the twos mean. You think I should have got excited when I found out you were mixed up in it. Maybe you think I should have run out and said I wasn't going to have anything to do with you. Maybe I should have got out of town and signed up with somebody else."

"We had a gentleman's agreement," Henneberry said, alarmed. "No contractual arrangements were insisted upon because I believed—"

"Look—" Jones interrupted "—we're off the subject. I'm tired of talking and answering questions."

"You'll do it as long as I say," Bauer threatened.

"I'm not going to argue with you." The pianist seemed near the point of exhaustion. "I think I know what your plans for me were, why you invited me up here today. You were probably going to drop me and try to use your influence to stop me from playing altogether. I guess you think you've built me up so high that I couldn't take a fall like that . . ."

"You're wrong," Henneberry said. "Paul was going—"

". . . But you made a mistake," Jones said coolly, appearing not to have heard the interruption. "You just couldn't believe I wouldn't be changed by what's happened to me this year. So now I'll tell you why I came up here today: I'm quitting. You can forget about your plans. Last night's concert . . . was my last time. I'm finished with all this." He stood.

"*Sit down.*" Bauer's body had curved forward like a scythe. His face was bloodless, his lips almost totally erased. Like a savage bird he kept his eyes on Jones until the pianist was seated again. For a very long time Bauer said nothing. Gradually his indrawn face took on color; his lips reappeared, moved:

"Quitting. I suppose you've saved a lot of money . . ."

"Enough."

". . . For the rest of your life, of course." His fingers shook as they explored the long blades of his desk-shears.

"That's my problem—you know that."

Bauer slumped back and put one hand over his face. For a moment Henneberry and the pianist stiffened as if they expected to see the old man gasp for help. But in only a short while the hand came away from the face, which was even more composed than before. Then Bauer reached for the telephone, dialed, waited—spoke, cursed, hung up by pressing a finger on the cradle-bar . . . lifted and dialed again.

They watched him as he dialed five times. And he watched Jones. The pianist did not move to leave again. Almost politely, he sat alert and patient, waiting for Bauer to finish.

On the fifth call Bauer relaxed and, cupping one hand over half the mouthpiece, spoke behind the shield in a voice barely audible. He nodded and grimaced. Repeated a name and a number, hung up.

"A friend," he explained. His face had become more relieved, more the master of itself and the situation. "All right—you're through, you said. There's not much I can do if that's the way it is."

"Paul—" Henneberry said helplessly "—this can't happen. Not like *this*."

"What can I do? What can either of us do? I've been outsmarted, that's all." He got to his feet. "Isn't that right, Jones?"

"I didn't hear everything you said . . ." The pianist also stood. From beneath a frown his eyes stared at Bauer's lips.

"I said I've been outsmarted—and that doesn't happen

every day. But when it does, I guess it's worth a drink, so let's go down to a bar I know."

"Thanks," Jones said, "but I—"

"*One drink*. Take us five minutes . . . and I'll drop you at your place when we're through. You haven't got a car, have you?"

For a few seconds Jones did not decide. He seemed to be weighing Bauer's sudden gracious acceptance of defeat against all the things he knew the agent to be. Finally he nodded and said he would have just one drink.

He rode down between the others in the elevator. Henneberry made weak, absurdly meaningless gestures with his hands and mouth; the sudden disintegration of his plans had made him nearly senseless. By the time the cage reached the lobby he had stopped trying for any answers and was sunk in mute depression.

The late Sunday morning street was sunless and quiet. The wind had shifted and was warmer; moving in low from the west were heavy clouds. Bauer turned the corner first and pointed at his Cadillac.

Henneberry offered his white Ferrari parked directly across the street.

Bauer commented acidly about ten thousand dollar cars that only midgets could ride comfortably in. He opened the door and motioned to the pianist, then told Henneberry to take his own car and meet them at an address.

Through the still-open door of the Cadillac Jones said that he thought bars weren't open until one or two on Sundays.

Bauer said that only nobodys had to put up with that rule. He closed the door and with his head signaled Henneberry to get over to his damned car and start driving.

Neither the agent nor Jones spoke during the short ride. Ahead of them all the way was the Ferrari. Parking tandem in front of a baroque wood door set in a wall of clay-colored brick, Bauer made a sound of authority and got out. The three grouped again on the sidewalk, and, led by Bauer, were admitted to the door.

Inside it was dark and rich with walnut and brass, and there was only a tartan-vested bartender who served with great deference and squinted almost imperceptibly at Jones.

Bauer raised his glass. "Here's to something," he said stiffly. Covertly his eyes followed the pianist's profile; then he set his drink on the bar and excused himself for a moment.

"Another drink?" Henneberry asked, ready again, still sullen and defeated. "Have another drink. Drink all day. Why not."

Jones shook his head, then held the glass up to the light, drank nearly all of his bourbon and soda. He did not seem apprehensive about Bauer's telephone calls, his "friend," or his absence now.

In a matter of minutes the agent returned. His face was tight and pale, but he managed to work a narrow smile onto it and ask if Jones cared for another drink.

"No?" he said to the reply. "All right—I know when I ought to stop forcing a man. Especially one like you, eh?" His laugh was short and brittle. "Well, I asked you for a drink, you've had one, and now we'll go . . . . . . stay here, announcer . . . I'll drive him. Here—bartender, *you* . . ." He put a fifty-dollar bill on the bar. "This will cover everything—for him, too," he said, eyeing Henneberry.

"Mister Bauer—" the bartender began.

"Cash. And I don't want change." Then he turned and without a word to Henneberry went out with the pianist.

They drove west on Division in the gathering unseasonal darkness of imminent rain. Traffic was heavy with church-crowded cars; the streetcorners surged and hesitated with the confusion of old ladies wearing outdated hats and cheap fur

348

neckpieces. Clearing the pack at last, Bauer stepped up his speed to forty-five and held it until the brick buildings separated and there were prairies and factories.

"I thought you were driving me home," Jones said.

Bauer did not answer as he made a turn.

"You made a wrong turn. You're going south."

"I've done a lot of things wrong this last year, Jones. More than I've ever done before—and this is where I make them *right*."

The pianist's wide-set eyes watched coldly. Then he turned his face ahead toward the onrushing cracked pavement bordered by bleak brown stubble. After ten minutes there was a series of turns, and on the isolated street ahead was a parked car. Bauer slowed. The car was an old maroon Buick with rusted bumpers and jeweled mudflaps. Its exhaustpipe was breathing heavily. The Cadillac drew alongside and braked. Instantly a huge Negro emerged from the car, opened the door on Jones' side.

"This him?" The Negro already had a hand clamped on Jones' upper arm. With his free hand he took the envelope thrust at him. Then, with the ease of handling a child, he pulled the pianist from the Cadillac, kicked shut its door, and transferred Jones into the front seat of the Buick. He put the envelope between his teeth and slid behind the wheel. Bauer's car sped away.

The big Negro looked around, grunted. He took the envelope from his mouth, ripped it open with a long shiny thumbnail, and counted. His skin was a peculiar olive color and his face was flat and hardlipped with eyes thickbrowed by scar tissue.

Satisfied with the count, he looked at an enclosed piece of paper. Then raised his eyes. And gaped. For a while his face twisted between three expressions before casting itself into one of immense superiority.

349

"*You* the guy," he said to Jones, who was sitting rigidly with his back to the door which had been wired shut. "Ah 'member *you*. You the real *cute* white boy messed with me, ain't you?"

Jones nodded.

"You mus' get in fixes *all* the time. What you do get him so down on you?"

"I wouldn't play the piano so he could live off me. That's part of it."

"Piano?" The brutal face frowned deeply. "Ah didn' know you was a piano player . . ." He put the car in gear and began to pull away slowly. ". . . You sure 'nough play the piano?"

Again Jones nodded.

Heading south, they drove along the perimeter of a thin, cold rain falling onto dead factories and stretches of stiff weeds. The sky was the color of mud. Wind whistled at the windows; the windshield-wipers struggled noisily and ineffectively. The rain came on.

"Ah nevah seed you play piano nowhere . . . what you name?"

Jones told him.

The Negro shook his head. "Nope. Nevah heard a you." He drove on, frowning. After a mile or so he turned east. The city was still a tundra. "You play boogie?"

"I can."

"Ah likes boogie. Gets me hot. You know."

Jones continued staring. His hands were open and motionless in his lap. He did not look at passing cars or trucks.

After fifteen minutes the Buick made a sharp turn, jumped a curb, and bounced along a corduroyed road and swung behind a building with not a single pane of glass intact. Jewel got out and waited for the pianist. The Negro wrenched open a hasp on a door and together they went inside. It was

350

cold and damp, and there were steel shavings and oilstains. Against one wall a thin pile of burlap bags made a bed on the cement floor. The Negro motioned. Jones sat with his back to the wall. Jewel kicked an orange-crate into a position less than ten feet away from Jones and sat with his hands between his knees.

"Got to wait," he explained. "It'll be dark by n' by."

Jones' wide blue eyes roved the littered room. He shivered from a gust of wind-soaked rain that rattled the broken windowpanes.

"Whyn't you say somethin'?" Jewel demanded. Far in the distance a diesel went through three gears. The rain continued hammering at the jagged sections of glass; the Negro's breathing was like smoke in the cold air. "You don' care to know what Ah'm sposed to do with you?"

Jones did not answer.

"Break you hands, that's what. Hear?" He scowled menacingly. *"Break you hands.* What you say 'bout that?" He himself shivered.

For reply Jones raised his left hand and began kneading his eyes with thumb and forefinger.

"You don' *care?"* He stood. Began pacing the floor. Kicked over the orange-crate. Put his hands on his hips and took them off and swore. Shook his head. Then he upended the crate again and sat.

There was not much time to the winter afternoon. The rain did not let up, and the air grew darker and colder. When it was too dark to see the pianist at ten feet, Jewel stood up. He walked a large oblong on the floor, then went to a window and frowned for a long time. After that he returned and stood over Jones and shifted his weight from one foot to the other.

"Okay," he said at last. "This it. Get up." Holding his right hand in a sledgelike fist, he pulled Jones up with his left. There was no resistance. For a few seconds they faced each other. "Ah don' too much like this. You kind of all *right* white boy. But Ah got this *job* to do . . . . . ." He reached with his right hand.

The pianist pulled free and backed up.

Jewel smiled. "Damn you, you don' take *nothin'* easy, does you?" He had taken just two steps forward when Jones hit him squarely in the middle of the face and leaped for the door.

The Negro barely staggered. With one motion he seized Jones and hurled him to the floor. The pianist struggled to hands and knees and finally stood.

Jewel came forward and was hit again. And once more Jones was caught and thrown heavily.

This time he did not get up as quickly. But he did, and braced himself, breathing deep, and waited again. And for the third time Jewel towered closer, and he swung with all his strength, but the Negro moved sinuous and gigantic and chopped a single crushing blow behind the ear. Jones toppled headfirst toward the cement, struck, and in openmouthed silence began writhing convulsively.

Jewel stared. Then he ran.

6

After parking the car she sat for awhile to organize herself. Rain was pouring through the darkness. It bounced like mercury off the hood and pelted heavily on the canvas top just above her head. No letup was in sight. Unless sometime during the night it would turn to snow.

Against the chance of a respite, however, and because she lacked the energy to move, she lit a cigarette and smoked thoughtlessly in the warm leather cave. There was a soreness in her pelvic bones, a memory of his surgings. Her calves ached. With each inhalation the thick smoke seemed more tasteless, but she continued dutifully and methodically to draw it into her. The rain came down silver, straight, and hard.

Finally, sensing the danger of falling asleep, she forced herself out of the Cadillac, flung the cigarette in a puddle, and hurried to the entrance of her apartment-building. She was ducking away from the rain and fumbling for her keys when the voice spoke close by.

"Don't be afraid, Helen."

Jones stepped out of the darkness. The center of his face was a smear of blood. His mouth was open and his hair was soaked flat. With glazed eyes he stood looking at her. He did not seem able to move.

She went to him. "What happened?"

He swayed, caught himself, and moved his mouth as though gasping. No sound came out.

Holding the sodden sleeve at his upper arm, she led him through the door. When she released her grip to fumble for her keys Jones staggered against the wall and tried to speak again. She opened the door, caught him by the arm, and saw that there was blood in his ears. He tried to pull away and climb the stairs unaided, but she held on. Close to her, his breathing was hoarse and liquid. He fell. As she pulled at him he tried to push her away, but his hand was bonelessly weak.

She unlocked her door and at once snapped the light-switch. He stumbled into the center of the room, his coat dripping, his face a wet red mask, his body, shuddering uncontrollably, trying to balance and find direction. Then in what was almost a lunge he made for the boxlike couch and threw himself on it heavily.

She did not take time to remove her coat.

"Ross? Darling—listen . . . Jones is here and—I'm all *right* . . . yes, *no* . . . *lis*ten to me . . . . . . He's hurt, another fight, I think . . . but this time a bad one—no, he's not drunk, he's *hurt* . . . I don't know what's wrong with him. Get a cab and come over right away, will you?" She stepped back and glanced into the livingroom. "As soon as you can. *Please.* This is bad. It's awfully bad . . . I'm calling the hospital right away. Yes . . . *no,* I'm all *right,* I told you . . . but get here as soon as you can." She hung up, looked in again on Jones, and then called for an ambulance.

Jones moved his head when she went in to him. "C-c-c-old," he chattered. His eyes were lost, loose and uncomprehending. He did not resist as she took off his coat and shoes and covered him with blankets; securing the satin edges, her hands could feel the spasms of his body. With a warm wash-

354

cloth she wiped his face, stared in surprise. His face was un-marked. The blood had not come from any cuts. And even as she gently cleaned him she saw it beginning to seep from his nose and mouth. She looked at his ears.

"You're going to be all right," she said. "Just lie there, and everything's going to be all right. There's nothing really wrong. Nothing. You're going to be all right, Virgil, all right . . ." She tightened her hands together in her lap and grimaced at the neat pale half-moons of the thumbnails. Then she put her hands in his hair and pressed all her warmth against him.

It was not long before Jaeger arrived. He let himself in and stood tensely, scowling and wet, as she told him how Jones had been waiting for her and how he had looked. Jaeger threw his coat into a chair and went to the couch.

"What happened?" he asked Jones roughly. He asked again. His face was constricted as he turned to her. "Where's that goddamned ambulance?"

"I called them right after you."

"*Yes*terday would've been better—maybe they'd be here by now . . ." He lit a cigarette and exploded smoke. "Some-body did a job on him—" his thumb jerked "—a *real* job. He's not with it at all. *Jesus!*" He reached down and wrenched back the blankets, peered, and with a deep breath of relief covered Jones again. "Thought somebody might've laid a knife on him . . ."

She shook her head. "No—it's his head. His ears. Look at his ears."

Jaeger bent, straightened. He put his left fist to his fore-head and closed his eyes.

"Where's that bastard *of an ambulance?"*

She aimed her words between his eyes.

"Man of action," she said.

"What?" His stare was unsteady.

"You heard me," she said quietly.

When the doorbell buzzed he was on it in three strides. At the open door he swore, came back into the room.

"Get a camera," he gritted. *"This* won't happen again in twenty years . . ."

Two long-faced, businesslike policemen walked in. The taller went directly to where Jones was encased and silent; the other approached Jaeger, who began talking before the first question was asked.

"Not so fast," was the warning.

"To hell with that," Jaeger said. "We want the ambulance. This guy's in bad shape."

"Jimmy," said the policeman with Jones. "C'mere a second."

While they were talking the bell sounded again. Jaeger stood in the hallway, looking down, then returned quickly. Behind him were three men, two of whom carried the metal stretcher. They wasted no time. In less than a minute the third man had finished with Jones and the others were expertly strapping him into the stretcher.

"Doctor—" Helen began.

"You can come along if they say so," the third man clipped.

"Okay, lady," said the taller policeman. "But *you*—" he pointed a blunt finger at Jaeger "—ride with us."

So they crowded into the hallway and she double-locked the door behind her and went downstairs past the triumphantly smug eyes of neighbors whose mouths were arrogant beyond whispering. At last they were right. There she was: mixed up with the police and that musician of hers and somebody either drunk or dead or shot getting carried down into an ambulance. She closed her eyes and tried not to think.

In the street people had appeared from nowhere. They stood in the rain and struggled to see. The red turret-lights on both the squadcar and ambulance flashed across their faces, spun, flashed at opposite buildings, back across the faces in the crowd. The rain made a million fountains on the headlight-bright street. Windows were up, people leaned out.

Jaeger turned and nodded reassuringly at her before entering the squadcar. She got in the ambulance. As she sat in the seat facing the locked-in stretcher she felt the knee of one of the men pressing against her thigh. The knee did not draw back. She shifted, leaned closer to Jones. She did not feel the pressure again. With a smooth surge and mounting siren, the ambulance moved, and in no time at all was screaming down a wide street so fast that she dared not look.

"How is he?" She saw that his eyes were open but that there was no thinking behind them.

The attendant shrugged, looked away. "Can't tell."

"But you know *some*thing! Just by looking you can tell *some*thing."

"Tell you this—" he said casually "—I wouldn't want his head."

She turned to Jones. Her fingers pushed back a curve of matted hair. That was all she could do. She could push back his hair and look at him.

At the hospital Jones was wheeled away and she was directed to a rotundalike desk. She could answer almost none of the questions. Tired of standing, tired of all the frustrations and uncertainties of everything, and with the excitement of shock wearing off, it was only minutes before she snapped at the nurse and said she didn't give a damn *what* she thought —holding back information or not—she was making a phone call.

Schwab said he would come right away.

She told him to bring some money. The hospital wanted money.

Jaeger arrived in half an hour with two plainclothesmen.

357

He was fuming at a cigarette but apparently in good standing with the law.

"Where is he?" he asked.

"How do I know?" she answered irritably. "They took him away—I don't know what they're doing. Hello," she said obliquely to the detectives. "I'm the woman in this . . . I'll tell you all I can when this gets straightened out . . ." Then to Jaeger: "I hope you have a few hundred. This butchershop wants us to pay the rent before they give him an aspirin."

Jaeger got out his billfold. "He's lucky," he said, "he's white."

After paying they sat on a bench and Helen told the detectives everything she knew. They were not satisfied. They were polite but firm. There had to be more.

"Enemies?" Jaeger said. He smiled wryly. "Sure. He had enemies. This town's loaded with them. You could call *me* one, I suppose. But I didn't do it and wouldn't, either. Sure, he didn't go around leaning on people, but he had enemies. It's just the way he was . . ."

"How so? 'The way he was.' "

Jaeger spread his hands. "I don't know. He just did the things he wanted to do, whether anybody agreed with him or not. Not salty or anything—just a real solo. The kind that won't take noise from anybody. You can get in a hell of a lot of trouble that way, you know."

The detectives said what they really wanted to know was more about Jones' past, his habits, whether he had any bad ones. Everything.

It was just as well that a reporter and photographer from the *Sun-Times* came in, because Jaeger was not much help to the police. The questions just couldn't be answered, and he didn't know anybody who could come up with what they wanted to know. The *Tribune* men hustled in next. Everyone wanted to know everything. The nurses threatened. The newspapermen changed tactics and tried to get information from them. In the center of the confusion Jaeger chain-smoked and looked at his shoes.

When after forty minutes Schwab arrived, Helen told him thanks, but the money had been taken care of. And that was all she was able to say before the detectives walked him into a corner and began the routine of questioning.

Flashbulbs had brought anger to Jaeger's face when she returned. She sat and listened to him swear. Suddenly he got up and coiled for a punch at an insistently whispering reporter. A flashbulb went off. His body went limp. He sat, slumped.

"Wait till they get this," he said wearily, indicating the newsmen with a toss of his head. "You'll be a punchboard and Jones and I'll be mainliners. Jesus. They just don't care at all. Write it real strong and sell papers. That's the pitch— sell papers. They just don't care." He stamped on a cigarette. "What a business this is. What a goddamned business . . ."

Time passed in a swift sweep of voices and smoke and more voices. Finally from down the hall came a nurse and a heavy, rust-haired man showing strong freckled arms against white clothing. He took only passing notice of the newsmen.

The detectives were on their feet. Helen stood between Jaeger and Schwab. The five of them faced the doctor. His voice came out of his chest in a deep professional monotone.

"What does that man do for a living?" The question was directed to no one in particular. "A prizefighter?"

"No," she said, seeing that no one else seemed ready to answer. "He's a musician—a pianist."

The red brows pointed in a frown. "A musician. Do you know if he ever engaged in violent sports? Football . . . like that."

They looked at each other. Shook their heads.

359

"How *is* he?" she asked. "We don't know what he might've done years ago . . . how *is* he?"

"Skull fracture," the doctor said. "He'll live."

"Can he talk?" The heavier detective pushed forward. "We want to ask him a few questions, doctor. Won't take long."

"No questions yet." He chewed a corner of his mouth. His face dismissed the police, who did not move. The doctor turned to her. "A successful musician?"

All three nodded.

"Who's the most interested party in his career?"

"No one," Jaeger said. "He hasn't got an agent—never had one. I guess we're the closest to him."

"He has no family?"

"No."

"No one?"

"I just told you—no."

"Then you get the bad news. I'm sorry. The reason I asked about his past was because this skull fracture isn't as—well, as *vi*tal as it might seem. You could even call it unnecessary. He should have been in here a long time ago . . ." He mauled his shaggy reddish hair and exhaled from his mouth. ". . . His head is in very bad condition. He's taken too many blows . . . I don't know when it was incurred, but he's had a hemorrhage in there. He's been carrying around a blood clot."

She closed her eyes. The voice went on.

"It might not have been painful, but it was pressing against the eighth cranial nerve—the auditory nerve. He probably suffered a loss of balance from time to time. Anyone notice?" He squinted at Schwab's faint nodding. "Yes. And his hearing was deteriorating—maybe by stages, maybe—"

"His *hearing*?" Jaeger said.

"Yes."

"But—"

360

"I know," the doctor said. "It's too bad. But it was merely a matter of time. This thing tonight took him the rest of the way."

There was a silence.

"Then you mean he's deaf," Schwab said.

"He is deaf."

"Is there any—"

"No," the doctor said. "There's nothing anyone can do. He has complete bilateral deafness. He will be deaf for the rest of his life."

7

Anonymous in shadow, she waited alone in a booth against the wall of the nightclub on Howard Street. In the two months since it had happened she had been compelled to learn patience.

During the first week or so she had been unable to see through to Ross' feelings. Withdrawn and reflective, he appeared not to be brooding but instead determinedly trying to arrange and understand a complicated problem. He did not mention Jones. She could only guess, and wait, and hope.

The assault had not been solved. Jones had refused to tell the police or anyone else a word about it. There was nothing the newspapers could do. In a matter of days the subject was dropped.

Soon after, guardedly, tentatively, Ross began talking about him. It seemed as though he was trying to free a judgment which had been in his system too long—a conclusion he had never fully understood but which he felt he could grasp if he brought it into the open.

And at the same time, in the same cautiously experimental manner, he came back to the piano. During the following several weeks she had often entered his apartment in the evenings to find him in the center of a day-long clutter of sheet music and cigarette-stubs, evidence not only of his efforts but of his uncertainty. Then one night the room had been orderly, he had not been drinking. And he had not tried to make a big thing of his decision when he told her.

Now, the underlit, smoke-packed club began to fill rapidly as nine o'clock approached. Ever since Ross had opened with his young quartet the crowds had been capacity. Jaeger had come back. When he had finished the first set on opening night half the audience had stood to applaud.

By the third night there had been a crowd of jazzmen on hand. A page-three story was in *Metronome* after a week. And from nightclubs in a dozen cities came offers.

Five minutes early, she saw him come in with Don Nicholis, his drummer who had a brush-beat that made listeners stare at his hands to see where the third one was. The pack of well-wishers delayed them only momentarily.

"Hello." She turned her head and touched her lips to the palm of the strong hand held against her face. She exchanged wry smiles with the swarthy drummer. Nicholis was wearing a blue sportcoat and gray flannel slacks. He had less than an inch of forehead.

"What you hear from Athens?" he asked.

"The usual. Earthquakes."

"Yeah." He shook his head. "Man, that town really moves." He blinked, cracked his knuckles, bounced on the balls of his feet and moved his tongue in his mouth. "This ain't making it for me," he said, grimacing at his wristwatch. "Any of you want to catch one?"

They both said no. Nicholis swung jerkily to the bar and with four fingers beat out a paradiddle to get attention. He plucked his lower lip and cornered challenging eyes at a blonde who was smiling worshipfully. Then the drink came and he tipped a mouthful of gin and ice out of sight. He turned his back on the blonde.

Ross sat down. He moved his hand and softly gripped the

363

inside of her elbow. She could feel the strength in his long fingers.

"Heard from the city again today," he said, meaning New York.

"Oh?"

"They've upped the guarantee. Twelve thousand."

"You'll be rich," she said, wishing for an instant that they were not sitting where so many people could see them.

"I don't want to be rich—I just want to live like I am."

"Don't we all."

"It's not so hard. I used to think it was, but it isn't."

"Nothing helps a philosophy like an offer of twelve thousand," she said through a smile. "Are you going to take it?"

For a moment his lean face tightened. He looked as if he wanted her to tell him what to do. But then he nodded in a way settling it once and for all.

"Fine," she heard herself saying, "it'll be good for you."

"Us," he corrected. With that he got to his feet and inclined his head in the direction of the door. "Well, they showed. Off to work, girl." Then he placed both hands on the table and loomed over her. "Us," he repeated. "And I'm not asking—I'm telling you. *Us.*"

With her eyes she followed his broad flat shoulders moving easily between people as he went toward the stand. She was still watching when bassist Tape Williams and guitarist Billy Bell passed her with warm wide smiles. Belatedly she raised her hand in greeting, but not in time. They grouped at the far end of the bar with Ross and Don, and stood chatting for a minute or so. Finally Ross nodded in agreement with something Williams had laughed, and then they ducked under the lid in the bar and took their places on the stand.

They did not waste any time. Ross got Williams and Bell tuned up in a hurry, and since Nicholis had only one snare and two bongos to work with, the quartet was ready to take off in less than three minutes.

The crowd quieted. Ross spoke over the top of the piano. Tape Williams frowned his rough pink face and pinched the adhesive on the first two fingers of his right hand. Nicholis flashed his brushes and hitched his shoulders several times. Billy Bell lifted his dark face lazily toward the ceiling.

Suddenly they were in it—an upbeat *Beguine*—the arrangement he had scored in five hours the week before. It was brilliantly new, imaginative, and above all, confident. They moved it along with flawless integration: the guitar note-for-note with Ross, the bass thrumming an underlay of rhythm and the drums a powerhouse of soft and steady drive.

At the corner of her left eye was an undistinguishable shape in the set-off darkness where she was sitting. She turned. Without invitation, Paul Bauer smiled and sat next to her.

Watching only the keys, feeling the solid pulse beating beneath every movement of his fingers, Jaeger drove the music home. His eyes and ears were buffeted by applause as he clawed down the final chord and sat back on the bench in the hot bluish light. Williams winked at him with sly, prideful satisfaction. The *Beguine* had come off great. It was going to be a good night. All the nights were going to be good.

"Let's go *Sunny Side*," he snapped. The others looked at him in doubt. "Do a head . . . you've all blown it enough before. Let's get with it here." He glanced toward Nicholis. "Lay it down, man . . ." He cocked his head and at the same time started his right heel *bump bump bump bump* on the threadbare carpet under the piano, and then his hands moved in quick sure precision and it was *Sunny Side,* all of them on it, for him, for themselves, for this night and this big hushed crowd, for Bern DeWitt—and it was as it always should have been: looking up, the way a jazzman had to be, doing what he wanted to do and had to do and being happy with it. He played a lingering, singing chorus and did not feel like ever giving it up to Billy's guitar. But he did, and filled in behind the metallically swinging bars with sharp, true chords, and when Billy was through he came back in for another break before letting Tape take over. Still the melody seemed to go on and on in his head, almost as if he himself was playing all the instruments, and when it was all over he opened his mouth and drew a deep luxurious breath and nodded happily into the applause and shouts of appreciation.

That was for Bern, he said to his fingers. *That was for 'Frisco and New York and all the times and places you've been brought down. And Romeo, too. He'd understand. You can count on that. Ought to look him up when we head east. Surprised to see me. Surprised I'm not in that graveyard of his.*

He had no sense of time. Not the kind people measured on faces of watches and clocks. The only time he knew was rhythm, the beat he was part of, the music. He was not tired. He had the feeling he would never be tired again. At least not in the way he had been this last year. Never that kind of tiredness again.

When he saw their eyes begging after *Perdido* he called for *April in Paris,* a quick run-through, and then they could take a break. A chance to back off and be human. There was no sense in driving a man too hard, or in a man driving himself too hard. You took all the living out of it when you did that.

So, reminding himself, he relaxed and led them through the final number, and they came off the stand.

At first he did not look toward her. He stood with the others at the bar and as they drank he told them of the New York offer.

Tape was not enthusiastic. He said he sure as hell would like to go, all right, but first he'd have to see how the wind blew at home. The woman wasn't exactly flipped on him booting around that town, with or without her. But, he guessed you had to put up with the strong scenes when you got tied down. He'd have to see. In a couple of days he'd have the pitch.

Nicholis and Bell didn't have to ask anybody. They were young, and hadn't yet rationed themselves to any one woman. By the time Jaeger had tagged the period on his last sentence their minds had been made up. Hell Yes. Chicago was good enough, but it was always better when you got away from it for awhile. When you got hung up in it too long you got to thinking one way; you forgot there were other cities and other ways of thinking. When was this deal going to start?

Jaeger told them in a month.

And again—the bread?

He said twelve thousand and listened to low whistles.

Tape started to say On second thought—when the blonde Nicholis had eyed at the bar touched Jaeger's forearm and asked him to hear what she had to say. Having stepped aside, he looked down at her worried face.

"I think you'd better get back to your girl," she said. "I got a hunch she don't go for that old yo-yo she's sitting with."

Jaeger looked, muttered a thanks, called to Tape and the others that they'd talk more about it later, and strode to the booth.

Paul Bauer rose, ancient and formal, smiling thinly and offering his hand.

"Ross . . ."

"Sorry, hon," Jaeger said to Helen, ignoring the greeting. He sat close to her and jammed a cigarette into his mouth and lit it.

"That wasn't very smart," Bauer said, clenching his refused hand into a fist as he sat again.

Jaeger said nothing. He could sense Helen looking at him out of cornered eyes. He smoked and watched Bauer's small silvery head scan the crowd. Finally the eyes came around to his.

"Nice, Ross—very nice. I can believe all the good things I've heard about you lately. You're doing well . . ."

Still Jaeger made no comment.

"Your young lady isn't very talkative either, Jaeger. Hasn't said a word to me since I came in five minutes ago."

Jaeger tapped an ash to the floor. When he saw where it powdered he raised his eyes and stared back at Bauer again.

"You're not being smart." Bauer's voice had changed. "Not one bit smart—I hope you know that. I'm not impressed with this act of yours . . . nor with yours either, young woman."

Jaeger held his cigarette between thumb and forefinger and drew on it. His eyes did not waver.

"I suppose you think you're pretty independent now that you've got all these idiots idolizing you again. Well, you're mistaken. You're forgetting, Jaeger. You don't remember how it used to be."

Jaeger closed his eyes and held them that way for a long moment.

"I'm warning you, Jaeger—you're just asking for—"

"Get out," he said, crushing his cigarette on the formica top of the table. "I don't know and don't *care* what you came down here to talk about. I'm not interested. I don't want to talk to you. I don't even want to listen. Get out."

Bauer's face reddened. As he put his hands on the table, they were shaking as badly as his voice.

368

"Nobody talks to me that way."

"And you don't impress me," Jaeger said. "So get out of here."

"If I do, it'll be the biggest mistake you ever made."

"No it won't. It'll be one thing I've done right this last year. I've done a lot of thinking these last couple of months, and this is the answer, Bauer: I don't want you. My boys don't want you . . . there isn't a jazzman going who wants any part of you. We've caught your act, you son of a bitch, and we're not buying it any more. *We know who had the arm put on Jones.* You couldn't make him dance step one, could you? All your *mus*cle, and you couldn't move him an inch, so you thought you'd 'win' by breaking his hands . . ."

Bauer leaned back and narrowed his eyes. His mouth was a ragged slit.

"You think you know a lot, Jaeger."

"I'm just as smart as your apes are dumb, man, and you've got a lot of them who aren't on to you. *Yet.* And let me tell you something else: it wouldn't have made any difference even if his hands *had* been broken. He had you beat going in. You didn't even score. Jones beat you so bad you aren't even in the league any more."

"Is that so?" He formed a cold smile. "And where is *he* now?"

"Around."

" 'Around.' Very interesting—'around.' But I haven't seen his name *any*where, have you?"

"Sure I have; it's out front right now. Take a look on your way out. Only it's spelled J-a-e-g-e-r. And B-e-l-l. And Nicholis, and Williams. Or go downtown. They spell it Jackson and Britton and Allred down there. Go out south. He's around there too. You haven't seen his name? Man, you're getting so old you've forgotten how to read, that's all."

Bauer smiled thinly. "Do you hear that, young woman?" he said, his eyes on Jaeger. "Your hero here has got all the answers now that Jones is out of the way. Isn't that so, Jaeger? The answers are easier *now,* aren't they?"

"Bauer—" Jaeger said with calm deliberation "—people like you can't think any other way, can you? You've got to tear things down because that's the only way you can build your-selves up. Well, man, you can have that kind of thinking . . . I don't care. I really don't care what the hell you think any more."

"Listen to me . . . you listen. . . . . ."

Jaeger turned his head toward the stand, flaunted attention to his wristwatch. He stood and rested his hand on Helen's shoulder.

"All right, Bauer—this is it. I've got a job to do. Just get out of my sight and stay out. And if you're still here and say *one word* to Helen in thirty seconds, I'm coming off that stand and out you go, old or not." He pressed his fingers into her shoulder.

When he reached the stand he looked back. Bauer was standing.

He sat and spread a chord. Once again he looked. Bauer was slow and small, moving toward the door.

He dried his hands on his pantslegs and shaped another chord as Tape plucked languidly at the thick strings of his bass and held it close, like a woman. Nicholis, standing front and center at his waist-high array of drums, turned and mopped his mouth, asked one of the bartenders to cut down the lights if he could. A blue and a white went off. Bell bent and adjusted the amplifier of his guitar. They loosened up: relaxed, subdued, fragmenting melodies.

Nicholis stepped back and rested his right arm on the piano. A frown roughened his forehead.

"What'd he want?"

Jaeger looked up at him, then at the closing door. He could feel the close, colored lights on his face. He made a mouth at the young drummer, put his thumb on middle C.

"Something he couldn't have," he said.

8

For the last time Schwab parked his sedan on the narrow, obscure street and stood viewing the ugly façade. Like a giant red crate on its side, the building extended its two-story height half the length of the block, and had four separate entrances to the maze of cramped rooms inside. Shutters were on some of the windows.

He climbed the familiar shallow steps and pushed the button next to the name pencilled on brass. He waited. Tried again. Waited. For a moment an expression of concern locked his face, but then he came out of the hallway and sat on the steps.

Shadows were coming over the limpid April afternoon. Reflected sunlight splintered from a window being washed by a woman wearing an Army dungaree jacket. Far down the street he could see three little girls hopping one-legged in a game; squeals drifted on the air. He packed his briar and puffed absently while eyeing the car. It was ready: low with weight, crowded, strapped, the tank full, oil up, tires good enough, the radio working. There was no undoing it now. He had made his decision. After all these months—years, to be honest—he had finally decided, and, surprisingly, it had been easier than he'd ever imagined.

Of course, he thought, vacantly watching the erratic motions of the woman at the window, the aftermath until now had been something else. He had not got his hoped-for price from the business. Sale of two minor local investments had been at another loss. Several times during the sale of his home furnishings he had fought back an impulse to tell the appraisers to wear masks to look more the part. He had had to put up with criticism, advice. All of a sudden he had found himself surrounded by management-experts, every last one of them telling him how wrong he was. It seemed that everyone thought they were more qualified to run his life than he was. And they had not merely offered advice; they had been militant about it. With a sad but resigned feeling he guessed he had lost two friends because he had not deferred to their judgments. Simplifying life could be such a complicated affair.

The encouraging part, however, was that day by day he was coming to feel less regret over his losses. They had been suffered, and he was still intact. He was still setting out to try what for too long he had been afraid of: Chance. Yes, afraid. He had feared the new, the unproved, the thing at which he might fail. He had clung to the safe world of no-risk, of small change. There had been less chance of failing there.

And another thing. In retrospect, it seemed that he had always oriented himself toward failure rather than success. He had asked *What if I fail?* instead of *What if I succeed?* It was true. Until now his life had been negative. He had actually sought to avoid failure, not to seek success. And even then, he had not known the real meanings of the words.

For some time he sat on the steps and watched the afternoon lose its color. Soft cirrus clouds had begun to form. He noticed that the woman had finished her windows and that the children had gone. Every so often he looked in the bowl of his dead pipe, but made no attempt to relight it. He watched an ant crawl along a matchstick as though on a girder. After an unbelievably thorough inspection of the blackened tip, the ant got off and began zigzagging elsewhere.

Finally, across the street and still in the next block, he caught sight of the white-haired, casually walking figure of Jones. With a sound of relief and effort, Schwab stood.

Jones had on a black corduroy sportcoat with a tieless, unpressed white shirt and oatmeal-colored slacks. Even from the distance his face looked as if he had been in the sun all day. It wasn't until he was less than twenty-five yards away that he nodded in greeting.

Schwab was careful to wait for Jones' eyes to focus on his lips. In the beginning he had spoken slowly, exaggerating word-formations, but it was not long before he realized that Jones could read normal speech with near-perfect accuracy.

"Where've you been?"

"The park. Out on the breakwater. They had pretty good luck fishing today." He turned his eyes toward the car. "Did you leave room in there for yourself?"

"Plenty. All set to go." His voice sounded loud and childish in his ears. He had never been able to keep from raising his voice when talking to Jones.

"Come on up," Jones said. "Somebody gave me a bottle. I can't take it, and I don't like to see good whiskey just sit there. Old Fitzgerald, but one shot drives me crazy." He pointed to his head. "This fracture. The doctors said no drinking for at least a year, and they sure were right. Only one drink and I didn't even know if the year was up." He let Schwab into the inner hall and then went ahead of him on the stairs, turning sideways in order to see anything which might be said.

But Schwab had no words. Perhaps, he thought, it was because he was seeing Jones for the last time that he felt this

374

sudden sense of a very great loss. He had been the only regular visitor Jones had had these months; the others, all of them, had defected one by one, and now, when he left, Jones would be alone. As he waited for the door to be opened he could not help thinking that Jones, too, was aware of it—yet here he was, sunburned and relaxed after a day in the park and at the beach, his face incorruptibly content as he opened the door to his soundless, solitary rooms.

"I'm getting to like this place more every day," Jones said on his way to a bookcase empty except for the bottle. "But next fall I'll probably move out. I like to move around."

Seated on a planklike couch, Schwab took in the straight chairs, the worn linoleum, the severe box-shape of the piano he had given Jones, the clear bulb high above which he knew lit brilliantly when someone pressed the bell downstairs, the bleakness of everything in spite of the dark cool atmosphere made by drawn shades. From the makeshift kitchen the refrigerator started whirring. He observed that Jones' back was to him.

"I don't know how you stand it," he said. "I couldn't live here alone for a week. Well, maybe I could—now. But God, I don't know whether to pity you, or what . . ."

Jones corked the bottle and crossed the room with a jelly-glass half full of whiskey. Schwab took it with thanks and said straight was fine. To no clear purpose he raised the glass briefly in the motion of a toast as Jones sat facing him in his usual interested-in-everything posture.

"You're going to California," Jones said.

He nodded, vaguely feeling that he did not want to talk about it here and now.

"I think you're doing the right thing. Even if it doesn't turn out the way you hope, it's better than wanting to go and not going and never knowing. But you know that."

375

"I know it now." The whiskey had burned itself out. "Have you heard about Jaeger?"

"The last I knew, he was doing a lot better."

"A lot," he echoed, watching carefully to see the effect of what he was about to say. "It seems that he had a run-in with this Bauer person, and from what I gather, Jaeger didn't lose. Apparently he told Bauer just what he thought of him and the way he operated. I understand he told him all the musicians here weren't going to take any more of his schemes and coercions. And finally, I heard that he accused Bauer of what happened to you."

"Good," Jones said mildly. He appeared not to have been able to read the last statement, or else, completely disinterested in it. "He'll be better for letting off steam like that. I always thought he would have liked himself more if he ever told people the things he was thinking about them."

"Virgil . . ." he said, shifting uncomfortably on the couch ". . . you don't have to answer this, of course . . . but now that I'm leaving, my curiosity is too much for me. *Did* Bauer have anything to do with this injury?"

Jones smiled. "I'm deaf. I can't hear a word you say."

"All right—that's your privilege."

"My right."

"Your right, then. I suppose I don't have any right to ask you to explain yourself, but going along with what you just said as to Jaeger being better off for telling people what he's thinking about them, I'll tell you now that *I* think, like almost everybody else, Bauer *was* the cause—and Virgil, if he was, for the life of me I cannot understand why you're protecting him."

"Did you say 'protecting'?" Squinting, he leaned forward.

"That's what it amounts to."

" 'Amounts to.' Well—" he stood and scratched his head "—you can look at it that way, I guess, but it seems like splitting hairs to me. What difference does it make? It's over with. Here, I'll get you another drink."

"Then Bauer *was* responsi—" Jones was not looking at him. He had taken the empty glass and was going to the bookcase.

"For the sake of your curiosity," Jones said over his shoulder, "it was my doing, this thing with my head. I'd do something about it if I felt somebody else was the reason. But I don't. *I* caused it, and it'd probably been different if I hadn't been the way I am. I wouldn't be surprised if I get hit in the head all my life. But it's my head, you know. I've never seen so many people getting all excited about a head."

Schwab pushed himself erect and with the tip of his shoe probed at a brown-edged hole in the linoleum. At times like this he was dumbstruck. He could not even begin to contend with Jones. Never had he seen anyone so willing to accept personal responsibility, so able to maintain confidence after such losses. And there was no falseness. There was no desperate bravado, no smug, arrogant self-satisfaction. His strength was real. Not even twenty-five years old, and already he had more faith in himself and in the world than ten thousand men found in their lifetimes. What was there to say? Nothing. Accept the drink, declare firmly it was the last because of driving ahead. Be sociable, ask the intent blue eyes questions already half-answered.

"You still haven't changed your mind about the piano?"

"No." He sat on the couch with his back against the pale green wall. "I have it here."

"Well, at any rate, your ability is good to have in reserve. You can always make a comfortable living from it if you're forced to."

"I suppose."

"You *know* you can."

"You're right. But I won't go back. Not for the money,

though, and that's all it would be. I don't want that, so I won't do it."

"I hope you can hold out," he said, and with one blazing swallow downed the whiskey. He blinked, opened his mouth. "I really hope you can do it, Virgil."

"It won't be hard. At least not as hard as you probably figure, you and a lot of others. Before I make up my mind I usually have a fair idea of what it's going to take to do something. I might have to put up with things I don't especially like, but that's part of what I knew when I started. So why get discouraged? You can beat yourself before you start, thinking of all the things against you. I could get run over by a truck tomorrow, or the world could blow up, but if I let that bother me I'd just climb in and pull up the covers and lose my mind. Fracture and all. Hell, this isn't new stuff to you. Right? right. Four days to get there?"

Four or five, Schwab said. He hadn't wanted to sit in Chicago and plan every stop. Oh, he'd thought of places he'd like to see, but he hadn't made a timetable or anything like that. Tonight he was simply driving, and if he felt like it all night he'd keep on going.

In the progressively uncertain light Jones twice interrupted to say that he hadn't followed the words, yet nothing was done about brightening the room. Before very long Schwab again found himself out of words. He jogged the glass in his hand.

"You want to go," Jones said, rising with the suppleness he had always given to every movement. "I'll walk out to the car. Just set the glass anywhere. I won't kick it over. I'm a lot better at seeing than I used to be."

They left the room and went down the stairs and out into cooling dusk. Jones preceded him to the car.

Close to his, the face was solid and unchanged. Even now, seeing it for the last time, Schwab could not heighten his perception and discover some new aspect of the wide-spaced eyes, of the set mouth or of the facial bones like granite beneath the skin. For a piece of a second he wondered how it had been possible to damage such a head; it looked like only a sledgehammer could have had any effect.

Before he could begin to say what he had been considering for over a week, the door was open and Jones had thrust out his hand.

"Good luck," Jones said. "It's been some year, hasn't it? And we're still alive. Don't think for a minute you're not doing the right thing. Well, one of these years I may see you there or you may see me back here. You still have my card, don't you?"

Schwab reached for his hip pocket.

"Keep it. A souvenir." With a powerful hand he guided Schwab to the door of the car and gently but inexorably forced until he was behind the wheel. Then Jones shut him in and stood with his hands clamped over the lower edge of the open window. Fingers together, his hands slapped once on the metal. And he was gone.

Schwab turned quickly, leaned, and started to open the curbside window to say *some*thing, at least goodbye, but Jones was already on the steps. There was no use calling out—he could not hear. His white hair disappeared into the dark hallway. The street was quiet and empty and growing darker; the tall lamp-posts stood like black poles against the sky and barren trees.

He pressed the starter and let the engine idle as he made certain his tobacco-can was within reach. Switching on the headlights, he shifted gears and pulled away without looking back. After several blocks he turned on the radio. Sounds of an interplanetary drama zoomed from the speaker. He swore at the pushbuttons and worked the dial. He went across the entire band three times, each time twisting through the unmistakable noise of the war going on in outer space. Finally, unable to find anything but popular music and news, he let the indicator stay on the station. Evidently a crisis had just passed. The characters were congratulating each other. They had thwarted another of the mad Doctor Fang's attacks. Some day he was not going to escape. Suddenly a crisp baritone cut in, saying they'd better hurry to the secret launching platform to find out if Professor Hamilton and The Ship were safe. Almost hysterically, the cast rushed off behind Commander Noble. Everything *had* to be all right. Just before the attack Professor Hamilton had been about to make the final tests of his secret self-generating rocket tubes, and if anything had happened to them, The Ship would never be able to reach Heliotron!

"*WILL Professor Hamilton and The—*"

"Yes, yes . . ." Schwab answered indulgently ". . . the old Professor will be just fine. And The Ship will probably have a damaged secret stabilizer or something, but Professor Hamilton will putter around and fix it, and one of these days they'll all be off for Heliotron." Ahead, he saw the highway laced by long pale beams of cross-country trucks. "And I'll bet they make it," he whispered. "By God, I'll bet we all make it."

The room was quite dark. He picked up the glass and inverted it on the neck of the whiskey bottle. Then he placed a chair under the bare lightbulb. With two twists he loosened it in its socket. He stepped down and locked the door and began to undress. Shivering, he rubbed the palms of his hands together.

The bathtub had claw-and-ball feet and fat porcelain knobs. On a ring above was strung a green pliofilm curtain dead to the touch. The warm water fell in thin bright lines from the showerhead.

When he had finished he dried and went to bed. For some time he lay with his eyes open and unfocused before going to sleep. As he slept the room became black.

Two hours later he got up and dressed in clean clothes. Over a bulky maroon sweater he wore the expensive topcoat given him by the woman in New York, and, as usual, left without a hat. In the hall he stopped at his mailbox and inserted a forefinger, felt. Then he went out into the silence.

He walked about a mile along the business-bright street until he came to a marquee advertising a technicolor musical on a seamless wide screen. Inside, he sat midway back and watched the famous redhaired showgirl move her mouth in song. Whole choruses of beautiful young women joined her in dancing while tanned men sat at tables in the nightclub looking captivated. Following the musical came an episodic western in which revolvers puffed and the hoofs of horses raised long swirls of dust. Every so often he lowered his head and rubbed his eyes, and when the musical began again, he edged out of the row and left.

He looked up and down the street and walked against the red light. At a Rexall he ordered the last of the pot roast dinner, ate it slowly, and did not raise his eyes to the waitress who cleaned his section of the counter four times. When she refilled his coffeecup he thanked her, and as she returned the glass bowl her right elbow brushed a small plate. He watched it strike and break into jagged pieces on the wood-strip rack at her feet. His fingers separated a bun, and he began mopping his plate.

On the sidewalk, he turned his coatcollar against the wind coming out of the north and started for his rooms. It did not take him long to reach his street, the steps, the hallway, the door of his key.

He put on the table-lamp and hung his coat in the closet. After exercising his hands and wrists he went to the piano

381

and raised its cover. He rested his fingers on the smooth keys before sitting on the bench.

But when he began, there was no music.

A faint clicking was the only sound in the room. The keys went down, the hammers moved—but that was all. With careful tools he had made it his piano. And alone he played, without loneliness or anger, certain of his hands and of himself in the knowledge that he had not been defeated.